THE MEANING OF THE MURDER

A NOVEL BY

WALTER B. LEVIS

ANAPHORA LITERARY PRESS

QUANAH, TEXAS

ANAPHORA LITERARY PRESS
1108 W 3rd Street
Quanah, TX 79252
https://anaphoraliterary.com

Book design by Anna Faktorovich, Ph.D.

Author Photo: Vic Puccio.

Published in 2025 by Anaphora Literary Press

The Meaning of the Murder: A Novel
Walter B. Levis—1st edition.

Library of Congress Control Number: 2025902446

Library Cataloging Information
Levis, Walter B., 1960-, author.
    The meaning of the murder : A novel / Walter B. Levis
    238 p. ; 9 in.
    ISBN 978-1-68114-618-8 (softcover : alk. paper)
    ISBN 978-1-68114-619-5 (hardcover : alk. paper)
    Kindle (e-book)
    ISBN 978-1-68114-622-5 (softcover: Ingram: alk. paper)
1. Books—Literature & Fiction—Genre Fiction—Psychological.
2. Books—Mystery, Thriller & Suspense—Crime Fiction—Murder.
3. Literature & Fiction—Genre Fiction—Religious & Inspirational—Jewish.
PN3311-3503: Literature: Prose fiction
813: American fiction in English

To my father, a kind and gentle man who understood violence.

"If the book we are reading does not wake us, as with a fist hammering on our skulls, then why do we read it? Good God, we also would be happy if we had no books and such books that make us happy we could, if need be, write ourselves. What we must have are those books that come on us like ill fortune, like the death of one we love better than ourselves, like suicide. A book must be an ice axe to break the sea frozen inside us. What we need are books that hit us like a most painful misfortune, like the death of someone we loved more than we love ourselves, that make us feel as though we had been banished to the woods, far from any human presence, like a suicide. A book must be the ax for the frozen sea within us."

—Franz Kafka, letter to Oskar Pollak, 1904

"...My concern was different from that of most of my comrades. Their question was, 'Will we survive the camp? For, if not, all this suffering has no meaning.' But the question which beset me was, 'Has all this suffering, this dying around us, a meaning?' For, if not, then ultimately there is no meaning to survival; for a life whose meaning depends upon such a happenstance—as whether one escapes or not—ultimately would not be worth living at all."

—Frankl, Viktor E., *Man's Search for Meaning* (First published in German in 1946 under the title: *Ein Psycholog erlebt das Konzentmtionslager)*

Chapter 1

Not raindrops—blood. Blood falls from the black sky. Head back, neck craning, she strains to see, wincing as the drops hit her face. Thick red drops, pasty, mixed with white dust, the pulverized concrete of the fallen towers. This blood-and-dust mush—it swirls. Fat flakes swirling over the street, over the rubble, over the New York harbor, swirling like a shaken snow-globe model of lower Manhattan, sticking to the strange grotesque almost-unrecognizable human body parts that hang in the air: a blown-off hand, a stump of leg, a headless torso oozing a gelatinous trail of red-and-grey. Cheshire-style, the parts drift past, a floating parade.

She feels nauseous and her throat hurts and she wonders why she must watch this—why? Why her? The thick dust gleams red-and-white and the sheer size weight and volume of it—a crazy, blood-streaked fog, it so attenuates the sunlight that she stands in utter darkness. Like inside a movie theater before the show starts, but darker. No faint glow from the screen, no emergency lights from under the seats, nothing. Where are all the people? There should be throngs running and screaming, but she's alone. Until her father appears. He seems to hover a few inches off the ground. Then he takes her hand.

"Follow me," he says, and leads her deeper into the darkness, inside a building, down an unlit hall, then outside again, onto a narrow street squeezed between cavernous buildings. They float together deeper and deeper into the darkness, into the oily, putrid odor of burnt plastic. And the sound—like the roar of a waterfall, she thinks. But strange—there's no water. Her throat scratches and burns—aches for water—while her father, glowing, ghost-like, looks over his shoulder and smiles. Does he have water? He wears a clean suit and tie, well-fitted. His hair is combed. Dust-free, no blood on his clothes. "The hooker," he whispers, then shrugs, squeezes her hand, looks away. Bashful, modest—a religious man. "Sex worker, I mean. If you knew what she knew..." She wants to ask: "What do you mean?" But fears if she opens her mouth, she'll ingest the swirling white dust, swallow the big red drops of blood falling from the black sky. So she breathes through her nose, teeth clenched. Hard heavy breaths, straining for air.

When Eliana Golden woke, her jaw ached, a tightness deep in the joint. The dream—again. Same dream, third time. Or fourth? She pressed her thumb into the knotty muscle at her jaw, sending a bolt of pain into her ear, behind her eye, across her forehead. Migraine trigger. But no throbbing headache, not yet. Water. That's what she needed. Her throat was parched. A cup of water by the side of the bed? No—another bit of therapeutic advice she failed to follow. Maybe she could fall back asleep. She reached for her watch. Brand new, a G-shock men's digital, set for military time. She looked hard at the numbers, started to drop the big watch back on the night table, then put it on her wrist. Fuck it, she thought. Four hours of sleep—I'll live.

She knew where Kitty strolled. And she'd find her—tonight, right now.

Eliana took a deep breath, then she threw her feet over the side of the bed and dropped straight into a close-grip push-up position on the floor in front of the nightstand. A quick set of ten, then a five-breath rest, and then another set, and another, until the muscles in her arms and shoulders burned. A good feeling—wide awake, ready for New York City at two in the morning.

The Queensborough Bridge cast a long shadow over 10th Street. A few sparse trees gasped for breath under the grey scaffolding at the corner. Further down the block, a temporary fence marked off a section for DOT parking, city officials only. Middle of the night, filled with cars—nobody bothered about the sign. Eliana sat in her beat-up Toyota waiting, watching. A cab stand at one end of the block, a parking lot for *Silvercup Studios* at the other—in between, girls of all sizes, ages, colors, and types. Teens with an easy sway in their young hips; middle aged vets fighting to keep some swagger in their wobbly knees.

#metoo.

The phrase popped into her head. Inappropriately, she thought, but, yeah, prostitutes still go to work. She thought of her sixteen-year-old niece, who along with a bunch of her nice suburban girlfriends used magic markers to draw hashtags on the palms of their hands before they went off to parties. Will the whole fucked-up world of sexual harassment really be different for them? Eliana didn't think so. Then thought: *shit, I'm getting jaded.* And that concerned her—exactly why her family thought becoming a cop was nuts. Why devote yourself to the ugliest parts of life? Her big sister Livi's question.

She shook off the distracting thoughts. It was a warm June night. That explained the heavy traffic. She recognized some of these workers. A wide-hipped, big-breasted girl—sixteen, tops—hair dyed blue, her short-shorts halfway zipped, the top button open. She stood under the streetlamp with confidence, shoulders back, chest out, the glow of yellowish light giving her skin—regardless of its actual color—a gold tint. A few feet away, an older woman, a redhead, hung in the shadows until a shiny BMW pulled up, then she hobbled to the curb and waited for the window to roll down. No window, no business. And not worth the effort to try. But sure enough—the window opened, and out drifted the smell of money. They sometimes called it that. The old redhead took a chesty breath, a small step, and in a flash leaned over, pushing her sagging breasts through the open car window. Yes, indeed, Queens Plaza South, a new place to party.

Not tonight, maybe, but soon enough cops would crash this party— or, rather, move it. Pest control, the detectives called it. Spray regularly and you'll keep the girls—and boys—out of your neighborhood, but they'll always find another block. And street-workers—just a fraction of the industry. Online "escort services" thrive in a world of their own, protected by intricate licensing laws almost impossible for police to penetrate. Providing companionship, giving a massage—nothing illegal about this, as long as you've got the license, which means any law-abiding citizen with enough money to control an indoor space can buy and sell sex with impunity.

Early in her career, Eliana struggled to accept this. Why pick on the girls working the street? What about the 1,200 "rub-and-tug" parlors all over the city claiming to offer facials, reflexology, waxing, or, as one place on the Grand Concourse advertised: "The Work Day Whistle," a special "happy ending" hundred-dollar massage, "hot stones included." And don't kid yourself: the New York State Division of Licensing Services required 500 hours of massage training. An army of regulators battle this paperwork, but meanwhile: a happy customer is a happy customer.

Eventually, she understood: cops keep their clothes on, which makes it tough to crack the criminal side of indoor sex. And prostitutes—well, not exactly criminals. Victims, mostly. And, if appreciated properly, these girls—and boys, and, of course, the transgender workers too—can be extremely helpful to police investigations. Hence, Eliana's approach: the criminal world as ecosystem. It was a way of thinking that allowed her to feel OK about her work. And maybe that's why she'd been so depressed lately: because she'd been forgetting the big theory, failing to trust the ideas behind it all. Not a pond or forest or grassland, but the criminal world is still an interactive set of processes that link the living to the non-living. And the system, like all systems, involves the transformation of energy into matter, and matter into energy. Bio-geochemical cycling. It can be mapped to show the importance of prostitutes.

She did this one night, laid poster board on the floor of her studio apartment and drew the "food web" of the "prostitution-system," studying the linkages, tracking the cycling of elements. She placed a

circle in the dead-center of the huge sheet of paper, and inside the circle, the word: SEX. Then she drew her lines and arrows, flowing from
the ground up, expanding in all directions, the irrepressible force of sex
like a fundamental nutrient supply to the higher trophic levels, where
predators reign over grazers who lord over primary producers, a.k.a.
street players. Sex, sex, and more sex. The precious resource. And bad
guys do it differently, she knew. They don't simply enjoy sex. They fight
for it, kill for it, die for it. Which means, for a cop, if you want to find a
perp— find the perp's girlfriend. In fact, finding her might be even better, more helpful. And why do so many of these assholes have hooker
girlfriends? Because in this ecosystem the capacity for genuine intimacy
fails to be a dominant, adaptive process. Sexual energy finds release
a simpler way: *bucks for fucks*. That's a cop-phrase she hated, though it
made an irrefutable point. Find a guy's favorite hooker—find the guy.

What a theory. She told almost nobody, of course. Most cops don't
like this sort of thing, although Danny, her ex, put up with it, for
a while. And—well, she admitted that her big ideas about prostitution were self-serving. Her career-bump—the gold shield—came from
playing dress-up. Undercover work accelerated her career. But her fascination with prostitution went beyond that. It amazed her what a
horrible, violent guy will say when he's horny. The connection between
sex and aggression. Love and war. A lot to learn here, especially for a
nice Jewish Jersey girl.

There—getting out of a minivan, blowing her john a kiss, giggling,
her small boney shoulders rising and falling in the dim light, Kitty, a
Ukrainian-Russian caught in the traffic at sixteen. Now, all grown-up
at nineteen: the sex worker from the dream? That's what she hoped.

"You want to get me killed?" It sounded like *keel-ed*.

"I just want—

"Get away. I seen talking to cop—"

"What—I don't—"

"Yessss—you fucking look like one—you—"

Kitty tugged on her stringy blonde hair, turned her head to look
down the street. Then took a step away. Her purple halter-top mini-
dress hung crookedly on slim hips, skinny legs, a paper-thin torso. A
scarecrow with a painted face—purple eyeshadow, same shade as the
dress, heavily rouged-up cheeks, thick dark lipstick and drawn-on eyebrows. All this failed to conceal a case of teenage acne.

"Bullshit, Kitty—I don't—"

"Your fucking arms—too much muscle."

In spite of herself, Eliana flinched, pulled at the bottom of her tight
skirt, adjusted the scoop-neck see-through blouse. Kitty was right, of
course. Too fit for the streets. That's why she tended to work the high-

end hotel sets.

"Look, we need to talk—"

"I answer you whole thing all in station. And you tell me—no more—and now—"

"Just a few quick questions—I promise."

"Uchh," Kitty turned her head, hard and fast, whipping her stringy hair across her face. "Fucking cop-promise."

"What time do you eat? You gotta eat, right?"

"I no eat—no *leaf*—till six a.m."

"Fine, 6:30. Court Square Diner, I'll be there. And you be there, too." She stepped closer, pushed two twenty-dollar bills into the palm of Kitty's hand. "Just a few questions, and I'm buying breakfast. See you at 6:30."

As Eliana turned away, she accidently caught a big whiff of Kitty's lavender perfume. Absurdly strong, it almost made her sneeze.

Chapter 2

A revolver's cylinder spins with a soft metallic click. A soothing sound to Vachik Savoyian. His monthly ritual, the first Sunday: dawn, a single bullet, a single spin of the cylinder. Then the barrel goes into his mouth.

And he pulls the trigger.

Nobody knows. Not even his favorite girls, the ones who invite conversation. But every month for the past year—what are the odds? Same odds, of course, each month—one-in-six. The gun, though it had belonged to his father in the Iranian military, was an American-made Colt Single Action Army .45, 4.75" barrel, with an ivory grip. "Cowboy popper," as collectors called it. This month, for some reason, the gun feels heavier than usual. Getting old, he thought, with a twinge of back pain as he lowered himself, fully clothed, into the bathtub. That's where he always positioned himself. If the gun fired, his brains and fragments of skull would splatter across easy-to-wipe tile. Vachik Savoyian—always thinking of others.

He leaned back now, elbows on the side of the tub, then looked down into the gun's long black barrel, its darkness like a tunnel with no end, the front sight at the tip, so integral. The Colt was a perfect gun, an archetypal gun, the weapon of the Wild West. And his father—a man he never knew—had used this exact gun, had left his sweat impregnated within this gorgeous hand-fitted mechanical sculpture created from forged steel. Yes, the fate of men shapes guns, and guns shape the fate of men.

But—silly feelings. It embarrassed Savoyian. Sentimentality. No wonder he'd told nobody about all this, not even that adorable Russian. A gun is a tool, like a screwdriver, a soulless instrument used to solve problems.

He thumbed the hammer, heard the unmistakable four clicks as it retracted, and quickly lifted his hand toward his mouth. The jerky move made his wrist ache—chronic tendonitis.

"Allahu Akbar" he whispered. And—although he'd told himself to bring the gun to his mouth, not his mouth to the gun—his head jutted forward, his lips wrapping tightly around the cool metal barrel. Then, a pause, a sniff—his nose felt stuffy, the smell of gun oil was faint. He swallowed hard, closed his eyes, and pulled the trigger.

Click.

Not a leaf falls, but He knows. Surah al-An am, 6:59

He pulled the gun from his mouth, wiped his lips, and got out of the bathtub. Then he dried the barrel, removed the bullet, and put the gun back in the same cloth bag his father had once used.

Now, part two: he lifted himself from the tub and sat down on the closed toilet seat, then lit a cigarette. He took a long hard drag. It helped him think. Helped him focus.

Unlike amphibians and reptiles, lizards and snakes, humans have neither a tough outer protection nor the ability to shed our integument *en masse* and replace it with a new coat. Savoyian had thought all this through, studied it. A voracious reader—autodidact, amateur philosopher. Minor sunburns, scratches, scrapes, and gouges create enough pain to remind us that we wear our feelings on the outside. A dangerous tendency. Either live or die, but don't complain. Pain—like fear—is an essential aspect of the human condition. Some jobs—some lives—are harder than others, yes, but nobody—nobody—escapes pain and fear.

He rolled up one pant leg and brought the lit cigarette to his calf about four inches below his knee. Then he watched the burning tip heat the layers of his skin. First the ordinary cells—which are, technically, already dead. The burn formed a circle the size of a quarter, producing redness, swelling, and moderate pain; then the germinal layer—the red circle blistered, fluid bubbling, increased pain; and, finally, the support tissue under the germinal layer of skin turned white, then olive-colored, and then black, achieving the full-thickness damage of a third-degree burn. He wanted to scream in pain; but, of course, that was the training. He pulled the cigarette away from his leg and brought it back to his mouth and took another hard drag.

Before going out, he'd cover the wound with a small bandage and antibiotic ointment. Bacteria can find its way into sterile tissue beneath burned skin and establish major infections quite quickly. A nasty, pus-filled wound—that could be annoying. That could interfere with his work.

Chapter 3

The 34th Precinct, serving the Upper Manhattan neighborhoods known as Washington Heights and Inwood, north of West 179th Street, covers two square miles, with 500 acres of parkland, including Inwood Hill Park and Fort Tyron Park. It's also home to the NYPD Cold Case squad. Eliana's former training officer runs the unit. Years ago, a large operation. Now, a total of about twelve detectives for almost nine thousand unsolved murders. That's dating back to 1985 when the records went electronic. Count the paper files and the Missing Persons and... well, nobody counts all those.

"Knock-knock," Eliana smiled, walked into the office.

Sergeant Jack Bayer, old enough to be her father, stood leaning over a big grey file cabinet drawer. When he looked up, Eliana realized she should have changed her clothes. The hooker costume: gold stretch sequin mini-skirt, scoop-neck fitted see-through top, her long, thick, dark auburn hair pulled and tied, but ready to drop as a prop, complementing the red eyeshadow and rouge accenting her already-high cheekbones. A naturally attractive face made gaudy for the streets. A good cover. An excellent cover, Kitty's critique of her muscular arms notwithstanding. The heels too, though she hated the damn heels. She'd dressed and raced out to Queens and—well, nearly twisted her ankle getting out of the car at that diner. Crazy fucking hooker boots. But it had been worth it. The breakfast with Kitty. The intuition—the gift of the gut. This could work. Especially with Jack's help. Always there for her. A cop's cop—thirty years on. Sergeant Jack Bayer knew how to take care of himself, how to balance the job and the rest of the world. A solid family—his wife a nurse, two kids in college. He coached girls' softball. Yes, Eliana respected not just the stripes, but the man. Though she thought his office smelled right now like gym shoes.

"Good morning, Detective," Sergeant Bayer said, and Eliana heard a forceful ahem in the older man's voice. "Or maybe not so good—I have bad news."

"I just talked to her, Jack—we had breakfast, and—"

"I know."

"You know?"

The file cabinet drawer slammed shut. Bayer stepped forward and dropped a thick manila folder onto a scratched-up metal desk cluttered with pens, folders, blank incident reports, a stack of exercise DVDs, and two empty coffee cups. Then he went to the window.

"What do you mean—you know?"

Bayer didn't answer. He muttered something about climate change and the scorching June heat and angrily pushed buttons on an air conditioner missing its plastic cover. The coiled metal insides were coated with grimy dust. When the unit finally rattled to life, he brushed dirt from his loose-fitting brown pants and white shirt. Built like an oversized teddy bear, a big firm belly, large thick arms, he stretched his thick, six-foot frame with a groan and reached to smooth a strip of grey duct tape running down the center of the windows cracked glass pane.

"Listen, Elly," Bayer turned now with his eyes carefully lowered. "This case isn't just cold, it's frozen."

He motioned to a metal folding chair in front of his desk. Eliana sat. The seat's hard cool metal stuck to her bare legs. The black lettering on the outside of the manila folder read: NEIL GOLDEN.

She knew the folder's contents, the dried-out, old-paper feel of every page, the excruciating dead-end emptiness of every investigative detail. Year after year, she'd checked and re-checked it all against the computerized Missing Persons records at 1 Police Plaza. Age of victim: 48; background: compliance officer at USBC bank; resident of Teaneck, N.J., married, three children; reported missing by wife; last seen March 1, 1994; according to canvas: faithful husband, devoted father, hard-working employee, synagogue board member, etc. Medical records, wills, insurance policies: nothing out of the ordinary.

Conclusion: triple zeros. Witnesses, none; body, not found; suspects, none.

The case: the disappearance eighteen years ago of Eliana's father.

"You've got to stop this poking around," said Bayer, his voice rising over the noisy air conditioner. He was still standing, his back turned to Eliana. She watched him adjust a two-year-old bird calendar on the wall near the windows. "We've been over this a million times," Bayer said, "the job's never going to permit you to investigate this case. And the on-your-own-time stuff—"

"Who told you I—"

"OCCB is set up out there."

"Oh, shit. Did I screw them up?"

Metal scraping grimy linoleum—there was a screech as Eliana drove her chair back from the desk, trying to face Bayer, who moved slowly from the out-of-date bird calendar to a dusty poster of the New York Yankees, a home-plate shaped pentagon of smiling players tacked to the wall with pushpins. Eliana recognized nobody, though she knew the adorable Derek Jeter was in there somewhere. To her, the headshots looked more like a group of uniformed, smiling salesmen than elite, world-beating athletes.

She waited in silence. Bayer continued to avoid looking at her. He pulled a pin from the wall, smoothed a corner of the poster, then pushed the pin back into the wall with a small grunt. He stepped back, examining his work, and without turning around said, "Doesn't matter." Now, finally, Bayer turned, and Eliana felt his eyes lock with hers. That old contest: who'll blink first? She always loved this game. Always won. Except against Charlotte, her little sister. Can't defeat Charlotte's spooked out stare. Radical politics glaze the eyes like—well, like Char's time in the psych ward. The gaze of the crazy.

"Eliana," Bayer said, lowering his voice. "I'm worried about you." She met his eyes and—game on—focused, not blinking, not moving. Until she saw a flash of light in her right eye and felt a bolt of pain shoot through the side of her head. A moment, a breath—then the throb. Pain on the pulse. A migraine. Four hours sleep—she'd asked for it. Still, she swallowed hard, trying to conceal. Nobody on the job knew about her headaches. Except Danny, of course. But ex-husbands don't count.

Bayer abruptly tugged on his tie, then turned and stepped out of his office. It caught Eliana off-guard. Had he somehow read the pain on her face? Was she slipping? No, no—inhale, two, three, four, pause; exhale, two, three, four, pause. And again... grateful to be alone, she massaged her temples as she breathed.

The door cracked open, and Bayer started to step back inside. She forced herself to stand up. Strong posture, shoulders back, weight centered. She leveled her eyes on Bayer, who angled himself in the doorway and, one hand on the knob, tossed her a sweatshirt. He looked at his shoes, boyish, and Eliana appreciated the sincere, old-guy embarrassment in his lowered gaze. "You still take your coffee extra-light, no sugar?"

"Good memory," she said, holding up the sweatshirt, a faded grey, long-sleeve hoodie with an NYPD logo on the front.

"You mug a tourist?" She sniffed, noting a smell like Indian spices. "Or—decoy squad, right? One of the cabbies?"

Bayer smiled. "You're good! Must have been that great training officer you had." He winked—his familiar, friendly, old-guy wink punctuated by that sharp clicking noise he made somehow in the back of his throat. Signature mannerism. Everyone knew Jack's wink-and-click. Even perps. Like a street tag, he'd arrest someone and the guy in cuffs would plead, "Yo, Winky, how 'bout some slack here?"

Eliana put on the sweatshirt slowly—head throbbing, even her hair seemed to hurt. She pulled the fabric carefully over her head. Then she sat and breathed into the pulsing pain, fighting the feeling of a metal hook stabbing her right eye. Re-image, she told herself, visualize: brain waves pushing across the cortex, neurons firing, nothing but chemistry. No metal hook, nothing jabbing, just tiny muscles and cells tensing—breathe. What's a headache, right? Hell, she'd taken a bullet. The three-inch scar on her right thigh always there to remind her. A headache, no big deal.

Bayer returned, opening the door with a burst of energy. He leaned over her to clear an open circle in the clutter of his desk, then set down her cup of coffee with an under-his-breath, "There ya go..."

"Sorry about the outfit—I should have changed. You know, all I did out there is talk to—"

"Without backup at three in the morning. You ever hear the phrase officer safety'?"

"I get it, Jack. I fucked up. I'll reach out to somebody in OCCB."

In her mind, she spelled it out: Organized Crime Control Bureau. Police jargon. She deeply resisted it, even now, after making detective. But she understood that her problem with cop-speak involved the question of whether she really fit in. On good days: protector of the social order; icon of justice; expert at the use of "legitimate force." Yes, on a good day she believed in being a cop. But on bad days she was just the crazy Jewish girl with a secret—that she became a cop because her father disappeared. On those days, the lingo felt like something she'd learned the way a tourist picks up a few phrases of a foreign language. Which made her no more authentic than a souvenir shop.

Bayer moved around to his side of the desk, then sat in a high-back swivel chair with a rip down the center of its black fabric. The way he settled in—Eliana knew: big daddy speech ahead. She swallowed a few gulps of the hot coffee. The burning in her throat soothed the pounding in her head.

"So... I know we've talked about this—"

"Nine hundred and forty-seven times, I think."

Bayer ignored her. "I'm worried about you."

"Copy that. I mean, '10-4.'"

Bayer smiled. "I'm serious, Eliana." He cleared his throat. "A lot of very smart people have already banged their brains against this case for a lot of years. And across divisions—Narcotics, Homicide, a Joint-Terror Task Force. And more than just our guys. Fed badges, too. And now? You're pissing people off acting like you're going to find something everybody else missed. Last month—cold calls to folks interviewed eighteen years ago? Showing up at people's doors?"

"That was one lady, and she was in the grocery store where my dad was last—"

"No—no. Don't explain—stop. Just stop and listen to me: you're chasing a ghost. And I've seen it before. A cop gets haunted and—" Bayer hesitated, mouth open, his eyes swollen with emotion. "Look, you're... what—thirty-five?"

"Thirty-six."

"OK, thirty-six. With a terrific future ahead of you, but if you don't believe in the future—the past will destroy you."

Good line, Eliana thought, but said nothing in reply. She didn't know how to reply. He was right... period.

Except for the dream—fourth time, same dream. Could she tell dear of Jack about her dream, her intuition?

Bayer shook his head, swallowed and opened his mouth again, as if to say more. But nothing came. She looked at him closely, noticing the way he'd aged. Only fifty-five, Bayer looked like a man close to seventy. Shoulders sagging, a wrinkle of skin flapping under his chin. His face, too. Cheeks drooping, loose, like a puffy sail lacking a strong wind. And his thinning, gray hair revealed a brown liver spot at the top of his narrow forehead. But his eyes—the bulging bags failed to diminish the power of his eyes. Large, dark, gleaming alertly.

Finally, he waved his hand, almost knocking over his coffee cup, which Eliana noted was balanced precariously on a stack of DVDs with the title "50 Days to Flat Abs."

"You're too good of a cop—that's another thing," he went on, his voice raspy with emotion. He was trying to control—contain—his feelings. Eliana appreciated it. He cared about her—it was that simple. "What you should do is give up the street crap and get your stripes. Sit behind a desk for a while. Boss people around, work regular hours. Hell, get married! Once you're off the streets, it's—"

He stopped mid-sentence, catching himself. Eliana knew he'd realized his blunder, and she wanted to say something about it. But the squeezing, pulsing migraine deepened suddenly like a nail hammering into the side of her head. She flashed on a famous homicide of a woman who'd been stabbed in the ear with a sheetrock saw.

Stop. Re-image, she told herself. Breathe. Feel the blood flowing, carrying nutrients, red cells. Healthy red blood cells, like the cavalry arriving to save and soothe. She fought the urge to lean forward, imagining, absurdly, that if she could press her head against the cool metal desk, she'd control the throbbing. Bayer, she could tell, was still feeling like a jerk for his memory lapse. He knew the story of her cop-crap marriage. Better than almost anyone. Hell, she'd cried on his shoulder.

"How is Danny anyway?" asked Bayer, trying to recover. He glanced at a pile of pens on the corner of his desk, picked one, checked to see if it worked.

Eliana just sat there. These migraines sometimes slammed her with such exhaustion blinking could be an effort. Keep punching, she told herself. Fight the fatigue.

She watched Bayer working the pens, scribbling on the corner of a blank incident report. If the pen wrote, he set it to one side. If broken, he threw it with a twist of anger into the green metal wastebasket across the room. The metallic ping of the pens hurt. Another symptom: heightened sensitivity to sound. Eliana concealed her wince. After firing off three rounds of bad pens, Bayer paused and looked up, waiting for Eliana's reply about her ex-husband.

"Sober," she said. "As far as I know, Danny's sober. Although..." Her voice trailed off. No energy for all that right now.

"I know your theory," Bayer nodded. "Still, if Danny's sober, that's good." He went back to the pens. Click, scribble, ping! Click, scribble... "All I'm really trying to say here, Elly, is that with your case record," he paused and put down the pens, looking at her now directly. "Your clean-as-a-whistle reputation, your ability to articulate yourself—"

"How about my legs?" She managed a small smile, though her voice lacked the force of sarcasm with a bite. Too tired.

"I'm being serious here—a few months studying, then start taking tests and talking to the right people—"

"Goddammit, I don't want to make rank—I want to make cases." She slapped the edge of his desk hard with the palm of her hand. A loud clear thwack. Her palm tingled, and she realized the outburst of anger unlocked the grip of her headache, a shift like the small adjustment of loosening a too-tight bandage. She inhaled, focusing her attention— micro-focusing. She felt the small steady stream of breath at the tip of her nose.

Bayer's eyes lifted—the desk-slap had gotten his attention.

"You know me, Jack," she went on, holding her voice steady. "Crime stat analysis, predictive modeling—fine, helpful. But look, this girl—"

He interrupted. "A hooker buying cop-love."

"She wants slack, yes, but—"

"Some guy gets his dick hard bragging about killing—nothing new there."

"It's not just—look, Jack, I've talked to her three times now, including this morning. You know how all this goes. Six weeks ago, we sweep up her block and I say, 'You help me, I help you.'—"

"Eliana—"

"I ask about guns or drugs—"

"Elly, you've told me all—"

"—And she says she knows about a murder. Her john told her he once killed a Jew-banker' from Jersey who—"

"Detective Golden!" Bayer barked, and Eliana felt the shout like a slap on her head. "Pay attention here."

She watched him lift his hand, then slowly spread three fingers across the upper sleeve of his shirt, tapping the spot where a uniform would show sergeant's stripes. "Chain of command," he said, in a low tone. "You understand?"

"Yes, sir. I understand, sir." She swallowed hard, forced herself again to lock eyes with Bayer. She wanted to tell him that she understood, sure. But she didn't believe. Not anymore. Chain of command, police work, street crime—vice, narcotics, the hell with it all. Let the prostitutes earn a living and legalize the fucking drugs and you could send home half the cops on the force. Everybody hates cops anyway. And the haters have a point: until this country starts to care about equality and take care of its poor—fuck it. Arresting people is like squashing roaches. The truth—no matter what detail she worked—only one crime really mattered to Eliana. Homicide. Her father's killer. And this time, in her gut, the dream...

But could she say all this to Jack? She kept her mouth shut and stared at the big teddy-bear man across the desk until, finally, she couldn't take it. The pounding of her headache returned—she needed to massage her temples. Blinking, looking away, she brought her hands to the sides of her head and said quietly, "She's gonna see the guy next week. I just want to follow them, then talk to him."

"You got a murder—bring it to homicide."

"I want to work it myself."

"Fine. Talk to your—"

"Jack, you know what they're doing to me in Vice—I'm the permanent high-priced working girl. Anytime there's an investigation anywhere in the five boroughs, I'm putting on the makeup."

"Hey, they call those details 'special' cuz they're citywide. And you wanted to be a detective."

"I'm not a detective—I'm a piece of ass."

"You want off the unit? I can get you back into a precinct."

"Right, the Five-O—I mean, Five-Slow, back up in Riverdale with the 'my people'? I just want—"

"All of the sudden prostitution isn't important? Trafficking, human rights. And with what's going on in the news these days? These people need—"

"You know what I'm saying, Jack. What I want—"

"I can't do it, Eliana. I can't take this hooker tip and open up a cold case, especially your dad's. It's not happening. You want to work your own homicide—great. Go above your lieutenant and talk to your C.O."

"He's a bigger jerk than the L.T."

"Hey, listen to me. We're playing cops-and-robbers here. And if you don't follow the rules, you can't play."

Eliana felt a strange moment of clarity—an intuition, like the feeling about her dream. The message. She knew, she understood, she grasped what needed to happen next: ignore chain of command, ignore Big Daddy Bayer, ignore the rules of the game. Get off the grid and take care of business—her own way.

All of this in a gut-flash, a break in the pulsing pain of her headache. She sat there—calculating, strategizing, concealing her thoughts. She suddenly felt strong, insanely alert. "You're right," she said, "I really don't know what's wrong with me. I—I appreciate your concern, Jack. I really do. I'm—overworked. Cooked. I just need—" She broke off and gulped the rest of her coffee. "Could you get me another cup?"

"You need to sleep."

"I know, but—"

"All right."

He picked up her empty cup and left her in the office, where she quickly leaned over his desk and rifled through the folder of her father's case. Not sure exactly what she was taking, she grabbed a handful of the top pages, folded them into a small tight square, and stuck it into the top of her boots. A moment later, Bayer returned with her cup of coffee.

"Here ya go."

"Thanks."

He nodded. "Fresh pot."

She smiled, drank. An awkward silence. Deceiving Jack, stealing pages—Eliana wanted nothing now but a quick getaway.

"You working a four-to-twelve today?" Bayer said, finally.

"Yeah. And I really should get home so I can grab a few hours of sleep." She stood, took a deep breath, then couldn't help sniffing the air.

Bayer laughed, a throaty chuckle. "Smells like a goddamn locker room in here, doesn't it? That fat beast O'Malley. Was in here for ten fucking years—with some cops you never get the stink out." He laughed more loudly, then got up from his chair and went absently to the air conditioner, as if the problem were there.

Eliana started for the door.

Bayer went on, "Anyway, shithole facilities, right? But—"

"—But glorious job." Eliana jumped in. Old line between them. Shared joke. "Hey, can I keep this?" She pulled on the sleeve of the heavy cotton sweatshirt.

Bayer nodded.

"Thanks. For everything. I needed a talk like this."

Chapter 4

The warm tub, bathroom lights off, a lavender-scented candle burning in a ceramic dish balanced on the edge of the sink. Like the *mikvah* of her youth, minus the blessings. Slowly, deeply, working through her migraine pain, Eliana breathed. And breathed. And felt the pounding in her head: pain, pure pain, plus words clattering, spiky memories, jangled fragments. And a prayer, in Hebrew—*Shema Yisrael...* That one, now? Yeah, right. The daily declaration of faith. As if she could claim to be a good Jew. That ended a long, long time ago. The crack, the break.

The night her father disappeared.

A thirteen-year-old girl sits alone in her bedroom. At a small teak desk, she's studying. Almost. Downstairs, her parents argue. Never before, not like this. Nasty, distant noise, their voices like angry music, undecipherable lyrics. But unmistakable emotion.

She should just focus on her homework, as her father told her to do. That was at dinner, when the atmosphere around the table grew mysteriously threatening, like one of those snap changes in the weather. A blast of cold, stilted conversation—the price of green beans, the kosher butcher s new assistant. The words swallowed. A hard, thick silence. The scrape of silverware, the sound of chewing. Both her sisters hunched over their plates. Now, she hears her mother's shrill voice, then her fathers, and she can't concentrate. Her geometry book stares at her, mocking. Strange pictures, curved lines like sinister smiles. *Identity Property, Inverse Property, Multiplication Property of Zero*—such phrases, dangerous, so pregnant with unintended meanings.

She gets up and stands in front of the mirror. The voices—what are they arguing about? She looks at her reflection and realizes she is still wearing her school uniform. She believes in this uniform, its purpose. She believes deeply but admits it to almost nobody, particularly her friends or her sisters. Intellectually precocious, unusually self-possessed, Eliana's the middle child—though she hates that pop psychology stuff. Like so much of what's "out there." Hollywood, etc. Shallow and... well, just plain dumb. Of course, she knows not to criticize others for the pleasure they find in popular culture. No self-righteous orthodoxy from her. We are the "modern" orthodox, yes? But even among her own—she takes herself seriously in a way hardly anyone does these days. Her sister Livi doesn't get it, that's for sure. And Char—too little. Her mother? No, not really. Fortunately, her father understands. A special bond exists between them. What drives, what motivates—yes, he understands. And the command is simple: *"To do justly, and to love mercy, and to walk humbly with thy God..."* Micah 6:8 *"He hath showed thee, O man, what is good; and what doth the Lord require of thee..."*

Her father's devotion to Torah; her devotion to her father. Symmetry.

She looks closely now at the uniform. Ma'ayanot Yeshiva High School for Girls. To Eliana, the school, the uniform—it expresses an identity befitting a *Bas Yisroel,* a Jewish woman. Every day: she makes sure the solid navy-blue skirt covers her knee. And the long-sleeved, button-down Oxford blouses—either solid white, light yellow, or pale blue—she tucks carefully into the top of her skirt. No T-shirts. No leggings or socks below the ankle. No backless shoes, no nail polish, no makeup. Jewelry permitted, yes—but kept to a minimum. Stars of David acceptable. But neck openings? Not to reveal the shoulder or extend below the collar bone.

All spelled out, the uniform's purpose reinforced by the teachers, the rabbis, and, of course, Mr. and Mrs. Fraylich, owners of the store where everyone shopped, where the uniform and official school sweatshirt were sold. Fraylich's Apparel—a Teaneck institution.

The Goldens moved to Teaneck for this exact reason: the modern orthodox Jewish community. Specifically, what impressed Eliana's father was the "eruv" agreement, a contract signed in the 1980s by Jewish leaders and Teaneck city officials allowing high-tension wires over two-thirds of the township, signaling an enclosed area for religious purposes. On the Sabbath, Jewish law prohibits carrying, which includes wheeling a carriage, except inside an enclosure. Under the wires, installed with Rabbinic supervision, carrying could be permitted. So every Saturday Neil Golden and his wife wheeled their baby daughters to and from synagogue, happily joining the throng of Modern Orthodox confidently observing their ancient laws.

Now, they argue. Eliana hears only fragments: "Not your place," her mother says. And something unintelligible, then: "...You're my husband, not some hero." And the retort, a deep-chested bark: "Blood, Miriam—they've got blood on their hands... Jewish blood!"

She's tempted to throw open the door, go downstairs, find out what this argument is about—but stops herself. Not my place, she thinks. That's what her mother just yelled. "Not your place." But to her father, not to her. His place, her place, your place. No, her ears playing mind-tricks. Just *fuhgeddaboudit!* That's what she tells herself—a foreign phrase. What the public school kids say, the tough-looking boys who hang out in front of Sal's pizzeria, their faces tinted orange from the neon sign flashing SLICES. Yes, toughen up, she thinks. Little argument between parents—it's their business. *Fuhgeddaboudit!*

She steps back to her desk, hits the radio, turns up the volume. The song playing is one of her big sister's favorites: Madonna's "Justify My Love." Dark, dirty, scary, especially the breathy parts, like someone in pain. Yes, her sister, Livi, going into her senior year in high school, Livi loves a boy named Avi Stimmel, one year older, who graduated top of the class from *Heichal Ha Torah* and went straight into a six-year medical school program at Northwestern University in Chicago. The distance kills, and Livi's young-love sadness hangs over the house like a bad smell. Nobody knows how to acknowledge it. Except five-year-old Charlotte, who was drawing pictures of Avi in his black hat and long coat every day for four straight weeks, until one night in October Livi snapped: "Stop it! That doesn't help me!" Which sent Charlotte running off to cry in Eliana's arms.

She hugged her little sister as she gazed at her big one. The middle child. Eliana understands the challenge of living in two worlds. Divided sympathies, conflicting loyalties—a sister on either side. Who am I? Whoever you want me to be.

Maybe that's why she spends so much time alone—because only then can she choose for herself who she is. Right now, listening to Madonna's dark breathy moans, she chooses the big girl in love, and she makes the song louder, trying to drown out the argument downstairs. Then she positions herself in front of the mirror and pulls off her kerchief, shakes out her hair, and unfastens her skirt, letting it drop to the floor. Her waist is slim, her legs long, her hair thick and dark. She unbuttons her shirt and looks inside—yes, decent-sized breasts—but too pointy, she thinks. Livi told her that's the way it is in eighth grade. Still, she's turning the heads of the Yeshiva-boys—the older ones, too. And the truth: the attention makes her uneasy. What she imagines they imagine under her knee length skirt. It's not that way with her. Her father knows, better than anyone, how serious-minded she is. It shows in her face. Slow to smile, quick to wonder.

Suddenly, a loud crash, dishes breaking? The house seems to shake as her father's voice booms, "Justice! That's why!"

Eliana hurries to her dresser, pulls out a pair of sweat pants and sweatshirt, and runs into the hall where Livi and Charlotte stand at the top of the stairs holding hands. Charlotte, dressed for bedtime, wears a cotton nightgown, a Disney princess on the front. Her face looks about to cry, lips trembling.

"What happened?" Eliana whispers to Livi.

Her big sister shakes her head. "I'm not sure—Dad wants to go to the grocery store, but mom is afraid. She doesn't want him to go out of the house. Because of the trial."

Eliana understands only partially. She knows her dad works at a bank in Manhattan. And that the bank is doing bad things. And her dad told his bosses, who did nothing. So he told the police, but not the regular police. Special government police. Which angered her mother. Because now he's supposed to be a witness at a trial—or hearing, or something. In two days, he testifies.

"It's a responsibility," her father says now, his voice hoarse.

To Eliana, he sounds sick or injured—or worse. Drunk? She's never known her father to be drunk. Except on Purim. And then the drunkenness was a *mitzvah*, wasn't it?

"You want to talk about responsibility?" her mother says. "What about your responsibility to me? To the girls?"

Hearing this, Eliana starts down the stairs, but Livi grabs her by the elbow. "No," she whispers. "Let them talk it out."

Eliana hesitates, leaning over the stair's landing, one hand on the wooden banister. She watches her parents. They stand with their backs to each other at opposite ends of the living room, her father near the bookshelves, her mother leaning on the small grand piano. Between them sits the empty couch. After a moment, her mother straightens up and gazes out the darkened front windows. Miriam Golden, a tall athletic woman, younger-looking than her forty-five years. "I couldn't sing today," she says quietly, almost as if she were talking to herself. "The children in the class looked up at me, waiting. But my throat— the tightness... One of the little girls finally said, 'Mrs. Golden, should we go get the principal?'"

She turns now to face her husband and, more loudly, says, "I can't take it, Neil. First my sleep, then my appetite, and now—I am scared. I am scared all the time."

Eliana watches her father shake his head, then he turns and takes several short jerky steps across the room. None of the natural grace of Eliana's mother. An odd couple. Her father almost six inches shorter, his shoulders rounded, posture stooped. Her mother naturally erect, chest lifted, the poise of a professional singer, though, in fact, she just teaches music part-time in a local elementary school. Someday she hopes to be a cantor. And beyond their physical appearance: their interests differed dramatically. Her mother loved opera; her father, the Yankees; her mother loved gourmet food and dining at expensive restaurants, while her father could eat sardines from a can with his head in a book. But their differences melted away when it came to the shared commitment at the center of their lives: a devotion to Judaism.

They had once seriously considered moving to Israel. They visited the holy land, looked at a home to buy, found a school for the girls, even interviewed for jobs. But ultimately, they chose to remain in the United States not for the convenience of an "easier" life, but because they deeply embraced the principle of Diaspora Judaism as a value in and of itself. Not necessarily superior to Zionism, they believed staying in the United States emphasized the resilience and adaptability of Jewish culture and identity across different geographical and cultural landscapes. By living as observant Jews in the United States, they were linked to the centuries and centuries of their people who had thrived by integrating into host societies while simultaneously preserving their distinct identity. Living as Diaspora Jews enriched both Jewish culture and history and the culture and history of the society in which the Jews happened to find themselves living. Yes, the Goldens knew they were Jews first, and Americans second. But maintaining this dual identity was important. And, of course, Israel—as a state—must exist. This was beyond dispute.

Indeed, right now, watching her mother and father argue, Eliana only partially grasps that all this Jewish history is at the center of the conflict between them. Her father seems almost out of breath, as if he'd just run a lap, as he scurries across the living room and takes hold of his wife's elbows. "A corrupt bank," he says, hitting the consonants so hard his head shakes at the end of each word, his yarmulke bouncing on his thick curly hair. "My bank has blood on its hands, Miriam. Jewish blood."

"You are not the bank. And you have done nothing wrong."

"But doing nothing is wrong." They stare at each other, unblinking, unmoving. "*The wicked flee when no man pursueth, but the righteous are bold as a lion,*" he says.

"Don't—" Her mother turns her face. "Please don't—"

But her father continues, voice rising, "*They that forsake the law praise the wicked: but such as keep the law, contend with them.*"

"I don't want to hear it," her mother yells, twisting her arms free, stepping away, turning her back. Then a deep breath, straining, "I don't want to hear Torah," she says, quietly.

And in the long stiff silence that follows, Eliana—shocked—feels her own body tighten.

"You don't mean that, Miriam," her father says in a low tone. "You don't mean that—"

"I do mean it," she turns, and Eliana watches, horrified.

Her tall powerful mother with the elegant poised posture looking down at her small fiery father. And the words of Torah. Rejected. Dismissed. How could her mother—so wounding. And so wrong.

Her father nods, lowering his gaze, as if looking for something on the floor. He takes a step forward, then turns away, shifting his weight oddly, foot to foot, like a man balancing on ice. Finally, he turns his back on Eliana's mother and goes to the front door. One hand on the knob, he stops. A familiar gesture, like when he forgets his keys or glasses. But now he turns and lifts his chest, a gulp of air. *"They that forsake the law praise the wicked: but such as keep the law, contend with them,"* he says loudly, clearly aware that he's repeating himself. Then he continues, "Do you hear me, Miriam? Do you hear those words? You can disagree with me. Disapprove of me. Disrespect me. I am just a man. One puny, insignificant man. But do not—please, Miriam, do not!—disrespect Torah." Her mother and father stare at each other like actors on a stage. In her memory, years later, that's how it plays: the living room a well-lit set, the couch, the bookshelves, the baby grand piano—props of a suburban home. The action: impassioned exit speech, *Proverbs 28, Verse 1*. Fade to black.

And she never sees her father again.

Chapter 5

The plan had been for Neil Golden to be protected by Federal Marshals, but the night he insisted on going out to the local grocery store, that protection hadn't yet begun. It was scheduled to start the following week, when Golden would be accompanied from Teaneck, New Jersey, to lower Manhattan, where he'd provide testimony before a federal grand jury in the U.S. District Court—Southern District of New York. Depending on the grand jury outcome, he might eventually have been taken—still under Federal protection—to Vienna, Virginia, where he would appear before the Financial Crimes Enforcement Network, a joint-effort of the Treasury Department, the Justice Department, the CIA, and the FBI. Why? Because eight months earlier, Golden, an Internal Compliance Officer at USBC Bank, had discovered a slew of transactions including money transfers, deposits, and other more arcane banking activity that showed USBC doing business with companies on the Office of Foreign Assets Control (OFAC) sanctions list.

Terrorism funding.

In the 1990s, banks started forming "anti-money laundering units." The new hot thing. And for good reason, Neil Golden thought, eager to move into the field, because six months earlier—WTC attack #1.

The headline that changed his life: February 26, 1993. Two men in a rented yellow Ryder van drove into a public garage beneath the World Trade Center. They parked on Level B-2, then lit a twenty-foot fuse connected to a 1,200-pound bomb contained inside their vehicle. Then they fled.

Neil Golden read and reread the news stories, which explained that exactly twelve minutes later, at 12:17 p.m., the bomb inside the van exploded, ripping a hole one hundred feet wide through four sub-levels of concrete. Fifty thousand people were evacuated. Amazingly, only six were killed, with one thousand forty-two injured. For some reason, beyond the obvious horror, what captured Goldens mind: the elevators. Hundreds of people trapped in elevators, including a teacher with seventeen kindergartners on their way down from the South Tower Observation Deck. For five hours they waited, suspended between the 35th and 36th floors, seventeen five-year-olds. Perhaps it was because his wife taught little children, but Golden found this particularly haunting. Seventeen five-year-olds stuck in an elevator for five hours—how would these children understand what had happened to them?

Terrorist Ramzi Yousef—captured in 1995 in Pakistan through a combined effort of the FBI and other international agencies—was sentenced to life in prison at the ADX Florence supermax federal facility in Colorado. Built in 1994, located about 90 miles south of Denver, nicknamed "the Alcatraz of the Rockies," the prison was specifically designed to house high-risk inmates such as terrorists, organized crime leaders, and other individuals deemed too dangerous for less secure facilities. Yousef is held in "administrative segregation," which means he is kept in isolation for up to 23 hours a day.

During his trial, Yousef explained the simple and clear purpose of the attack: to avenge the suffering Palestinian people had endured at the hands of U.S.-aided Israel.

Ah, yes, of course, Israel, the Jewish Question—to Neil Golden, that's what it came down to: Jewish life and its threat of extinction. At the bottom of the World Trade Center rubble, like a tiny particle of iron at the center of a huge magnetic field, lay one indestructible, eternally problematic little nub: the Jew. Like a puzzle of nature, mysterious in its power, deflective, as impossible to diminish as the spinning motion of electrons orbiting the tiny atoms of which they are composed. And the heart, the vector of Jewish life: fear, unceasing Jewish fear, coupled with an unceasing Jewish determination to fight. Golden accepted that he was not a hardcore Zionist but a proud Diaspora Jew. Still, he believed everyone needs a home; Israel must exist.

Within a week of working in the new compliance department he discovered disturbing information. Violations were obvious, and everywhere. He explained to his wife.

"It's not rocket science," he said. "I'm not even investigating. I'm just looking at this list of companies that the U.S. cannot do business with—and, for example, there's Caribe Supermarkets. It's right there on the list. A chain based in Khartoum, but it says right on their financial statements that they are owned by Tadico, which is a holding company owned by KhailahTajideen and his brother, both of whom live in Beirut, and are known financiers of Hezbollah. It is all right there—in black and white. All you have to do is look at it."

Business never intimidated Miriam, and at first she entirely supported her husband's whistle-blowing. He brought home documents; they looked at them together. He drafted memos; she proofread them. He rehearsed his presentation; she improved his "performance skills." But USBC upper management heard none of it. Suspicious Activity Reports slow business. The message to Golden and all compliance officers: make the SARs go away. Clear as many alerts and investigations as possible. And to clear them, Golden learned, was easy—just add a dot or dash or a different numeric coding. Poof! The OFAC screening was defeated, the wire went through, and the bosses and the customers were happy. Everyone got their money and went home on time.

The media, eventually, would call this "stripping the payments."

Neil Golden called it evil.

Ancient history, yes. She'd been over all this a million times. The night of "the argument," the night her father never returned from the grocery store. But Eliana couldn't stop thinking about it now as she sat in the tub with her full-blown migraine. Seeking relief, trying to clear her mind— the warm, wet, heat suffocated. Her head felt like a huge deformed gourd, swollen. And instead of soothing—the candle, the lavender smell, it made her want to puke. Sweet, cloying, like cheap perfume. Like Kitty's perfume, right. Would she barf in the bathtub?

The body. She'd figured it out a long time ago—how to get away with murder. Hide the body. That simple. No body, no homicide. That's why her father's case lingers in "missing persons" limbo. And that's why Charlotte—back in her days on the locked ward for adolescents—told the psychiatrists she'd get better as soon as they had a funeral for her father. A need for "closure," as they say. Now, of course, Charlotte's over all that. Done with doctors, she found "closure" another way— by deciding the whole country is fucked, including the corrupt bankers who murdered her father. And that's why... that's why that's why that's why that's why—the words nagged, knotted, nauseated. Eliana grabbed the side of the tub, suddenly needing to hurry for the toilet, but she fell back with a splash. Water sloshed onto the bathroom floor. Who gives a shit, she thought. I barf where I barf. And she waited, expecting, breathing, a sour taste rising into her chest. But nothing came. She sat there, head pounding, her hands floating, her fingers like fat white worms under the water's surface. The wave of nausea passed with a burp and stab of pain under her ribs, then a fuzzy feeling of uncertainty: Kitty. The lavender smelling teenage sex worker whose lead Eliana wanted to follow. Crazy? A good hunch? Or just stupid?

This morning in the diner Kitty sat there in the harsh fluorescent light, her face inches from her plate, eating her eggs like a dog working a bone. Eliana watched. All that makeup Kitty wore—it couldn't be healthy, she thought, and suggested to the girl that she go wash up. But Kitty refused. A silent headshake, eyes lowered.

They'd been through the story a few times already when Eliana said, "What you're telling me is very serious, Kitty. So I just want to ask again: do you really believe this guy actually killed someone?"

Bad question. Eliana shouldn't have asked it. Not fair to ask Kitty what she "really believed"—about anything. When Kitty looked up from the empty white plate, her dull, grey, heavily lidded eyes, in spite of the makeup, sat deep in her pasty face like empty windows in a vacant house. Someone once lived there, maybe. Eliana looked carefully at the girl's pale skinny arms: no needle marks. Not yet, anyway. Kitty just sat there staring, then looked at Eliana's barely eaten pancakes as if unsure what they were.

"Still hungry? Want some of my pancakes?"

Kitty nodded.

"OK. Just... one more time—did this guy say anything—anything at all you haven't told me—about who he killed?"

"He tell me a Jew. He tell me he responsible for Jew-banker killing."

"Yes, you told me that. But responsible? Responsible how? Did he say he actually killed the Jewish banker? Or he was just responsible for the killing?"

"What difference is it?"

Eliana leaned back in the booth, frustrated. "Right, good question, Kitty. You ought to be a lawyer."

Again, a tremble from Kitty's bare bony shoulders. Was she cold? Or frightened? Watching her shiver, Eliana felt a wave of regret for the lawyer crack. This poor kid is doing the best she can, she thought. Eliana pushed the pancakes forward, but kept her hand on the edge of the plate.

Kitty looked hard at the food. "He—he's a very nice man. I could ask him more."

"What do you mean 'nice'? How is he nice?"

"Gentle. And old, sort of."

"A nice gentle old man?"

Kitty nodded and took a deep breath and clearly wanted to say more. Maybe the promise of those pancakes, Eliana thought, and almost smiled at her masterful moment in the fine art of interrogation. She pushed the plate forward until it was right in front of Kitty, who immediately covered the pancakes with syrup and started to eat.

Eliana watched her chew. Instead of shoveling the food into her mouth like she did with the eggs, this time Kitty took small, deliberate, polite bites. It made Eliana wonder what kind of life Kitty might have if she didn't have this one. It also made her wonder about Kitty's real name. She almost asked, but instead said, "You want some more eggs? I could get you some more eggs."

Kitty shook her head. "No, thank you."

"Sure?"

Kitty nodded.

"OK," Eliana leaned forward, her elbows on the table. "Listen, Kitty, I need you to think hard and try to remember. Is there anything—anything at all—about this nice gentle old man that you haven't told me?"

"He sometimes bring a friend. A man in a chair. You know, without any legs."

"What?"

"The chair—I mean—the man. He has no legs. I mean, no legs that work."

"He brings a friend in a wheelchair?"

"Yes, that's it. But only sometimes. Usually he come alone. And he—well, last time he come alone, right after he brought a friend, two days after, and he started to cry." Kitty looked away. "Not hard—but there were tears when he talked about—" She hesitated, as if trying to remember the moment. Then she ran her hand through her oily hair. "He like to talk about guns."

"Did he have one?"

"I don't think so."

"Did he ever show you a gun?"

Kitty suddenly squirmed and pushed away from the table and yanked her feet into her lap. She unlaced her faux suede boots. Classic hooker shoes: stiletto heels, peep-toe opening, round cut-outs in the fabric, leaving her calves exposed. Eliana wore a similar pair.

"Itchy," Kitty said, loudly. "My feet are horrible itchy."

Athlete's foot, Eliana thought. Now there's a serious problem.

"Guns, Kitty. Did he ever show you a gun?"

Feet free from the boots, Kitty scratched her arches, both of them, hard, fast, the sound of fingernails scraping skin.

"No gun," she said, finally, still scratching. "He never showed me guns. I tell you already—a Jew, he said. He killed a Jew banker from Jersey."

But the way Kitty had hesitated before this last hurried little summary, all the while scratching and scratching her feet, thinking back on it now, Eliana sensed something wrong. A false note. Was Kitty simply lying?

A weird panic came over her, a feeling of claustrophobia. The bath water rising. She tasted it. Warm soapy soup up to her chin, lips, nose. Her breath tightened. She was sinking. Sinking down into it. She heard Bayer saying: *I'm worried about you, Eliana... You need to stop chasing this ghost, you need to get off the streets. Before something bad happens.* No, no, not sinking—drowning.

She pulled herself fast out of the tub, stepping onto the slippery tile floor with a lunge, nearly falling. She grabbed the sink, steadied herself. I need help, she thought. Following this hooker-tip? Ignoring chain of command? I need—*yes,* help. To talk. To someone. But—

Head pounding, she slowed her breath, catching a glimpse of herself in the bathrooms candle-lit mirror. A shadow fell over her bare breasts, rising slightly as she inhaled. Then she looked at the small white spot on the outside of her thigh—a thick, ropey patch a few inches above the knee—her bullet wound. Still no plastic surgery. Why not? Doesn't matter, she thought. I need—right now—Danny. Her ex-husband, in spite of everything, he cared and understood and wouldn't turn her away. A solid cop and a good man... yes, I need Danny, she thought.

And the thought angered her.

Chapter 6

A radio run on the Upper West Side: "Two-Four Charlie, 10-34, Broadway & 112, female, early twenties, caller says she's fighting back, no weapons identified—but be advised: four males. Repeat: 10-34, four males, one female, Broadway & 1-1-2."

The female, a Columbia University undergraduate, was Eliana Golden.

Lights and siren, right off the TV shows, Danny jumped the curb, rolling his RMP onto the sidewalk twenty yards from where Eliana held a big blond-haired guy in an arm-lock on the ground, shoulder hyper-rotated, elbow hyper-extended, her full-body leverage giving her complete control over a man who outweighed her by a hundred pounds.

As Danny stepped out of the car, Eliana looked up. Later, she'd recall seeing a trace of a smile on Danny's face. An expertly executed submission hold, she knew. Danny walked straight up to her, but said nothing. Neither did she. She just adjusted the slight sideways angle in which she pressed her knees into the big guy's back.

Finally, Danny said, "What's goin' on here?"

"I was waiting for some friends over at the West End bar, and this guy laid hands on me, then he and his three friends over there followed me down the street," Eliana said quickly.

Danny looked away. The three friends, he assumed, were the guys standing under the red awning of Famiglia's Pizza, holding in their drunken laughter. The guy on the ground started to lift his head and say something, but Eliana went on, "He's lucky I haven't dislocated his shoulder."

Danny nodded.

Eliana watched him throw his shoulders back, adjusting the collar of his uniform. Calm, deliberate. He seemed to be gazing into the distance, trying to remember something. Until his attention snapped back to her. "Kodokan Judo?"

"Yeah," she said, quietly. The question surprised her. "And an Aikido take-down."

Danny nodded, looking off again into the distance.

"Officer," the guy on the ground started to speak, "this is a big misunderstanding."

"I bet it is," Danny said, and this time Eliana definitely saw a small smile. Just then another police car pulled up. Much later, it would occur to Eliana that Danny had been waiting for backup. As two other cops approached, Danny stepped forward and tapped Eliana on the shoulder. "OK, let him up. We all need to talk."

In the end, before it was all over, Eliana had asked Danny for his phone number and explained she was thinking about a career in law enforcement. Being this forward surprised her, but something had come over her, something she didn't know how to control. Maybe it was the adrenaline-rush of violence. She'd never before used her years of martial arts training, not on the street like this. That was part of it. But—something else too. Something truly significant. Being up close to a cop—the uniform, the badge, the gun. For so many years, since her father's disappearance, law enforcement—its failure and its promise—hovered over her life in the form of a grand meta-narrative that explained everything, and nothing. Justice, her father's principles, his brave action, his willingness to get involved in important affairs, to be an integral part of—what? What was all this business about terrorism and safety and security and locking up the bad guys? Now, standing in front of this flesh-and-blood cop with the steady blue eyes, she felt these questions like a pain rising from somewhere in her stomach—or deeper, the gut-level of muscle fibers and blood cells. Yes, the urge for justice, like a physical ache. She wanted this man. A desire stronger than she'd ever dreamed possible.

When Danny scratched his phone number on the back of a gas receipt and handed it to her, Eliana felt her heart pounding. Then her face relaxed and she settled into a pleasant calmness, a tingling in her center, warmth rushing into her cheeks as she moistened her dry lips. He was staring, checking her out. She knew it. This man, this cop, this guy with the steady blue gaze—she had a weird sense of imagining herself right now from his point of view. Her lips. She'd put on a bit of makeup before going out, and she knew now her lips glistened a deep red in the hazy light from the streetlamps. They were full lips—but not perfectly symmetrical. Instead, bow-shaped, her lower lip slightly heavier, suggesting the beginning of a pout. Over the years, she'd stood in front of the mirror for more hours than she'd like to admit, trying to make peace with her too-big lips, her permanent trace-of-a-pout expression. Her conclusion: *fuhgeddaboudit!* I am what I am.

The silence lengthened as they stood looking at each other. She expected the moment to become awkward. But it didn't. Danny's eyes were calm, his head still, his shoulders back—everything about him suggested authority, strength, power.

"Ollie's," she said quietly, flicking her head toward the Chinese noodle place up the block. "You ever eat at Ollie's? I see cops in there all the time."

She almost invited him to dinner right on the spot, but hesitated. A flicker of self-consciousness broke through, thank God. She'd almost made a fool of herself. It's mythic, she knew. The whole rescue-bit, the knight in shining armor, how some women—the wounded ones, especially—throw themselves at cops or military guys, the man-in-the-uniform saving their lives. But she knew better. This cop didn't save her from anything. She'd taken care of herself, thank you very much. Of blue-eyes here just showed up after the asshole in the bar made a mess. Cops, she thought, are clean-up guys, not saviors. And no cop has ever figured out what happened to her dad.

Still, she couldn't stop the feeling of attraction, the pinch of excitement in her stomach. It embarrassed her, thinking how this man lived somewhere beyond the ordinary, on the edge of reality, a place buzzing with vitality—where "good" meets "bad," where crimes occurred, where the moral universe mattered. Yes, he lived for something greater. Law, order, justice.

Years later, she'd think of this moment, talk about it in therapy, and understand that what she felt toward Danny—pure projection. It had almost nothing to do with Danny himself.

The truth: Officer Danny McPartlan never wanted to be a hero or a savior or even a detective or a boss. Nothing but an ordinary patrol cop. Roll up in the RMP, step out wearing the uniform: no confusion. Everybody knows who you are. And making rank? Well, wearing stripes means other cops' problems become yours. No thanks.

Over the years, Eliana learned to appreciate Danny's approach to the job—up to a point. The context: a cousin of Danny's working undercover had been shot by another cop. A mix-up about the COD—color-of-the-day. Blue bandanna supposed to be red and worn on the left side, or was it red and on the right—whatever. The cousin survived, but so did the family embarrassment. And fear. Danny had a recurring nightmare where his father, a tough-as-nails lieutenant, doesn't recognize him. "Police, don't move! Police, don't move!" his father keeps yelling in the dream, pointing his Glock, while Danny squeals, "Dad, it's me! It's me!"

And the media—they loved the Keystone Kops bit. Who needs bad guys when the good guys shoot each other? The hilarity of incompetence.

Except of course it's not funny. And Eliana came to see that Danny's fear involved not just the rare occurrence of a cop-on-cop shooting, but the always-present possibility of making a mistake of any kind. When cops fuck up, it's bad. Real bad. And these days, especially, every cop

in America is nervous. Hence, the Patrol Guide. Danny didn't just follow it, he lived by it, observed it like a religious Jew observing *halakha*.
That's how Eliana thought of it. For the orthodox, no button-pushing
on the Sabbath, so forget elevators, appliances, even turning on a light.
For Danny, no casual actions without considering the consequences, so
simple questions could trigger his famous pause-and-thousand-yard-
stare, and then a response like, "That's Information Concerning Official Business of Department—P.G. two-one-two dash seven-six. Let's
check with the Sergeant."

Fear of mistakes. Eventually, Eliana saw this quality in Danny—
and saw nothing else. It repelled her. No, stronger: she hated it, hated
the way Danny concealed his fear. He fooled everyone. The way he
looked, walked, talked—everything about him said: "tough cop, good
cop, guy in charge." Uniform always pressed, shoes shined. What cop
actually shines their fucking tactical boots? When other cops broke his
balls about this—he smiled, impervious. Broad shoulders, slim waist, a
relaxed-but-confident posture. And his face—flat-nosed, square-jawed,
a cool thin-lipped gaze. Eyes pale blue. Effortlessly, he intimidated.
When he got out of his car or walked across a room or approached a
crowd on a corner, he moved with—well, a kind of fluidity, grace. The
natural power of a light heavyweight boxer was coiled in his smooth
step. Golden Gloves, USBO, he'd been nationally ranked. And knowing that damn Patrol Guide so thoroughly—that also gave him a deep
confidence. Like the observant boy in the front row, keeping up with
the rabbi, quietly proud of how well he knows the prayers.

When they first met, Eliana fell for all of it. Under his spell in a
heartbeat, she didn't stand a chance. It took being married two years,
but Eliana eventually understood that Danny approached being "on
the job" the way most cops do: wear your vest, wait for backup, and
make it to retirement. The "edge of reality buzzing with vitality," the
"moral universe?" Those were Eliana's issues, not Danny's. Yes, a brave
man, like a lot of cops. And, sure, he drank too much, like a lot of
cops. But the bottom line on Danny: an honest guy who does his job,
nothing more or less.

Standing over the copy machine, surprise rippled through his
body—a goose-necked double-take. Danny spotted Eliana pushing
through the heavy glass-and-steel door. What the—?

Three years since the divorce, over a year since they'd seen or spoken to each other; but he still ached for her. Last month, March 20th,
her thirty-sixth birthday, a bourbon-inspired swell of emotion—yes,
drinking again, skipping meetings—he sent her a store-bought card,
a cliched illustration of a brightly colored cake with the words: May

Your Day Be Sweet and Delicious. And he followed up with a call, then a text. But— nothing, no response. Of course: a divorce is a divorce. Stupid of him to reach out. He suffered two sleepless nights and then let it go.

Now, he positioned himself in front of the vending machines in the muster room, where he could keep an eye on the front desk. Eliana was showing her ID. She looked—well, as always, terrific. Worn faded jeans, snug-fitting cotton blouse, her long, thick, auburn hair fell casually over her shoulders, an effortless sensuality. She held, neatly folded, a lightweight summer windbreaker in the crook of her elbow. So poised, unhurried, that quiet confidence of hers. What she lacked in natural street smarts she'd made up for with "presence." Danny's word for it, her pure high-octane intellect, combined with her crazy, crazy determination to be a great cop.

The desk sergeant pointed, and she headed for the wooden partition. Danny stepped quickly to meet her straight on.

"Hey," he called across the room.

She kept walking without breaking her calm smooth stride, then smiled, offering a small nod. But Danny saw the tension in her eyes. It took a while—two years of marriage—before he could read those eyes. The pain, the headache. She concealed her feelings with the best of them, a natural undercover.

"You free?"

Danny considered cracking a joke, but caught himself. "Sure. You looking for me?"

Another small smile. He motioned. She followed. At an empty interview room, he pulled open the door, stepped aside for her to enter, catching the scent of her perfume as she swished past—or, not her perfume, her shampoo. It launched him, sent him flying backward, into the past. Yes, that floral smell, roses. Subtle, gorgeous, the deep purple bottle sitting upside down in the metal basket hanging over the showerhead— she'd sometimes call to him from the bathroom. Start a conversation, or continue one. Through the shower doors frosted glass, he'd watch her soap up, transfixed, hypnotized, feeling utterly destroyed by his lust: the curve of her hips, the strength in her long lean legs. That body—she trained like a professional athlete. Six days a week, alternating workouts, keeping a log, drinking protein shakes. Her arms, shoulders, abs—muscular, toned, hard. But still, at least in Danny's opinion, her body was deeply feminine. She worried about that. Losing touch with what she called her "softness."

The shampoo scent faded. She slid into a hard plastic chair on the far side of the table, and he fought a wave of embarrassment at his racing memories. Physical heat had fueled their intimacy. Shameless lust, spontaneous sex. At their peak, unapologetically raunchy, they made love anywhere, everywhere—the living room rug, in the car, and, once, during a boring Christmas party they slipped into the host's bathroom. Good—no, great sex. Eliana joked about Danny's stamina, invoking Celtic mythology. But all that was a long time ago. His thinking about this now was completely inappropriate.

He sat down across from her. What happened next confused him. It was a small gesture, but disturbing. She glanced at her fingers, then picked quickly at her pinky, a clicking sound, pick-pick-pick, until she ripped off a piece of nail. It bled. She ignored it and went fast to the pinky on the other hand until a hunk of nail came loose, and again she ripped. Such an obvious tell. A display of nerves. In fact, Danny wondered if it might be fake, a calculated play? With a quick breath she folded her hands, and her usual poise and confidence returned. Level gaze, her large brown eyes soft but focused.

"I need some help," she said, her tone controlled, flat.

Danny felt his stomach drop. "What kind of help?"

"A murder."

"You're on a—?"

She shook her head, started to speak, but Danny raised his hand. "If it's not your case—?" He heard the edge in his voice and saw Eliana's eyes react. And in a flash of intuition, he understood. Everything. The whole story: beautiful Eliana Golden, the innocent crime victim, the woman on a mission. Find her father's killer, save her messed-up sister, live happily ever after...

He watched her lean forward, her hands pressing hard into the scratched-up interview room table. Blood seeped from one of her ripped cuticles—the left hand, the ring-finger hand. That felt significant. To Danny, at least. Everything about the moment felt significant.

"Vice is making me crazy," she said, quietly. "I've got to break out of this."

"Shoot your pimp." Danny tried for a light tone. Saw it failed.

Eliana said, "I got a tip from a working girl—"

"—And you don't want to give to Homicide?"

Eliana nodded.

Danny went on, "You ever notice all these forms and reports in police stations, the computers and printers and all that stuff? You know, that's because we don't just give out a badge and a gun and say, 'go solve crimes.' We try to keep track of who's doing what, and we've got one or two rules we try to follow."

Eliana's eyes narrowed, closed, and when she lifted her hands to massage her temples Danny knew what he was seeing.

A pause. He said nothing. He felt bad about his sarcasm. Unnecessary, not helpful. The silence lengthened. "Migraine?" he whispered, finally.

A nod. "Yesterday—just about gone."

"Could see it when you came in," he went on. "That left eye, always sags a little after..."

He let his voice trail off. Then he took a deep breath and looked at Eliana's mouth—her beautiful full lips, twisted slightly, the lower one protruding.

"I've got eight-to-fours next week," he said quietly. "Just let me know where you'll be."

Eliana opened her eyes, stopped massaging her head and lowered her hands. "She strolls in Queens. Most nights around 68th and Woodland. I figure her guy will show, or set something up by internet and—"

Danny nodded. "You're gonna tail your murder suspect?"

"He bragged to her about—"

"Just let me know what night."

Danny felt suddenly impatient and pushed his chair back from the interview table and stood up. But then he hesitated. Eliana didn't budge.

Stone still, eyes wide, she sat looking ahead, as if he hadn't just risen. She stared at the empty space where he'd been sitting.

"I know you don't like this kind of thing, Danny," she said. "I appreciate the help."

"Don't worry about it."

She nodded, and then stood. They both pushed in their chairs and moved toward the door. Danny touched her elbow. "Be careful with this, Elly. I mean, off-duty back-up—for me, hey, I happened to be in the neighborhood. But you're gonna piss off somebody in a suit and—"

"I know. The dirty little secret: it's not the assholes on the street—it's other cops you've gotta worry about."

"The job is not your friend. That's all I'm saying."

"I'm just—I know, Danny, I know. I'm just going to see if I can find this guy. I can always pass it up the ladder."

Danny nodded. He liked that answer. Together they walked from the interview room to the front door. All eyes seemed to follow them—juicy story potential. Nobody loves gossip more than cops. As the saying goes: a precinct is like a high school with guns. The attractive female detective, yes, that was part of it. But no doubt some folks knew more: this was Danny's ex-wife in the house.

At the exit to the street, they stopped, inching close to the heavy door. The desk sergeant was out of view. Above them, on the wall, hung a recruiting poster: *ONE NYPD, MANY WAYS TO SERVE. BE PART OF PROTECTING TOMORROWS FUTURE TODAY*

"She says this guy's a regular," Eliana began. "Thursdays, usually. If he sets a date on the internet, she's supposed to call me. They'll pick a corner, you know, and cab it to a hotel. She's got a few places."

Danny nodded. He wanted to say more, but couldn't think what. Eliana seemed to be waiting. As the silence lengthened, a familiar, ugly feeling came over Danny: a feeling of failure, disappointment. It was moments like these, his inability to engage, to meet her expectations—that's what killed their marriage.

She asked, "You still hate those eight-to-fours?"

"Getting used to it. Adapting, you know. I eat protein bars now. Quick breakfast. Eat 'em on the way in. And, you know, I'll always be a vampire, but it's good to see a little sunshine once in a while."

They both laughed, and Danny felt a rush of heat in his chest as Eliana lowered her gaze, became still, and again she seemed to be waiting. And, again, he failed to find words. It was the old feeling. Standing next to her, comparing himself to her—he felt small, inadequate. Dumb. Unless he could be physical... that's when he knew—the only time, the only time he felt sure, yes—in bed he really pleased her. If only they could—? But no, of course not. He cleared his mind.

"You look good, Danny," she said, finally, without looking up. "Like you're taking care of yourself."

"I slip up sometimes," he said. He wanted her to know this, about his sobriety, that it wasn't perfect. He could tell her that, at least.

But she didn't react. She just kept her gaze fixed on the floor. "I got your birthday card," she went on, her voice so soft now he could barely hear. "I'm sorry I didn't respond. And your messages, too. This has been—well, I don't know. Was a tough birthday this year. I was going to take Char to visit Mom's grave that week—ten-year *yahrzeit*. But—we got into a thing because she's dating this guy, a new guy. African-American. A BLM type. We've had some serious arguments about it. He claims to be a leader of some kind. She shows up with him. Brings him to my apartment, but, you know, like he's coming with us to the cemetery? I try doing the open-minded thing—figure, in spite of the arguments, this is her new boyfriend so... whatever. And we get in the car, and he starts in—talking about how every Black man in America should be armed to protect themselves from the police, and—it's clear he's just trying to provoke me—he says that if he had a gun and got stopped by a cop, he'd shoot first. Finally, I just pulled over and said I want to visit the cemetery by myself."

Eliana stopped talking and shook her head, still looking at the floor. Then she said, "Char—that girl is heading for real trouble—I can feel it."

"What about that women's softball thing—becoming an umpire.

I thought she was taking classes and—seems like a nice wholesome activity."

"If she'd stay with it. But with Liv giving her money—sends her a check every month. It doesn't help."

"Does Liv know about the new boyfriend?"

"I doubt it. Liv sends Char money so she can avoid being a real sister. Out of sight, out of mind. If Livi could have it her way, she'd put Charlotte back in a locked ward."

Eliana hesitated, shook her head, still not looking at Danny. "All right, I exaggerate. Liv's not a monster, but she's... I don't know... I'm not sure I help much either. Sometimes I think I could use a few weeks in a hospital—nice padded walls, somebody to fix my meals, Jell-O for dessert. I like Jell-O."

A small smile, Eliana finally looked up. Danny met her eyes.

He wanted to reach out and take the jacket from her, then relax her fingers into his and turn her gently toward him and touch her face, rubbing her cheeks lightly with the back of his hand, the way he knew she liked. But he remained still, kept his hands to himself.

After a moment, she relaxed and folded the jacket over her arm. "Hey, I saw Jack yesterday."

"Yeah, how is he? Have been meaning to give him a shout."

"Seems OK. Had these exercise videos on his desk. 'Fifty Days to Flat Abs.'"

"Jack doing sit-ups? Would love to watch that. Like a circus bear doing tricks."

They both laughed.

"Throw him a marshmallow and he'll do another set," Eliana added.

More laughter, but Danny felt himself pushing it. Laughing too loudly. Thinking about Bayer, it occurred to Danny that the sergeant must have told Eliana to leave this murder suspect alone. That's why she came to him.

"Yeah, Jack—he did the big-daddy bit, you know. Wants me to take exams. Get off the street."

"That's a good thought. You'd be a helluva boss."

"Yeah, well..."

Eliana shifted her weight from one foot to the other. And Danny knew he'd said the wrong thing. Another moment of failure. She didn't want to make rank—so why did he say that? What he should have said— it's obvious—something encouraging. Stay on the street, catch this killer, and then another, and another, and another, until she finds the guy who killed her father, and the family curse is finally gone... but he couldn't support that dream, not anymore.

He looked closely at her. A small, thin frown creased her brow, then her lips twitched slightly, and for a second he entertained the crazy thought that maybe she'd lean forward and kiss him goodbye.

"I'll text you next week," she said without looking up, and pushed her hip into the side of the door. "Thanks, Danny."

And just like that she was gone.

Chapter 7

The subway door scraped open and then shut. A slim, curly-haired woman in her mid-twenties stepped on. Dark leggings, a loose-fitting summer shirt. College-girl, probably. Fair-skinned—freckles dotted her attractive face. The air brakes whooshed and the car lurched forward. She kept her balance—strong, athletic legs. She stood absorbed in her phone, then moved to a spot a short distance from the door. A moment passed. Two men standing nearby looked at each other. They moved closer to the woman. And closer—and closer. Savoyian watched, waited, listened. Her voice rose above the subways rumble.

"Excuse me—please. Please—I'm—I'm standing here—you're—you're too close—I'm—"

Two burly white guys with military cuts—they sandwiched her, one in front, one in back. Stupid grins on their faces, tattoos covering their thick necks, a skull and snake decorated one guy. Savoyian, sitting at the far end of the car, couldn't make out the tattoo on the other guy's neck. A sword? A flame? Didn't matter—the guy's hard, pockmarked face was ugly. The #7 train from Queens. Rush hour, yes, no open seats, but no need to squeeze this woman. Savoyian leaned forward to get a better look. The train shook, rattled, creaked, squeaked—then, above the din: "Please. Please let me get by."

And Savoyian recognized the sound in the woman's voice: fear. It's a tinny, high-pitched stress, like someone trying hard to sing in tune, but unable to keep the wobble from their pitch. "Please—I want to get by." The men didn't move.

"Hey assholes." Savoyian called out, then stood, stepped forward, and waited for the tattooed men to look at him. "I'm offering her my seat." Heads turned, phones lowered, earplugs were removed. Savoyian felt the eyes of the subway riders fix on him. Heart rate elevating—he'd control it, he knew. The inverted U-shaped performance curve. He knew how to be adrenalized enough for maximum alertness, coordination, and power, without diminishing complex motor skills. Approximately 115 beats per minute. The sweet spot of survival stress. Control the heart rate—you control the stress.

"Who the fuck you are?" said one of the men.

An Eastern European accent—Romania, Savoyian thought. Burly guy number one, with the snake on his neck, had spoken, then looked hard into his friend's face. "You believe this?" The other's pockmarked cheeks reddened, jaw clamped shut, balls of muscle bulging around his chin. Then, weirdly synchronous, both men moved closer to the woman, who shrieked "No!" The first guy looked down the subway car and said, "Go back to your seat, old man. This not for you."

"Don't—don't touch me—" the woman continued.

"I not touch you, sweetie—you want see what it feel like if I touch you? You mean, like this?"

He slipped his hand on her ass.

"Stop! Stop it—"

Savoyian didn't rush. The thick rubber sole of his tactical boots made no noise as he stepped calmly, rhythmically, almost like someone marching to a beat. Precise timing—the secret of life, the secret of fighting. Knowing how to close the distance, how to use the right tactic at the right time. Violence involves a fusion of instinct and decision making, whether to preempt an attack, move out of the way, or deflect and redirect a weapon. In simple terms, to fight is to control an encounter with whatever tactic you can. There are no rules.

Savoyian felt his hands curl into fists. A tingle spread through his arms, then swept across his chest, and down into his legs. A faint bite of pain on his calf from the burn, but no distraction. His attention landed on the subway car's vertical pole. Extending from floor to ceiling, its smudged silver gave the steel a grey tint in the yellowish light. And there—ah... not a conscious thought, exactly. Just an obvious point of focus. The big guy with the pockmarked face, holding the pole for balance—he and Savoyian locked eyes, and without stopping his steady march, before the man knew what had happened, Savoyian had pinned the man's hand to the pole and grabbed his elbow, pulling hard, snapping his wrist. While the man howled in pain, staring down at his limp, lifeless limb, his fingers dangling now like strips of boneless meat—Savoyian turned to the other man, who stepped back and pulled a knife from a pocket clip on his belt. Savoyian recognized it. A foldable ONTARIO XM-1—military grade. One of the heaviest folders made, weighing six ounces, with a drop-point blade of over three inches and dual thumb studs. Savoyian watched the well-made knife open smoothly and quietly—then lock. And then everything seemed to happen at once: the woman who'd been harassed hurried out from between the two men. Someone yelled "Knife!" Other passengers stood, shouting, "Help! Help!" And a recorded voice over the speaker announced, "Next stop: Forty-sixth Street and Queens Boulevard."

Savoyian remained still. The subway car lurched, shimmied. A snap of electricity flashed in the dark tunnel. Hyper-vigilance kicked in and his senses amplified. He heard screams and the rattle of a newspaper from a frightened rider moving to get away from the fight. And other sounds: the rustle of plastic bags, the scuffing of fabric and leather, the groans and grunts of people shifting, huddling, curled in fear. From the corner of his eye, he noted a fat woman with red hair drop her phone, and then a skinny teenage boy's backpack thudded to the floor and spilled, and somewhere in the back of the car, a baby cried.

Looking directly at the man with the knife, Savoyian spoke in a low tone. "You have a choice," he said. "Come at me—and I'll kill you. Or get off at the next stop—take your friend with you, and it's over."

A beat, a moment—the subway cars lights flickered, then the brakes squealed and the next station, crowded with people on the platform, flashed in the windows. Security call boxes, signs to stay back from the door, a map of the subway system, rows of faces, the mass of indifferent commuters—in his peripheral vision, Savoyian caught the flow of fast-moving images slowing, and slowing more, then coming to a full stop. The man folded his knife shut, grabbed his friend by the shoulder and—the instant the doors opened—they both disappeared into the sea of strangers.

New riders crowded onto the train, looking around, sensing something odd. But nobody spoke. Savoyian moved to the front of the car. He kept his face in his phone, pretending to read. In fact, tactical breathing. He needed to recover his equilibrium. That knife, he knew, would have done real damage. It would have killed the man.

A few stops went by. The woman with the attractive freckled face started to weave through the crowded train, murmuring, "Excuse me, excuse me." Savoyian didn't look up. As she grew close, the train pulled into 42nd Street, Grand Central Station. Savoyian hurried out. The woman followed.

"Excuse me," she called out. "Sir—excuse me, wait, please!" Savoyian didn't turn around. Then he heard the pat-pat-pat of her starting to run, and she called louder, "Wait, please."

He stopped, waited, turned to look. She caught up to him, a little breathless. Up close, her eyes contained a trace of green, sparkling. Color had crept into her face, her cheeks pink, the freckles fading.

"I just want to say thank you."

Savoyian looked at her.

"For what you did, I mean."

"You're welcome."

She smiled, shyly, holding him with her eyes. Quite beautiful, he thought.

"I really admire—"

"Don't," he said, sharply.

"I mean, the way you—"

"Don't admire me, please. You said thank you, fine. But—don't admire me."

Silence. Her mouth partly open. The look of surprise twisted her attractive features. Before she could say anything more, Savoyian turned and walked away.

Chapter 8

Vodka with a splash of cranberry juice. Joe & Joe's offered every third drink for free. Savoyian sat on the last stool in the far corner, his back to the wall and looked into his glass. Thumb to fingertip, he counted one, two, three, four. Or was it five? Trying to recall. He intended to get drunk, very drunk, and this was a good seat.

In front of him, the room's six small tables were empty. A couple sat on the couch near the restored fireplace—not used, against fire code. Instead, the hearth held oversized scented candles that threw shadows on the pressed-tin walls and ceilings. No television screens, no music. The click of billiard balls could be heard coming from the room in the back.

The name had changed several times, but Woodhaven old-timers insisted Joe & Joe's was the first bar in Queens, dating back to the 1820s, when the neighborhood was still called Woodville. The place didn't look, sound, smell, or feel like a bar, and that's why Vachik Savoyian liked it. Although he grew up not far from here, to him the bar felt exotic— reminded him of Syria, Lebanon, Iran, Kosovo, Afghanistan. In plenty of far-away countries, the bars appeared right alongside the homes, just like Joe & Joe's sat nestled among the Queens row houses—those signature New York squares of cement with no porches and nothing but a few inches of air between neighbors. On this quiet block, two streets away from the commercial strip of Jamaica Avenue, Savoyian felt safe. Nobody drank at Joe & Joe's who didn't belong.

For all its intimacy, he remained comfortably anonymous here. The Queens ID, he called it, along with his various "papers," as he liked to say. Nobody knew his real name. To the two Joe's and their regular customers, he'd made it clear years ago: a quiet hard-drinking man who left big tips as long as you left him alone. Need more? Oil rig work— in-and- out-of-town, gone for long stretches, a loner. It all made sense. A good cover always does.

The couple on the couch giggled and Savoyian fixed his vodka-gaze on the young man, clean-shaven with a military cut. He was laughing and pouring from an open bottle of champagne. The girl next to him—a healthy-looking, fair-skinned beauty with red cheeks—she caught Savoyian staring. He was trying to calculate her age because she looked considerably older than the man, a crease in her brow, the hint of mature lines around her eyes. Still, she was young enough to be Savoyian's daughter, if he'd had one.

Or, no, that's not the correct way to think, he told himself. I'm old enough to be her father—not the other way around. It's me, old. Not her, young. Was she still looking? Smiling now—at him? Couldn't be. But the thought made him—well... hungry. That's the word he used. Stupid euphemism. The woman wore a short tucked-up striped skirt and a plain white blouse, and Savoyian suddenly imagined her standing in a field playing bagpipes wearing no underwear beneath a kilt— he'd seen that somewhere, a porn magazine in Europe. Out of the blue memory. Pathetic. Yes, he was pathetic and hungry, and drunk, and the booze didn't help, not yet anyway. He looked away from the couple on the couch, not sure now if the woman had even been looking at him in the first place.

Alone with his thoughts, that's what he wanted. To let his mind roam, to transcend the past, to see the big picture, achieve a higher state of consciousness—and then write and write and write and write. Like the multi-armed Hindu goddess Durga, except instead of weapons— Savoyian's many hands would hold pens and pads and journals and pages of scribbled notes on clean lined sheets or torn scraps or folded dirty napkins and... yes, his obsessive writing is what caused all that trouble so many years ago. Now, he's more careful. Now, he uses only a carefully selected notebook. But the ambition—if he got drunk enough? The poem, the story, the book—there would be a work of art to serve as an act of self-redemption. Yes, if he got drunk enough, he still believed it was possible to get beyond the past. Understand it differently. Change the meaning of the past and you change the meaning of the present. Yes, Savoyian could still change his life. Or end it. That's the other side of it. The other way to move beyond his pain—kill himself with his father's revolver. But, right now, maybe right now, he thought, what I need is some beer with my vodka. Or maybe to mix the beer and vodka together in one glass—Russian lemonade. That's what they called it in Kosovo. Here, the beer tastes especially cold because Joe & Joe's use an ancient tap system in which a range of coils are cooled by ice. One of the Joes had once explained how it worked. Details like that mattered to Savoyian, or used to matter. These days, nothing mattered, except the drunken dream and the occasional hunger. Women, Kitty. But the hunger—well, he couldn't always get it to work.

He looked across the room at a floor-to-ceiling wooden hutch, its shelves filled with old books, softball and bowling trophies, random photos of the neighborhood brought in by bar patrons. The whole dark-wooded structure had settled with the building over the years, collapsing into itself, taking on the posture of a bent old man.

Slowly, Savoyian reached for his drink, then finished it in a large, deliberate gulp and ordered another—more vodka-and-cranberry, and a glass of house ale. Joe, a big-bellied man with white hair and a red-veined face, was leaning over the bar at the other end, reading the newspaper. He looked up and waved, holding three fingers, indicating this one is on the house. Savoyian felt pleased. Drunk enough, if he could just get drunk enough, then maybe he'd get it: the click, the release, the small measure of hope that someday he will change his life.

Eliana sat in her car feeling stupid. She'd followed Savoyian from Kitty's hotel to the bar and now sat across the street, with Danny a half-block behind her, out of uniform, hunkered down in his "personal vehicle," as he'd put it. She'd texted him, and he showed up, as promised—10-84. Arrived at scene. Was he using radio codes just to keep things professional between them? Whatever. It all felt like a waste. No danger here. Middle-aged boys with their hobbies: favorite hookers, favorite bars. What exactly is the crime?

But, of course, this guy bragged about a murder—and there was that damn recurring dream about her father.

"Focus," she told herself, saying the word aloud. Then she slipped out of the car and headed for the bar. The plan with Danny: twenty-five minutes inside.

The cold beer notched up the vodka-kick as Savoyian registered Eliana's entrance. It came effortlessly, but he resented noticing her. His heightened "situational awareness" was like an injury that never healed. A limp, a scar. Years of habit—he couldn't turn it off. The more profound and intense the undercover work, the hotter the flame, the deeper the burn, the more permanent the scar. He'd failed to take care of himself properly. Most UCs go in-and-out. Come up for air. Get to a ball game, attend a family picnic, grind out a few ordinary shifts at a desk or on patrol. Because going under can brand itself on the soul, cause you to forever view the world and all human interactions through a unique set of mental and emotional filters. It boils down to this: nothing is frightening, but everything is dangerous.

When he spotted Eliana, he knew right away that she didn't belong. But he didn't care, not at first. The danger needle moved only so far because—fuck it, he was here to drink, to think, to contact some higher consciousness about the meaning of his life. Today, for example—big success, good day at the office. Oh yeah, sure, the bullshit on the subway, that was a mistake. He'd failed to control his impulses, become involved in something that he should have let alone. But the Park Avenue assignment with the Sudanese businessman and his "injection." Mission accomplished, yes sir! Success, success, success!

But failure—spectacular failure, world-famous, historically signifi-cant failure—this is what defined Vachik Savoyian's life. And for the millionth time his thoughts went back to it.

Operation Eagle Claw. April 1980. Like an old song it stuck in his head—a brainworm. Right now he heard only fragments: helicopters. The whir of the engine, main rotor, tail rotor—that rhythmic "wop-wop-wop" sound coming from the two-bladed Navy birds. Fucking Navy. It had to be the Navy, even when those goddamn *Navy* helicop-ters—it was widely known—wouldn't work. The Air Force owns the sky. That's why it's called *Air* Force. But—turf wars, naturally—it was the fucking *Army* calling the shots. Two-, three-, and four-star generals against a twenty-year-old field-grade guy—forget it. No chance. Bu-reaucratic power destroys everything it touches, especially urgent com-munication. Nobody would listen to Savoyian.

Speaking Farsi had elevated his status slightly, but Savoyian re-mained a mere soldier—a low-level nobody—in the infamous failure of the 1980 mission to rescue fifty-three American hostages held in the U.S. Embassy in Iran. Burned into his memory: the sight of a broken helicopter propeller resting on a dry lakebed two hundred miles south-east of Tehran. Disaster at Desert One. Eight unnecessary deaths, one of which could have—should have?—been his. The meticulous plan that didn't work, the crucial details that can't be erased. How 'bout them pills, doc? The memory erasure pills. The past—swallow, gulp, gone. No, he couldn't shake the night, the list: eight US Navy RH-53D minesweeping helicopters, six US Air Force C-130 cargo planes, four additional Air Force C-14ls, and three MC-130s. And fuel—oh, god—nobody knows exactly how much fuel. That's what exploded—the fuel. After the sandstorm, after the communication failures, after the first two birds fell, then came the 2:30 a.m. command to abort, and Savoyian found himself inside a C-130 airplane that carried extra fuel in huge flat rubber bladders spread across the central body-portion of the craft, the area designed to accommodate the crew, the passengers, and the cargo. But that night: only fuel, and eighteen soldiers—angry, disappointed, tired and hot soldiers sprawled on a giant waterbed of jet fuel.

What came next started with blue sparks overhead and up front. Savoyian thought a bank of electronics between the flight deck and the cargo area had shorted out. Not good, the sparks, considering all this jet fuel. His chest tightened with every sizzling blue flash. But it wasn't an electrical short causing the sparks. As the whole world would learn, a helicopter next to them had been refueling, and when it lifted and banked away, its rotor sliced through the main body of the C-130. Mo-ments later: both chopper and plane burst into flame.

Why did he survive? Savoyian didn't do anything better or different than the eight men who died that night. When the crew door blew, the blast of heat shot one man through the hole as if he'd been fired from a cannon—that soldier died. Maybe from the impact of hitting the ground? Who knows. But Savoyian—burning fragments of metal showered down on him as he slammed into a jump-door ringed with fire. His field jacket started to burn, the flames scalding his back and neck, but he made it out, launching himself—absurdly—in a hard-arched skydiving position, as if the plane were in the air and he had a cord to pull. After a half-second of free fall, his body slammed into the cold hard desert. He screamed and rolled and extinguished the flames scalding his back. Later he would realize that had things happened differently, just a tiny bit differently—his life would have ended. Just like that—over. He'd almost burned to death.

Eliana looked around the bar. She seldom used words like "exceptionally handsome." That was the kind of phrase her sister Livi might use. But the words popped into her head as she caught sight of Savoyian perched on his stool in the corner. His physical presence was arresting.

He wore a black V-neck T-shirt and khaki pants. No belly, no flab. Dark hair streaked grey at the sides. Mid-fifties, late forties? Hard to tell. He seemed to look up at her as he crossed his legs, and she noticed his black leather tactical boots were well-worn.

She had to force herself to pull her eyes from him and keep scanning the room. For show, she glanced down at her watch. Savoyian—the "subject," as they say—seemed to ignore her. Good. That's what the subject is supposed to do. But she felt off her game. His appearance threw her. Get a grip. It's a fucking investigation, not a blind date. The distraction, she decided, was her sister's fault. Livi was constantly trying to set her up, at least one date a month. Jersey bankers, doctors, an English professor from Princeton. No cops or lawyers—that was a rule. Nice men, yes, of course. But every date ended in disaster, and now... screwing up her street skills? She'd tell Livi—no more blind dates.

She hovered near the door checking her watch as if deciding whether to stay or go. Then she spotted Savoyian slide smoothly from his bar stool. He stood, taking something out of his back pocket, a small notebook. He looked about six feet and remarkably fit. Lean, muscular. Eliana kept up her room-scan, but found it difficult not to look at him. Was he looking back at her? She couldn't be sure. After a moment, he sat down again and opened the notebook. Journal writing? She'd kept a journal, back in college. Wanted to get back in the habit. That's a good connection—authentic.

She approached the bar. "Your house vodka on ice with a splash of cranberry juice, please." She sat one stool away from Savoyian.

The bartender smiled, heightening Eliana's off-balance feeling. What's he smiling at? She knew Savoyian's eyes were on her now.

"Good choice," Savoyian said quietly, and lifted his glass, swirling his drink. The ice cubes clinked. In the quiet Eliana heard the soft crack of billiard balls coming from the other room. No music in this place— unusual. She smiled and then looked away. Same drink, she thought, a useful coincidence. Play it.

The bartender set her glass down. "On the house," he said, folding his arms across his big belly, elbows resting on the bulge as if a pillow were stuffed under his shirt.

"Wow, friendly place. Thank you." Eliana smiled. But the strangeness of the moment—were these two working together? Not likely. But that would, indeed, be dangerous. And anything's possible. She flashed on Danny sitting outside in his car—the twenty-five-minute plan.

Either she comes out, or he comes in. A relief. But her off-balance feeling remained. She'd expected to get some attention, obviously. That was the whole point. Establish contact with this guy, work him, lay down some carpet so that, eventually, he'll tell about the murder, if there really was one. A process, she knew. And the key involved attraction. Old line— when in doubt, seduce. But it should be him drawn to her, not the other way around. That's why this feeling—weird, yes, very weird. And older men? Never. Not her thing. Older men had never interested her.

She took a sip of her drink, annoyed with herself. Focus, damn it. She crossed one leg over the other, her bare thigh slipping through the front of her wrap-around skirt. She'd carefully calibrated the outfit: sexy, but no working girl. A professional look, tarted-up just a tad: the snug-fitting wrap-around was slit, yes, but reached almost to her knees; and she wore a long-sleeve blouse buttoned to the neck. The top included a lacey floral design, a partial see-through, but she wore a plain vanilla T-shirt bra, extra modest, the thin layer of foam hiding any possible nipple bulge. She knew the drill. Also, she knew to bring her favorite concealed-carry purse, which included an extra zipper in the back with access to her Glock 43, a smaller version of the standard police-issue G17. She could fire right through the leather, a trick she'd practiced, ruining three purses. But nobody at the range laughed. From ten yards out—she didn't miss, and the purse strap never left her shoulder.

With her bare leg exposed, Savoyian glanced up from his notebook. Game on, Eliana thought, and tried to concentrate on the details around her. You never know what might come into play. She watched him set down his pen and notebook. High end items—full-grain leather, smooth, like an expensive, oversized wallet with a loop for his shiny, gunmetal mini-pen. He placed the pen inside and closed the cover, then hesitated and re-opened it. While closed, Eliana saw the embossed design—or was it writing?—carved into the soft leather. Looked almost like Hebrew, at first. But no—ridiculous. It's Arabic, she thought. Yes, an Arabic word. But how unusual—an Arabic word embossed on the cover of this man's leather notebook? Terrorism funding, yes. This fit. She was on to something. But then that off-balance feeling returned; the sense of being distracted, as if—what?

"Excuse me," he leaned forward, looking directly into her eyes. "Do you know the meaning of the word 'synchronicity?'"

"Synchronicity?" she repeated, unable to keep the surprise out of her voice.

He nodded slightly, but said nothing more. Just held still, looking at her. The features of his face—thick dark eyebrows, deep-set eyes, a long thin nose, light brown skin. Ah, right, a dark swarthy Persian. That was it—a neat little label like this might keep things straight. And she felt herself trying to clear her mind like putting a mess in a box, then shoving it off to the side.

"Yes, I'm working on..." He tapped the front of the notebook. "Just notes, actually. For some poetry I hope to write."

As he spoke, she found herself captivated by the strange, indefinable, faint expression on his lips, something covert— a smile—or not a smile. She couldn't tell.

"I'm sorry," he went on, "I don't mean to be too forward—about the word, I mean. It's an odd question, I know. But you have a kind of intelligent, educated air about you, and I just thought—"

"I know the word, yes. Synchronicity. It means..."

She stopped and again focused on his lips. The hint of a smile intensified for an instant at the end of his words like a seal applied to the phrase, a sign, an indicator of double meanings, almost as if he were nodding and winking, but far more subtle, inscrutable.

"Synchronicity means, basically, a meaningful coincidence," Eliana said quietly.

He broke into a bashful grin, lowering his chin, his face now a smiling heart, like an *emoji*, she thought, with the V-shaped point in his hairline marking the center of his broad tall forehead. A widow's peak, her sister would say. Yes, but what the hell—? Again with her sister's vocabulary?

"I am mixing it up with synchrony, or synchronous," he said, shaking his head.

"Those words aren't unrelated," Eliana continued, and noted a racing feeling inside her. Was she trying to make a good impression? Show off her Ivy League vocabulary? She knew undercover work required exactly the opposite impulse—slow, slow, slow. Sliding under means you get yourself accepted without drawing attention, holding brief conversations without needing to make a friend, dropping hints without revealing too much. And it means, above all, demonstrating that you know the law of the street: trust nobody until they earn it. Yes, going under is a narrow, winding one-step-at-a-time process. Move too fast—stumble—and you get tagged a cop.

Eliana understood all this, but still went on, launching into a mini-lecture: "The word synchronicity—yes, the Swiss psychiatrist Carl Jung—he coined the term in the 1920s. It can be boiled down to meaningful coincidences, but it's really trying to suggest that everything in the universe is intimately connected."

She felt herself gushing, like a broken faucet, spraying sideways. Bayer's warning flashed: get off the street, before something bad happens. Was it too late? She watched as Savoyian's smile faded, his expression darkening, his eyes growing serious and heavy.

"That's a compelling notion," he said quietly. "Everything in the universe..." He paused and his lips twisted slightly into that mysterious little hint of a smile, but not a smile, something else. Then it vanished, and he finished his thought, "Intimately connected." He looked into his glass, nodded, and then lifted his eyes back up at her. "Well, I was right about one thing—the intelligence. I had a hunch you'd be able to explain this."

Eliana found herself laughing nervously—bad sign, very bad. He controlled the conversation, not her. She smiled, trying to recover some composure. "I used to be sort of a bookworm," she said.

"Hmmm, yes, books—books keep me alive. And this—" He pointed to his drink. "Every third one's free here at Joe & Joe's. Or, in your case, the first one. I've had—well, I'm OK. Can I get you another?"

Finally, she recognized a beat here, a point of contact, a way to work the subject. She felt grateful for a sense of police technique kicking in. Books. That gave her something with more substance than vodka and cranberry juice. She looked at her watch. Plenty of time before Danny came inside.

She sipped her drink, trying to regroup. The book connection—she could do this. Get a title and read it and come back and she'd be in this guy's head within a few days. And then give her a week—if this guy killed somebody, she'll know it. Yes, she felt her confidence returning. Like finding the downbeat in a song. Getting the rhythm. When undercover work falls into place, what a feeling. The sense of purpose, the certainty of making a difference. And the freedom—here she was, on her own, one puny person, calling the shots, working the case, pursuing... yes, she wasn't afraid to name it, her lofty goal: justice.

She wanted another drink. She wanted it so badly it frightened her. In fact, she felt like getting smashed.

Get a fucking grip, she told herself, stop the crazy thoughts. Then she spoke, "I have sort of a one drink rule during the week."

"Good rule, I understand."

He shifted his weight on his stool, pulled back, started to reach for his notebook, but Eliana didn't want to lose him. "Who's your favorite author right now?" she asked.

He answered quickly—almost before she'd finished the question: "Jalaluddin Rumi, the 13th century Sufi poet. I'm reading the translations right now by Coleman Barks."

The swiftness of his reply threw her, as if he'd been expecting the question. As if he was working her? That strange little twist in his lips appeared again, then vanished. "Are you a teacher?" she said, trying to stay steady.

"No," he shook his head.

"What do you—"

"Government work," he said, and again Eliana felt him anticipating her questions, controlling the tempo.

She tried to slow things down. She sipped her drink. She let an ice cube slide into her mouth. She chewed. After a moment, crunching the cube, she said, "What kind of government work—"

But he waved his hand. "Aaaah—let's just leave it at that." Then he leaned forward. "How about you?"

She had worked out a cover, of course. A secretary—"administrative aide"—at Queens County Savings Bank. A new job, with its offices on Jamaica Avenue. But just a day-job; she hoped to be an actress; had moved from the Midwest—Royal Oaks, suburb of Detroit; and on and on. But instead she blurted, "Government work."

His eyebrows lifted. "You too! Synchronicity!" He opened his mouth wide, revealing a row of white pointy teeth. Was he smiling—or baring his fangs? For a second Eliana felt dizzy, a short quick wave like stepping off a curb without realizing it, an out-of-nowhere drop. What the hell had she just said? Why had she ignored her cover story?

She grabbed the side of the bar. Booze gone to her head? A spiked drink? Would Danny find her here on the floor? But, no, it passed. She wouldn't fall off her stool. But she was losing it. That was the simple truth. This homicide investigation belonged with a homicide detective. Ignoring chain of command was the first step. Now she was ignoring basic undercover procedure, and putting her life at risk.

Dear ol' Jack again: I'm worried about, Elly...

The twist in Savoyian's lips returned, hinting at a smile, which, along with the twinkle in his eye, one dark bushy brow arching, telegraphed a question coming. But this time, instead of lagging one step behind, Eliana anticipated, and cut him off.

He began to say, "What sort of government work do you..." but Eliana waved her hand dismissively. Then he picked up on the meaning and together, in unison, they said, "Aaahhh, let's leave it at that."

The timing, the shared line, the synchronous laughter. Like a couple of old friends with an inside joke. Eliana was on autopilot now, not thinking, just reacting, but knowing that she'd fucked up big time. She'd ignored her cover and said way too much and needed to get the hell out of there right away. She gulped the rest of her drink.

Savoyian, still laughing, said, "One more?" he wiggled his index finger, like a windshield wiper, like a little kid.

"No thanks."

"The rule, right." He nodded firmly.

"That's right—and I'm tired." She unzipped the top of her purse, pulled out her wallet, and grabbed a few dollars for a tip.

"Well, I'm a regular here. Maybe... another time."

"Yeah, maybe."

She put away the wallet, zipped the purse, and slid off the stool. He was watching her closely. She could feel it. The way he leaned toward her, his forehead lowered, his dark eyes latched on to her every move. But his hard-steady gaze—something was odd. It lacked... what? A sexual energy. That was all on her side. Yes, he wasn't checking her out the way she expected, the way men always do. Were the changing times inhibiting him? Weinstein, Cosby, Kavanaugh? No doubt he was closer to that generation than to hers, although his fit and trim body made his age difficult to determine. In any case, instead of a sexual vibe, he gave off the sense of studying her, analyzing her. And he looked closely at her purse. Oh no—she thought, and checked the back zipper concealing her gun. Zipped up, no problem. But maybe she should unzip it and slip her hand inside so she could fire without even removing the gun—just like at the range? Force options, yes, always know your force options. Exactly how dangerous was this situation? Was she outnumbered? The bartender working with the subject? Danny was in his car, right outside. That reassured her. But these jumpy thoughts—she felt so off-balance, so off-her-game. At this exact moment no conflict even existed, let alone an escalating confrontation.

Just then Savoyian stood up, clearing a space, pushing his stool away from the bar. "How about I walk you to your car?"

"No thank you," she said quickly.

But he stepped forward and took hold of her elbow. Then he leaned so close that she smelled the weird mix of beer and vodka and cranberry juice on his breath. His exhale whistled in her ear, and he pressed his nose against the side of her face and whispered, "You're the cop, aren't you?"

She said nothing. What registered most strongly, most strangely, was that little word: "the." She'd been called out before and done fine, denying it. And she'd spoken to plenty of buy-and-bust UCs who'd faced these panicky moments too. But what threw her right now: he seemed so certain. What he wanted to know: not whether she was, in fact, a cop—but which cop? The cop. The cop who...?

As if reading her mind, he squeezed her arm firmly and went on in the same heavy whisper: "I heard Kitty got pinched. Are you the one? Was she telling you stories about me?"

Eliana stood frozen in confusion. But oddly, she felt no hurry to answer, and no hurry to step away either. Instead, she felt wonderfully alert, alive, as if there were something specific she needed to say and do and if she could just pay careful enough attention to the moment then clarity would emerge. But... what about fear? Why no fear? She had blown her cover and... *Fear is your friend—when you stop feeling afraid, it's time to get off the street.* "Another Bayer line. She looked down at Savoyian's grip on her elbow. His long, elegant fingers squeezed hard enough to hurt, but the sensation pleased her, like rubbing a sore muscle. Finally, Eliana said, "Yes, I spoke to Kitty, but right now, you need to let go of my arm or—"

"I understand," Savoyian cut her off, loosening his grip on her elbow. "Never come between a woman and her purse." He stepped back, turning his palms up. "I don't want you to shoot me—not yet, anyway." He smiled oddly at her. His soft deep voice reaching her faintly. He'd spoken while barely moving his lips, as if his words were a grave, profound vibration coming directly from his chest. "But, here..." He turned back to the bar, tore a piece of paper from his notebook, scribbled, then folded it once and pressed the small sheet hard into her palm. "My digits, as the kids say. Call me—or text. Or—well, I don't use email much. Hell, just show up. I included my address. And that's my real name—no kidding!"

Now, finally, the faint, mysterious smile appeared clear, obvious, and ironic, but his voice sounded utterly sincere, without any trace of a taunt. "I will look forward to it." And then added, "I believe—well, how did you define synchronicity? That the whole universe is intimately connected?" He nodded, as if saying goodbye, but smiled once more, then, finally, turned back to the bar. He didn't look at her again. He just opened his notebook and started to write.

***

On Jamaica Avenue, Eliana pulled into the Burger King parking lot where she and Danny had arranged to meet. She sat in a corner of the lot waiting for him and unfolded the piece of paper with Savoyian's address and phone number. His handwriting surprised her. Feminine-looking— curved and slanted, with loopy lines and big open circles. He'd printed in simple block capital letters: VACHIK SAVOYIAN, 347-548-4527, 7813 87th ST, #3-B, QUEENS. She wondered about his that's-my-real- name riff. Weird—he'd clearly found that funny. But was he joking?

She didn't notice Danny's car pull into the driveway, but when she saw him walking toward her, she folded the paper and put it into her purse. Then she rolled down her window. He crouched at the side of her car.

"Well...?"

Eliana shrugged and shook her head. One part of her wanted to confide in Danny. Tell him exactly what happened. Admit she was falling apart. It would be easy. In a heartbeat, he'd slide into the passenger seat, and she could cry on his shoulder. But would that help? Would it feel good? She couldn't remember the last time she'd cried—about anything. She turned now to Danny. The features of his face—his pale blue eyes, flat nose, square jaw—it all looked so simple, so open, so straight-forward. "This was stupid," she said. "I'm sorry about dragging you out here."

"You get anywhere with the guy?"

Eliana hesitated. "No."

"Nothing? You wanna come back?"

"No, I don't think so."

"You don't like the guy for the murder?"

"No."

"Doesn't surprise me. Hooker tips."

"Yeah, well..."

"Sure, you can't blame the girls for trying, but—you're done with this thing then, right?" Danny asked.

Eliana looked straight ahead. An Asian family exited the Burger King. A mom, a dad, and two little kids wearing paper crowns. The dad wore a camera around his neck. Tourists? At this time of night? And what the hell is there to photograph inside a Burger King?

"Yeah, I'm done with it," she said finally to Danny, and felt bad for lying. Especially to Danny.

Chapter 9

Some sites advertised "GF" in their description, which indicated a worker's willingness to be social, to talk, to kiss on the mouth. You paid extra for this, but Savoyian found that most women—well, no charge. They liked him.

A sexually dysfunctional man. That's how he thought of himself. Too much scar tissue, he said, if they asked why he sometimes skipped sex and just talked. And he didn't elaborate.

He and Kitty cuddled that night, yes, and chatted, though he couldn't remember exactly what he'd told her. He sat now alone in his apartment, trying to retrace his steps. Very damn drunk—that's what he'd been that night. He'd tried but was unable to perform. And it was his second time with her that week. The previous night—he'd brought a young-guy soldier he met at the gym. A Special Forces hotshot just back from the mountains, once a devout Christian, once a tall, serious-looking athlete with muscles of steel.

Until he stepped on an IED—"Improvised Explosive Device"—and lost both legs. Fucking Afghanistan.

"Lost two friends," he told Savoyian, who'd been listening patiently, then asked point blank.

"How about your pecker? It still work?"

The guy looked surprised, then swallowed and smiled sheepishly.

A few hours later he pushed his new friend's wheelchair into a room at the New Farrington hotel, where Kitty was lying on the bed. She was ready and waiting, dressed in one of Savoyian's favorites; a two-piece stretch mesh corset with black lace overlay, and a matching ruffled panty.

She sat up and waved, "Hi."

"This is a friend of mine, Kitty. He—he needs some special attention. Just back from—"

"I understand," she interrupted, and motioned for Savoyian to push the wheelchair closer, all the way to the edge of the bed. "A soldier?" she asked, softly. "What's your name, soldier?"

The soldier didn't answer. Neither did Savoyian. Nobody said anything. Kitty massaged the man's thighs.

Then, finally, Savoyian tapped his friend's arm. "She asked you a question."

"I'd rather not tell my name."

"I understand," Kitty said. "I just call you soldier, OK?" She started to unbuckle the man's pants. Then she looked up at Savoyian. "You going to watch?"

"No—I'll be back in a while."

The soldier in the wheelchair grabbed Savoyian's arm. "Hey, I don't think I can do this—" And then he lost it. He burst into tears, like a child who'd been suddenly scolded, slapped, shamed.

Kitty leaned forward and wrapped her arms around the wounded man's waist and laid her head in his lap. Then she said in a thick whisper, "You go risk your life for others and then this—" She stopped and lifted her head, and Savoyian saw her eyes glazed with tears. She looked into the soldier's face. "You are a man—so... you let me help you."

Savoyian was impressed by Kitty's emotion, moved. That must be why he himself had opened up so much to her, talked about killing, tried to tell her what it's like. Yes, that must have been what had happened. He must have tried telling Kitty how it felt, and how it all got started for him. Guns, she liked to hear about guns, and he'd explained about calibers, how a Glock .45—had he told her the model's name?—is best because a smaller bullet might not destroy enough of the cerebral cortex to prevent the person from feeling anything. A death without suffering. That's what he wanted for his victims. What he always wanted. And how you have to be sure not to fire at an oblique angle because even a large caliber bullet might just severely wound, causing intense pain. If the angle is wrong—disaster. You need to level the barrel and push the muzzle hard into the exact spot—the base of the back of the skull—so the bullet destroys the brain stem. Then there's no pain.

Had he told her all of this? And what exactly had she told the cop?

Savoyian went for his phone. Not his personal phone. He needed real information. Cut through the bullshit.

"CFC Recovery Appointment Request, please. 4-5-8-3-T-T. Adam, Bravo, William." He waited, then continued: "An NYPD cop—female—working vice, probably citywide special detail," he paused, not recognizing the voice of the person on the other end. "NPIC, NGIA, who cares. Get me images and I'll identify her, and—"

He didn't like this guy. New kid. An interrupter. Kids today—don't know how to listen. Maybe the youngster needed it spelled out: National Geospatial-Intelligence Agency.

"Sure, yeah, classified, I'm Batman—OK? I gave you codes. Were you paying attention?"

More verbiage from the kid.

"Yes, that's right, I just said—listen, son, have you got a pencil?"

He repeated himself, asked for a read-back, then hung up. No matter about the cocky kid. Crap like that—Savoyian knew it shouldn't bother him. The info he wanted. That's what mattered. He'd give the kid an hour, then call back.

Agitated, he sat down on the edge of his bed and opened his journal, the smooth leather, the embossed cover with its one-word Arabic script, "رفاسُم," meaning "Traveler." Often he simply copied passages from books, then read and re-read the words of others. Call it an assassin's fascination with philosophy. He often fantasized about meeting various writers, some of them long dead. He craved their knowledge, their eloquence—it could almost substitute for faith.

He read:

> *...the study of killing in combat is very much like the study of sex... A virgin observer might get the mechanics of sex right by watching an X-rated movie, but he or she could never hope to understand the intimacy and intensity of the procreative experience. As a society we are as fascinated by killing as we are by sex—possibly more so, since we are somewhat jaded by sex and have a fairly broad base of individual experience in this area... Many children, upon seeing that I am a decorated soldier, immediately ask 'Have you ever killed anyone.*
> *On Killing, Lt. Col. Dave Grossman.*

He wished he'd written that damn book. More flipping through the journal, then he found another passage, this one from a book called *Thank You for Your Service,* by David Finkel. He had copied these lines into his journal:

> *...twenty to thirty percent of soldiers come home with post-traumatic stress disorder...Depression, anxiety, nightmares, memory problems, personality changes, suicidal thoughts: every war has its after-war...*

Yes, he'd underlined that last sentence. But the stats, he thought now—only twenty to thirty percent?

Chapter 10

Eliana stood in the living room of her one-bedroom apartment looking at a pile of unfolded laundry: bras and panties, T-shirts hanging over the arm of a rocking chair, her socks balled up in the corner of a seat cushion on the couch *"Keep your home clean and organized,"* Bayer warned. *"Out there, it's filth and chaos. But the streets are where you work, not where you live. Separate the two, or go crazy."*

Yes, that's what she feared—going crazy. That's what she felt was happening to her in the bar. And that's why she came home and tossed Savoyian's address into a pile of unopened junk mail and told herself: let it go. A strange, weirdly attractive man—but not her father's killer. Forget him—move on. Cops learn to do this: lockbox their thoughts and feelings. The rape's over; onto the burglary; start the paperwork, finish the tour. It's a question of survival.

Numb, detached—early in her career she'd accepted the challenge of toughening up. She knew what some cops thought of her: Ivy League- educated but street-dumb. Bookish, over-sensitive.

Her first test—she failed miserably. A radio run: foul odor coming from an apartment on the twelfth floor of the Patterson House in Mott Haven, public housing in the Bronx. Long live NYCHA—New York City Housing Authority. The building's elevator—broken, of course. Urban mountain-climb, up the piss-filled canyon, a twelve-flight hike. Eliana's partner, a veteran who kept a can of Folgers in the car, handed her the container while taking a wheezy breath on the last landing. Apparently, he assumed she'd be the one to execute this old police trick: cut the smell of a rotting corpse by burning coffee grounds. He'd warned her that's what they were going to find: a dead body. But why should she be sent to the kitchen? Women's work, huh?

She wanted to say something, push back—but when the apartment door opened, she gagged, overwhelmed by the sour, putrid smell of rotting flesh. It was like being gut-punched. She doubled over and turned away, a pure reflex. She almost stepped back into the hall, but her partner, holding a handkerchief over his mouth and nose, glared at her. Dark eyes, sweaty forehead, the rest of his face concealed. She got the point.

Inside the apartment, down a narrow hall toward the back, she found a tiny kitchen where she ignored the back wall dotted with cockroaches and poured the coffee grounds into a disgusting little pan, then turned the flame up high. After about a minute, the acrid smell started to cut the odor, but she still found it hard to breathe. Couldn't they give us some kind of special odor-cutting gas masks, she wondered? And imagined Danny rolling his eyes.

She knew what she needed to do next: go see the body. And then...? The patrol guide, what she'd learned in the academy, just follow procedure, do whatever the uniformed cops do—which is mostly wait around for other people to show up, right? That's how it came to her as she turned away from the kitchen, then suddenly felt something crawling on her neck—a cockroach? She slapped at her head and shook out her hair. Spastic, jerky—her thoughts jumped like that too, racing through patrol guide training: *upon arrival at scene of an apparently dead human body the uniformed member of the service must request ambulance and patrol supervisor to respond; exclude unauthorized persons from scene; obtain names of witnesses; detain at scene if death suspicious; screen area from public view; cover body with waterproof covering; ascertain facts; and notify desk officer and then... and then?*

Her mind shut off when she stepped into the living room and looked down at the center of the bare floor where a small brown-skinned man lay swollen like a rotten piece of fruit. The medical term, she knew, was "distended." The skin on his hands and feet were stretched tight—a balloon about to pop. But his face—that's where she couldn't stop looking. Jaw hanging open, his tongue, a thick blue slab, like spoiled meat. And his eyes—a buttery yellow—so bulbous they seemed to have popped out of their sockets, a cartoon character's expression of surprise. Then at the tip of his nose she saw something move. But couldn't be—dead men don't move. So she leaned closer, determined. Yes, something moving there. Her heart quickened with a sense of ambition, edge, competitive drive. Whaddya got—crack the case? Grab the flashlight. Investigate. Get to the bottom of—

Leaning over the dead man's face, her stomach rumbled just once before the unstoppable swell and surge. Then at the last possible moment she turned away to avoid puking all over this poor, foul-smelling dead man who had bugs crawling in and out of his nose—hundreds and hundreds of tiny black bugs. She made it to the corner of the room and vomited near a steam-heat radiator.

Maggots, she later learned. Very common.

Her first corpse, and she blew it. Lost her cookies. But she made a vow that night: never again would emotions like fear or disgust overwhelm her self-control. Cops deal with death—she'd learn to deal with it too. Danny, reluctantly, agreed to help. This was before the divorce.

And so Danny took her to the city morgue, where she had a simple, single goal: toughen up. Once upon a time, the academy took all recruits on a field trip to 421 E. 26th Street. But—budget cuts? Whatever. Eliana had never been. Until now. The building, on the one hand, reminded her of a hospital: wide sidewalks, huge cement columns, brightly lit overhead fixtures. But tire spikes and a steel rampart blocked the driveway leading up to the entrance. It was part-hospital, part-fortress.

Near the driveway, two ambulances, a patrol car, and a Fire Department van had pulled up over the curb, parked at jagged angles, as if they'd been in a rush. A rush with a dead body? The thought made Eliana laugh—almost. But no jokes, not now. She knew that Danny, who had expected to accompany her the whole time, found nothing funny about her insistence on doing this alone. They had both just finished a four-to-twelve on a Friday night, and Danny had reached out to a cop who worked in the Medical Examiner's office. Jimmy Gallagher, old friend of the family, had worked with Danny's father.

She allowed Danny to accompany her inside, and they walked through the lobby in silence until they found Gallagher's office, where Danny made the introduction. When she nodded, dismissing him, he stepped away, failing to conceal his anger. A clipped tone, teeth-clenched, he tossed a line over his shoulder: "Have fun."

Gallagher, a pasty-faced older guy with a beer gut, looked vaguely amused, a sideways smile, head tilted at a cocky angle. He stood with his arms folded, weight on his heels, looking out from behind a long counter stacked with manila envelopes, boxes of forms, and an old-fashioned radio that looked straight out of the 1960s. Square brown box, speaker in the center covered with a gold fabric, two bright red dials, rabbit ear antenna. Eliana couldn't help wondering if the machine actually worked. Almost seemed like it could be a valuable antique—but why here?

"You and your boyfriend there," Gallagher said, a huge ring of keys jingling as he stepped around the counter. "You in a fight? Funny place to bring it—but, hey, I'm not lookin' to get in the middle of nothin.'"

Eliana lifted a hand, palm out, a small wave. "Actually, we're married. It's fine. No big deal."

"Yeah, well, I knew Danny's father. One helluva cop. That's the only reason I'm doing this. Danny's dad was the best."

She motioned again—steady-there-steady—afraid this Gallagher might launch into war stories about Danny's dad. Last thing Eliana needed right now: to be reminded of Danny's famous cop family. "I appreciate it, really."

A quick nod, military-style, then he stepped past her, motioning with a head-flick to follow. Together they walked down a long, tiled hallway to a thick metal door that read: OIC EXAMINATION

GROUP INITIAL HOLDING.

Eliana had no idea what the sign meant—OIC = Officer in Charge, but a "group?" A group of what? Medical Examiners? And bodies held "initially?" She wanted to ask but kept her mouth shut.

Gallagher unlocked the door, which opened to a long brightly lit stairway. Very narrow. Two people could never fit side-by-side. One way, one-at-a-time—down. One step, one step, one step—down, down, down. Bodies in the basement, she thought. And remembered Livi once pulling an evil-big-sister stunt telling her and Charlotte that their Jersey basement smelled musty because someone had died down there.

"Dead body odors never go away," Livi had said. "And if you play down in the basement for too long, you'll start to smell like that too."

At the time of this little joke, their dad was not yet missing. Livi was a mean big sister, but not cruel. Still, Charlotte, the sensitive one, freaked out. Even now, she goes through phases of sniffing her hands every few seconds. Once, when a psychiatrist asked her why, Charlotte explained: "Need to be sure I don't smell dead."

A crazy idea—or maybe not. The night of the Mott Haven corpse when Eliana barfed in the corner, she spent almost an hour that night in the shower. Needed to be sure she didn't smell dead.

Now, Gallagher lumbered down the stairs, alternating his feet to favor one leg. As they descended, Eliana felt her throat tighten. The smell, yes. But not Livi's musty basement-smell. This was medicinal.

The odor of antiseptic cleaning products and... something else, hard to name. Cat litter? No, not quite. Rotten. Like spoiled vegetables. Or— not rotten-spoiled, but rotten-sweet. Something overcooked?

When they reached the bottom of the stairs, Gallagher paused before moving into the bright room. For a moment, complete silence, then Eliana heard him breathing, a slight wheeze on the inhale, followed by a weird, back-of-the-throat cluck, like he needed to cough.

A dramatic pause? She was about to ask, hey, are you OK? Then he exhaled loudly, and they stepped into the room, brightly lit, a long rectangle of white. Everything white. White floor, white tiles, white walls. Florescent lighting, too. She noted the hum, a buzz of energy coming from the ceiling, as if something up there were alive. She glanced up. The glare hurt her eyes. A headache coming on? Oh, no, she thought, please, not now. Then Gallagher stepped in front of her, motioning as if he were an usher showing her to a seat. At the far end of the room, the wall resembled a giant file cabinet, floor to ceiling, a gray metal grid of four-foot square drawers. Organized in rows of eight stacked three high, she counted, and re-counted. Each drawer, she knew, contained a body.

"So whaddya need?" Gallagher asked. And turned to look at her, straightening his shoulders and holding himself with a vigor that caught Eliana by surprise. In spite of the beer belly, the sleepy eyes, the been- there-done-that smirk on his face, Eliana realized that once upon a time this old cop had been quick and sharp. "Your missing person is...?"

"Missing person?"

"Yeah—whatddya got?"

A confused moment, then Eliana understood: Danny had concealed her "stress inoculation" idea from Gallagher. "Uhh, a pattern," she stalled, taking a small step forward, "We're trying to link some homicides, looking for a pattern."

"What kind? I got a crushed head, a carved-up little girl, a guy with thirteen bullet holes—what kind of pattern you got?"

Eliana felt a pinch in her stomach. She feared getting too far into a bullshit story about investigating homicides—wouldn't take much for that to blow up in her face.

"There are a few more in the cold room," Gallagher went on. "Pre-autopsy, still in the bag. Not sure what they look like."

He flicked his head toward another door in the corner. Eliana flashed on Danny's warning to stay out of the cold room unless she was prepared to go sleepless for a week. Amputated body parts. Samples of organs stored like food in to-go containers. And when she winced, Danny had pushed harder, explaining that she'd find severed limbs on grey dishes like cafeteria platters. Would you like a plate of fingers, an arm on a tray?

She looked at Gallagher. "I'll take a look at the girl," she said.

He walked quickly to the wall. Eliana stood frozen in place and watched him pull open the first drawer, then the second, then the third. The sound struck a chord: drawers opening and closing, wheels gliding, a smooth *kerchunk* at the end—all of it accompanied by Gallagher's labored breathing. Exercise noise, she thought, as if she were in a gym, watching a guy with a gut huffing and puffing, getting a workout.

Crazy, but—yes and no. A mind-trick, but the gym association fits, she thought, because the whole purpose of being here: get strong. Overcome fear, toughen up. Prepare, train, practice. She'd read about what to expect. The trauma, what might happen, how she might experience perceptual distortions, her hearing, her eyesight. Diminished sound, possibly tunnel vision, maybe a tingling in her limbs. Mild, all of this, compared to the disgusting likelihood that she'd lose control of her bladder and bowel. Perfectly normal stress response, the literature makes clear. It's common as hell, though few admit it. Another cultural conspiracy of macho silence. Men and their egos—their power of denial. But she was here to face reality, not deny it. Still, she knew that her conscious mind might simply shut down, resulting in what some call the "wild brain" taking over. She imagined it like a car rolling downhill without a driver. In that case, she figured, she'd collapse, knees buckling, and faint. And so—worst case scenario—she embarrasses herself with a friend of the McPartlan family.

"Ah, here she is..." Gallagher stepped back, motioning for Eliana to come closer.

She moved forward, taking several steps until she found herself standing over the open metal drawer. Breathe, she told herself, and lowered her eyes, looking down into the drawer at a white cotton sheet, smaller than she'd expected. It reminded her of a beach towel. Yes, right, a child's body. Her teeth clenched at the thought. But—teeth apart, teeth apart, relax the jaw. And breathe, breathe, breathe.

After a moment, she pulled off the sheet and let it hang from the drawer, then looked down and studied the death in front of her. A small pale blonde-haired girl, maybe seven or eight years old. The dead girl lay naked on this cold metal rack with her head flattened, the skull a squashed gourd, like a pale pumpkin, smashed. Eliana forced herself to look more closely. One of the girl's eyes was missing, its socket jet-black but tinged red in the center, as if to add a cruel touch of color. The crushed forehead, its fair skin purple at the edges, oozed grey-green. But no bugs, Eliana thought, closing her eyes. Yes, that's good, no bugs, no bugs. No bugs is good. But the words alarmed her because she couldn't stop repeating—no bugs no bugs no bugs—and with her eyes closed she felt her pulse start to throb, blood rushing through her ears, a tingling sensation sweeping across her body, like tiny droplets of rain, wet sharp needles. Chest, arms, legs, neck, forehead, face. A sudden sweat. And then came the urge: bladder, bowels. She squeezed, holding it in, activating, as she'd practiced, the *pubococcygeus* muscle. Kegel exercise—a way to hold in piss, but the intestinal pressure rose into her stomach, chest, throat. Hard swallows, gulping air, gagging—

Just then Gallagher cleared phlegm from his throat and said, "Damn, I thought she was carved up, not bashed in. Where the hell is that carved up one?" He stepped away, heading down another aisle.

Grateful to be alone, Eliana stood with her eyes closed, squeezing hard, thinking that maybe she should pray. Yes, the mourner's *kaddish*. Had anyone prayed for this child? But the *kaddish* wouldn't come. No Hebrew. Instead, just a dumb line in English: *the spark of divinity exists in all things—or not at all.* The words surprised her, not even sure where they came from—a reading, a rabbi? Did she even believe this? She leaned closer to the small body and, her eyes still closed, forced herself to inhale the smell—formaldehyde. It reminded her of cat urine. Blindly, eyes shut, she extended her hand, feeling for the body, a delicate object in the dark. She wasn't sure if it was OK to touch the body but leaned forward slightly and lay the tips of her fingers lightly on the little girl's bare chest. She felt stitching on the girl's skin like the seam of a base-ball. And understood: the medical examiner's incision. Yes, under the tips of her fingers, that's what she was feeling, and—squeezing her eyes shut tighter—she traced the bumpy groove slowly along the line where a technician had inserted a scalpel into this little girl's shoulder, slic-ing down to the tip of her breastbone, and then, curving around the belly button, continuing the cut until she reached the pubic bone. And then—other side—the famous "Y" cut. Eliana followed its shape, mov-ing her fingers slowly and lightly along the cool, rubbery seam of the skin.

What she felt was a certain kind of fascination—and pride. A sick pride, yes. The way her mind had calmed. And the cat-piss smell had faded into something tolerable. And her breathing was easy, smooth. And the throbbing in her ears, even the sweaty, clammy feel of her body—all of it seemed to clear. So she opened her eyes. She looked down at the corpse. This little girl's dead body, her head grotesquely crushed, her skin rubbery and lifeless—the corpse no longer frightened Eliana. And the incision—yes, it had such a clear purpose it looked almost beautiful in its own way. She'd read all about it. How the sym-metry of the "Y" allowed the medical examiner to peel the girls skin back so the surrounding tissue could be more effortlessly pulled away from the chest, exposing the ribs, making it easier for the bone-saw to cut through the plate of the sternum, which, in turn, allowed the stomach and interior organs to be scooped out and examined and... Autopsy. The word itself—Eliana repeated it now softly: autopsy... au-topsy. From the Greek *autos* "self" and *optos* "seen." As if peering inside a dead body is a way to look for one's self.

Chapter 11

Several days passed. Eliana tried to forget all about Vachik Savoyian. Family, ordinary life. Keep the police world on the other side of that line—that's the key. That's what Jack Bayer did so well. Right now, driving across the George Washington Bridge, noting the late afternoon light fading into a perfect June evening, she told herself to let the tension release from her body like a tangle of knotted cords being untied and smoothed into nice clear strands. Yes, she was headed to her niece's birthday party in Jersey, a relaxing celebration of normal family life.

Traffic was light. Absorbed by the river view, she failed to notice Vachik Savoyian's grey Honda Accord following two cars behind. She turned up the radio and looked out the window, admiring the green-and-grey cliffs of the Jersey Palisades. A geological wonder, her father used to say. Trees sprouting from rock. Forty-two different species, six endangered forms of plant life. The formal name: a "talus slope community." Very rare piece of nature, he explained.

Hard for Eliana to think of Jersey this way—rare nature—especially where her sister lived. Livi had traded the sheltered world of their modern orthodox childhood for the sheltered world of rich investment bankers. Ah, yes, *meowww-hiss-scraaatch*. Eliana hated herself for being so judgmental, but that's how it came. Livi's husband Richard (call me Ricky) was loaded. A hedge fund guy, or something. He drove one of those low-to-the-ground sporty cars with doors that open like airplane wings. Livi drove something fancy too, and they owned a gorgeous country place upstate which they practically never used. Their home, a McMansion located in Jersey's wealthiest county, Hunterdon, overlooked the Round Valley Reservoir, a beautiful, man-made, artificial piece of nature, which, to Eliana, symbolized the essence of her sister's life: a gorgeous fake.

And Char lived the opposite extreme: hated everything to do with money. White people rule the world because of their money, bankers killed their father, and on and on.

But what right had Eliana to judge her sisters so harshly? The nice Jewish girl pretending to be a tough city cop—talk about a gorgeous fake! No, especially since their mom died, Eliana hated when this compare-your-life-to-mine game crowded out her affection for her Livi. And she hated when she couldn't shake off her own feeling of superiority. Police work versus housework. And the winner is—?

She thought of her father—how he'd feel about her swollen sense of self-importance, the cop swagger. Ridiculous. Totally unacceptable. He'd give her that stern look, brow squeezed, and start in with the old Hasidic "tale of two-pockets," the story how every human being needs to carry two notes, one in each pocket. In the right, the note says: "For my sake was the world created." Feeling low, reach in and pull it out. But feeling high and mighty, then you need the other pocket, where the note says: "I am but dust and ashes."

Yeah, sure dad, two pockets—impossible contradictions. The responsibility to care for the whole world together with the knowledge that we're puny and insignificant. So—everything matters and nothing matters. Therefore: what? Pursue pleasure, avoid pain. Join the good life in the 'burbs?

Another twenty minutes, agitation growing. She tried to push back on the old childhood crap. Be cheerful, she told herself, this is the only family you've got.

Still no awareness of the grey Honda Accord following her.

When she pulled into Livi's circular driveway, Savoyian's car drove past without her noticing. Totally absorbed in herself, determined to enjoy this family event, her niece's birthday, Eliana turned off her car and took a deep breath.

The driveway was beautiful. Red brick, hand-laid, an old-world European design. In the few months since she'd last visited, a landscaped island had been constructed in the driveway's center, a patch of manicured lawn with room for a black iron bench, two chairs, and a Weeping Willow tree. The tree's curved branches sloped now to the grass in a dramatic arc. Gorgeous, gentle. There was a song, wasn't there? Something her mother sang: *Willow weep for me / Bend your branches down along the ground / And cover me...*

No mistake, Livi must have selected the willow deliberately. For Mom? Ah, yes, and because the willow's one of the four species used to *celebrate Sukkot. Leviticus 23:40...* branches of palm and boughs of leafy trees and willows of the brook...

Weird. Her memory's chapter-and-verse precision surprised her—and came with a strange feeling of heaviness. Her shoulders and neck suddenly ached, as if she'd just lifted something too heavy. Holy days, meticulous observance of ritual, her past seemed so distant—her Jewish life, her family. She wondered if Livi really viewed her as the conceited little sister, inflated with her hero-cop-fantasy? And was it, in fact, nothing but a fantasy? Maybe Jack's right, she thought, I'm haunted and should get off the street before something bad happens. Or quit the job altogether. Go to law school. That's what Mom always wanted... but— *oy, don t go there, what mom wanted!*

She thought often of her mother, who died of ovarian cancer just before Eliana went into the Police Academy. Her mother disapproved of police work, but—well, the family joke was that if Mom had been alive when Eliana married Danny (an interfaith wedding without a rabbi!), that would have killed her. Still, her mother's final words remained important to Eliana: "Take care of Char. Because Livi—Livi can't do it."

For chrissake, Eliana thought, the family-shit button being pushed and the party hasn't even started. She turned the car back on and accelerated—a little too fast—then pulled past the Willow tree to park in the shade at the edge of the driveway. She wanted to avoid being boxed in by other cars. In case she needed to—as they say—make a quick getaway.

She got out of the car and walked up the driveway. Her agitation gnawed like the trace of an upset stomach, a gassy, full feeling. Then she inhaled the suburban smell of grass and leaves and trees. And the fake reservoir? Am I smelling that? That fake shit? She pushed the question aside.

The front door stood wide open. That's nice, she thought—why inconvenience some hard-working burglar? Simply take the "break" out of "breaking and entering." She stepped inside and started down the hall past the living room, but stopped a moment. The room—stunning, truly. She had to admit. Luxurious, sunken, surrounded by the higher flooring of the main living room, with a recessed sitting area, a circular leather couch—it created the feeling of a separate space without using walls. Her niece, Ariel, called it the "convo pit" because that's where "family talks" were held. Eliana remembered when her sister first showed her the idea—on paper, it looked like nothing but a big hole in the floor. But now, the space felt truly inviting. The "convo pit," yes. If only she and her sister could really talk.

She went into the kitchen—absurdly spacious compared to the cramped alcove in Eliana's apartment. This was really two rooms: one for the stove and sink and every possible appliance, along with a butcher-block chef's island in the center; plus, behind this, a drop-ceiling breakfast room opened onto a stone patio with an outdoor fireplace. Over-the-top, Eliana thought, but, she admitted, beautiful. The other wall contained a picture window overlooking the giant wooded land behind the house, and beyond that: the reservoir. In spite of herself, Eliana found the view exhilarating, and she felt a presence that almost disturbed her with its joy: the thick woods, the setting sun, the blue water—it looked so real. So pretty. There are moments, she thought, when something pretty simply dwarfs the worlds ugliness. Yes, she needed this—to get out of the city.

A caterer entered carrying a crate of oranges and two crates of bananas. Eliana turned from the windows. Male, early twenties, short blond hair, black pants, white shirt, the handsome face of a wannabe actor—he set the crates on the granite counter and said, "Hi! I'm Aaron. You know where the blender is?"

Something about his tone bothered Eliana. Too friendly, too confident.

"Homemade smoothies," he went on. "I understand that's one of the birthday girl's favorites?"

Eliana hesitated, taking in this guy's cocky smile. "Yeah, that's my niece. She loves smoothies. I think the blender is in that cabinet near the fridge."

"Hey, thanks. Appreciate it. I can make one for you too, of course." He nodded firmly, tucked his chin, still smiling, another whiff of arrogance in his smirk. He held Eliana's gaze way too long, and she understood: this guy, fully aware of his soap-opera good looks, this little twit, he was checking her out.

"No thanks. I don't care for smoothies," she said, and turned back to the window. Outside, she saw four more young-guy caterers working a tree-cutting lift to hang colored lights in the falling dusk—hundreds of colored lights, enough to make a Christmas tree out of the fifty-foot maple at the back of the lawn. A lit-up tree, in June? And the cost of renting that tree-doctor equipment? All this for a sweet sixteen— what will the wedding look like? A portable dance floor had been set up a short distance from the soon-to-be twinkling tree. Ripped right out of a nightclub—that's what it looked like. Glossy black-and-white squares, illuminated with LED strip lights—they flashed in the growing darkness.

Eliana found herself counting the number of event staff: four in the tree, two at the grill, one making drinks, another on the dance floor, and Mr. Smoothie behind her. Nine, all male. And how many teenage girls will be here? A security nightmare.

"Hey, didn't hear you come in," Livi called from behind her.

Eliana turned and gave her sister a hug. She considered saying something about the open, unlocked front door. But Livi held up her cell phone.

"Just got a text from Char—last week she said she couldn't make it tonight. But now—I don't know. Sounds like she might come. And maybe bring a friend."

"Oh no—"

"What?"

"Her friend."

"Yeah?"

"I don't want to sound like a racist cop—"

"Then don't."

"I met him."

"And he's Black, right?"

"Yes, but that's not—"

Ariel came in from the patio, calling: "Auntie Em, Auntie Em!"

Old joke. Once, when Ariel was about eight years old and home from school with a fever, they spent the day together watching *The Wizard of Oz*—twice, from beginning to end, back-to-back. Jell-O at the intermission.

"The birthday girl!" Eliana turned to Ariel, but instead of a hug, Ariel stepped back and spread her arms.

"Like my outfit? New leggings."

Skintight, part polyester, part spandex, a black-and-white pattern of splotches and squares—a little like the dance floor. Eliana, in fact, disapproved. Way too revealing. She spotted the smoothie-guy peering over his crate of fruit. Ariel's shirt—a thin, gauze-like, loose-fitting T-shirt, practically see-through—hung just over her ass, suggesting a too-short skirt. Hooker clothes pretending to be "sportswear."

Ariel stood holding her arms out and then made a quick spin, her long dark hair flowing across her face. A natural beauty; long, athletic legs, an hour-glass shape, high cheekbones, easy smile—the family line, sort of: Ariel looked more like her aunt than her mother. This touched a tender spot between the sisters because Livi had inherited their father's Polish features: stocky, short, big boned and thick with muscle. Livi's face also resembled her fathers: a flat nose and straight lips on a large square head. Her best feature was her smile, but she couldn't escape a sort of jack-o-lantern look, especially when she puffed up with extra weight. While Eliana could eat junk all day long, Livi added pounds the minute she came off the veggies. Eliana knew all about it, her sisters constant struggle, the curve of Livi's hips battling her box-shaped trunk. It was a war her sister fought and won through sheer force of will: exercise, exercise, exercise. The basement was stocked like a small health club. Treadmill, elliptical, stationary bike. Bands, balls, brackets attached to the walls. And three times a week: a personal trainer.

On the other hand, Eliana—and Ariel—took after their mother, a Slavic beauty. Tall, slim, with a fine light bone structure, not muscular, but robust, lithe. Somewhere in that side of the family line was a ballerina who'd danced with the Kirov. Not hard to imagine. Glamor had radiated from their mother's face too: heart-shaped, with high cheekbones, full red lips, and dark almond-shaped eyes.

"Welllll?" Ariel still stood there, her own body a delicious combination of teenage curves and angles, dripping with sexuality, like drops of dew on a blossoming tree. "You like?"

Eliana stepped closer. "Ahh, there's a little too much—uhhhh..." she paused, motioned to her chest, then whispered. "Your bra shows right through the shirt."

Ariel ignored this and glanced side-to-side, then—coast clear—leaned forward, an impish twinkle in her eyes. "Can you believe how cute these waiters are?"

"They're not exactly waiters. And they're way too old for you."

"Whatever," Ariel said, and took Eliana by the arm. She pulled her into the hall just outside the kitchen.

"Did you hear me about the outfit? I said I can see—"

"It's a sports bra, Auntie Em, like a halter top. It's no big deal, really." Ariel leaned closer, pressing her mouth to her aunt's ear. Eliana smelled potato chips on Ariel's breath. "Auntie Em, listen, I really need a favor, OK? Did you see the guy at the juice machine?"

"What about him?"

"I need you to cuff him."

Eliana laughed, as much at the cop-slang as anything else, and she couldn't resist playing along. "What did he do?" she asked.

"Nothing, yet. But once you put the handcuffs on him, bring him up to my room. I'll take it from there."

Ariel's breathy whisper tickled Eliana's ear. They both laughed, then they started together back toward the kitchen.

"Where's your little brother?"

"My what? Do I have a little brother?"

"Very funny."

"There's some kind of a large rodent running around upstairs, but—" Eliana grabbed Ariel around the neck from behind, pretending a choke hold.

"What happened to the cute little girl I used to know?"

"What—I'm still cute."

"No, you're not." She released her grip, then smoothed Ariel's thick dark hair. She really was a gorgeous girl. "You're sixteen, and—well, outfits like this—I mean, hey, it's dangerous out there."

"Yeah, but, come on—my aunt's a cop. Like, nobody's going to mess with me, right?"

Eliana experienced a weird involuntary surge of anger. She felt suddenly aggressive, and, although she didn't intend it, she turned Ariel toward her with a hard quick grab-and-pull, her hands placed on each side of the gauzy shirt, a show of force, as if she were on the street.

Shock registered on Ariel's face. And fear. Head back, eyes still, the skin on her face tightened.

"Don't joke about that, Ariel."

"What? About you being a cop?"

"I can't protect you."

"I was—what—I'm sorry. I was just joking."

"Yeah—well..."

Ariel's eyes filled with tears. Then with a quick sniff she blinked them away. "You were laughing too, Aunt Elly. I mean—about the waiter and everything. I was just making a joke."

Yes, of course, a joke, an innocent joke, but Eliana heard something else. The cop world and the ordinary world—keep the two separate, or go crazy. But what if the separation itself—the gap, the split—what if that makes you crazy? She massaged the spot of soft cartilage where she'd grabbed Ariel's shoulder. "I'm sorry. You're... you're right. You didn't—you didn't do anything... I just—I don't know. Things have been a little tense at work. Actually, I'm thinking I might quit."

"Quit being a cop? Does my mom know?" Ariel's eyes flashed—hurt gone. She looked alert now, suddenly intense. Alive to the darkness, the conflict, the family wound. No doubt Ariel understood that her "aunt-the-cop" was nothing but the proverbial tip of the iceberg. Under the surface, a huge dark mass of family pain—frozen, ancient, feared.

"*... behold, I will bring a flood upon the earth...*"

Don't go there, Eliana thought, and wondered why she'd just dragged her niece into this. In fact, the surprise in Ariel's eyes mirrored the feeling in Eliana's gut. Had she really just said that she might quit being a cop? Where did that come from? Like an unexpected belch. Her body heated up with a strange feeling of embarrassment. And then she noticed her sister had been standing there, listening.

"Did I just hear—no more police work?"

"No," Eliana said quickly, turning to her sister. "I mean—I'm just going through kind of a rough spell. But I do want to talk with you about something."

The blind-date business, Eliana thought. She needed to put a stop to that nonsense.

Livi smiled—spontaneously, unforced, and the warm, curious look in her sister's eyes melted something hard and tense in Eliana, weakened her resolve about no more blind dates. Her sister just wanted to help, right?

"Sure," Livi said, nodding. "Let's talk." Her big toothy smile hung there pasted a little sideways on her square head like a crooked sign. Her funny-looking big sister—Eliana felt a wave of affection for Livi. Old tensions loosening? In fact, that's exactly what Eliana wanted. She wanted to feel connected to her sister, to belong to a family, to be firmly grounded here—far from "the job."

"Ricky won't be home for another half-hour," Livi said. "Come, let's sit in the living room. You want a glass of wine or something?"

"Wait, mom, if you guys are heading for the convo-pit—is Dad meeting the 6:30 train, because—"

"Oooh, I forgot, your friend Jenna needs—text Dad right now, will you?"

"Mom! You didn't tell Dad to—"

"I'll go get Jenna if Dad doesn't respond to the text."

"Ughhh—I can't wait until I get my driver's license."

"That makes two of us."

"Depending on you and Dad for every ride is like—"

"If she were getting behind the wheel herself," Eliana cut in. "I'd make her change that outfit."

Ariel froze, head cocked, jaw clenched. If looks could kill...

Eliana immediately regretted saying anything. She watched her sisters head swivel from her to Ariel, then back again. For a long minute— awkward silence.

Finally, Eliana jumped in, "I'm just saying—hey, there are cops out there who'll stop you for some made-up traffic crap just to get a closer look. Why invite trouble?"

"Because it's, like, a free country?" Ariel said quietly, lowering her eyes, a definite sass in her voice.

"A free country, right, just watch your tone," her mother said. "And don't forget the restrictions on your freedom tonight, young lady."

"I know, Mom, you've told me like twenty-five times: no boys upstairs. I get it."

A loud sigh punctuated the end of her sentence. Then Ariel turned away, heels pounding the floor as she headed down the hall.

"Sorry," Eliana said quietly. "What do I know about teenagers, huh? I should've kept my mouth shut. She's gonna be pissed at me now the whole night."

"Don't worry about it. In twenty minutes, her friends will be here— and she'll forget the whole thing. But I do think it's time for a glass of wine."

Zig-zag emotions, yes—Eliana told herself to stick to the positive. Like working a cover—act a feeling, and the feeling will come. Act comfortable, act confident, act connected to your sister. This little drama? Families fight. Yes, and that's because—well, it's family. It's normal. Be part of it. Normal.

She settled into the recessed leather couch and sipped her white wine. Expensive, she knew. Livi's husband could talk for hours about flavor profiles and grape-growing regions and "oaking" in old-fashioned wooden barrels and—Eliana's favorite—the aromas derived from "*malolactic fermentation.*"

"Soooo... you know, I've got to ask," Livi said, "I mean, the idea that you might quit—"

"No. No, no, no—I don't know why I even said that. I'm not leaving the job."

Disappointment transformed Livi's expression—the happy jack-o-lantern smashed. Yes, now she looked just like their father. Her face worked into that same heavy-lined expression of moral judgment. Eliana found her sister's familiar look of disapproval disturbing—no, worse: destructive. It shattered the moment's intimacy. They both took big gulps of their wine. Just like that, a single look—gone was the warm family feeling.

Instead: the ancient split. How their lives pointed in opposite directions—Eliana facing the world of crime and violence because that's precisely what had destroyed their family. While Livi turned the opposite way, moving forward, as she put it. Livi's argument against Eliana becoming a cop included a mountain of facts, which she basically boiled down to one line: "Look at the statistics, Elly. Most people—more than ninety-nine percent—never experience violence in their lives." Then the week before Eliana graduated from Columbia, when she told Livi that she'd applied to the Police Academy, Livi shook her head and said to her, "Look, what happened—to Dad, I mean—it was horrible—yes, horrible. But... Elly, I worry—this one horrible thing doesn't have to define the whole meaning of your life, does it?"

The question still lingered—after all these years. Here in the sunken living room, it felt like Livi had just asked the question again. Awkwardly, silently, they drank their wine. Finally, the moment passed. Livi's expression softened. She took a swallow, looked up, and said, "There's a new guy at Ricky's office. Single. Very nice—I met him a few weeks ago. And—well, cute. I mean, seriously cute. He played professional tennis before getting his MBA."

"A tennis pro! That's one I haven't tried." Eliana laughed. Hadn't she just promised herself no more blind dates?

"We asked him to join us tonight. Totally casual. He lives nearby. In fact—"

Livi looked up. Just then Richard arrived. He waved, smiling, calling hello from the entrance to the living room. Behind him stood the new-guy-former-tennis-pro. They stepped down into the recessed area of the living room.

Then Ariel poked her head in: "Who's picking up Jenna?"

Livi excused herself and rushed off. Richard went for drinks. This left Eliana and the former tennis pro sitting across from each other on the matching leather couches. Between them was a glass and chrome coffee table.

"Steven... Steve."

That's how he introduced himself—first formally, then more casually, with a nervous shrug. He wore a pair of dark brown, grained-leather shoes, and a traditional dark blue suit—sharp-looking and well-fitted, exactly the sort of thing a successful businessman would be expected to wear. But her sister was right—cute, very cute.

He leaned back on the couch and looked around the room, commenting on "what a beautiful place this is." Then he fidgeted with his hands, rubbing one wrist, then the other. Like perps when the cuffs come off. The association made Eliana want to smile, but she controlled herself. "So you work with Richard?" she said.

"Yeah—actually, he hired me. Just three months ago. Great guy." Steven—Steve—was lying. Eliana knew it by his voice. After a while, cops know the sound of a lie like musicians know bad singing. It's a tone. The muscles in the guy's throat working too hard. Even if, technically, the right notes are being sung—it's still not music.

Eliana felt unsure what to do with this realization. She looked at his face. Diamond-shaped, with a long straight nose—classic, chiseled—it gave him a strong, determined look. But something undercut the determination: his eyes, yes. He had unusually long eyelashes for a male. "What do you do at the firm?"

He seemed surprised by the question. "I'm a fixed income specialist. Right now, I'm tracking credit migration patterns on high yield corporate debt trading in the secondary market."

Eliana cleared her throat and took a sip of wine, then said, "There are a bunch of words in there I know, but I've got almost no idea what you're talking about."

"Sorry," Steve said, laughing nervously. "It's kind of technical. Basically, I help the guys trading bonds. It's actually very interesting in a way, and I like it a lot—"

More lies. Eliana registered this with a twinge. Unfortunately, it made this guy a little less cute.

"But basically, what I'm really enjoying most is the overall atmosphere at the firm," Steve went on. "I mean, Ricky is just a great guy to work for."

He was belting it out now, top of his lungs—but painfully off-key. Eliana couldn't take it anymore. "Really?" she said, and slid forward, sitting on just the edge of the couch. Steve picked up on it, sliding forward too, a bit of conspiratorial intimacy between them, closing the physical distance.

"I'm kind of surprised," Eliana continued, "Because I find Richard to be an uptight, pompous asshole." She paused and watched the shock hit Steves good-looking face. "But, hey, he's married to my sister—so what can I say?"

The shock melted into an amused, crooked grin that gave Steve's face an entirely new dimension. Aaah, finally, the cocky tennis pro—a little swagger on the court. "Yeah," he said, holding in a laugh, "I know what you mean, but he's my boss—so what can I say?"

Richard returned to the room holding drinks for him and Steve. Eliana finished off her wine with a quick gulp, then gave Steve a quick nod-and-wink and said, "You boys can talk business, I'm gonna see how things are with Ariel."

Darkness fell. In the huge backyard behind the house: blinking lights, blasting music, the smell of grilled meat. A throng of teenagers danced and squirmed and giggled and gossiped and wrapped themselves into little clumps of flesh, disappearing behind trees, in and out of the shadows. Eliana stood on the patio deck. Watching. Or, rather, patrolling. She couldn't help it. Fifty, maybe seventy-five kids—this could easily get out of control. More than once she'd smelled pot. And the no-boys-upstairs rule? Violated, definitely. But—kids will be kids, right? That's what she told herself, trying to relax. No alcohol being served, of course. Still, plenty of these little boys and girls showed up with a nice ripe glow, and once the soda can is opened, no telling what gets added. She wondered if her sister missed the orthodox Jewish community of their childhood. Problems there too, of course, but you don't find too many parties like this.

Eliana recognized some of the kids. Older versions of sweet little ones she used to know. The Tarleton triplets—who still looked freakishly alike—leaned against one wall of the temporary dance floor. They stood side by side, inseparable as usual. Little Reyna Cowan had turned into a blonde bombshell, circulating among the crowd as if there were a spotlight on her, a small group of girls hovering like worker bees around their queen. Right now, the hive occupied the dance floor, Reyna in the center. A natural athlete—hips swiveling, butt shaking, her big breasts bouncing—she was torturing one boy after another, rushing between songs to whisper into the ears of Cathleen Munroe and Alexis Rossini, sending the girls into gales of giggles. Once upon a time, didn't those three play travel softball together? Ah, the good old days: little girls wearing uniforms, following rules, hoping to hit a home run. A simple, wholesome homerun.

Eliana couldn't see Ariel right now, although about an hour ago near the grill they'd made eye contact. Anger, yes, but Eliana also saw that her niece had a wanting-to-please look in her eye: Ariel had changed her shirt from the gauzy see-through into a modest V-neck tee, and the way she held Eliana's gaze, longer than necessary, made it clear she wanted her aunt to notice. It somehow broke Eliana's heart. She had not wanted to make her niece feel bad, but only—to protect? Make the world safe? But, right, there it is: the grandiosity, the wound, the family curse. Crime and violence once broke into their lives like monsters from another world, and now—

Steve tapped lightly on her elbow. He'd remained with the small contingent of grown-ups who camped out in the sunken living room. But now he stood there smiling, swirling his glass of wine. "We'd be crazy to try dancing with them, don't you think?" He laughed softly.

"Yeah, my niece would kill me."

"Which one is she?" Steve brushed lightly against Eliana's body as he stepped past her. It was definitely a move. She'd felt his hand on her arm, inviting her to join him at the balcony's railing.

"She's not out there, I don't think," Eliana spoke without stepping forward. "I'm not sure where she is."

Steve hesitated, then turned around. But he didn't move to where Eliana stood. Instead, he leaned back, elbows on the railing. The gesture marked the space between them. They looked at each other—the ball, so to speak, clearly on Eliana's side of the court, though she also experienced another analogy: police tape, do not cross.

In the dim patio light, the sharp features of Steve's face looked handsome in a rugged sort of way. And his relaxed posture—the confident lean, wrists limp, holding his wine glass between two long fingers. Attractive, definitely—but Eliana couldn't tell what she herself was feeling. Like wondering if she were hungry or thirsty or—neither, just tired. And if you've gotta ask...? Still, sometimes you just eat because you know it's good for you. Right?

She stepped forward. Steve's face brightened, eyes opening a bit wider.

He wanted to play—and she couldn't blame him. After all, she started the game with that seam-splitting smash back in the living room—her crack about Richard being a jerk.

"Want another drink?" he asked.

She hesitated. "How about a sip of yours?"

He lifted his glass. As she took it from him, her fingers rested way too long on his hand, and then she pulled away slowly, gently, lightly rubbing the inside of his palm. A not-so-subtle tease. She couldn't believe it. Without trying, without intending it, she'd flipped into hooker mode. She wasn't flirting—she was working this guy. And couldn't seem to stop. With the glass to her lips, she said, "Before I sip this—anything I should know?"

Steve smiled the same crooked grin he'd flashed during their confidential moment in the living room. "What do you mean?"

"Accepting drinks, you know—we teach girls to—"

Steve cut in, laughing. "You mean is it spiked?"

"Here," she pushed the glass up to his mouth. "You sip first."

"What—so if it is spiked—"

"Then you pass out and I get to take advantage of you."

She held the glass against Steve's lips. He played along, swallowing a big mouthful. Eliana pushed her unease off to the side, ignoring the voices inside her, like blocking out the sound of people talking at the table next to you. It's there—this other conversation. Vague voices, fragments of an argument, advice ignored: *don't let the job become your life; never forget you're a person first, a cop second; in your personal life live not by the laws of the street, but by the laws of love—which means: cut the crap, keep it real, let people know you.*

"Hmmm, delicious," Steve said, smacking his lips. "Now, if I collapse right here on the deck—do I get mouth-to-mouth resuscitation?"

"Actually, my sister has a defibrillator, so I'll be ripping open your shirt and strapping electrodes on your chest—"

"No, no—that's no good."

"Though—I would first stick my fingers in your mouth. Obstructed airway check. Be sure you're not choking."

"Well, that's sexy."

Eliana lifted the wine as if offering a toast. She took a small sip, then handed him back the glass.

"So Rick told me that you're a... a..."

She waited. It was cruel, yes, but she enjoyed watching him struggle. Would he call her a cop, a police officer, a detective? Or would he backtrack and ask if she "worked in law enforcement?" Or maybe he'd quote a cop show, fake the insider's approach and ask if she was "on the job."

"A... yeah—" he stammered. "—he said that you—you work—"

"I'm a detective with the NYPD." She rescued him—so big hearted. Steve's brows lifted. "Wow, yeah, I've never—well, never known a— never even met a... a—"

"A detective with the NYPD?"

"Or any cop."

Eliana smiled. Drop the tennis racket and keep your hands where I can see them, she thought. Steve had never met a cop, right. But so what? She'd never met a tennis pro. She felt bad about her attitude, her condescending bullshit. He knew plenty about the world that that she didn't. And so...

Just then Eliana's phone went off. She checked the number.

"Sorry, I have to take this," she said. She walked to a corner of the deck. "What's up, Jack? Are you going to ruin my weekend?"

"I thought you'd want to know this. Your girl, Kitty, the hooker, she was found dead."

"What?" The shock hit Eliana like a gut-punch. She gasped, "How—where?"

"Prelim is she was strangled. No suspects yet. A hotel on Southern Boulevard."

"I know that hotel. I'll get right over and—"

"It's a Queens homicide, Elly. If they want your help, they'll call you. They're tracking down her pimp."

"That should be plural. These guys are corporations. I'll be there in an hour and—"

"No, you won't. It's not your case."

She registered Jack's sharp tone.

"Listen, Eliana," he went on, his voice low. "I'm calling you—as a friend. And a sergeant. It's not your case. Do you hear me?"

"Right," she said quietly, "I understand. Not my case."

She hung up and stood there leaning on the railing looking out at the night sky. Beyond the party, out over the reservoir, the darkness grew thick. *Savoyian,* she thought. *Did he kill Kitty?*

Just then a squeal of laughter came from the yard below, rising above the thump of dance music. She started to walk back toward Steve, then stopped. A noise. A shout. Low, guttural, a man's voice. Her brother-in-law? Yes, and it came not from the yard, but from inside the house. "Out! Out right now! Or I call the police!"

The rage in Richard's voice—hoarse, crackling.

Eliana bolted past Steve and into the house, hurrying through the kitchen and down the hall where she found her brother-in-law standing now at the front door. Ariel stood next to him, her shirt torn, her lip bleeding. She was crying, trying to control her hard choppy breaths while her mother held one arm around her shoulder.

"What's going on?" Eliana said.

Richard flicked his head toward the driveway. "Forget it. He's leaving—if s over."

"No, it's not," Livi snapped. "We should press charges."

"Charges?" Richard answered, with that pompous whine in his voice, exactly the sound Eliana found so irritating.

"She's underage," Livi said.

"And she was drinking."

"Daddy, I wasn't—"

"Don't lie to me."

"But I—"

"There's alcohol on your breath. I can smell—"

"I took one sip."

"And that's—"

Livi cut in. "So what, Richard. Even if she drank—that doesn't mean she deserved to be attacked."

Eliana turned to look out the open door. A white shirt, faint in the darkness, floated slowly down the driveway, a cocky lilt in the step, shoulders swaying, blond head bobbing. Even from this distance, she knew who it was: Aaron, the smoothie guy.

Before anyone could react, Eliana grabbed Ariel by the elbow and walked her down the hallway and around the corner, then stopped and stood directly in front of her niece, just the two of them, their faces inches apart.

"What happened?" Eliana asked. "From the beginning."

The force in Eliana's voice shut down Ariel's tears immediately. Her puffy eyes blinked fast, as if she'd been splashed with water. Collecting herself, straightening her posture, she seemed to be gathering her thoughts, pursing her mouth and sucking in her cheeks. She winced when her tongue passed over her swollen bloody lip. But she didn't speak. Too scared.

Eliana put her hand on her niece's shoulder. She squeezed gently, spoke quietly. "Ariel, whatever happened—it's OK. I just need to know." She gave her nieces shoulder another gentle squeeze. "Did you invite him upstairs?"

Ariel shrugged.

"Ariel, it's OK. Is that what happened?"

"Kind of—but not really. He was in James' room. And I—well, some of my friends brought alcohol and I put it in my closet, you know, so they, like, wouldn't drink it."

"But you drank it."

"It's not like I'm drunk, Aunt Elly. I just—"

"OK—you invited him into your room to have a drink, right?"

"Yeah, and then, you know, we started fooling around, and then..."

Ariel lowered her eyes—tears again, almost. She held them back, then continued in a choked voice: "It got kind of intense right away. And I got, you know, scared—because he was grabbing for my leggings and pulling them down and everything and he started saying this stuff about how he was going to 'break me in' and I just got more and more scared and tried to get him off of me and then when I heard my shirt rip, I yelled—and that's when he hit me."

Ariel stopped.

"He hit you?"

Ariel took a small tight breath, then nodded.

Eliana took off down the hall.

"Aunt Elly—"

"Go to your parents, Ariel," she called without looking back.

From the bottom of the driveway, she saw him standing at his car. He'd parked on the street and stood finishing a cigarette. He threw the butt on the ground, then leaned over and started to open the door of a beat-up four-door. Eliana noted make and model—Chevrolet Sonic, two-toned, blue with a grey roof, right fender bent, Jersey plate: Frank Harry 5-9-5 John. She knew exactly what was happening: high situational awareness. Adrenaline pumping. No gun, no cuffs. But it didn't matter.

She headed straight for his car. "Hey, Aaron, don't go anywhere." Her voice, though she'd called loudly, sounded far away. The mind flips over in seconds, she knew, though she also understood that from the perspective of the more advanced, slower thinking, time-conscious cerebral cortex, it can feel like you've stepped into a slow-motion movie. Surreal—you see everything clearly, your breath flows, your heart pounds, your blood thuds in your ears, and your muscles tingle: ready, ready, ready. A sweet, pure, adrenaline-high. Eliana never felt more alive.

"...*The righteous are bold as a lion.*"

"What do you want," he said, "I'm leaving."

"Step away from the car."

"Why? I'm just—"

Theres an old cop line: if it's s a fair fight, you didn't plan right. Back in her judo and aikido days, Eliana took pride in her technique—the "art" in martial arts." But—Danny was dead right about this—the streets are different. Forget grace and beauty. Instead: Krav Maga, the Israeli fighting system. The words in Hebrew mean, "close combat." Popular with the NYPD—the Jewish connection felt special to Eliana, though nobody else gave a shit. As one ex-Israeli commando turned teacher put it, "Hey, this is not a sport—it's violence."

Before Aaron finished his sentence, Eliana executed what's called a "Front Straight Web Strike." Hand parallel to the ground, the "web," which is the patch of skin between thumb and forefinger creates a V-shaped striking tool that's thin, strong, and capable of sliding under the chin. Her blow landed directly on Aaron's windpipe. She checked the punch just enough to avoid collapsing the trachea—killing him.

He dropped his car keys, gasped and coughed—and brought both hands up to his throat, which left his groin completely exposed. Next move: Eliana rocked back on her heel, a brief pause to gather her breath, then launched her whole body forward, using the power and strength of her hips and legs to maximize the power of the kick. And, as she'd learned: angle upward, rather than straight in. Striking the testicles from below maximizes the pain.

He doubled over and fell forward, his face hitting the street with a quiet smacking sound. A moment passed, then he lifted his head a few inches, groaned, and puked. Eliana stepped back, looked at the vomit and imagined rubbing his face in it. Almost started to do that— then stopped. Her rage left her and now, suddenly, she felt drained. Unsteady. And, too late, she realized what she'd just done: violated every principle of law enforcement, embarrassed the badge, as they say, and dishonored the essential spirit of Krav Maga. This wasn't justice— it was revenge. Not self-defense, but a vicious attack. And yet it felt good. Plain and simple: she'd punished the asshole for attacking her niece, and it felt good. That's what unnerved her: The swift righteous justice of it and how good it felt.

She straightened herself and looked off in the distance taking several deep breaths. Then she stared down at the strange sight of smoothie boy twitching in spasms of pain, his body occasionally moving in synchrony with the rhythmic beat of the dance music coming faintly from the yard. Looking at him, she felt nothing. No thought, no feeling, certainly no remorse—and she knew then this moment changed everything. It marked a step across a line. Every dirty cop's delusion: it's not wrong— because it feels so right.

Chapter 12

Eliana left him on the ground—he'll recover, she thought, and considered returning to the party. But there was enough anger and chaos at the house. It was Livi's job—not hers—to comfort Ariel. Instead, she decided to head home, but she'd driven only a few miles when high beams flashed in her rear-view mirror. When they flashed again, she slowed and pulled toward the shoulder to let the car pass. The other car also slowed and followed right along behind her. And again, the high beams flashed.

What the hell? Then her cell rang. She didn't recognize the number.

"Who are you and why are you following me?"

"We need to talk."

Her heart raced when she recognized Savoyian's voice. And she thought: he murdered Kitty, and now he's coming for me. But why flash his beams? Why call her? That made no sense.

"How did you find me?"

"Look, I don't mean you any harm, believe me. I just want to talk. Please."

He didn't sound threatening, but still this was dangerous. No back-up, no gun, no cuffs. A public place, she thought. Plenty of eyes on us both.

"There's a strip mall a few miles up the road and an all-night diner called Pappy's. I'll meet you inside."

She got there first and took a booth close to the waitress' station and ordered coffee. She watched Savoyian sitting in his car for a few long minutes, then finally he came in and sat down across from her. It was the first time she'd seen him in full light. Thick dark eyebrows, deep-set eyes, long thin nose. Yes, handsome; the dark swarthy Persian—that line popped into her head again. Distracting. She told herself to concentrate, but her mind also kept flitting back to smoothie boy lying in his vomit. *What the hell's wrong with me? Beating up that kid? Jack's right—I'm falling apart.*

The waitress came. Savoyian ordered coffee.

Eliana looked directly into his eyes. "Why are you following me? And how did you know where I'd be?"

"It doesn't matter."

"It matters to me."

She watched his lips do that strange curl, his indefinable, faint half-smile. "You're right. I'm sorry," he said. "That's rude. It matters to you—yes."

He was silent a moment, thinking, and then he lifted his head and looked directly into her eyes. "I used to be a cop."

"Ahh... I should've thought of that. When you made me in the bar. What precinct did you—"

"Not exactly that kind of cop."

"What does that mean? What kind of cop were you?"

"Long story. But you, Vice, right?" He paused, then with sarcasm added, "And apparently with jurisdiction in Jersey! Never knew the NYPD could—"

"You—you saw all that?"

"You seemed to be enjoying yourself."

"Yes. Which bothers me—or should bother me, right?"

He nodded. "What did he do?"

"Assaulted my niece."

Another nod. "Little shit deserved a beating, I'm sure. Don't give yourself a hard time about it." He paused, put his hands flat on the table. "But don't tell anyone, either."

"Right. I wasn't planning to."

"Just our little secret," he said and pulled his cell phone from his front pocket.

"I could tell the way you were walking toward him you had something in mind. A front web-strike—you're lucky you didn't—"

He held his cell in the air.

"A video? You recorded—"

"You could've killed that kid. Eight pounds of pressure on the trachea—"

"I know how to calibrate the punch. Why did you record me?"

"Why not?"

She felt it happening again—just like in the bar. How he managed to control the conversation.

He slipped the phone into his front pocket. "Hey, I'm on your side. The asshole attacked your niece—and in her own home."

"How did you know it was—"

"Your sister's house, right? She's done well. That Richard is kind of a jerk, but—loaded, huh?"

"How do you know all this?"

The calmness in his manner, the quiet way he spoke, the slight almost intimate forward slouch in his shoulders—it was unsettling to Eliana, but it didn't suggest danger.

He shook his head and smiled.

"Don't tell me it's because you're a retired cop—"

"I didn't say I was retired. I said I used to be a cop. You need to listen more closely, Detective. Look, the reason I followed you is simple: I want you to promise you'll leave me alone and also stop harassing Kitty." He sipped his coffee. "She's a good person."

He doesn't know, she thought. Or is this just another play to throw me off?

"So you plan to hold the video over me unless I drop the investigation. Is that it?"

"Is that what this is—an investigation? Going around bars in Queens with that police academy purse?"

"I had backup."

"Well, I'm glad to hear that. You know, the streets of New York City can be very dangerous. Look, the point is I can't have a cop poking around in my life bothering—"

"Kitty's dead," she said.

She saw the shock in his face. That was real. You don't fake that. He swallowed hard, looked away, then swallowed once more and said, "What do you know?"

"Not much." Eliana took a breath, a deliberate pause. "When was the last time *you* saw her?"

"Me? What—you want to read me my Miranda rights?"

"You told Kitty about a Jewish banker. You said he—"

"I told Kitty all kinds of things. Scary stories were a turn-on for her. Look, don't play cop with me. Whoever killed Kitty—I will find him."

Eliana felt her blood rising. Savoyian's arrogance angered her. "You make it sound easy."

"I have resources. Give me the address of where she was found."

"I can't do that. Police procedure. And this is not my case."

Savoyian leaned forward, holding his eyes steady. "I don't want to send video to Internal Affairs—but I will."

Eliana felt her energy drop, a heaviness in her shoulders. He had outmaneuvered her. Played—defeated.

"You probably know the hotel on Southern Boulevard," she said, "but here..." She took out a small notebook and wrote the address, then tore off the piece of paper and handed it to him.

He glanced at it, nodded, then looked up at her but didn't say anything.

They sat for a moment gazing across the booth at each other. Eliana felt a strange sense of intimacy, as if they'd agreed to share a "moment of silence" in memory of Kitty. After a while, she turned and looked out the window. Two squad cars had pulled into the diner's lot and were parked facing opposite directions so the drivers could talk. The sky behind them was a strange blue-grey, like the color of smoke.

"My father disappeared eighteen years ago," she said quietly.

"Disappeared?"

"He was scheduled to testify in federal court against his bank's involvement with a terrorist organization's financial activity. Left the house one night and was never seen again."

Savoyian folded his hands in front of him. Eliana stopped looking out the window and watched him take a long slow breath. He was silent for a good five seconds and then gravely said, "I see. All this—it's personal."

"Yeah, it's personal."

"I am sorry. That is no way to lose a father."

He looked at his watch. "I wish I could stay here and talk with you, but I have to go." He started to slide out of the booth, then stopped. "Let me give you some advice, Detective." He spoke without looking at her, gazing down at the floor of the diner. "This will sound cold, but you're not the first person in the world to tragically lose a parent. You've got a soul, I can tell. Whatever happened to your father—don't let it destroy your soul." He took out a five-dollar bill and put it on the table. Then, finally, he made eye contact with her. "My treat," he said, quietly, and his lips twisted slightly into that mysterious little hint of a smile, but not a smile, something else. And as quickly as she noticed it—it vanished.

She slid out of the booth and they left the diner together. Outside, following two steps behind him, she wanted to say more but couldn't find the words. He didn't turn around.

I need to follow him, she thought uneasily, realizing that by sharing the hotel information she might have just motivated a vigilante killing.

When he got into his car, Eliana hurried to hers. She watched him exit, turning left onto the road leading to I-78. She knew he'd be looking so Eliana turned right. But she drove only a few hundred yards before turning around and following. He took the entrance to the Interstate toward the city. She followed, staying back a good distance but keeping his Honda Accord in sight. A few miles later, he pulled off exit 29. She pulled off too, but cut her lights and pulled over on the shoulder. She watched him drive down a service road until he reached an empty lot with a large wooden sign advertising a new shopping mall that would be coming soon. He pulled over and parked his car in the corner of the lot near a big green dumpster for construction trash. After a moment, he got out of his car and stood holding his cell phone to his ear, his face titled up to the sky. Eliana rolled down her window and craned her neck to look up. Nothing but moonlight and the dull glow from the highway lights. What could he be looking for? She took in her surroundings. Deserted. No cars coming or going. The lot sat tucked behind a bank of trees and there was a long flat warehouse in the distance.

She watched Savoyian who continued looking up at the sky, then down at his watch, then back up. Finally, Eliana heard it, a helicopter. The sound grew closer and she watched it descend, the blade-slap of the rotor growing louder and louder until it sounded vaguely like machine gun fire.

After it landed, Savoyian jogged slowly across the lot. She couldn't pick out any identifying agency insignia on the helicopter. She watched as he jumped onto the landing skid where he balanced himself for a moment looking back over the area before disappearing through the open side door.

The helicopter lifted off and slowly turned east and vanished into the darkness. Eliana dropped back against her car seat stunned, thinking, *who the hell is this guy?*

Chapter 13

No migraine that night, but Eliana couldn't sleep. Lying in bed, she kept thinking about Vachik Savoyian's bizarre disappearing act—the helicopter rising above the empty lot, growing smaller and smaller as it disappeared into the dark sky. She also kept flashing on Aaron the smoothie guy twitching in pain. And the odor: she couldn't shake the stink of his puke.

She told herself that she'd done nothing wrong, not really. Beating up the kid? Not even a felony assault—no serious injury. Pretty boy would be fine. Unless—unless she'd ruptured one of his testicles. Possible, yes. In that case... a felony charge. Which brought to mind Savoyian's video. She'd fucked up not asking him to play it for her. Could he be bluffing? Where the hell was he standing when he took that video? But suppose he did have it—then what? Was she going to let this ex-cop (assuming that part was true) hold this little incident over her for the rest of her life? And this crazy shit with the helicopter? Military, she thought. But no insignia? Whatever—she felt sure Savoyian knew something about her father. It was the way he had given her "advice." *Don't let it destroy your soul* Why did he say that?

Of course, this has been her sister Livi's point for years: that Eliana had let a childhood trauma define her whole life. She needed to grow up and move on.

But at this moment, everything about this increasingly strange man felt linked to her own increasingly strange behavior: stealing investigative notes, lying to Jack and Danny, beating up the kid at the party. She was, as they say, shaming the badge, and heard a little Danny-speech inside her own head: *When an officer engages in misconduct, corruption, or any abuse of power, it's not just one reputation at stake but the credibility and integrity of the entire law enforcement community.*

She tried to stop these thoughts but couldn't. And another phrase: "moral anxiety." Not her words, left over from her college days at Columbia University. Now, she knew she was in trouble. She could feel one part of her mind racing while another part tried screeching to a halt. Not the philosophy stuff, she thought, please, not now. That's the last thing I need.

As often happened to Eliana, her mind was keeping her body from falling asleep. She tried to resist. "Moral anxiety," she thought. Who needs a fancy concept like this? In this day and age of sound bites and tweets, nobody takes a fancy idea like this seriously. Anxiety, sure. Take a pill. Or see a therapist. But *moral* anxiety? All that... now?

She surrendered, and let her thoughts run: in her college days, the word "moral" had cut to the center of Eliana's struggle with her Jewish identity. After the disappearance of her father, nothing made sense. Morality? What was morality? When her father disappeared, morality disappeared with him. And then she went off to college and met Professor Roberta Ammerman, one of those "change-your-life" teachers, a fiery little curly-haired philosophy professor who, lecturing with the performance power of a rock star, persuaded Eliana that, yes, indeed, "God is dead." The class was focused on the German philosopher, Friedrich Wilhelm Nietzsche, who coined the famous "God is dead" phrase, explaining that it is we who have killed God with our rational scientific thought, leaving us with this horrible human predicament, our tragic struggle, which is to see the world through a moral lens, judging it in terms of good and bad, even though there is no ultimate authority to make the moral judgement. Hence, we suffer "moral anxiety."

Her father's disappearance triggered the basic question: if God let this happen, how could you trust anything? And the synagogue, the religious answer? Well, Eliana would never forget the day the rabbi came to visit her mother. It was weeks after her father had disappeared, not a condolence call, of course, because—although nobody believed it—the possibility remained that her father might still be alive. So there were no covered mirrors, or *shiva* candle, or low-to-the ground stools, and no ritual torn garment to signify grief for the loss of a loved one. No, when the doorbell rang, Eliana and her sisters, wearing their usual school clothes, led the rabbi into the brightly lit living room, where their mother sat on the edge of the couch, her legs crossed, her hands folded in her lap.

She greeted the rabbi with a silent nod, white-faced and rigid. Eliana had been told to bring in a tray of tea and crackers and then leave the room. But she stood with Livi and Charlotte in the dining room alcove, watching and listening.

"I could claim theological modesty," the rabbi began. He spoke with a soft, high-pitched, distinctly feminine quality, which struck Eliana as very strange. She'd never noticed it before. His sermons on the Sabbath were always amplified by a microphone, and his body, with its broad shoulders and thick neck, made him look like a football player. His voice should sound deep, husky, masculine. But it didn't. It sounded like a woman's voice. "The traditional rabbinic approach right now would be to say, who am I with my limited reason to penetrate into the ways of God," he went on in his flute-like register. "That—that would be the traditional approach."

"I don't expect answers from you," her mother said quietly, barely moving her lips.

The rabbi nodded and started to reach for his tea, but he paused with his hand hovering over the cup. He spoke without looking up. "Many of the sages in the Talmud argue that suffering implies some fault in human beings. Or, that the suffering is sent by God to test our faith, much as Abraham was tested—called to sacrifice his son—or Job, who..." The rabbi broke off, and lifted his tea. "Of course, you know Torah." He blew into his cup for a long while, but then put it down without taking a sip. Something about this bothered Eliana. Then the rabbi turned all of his attention to her mother, leaning forward, the fabric of his dark suit jacket stretched tight across his enormous shoulders. And he went on in his soft, high voice, "It's one thing to look deep into a sacred text and another to look deep into the eyes of an anguished wife. Yes, I say *'Baruch dayam emet*—blessed is the Truthful Judge', but I am not here to be God's attorney. I cannot take away your pain, but—"

"Why exactly are you here?" her mother interrupted, and it occurred to Eliana that she'd never before seen anyone interrupt a rabbi. "I didn't call you."

The rabbi nodded slowly, adjusting his weight in his chair. "I'm here because people who cease to believe in something do not believe in nothing, they believe in anything." He paused, and Eliana watched her mother hold completely still, leaving the rabbi's words unacknowledged, as if she hadn't heard him at all. "Miriam, listen to me, please. Neil was— is," he stopped, swallowed hard, "a good man—a good man. I know that he went up against the people in that bank because—"

"Please," her mother interrupted again. "I know exactly what my husband did."

The rabbi stopped; his mouth parted. Maybe he too was shocked by being interrupted? He appeared frozen for a moment, then swallowed, regrouped, and prepared to speak again. The house seemed to be so silent that Eliana felt she could hear the rabbi s lips separating as he spoke, as if his mouth were excessively dry. She thought again about how he had blown into his tea to cool it but failed to take a sip.

"In Judaism there is One God," he began quietly, "but it is One God with two names—*Adonai* and *Elohim*," he paused, took a breath, and then continued with that nervous high pitch in his voice. "We have no devil to scapegoat, no anti-Christ on whom to blame evil, we have only *Adonai* and *Elohim*—with *Elohim* in the first chapter of Genesis, and *Adonai* introduced in the second. You know all this, yes, and Neil knew it too—he understood the significance."

The rabbi seemed about to reach for Eliana's mother, to put his hand on her shoulder as he went on talking. But her mother leaned away from him. "Excuse me," she said, uncrossing her legs and standing quickly. "I'm not feeling well. My daughters will show you to the door."

She stepped away quickly, exiting through the front of the living room, without passing by the girls.

Livi moved first. Eliana watched her. The way Livi lifted her chest, extending her carriage, lengthening her neck—a perfect imitation of their mothers singing posture. Poised, controlled. Livi went into the living room and motioned for the rabbi, who followed her to the front door. Eliana and Charlotte trailed behind. Then Livi impressed Eliana further by finding the presence of mind to say, "Rabbi, please understand that my mother doesn't mean to be disrespectful."

"Yes, I understand," the rabbi said, and Eliana noticed that his voice finally sounded normal, an ordinary middle register. "Your mother feels cursed by God, and I, your rabbi, represent that God of malediction."

Years later, after joining the police department, Eliana would sometimes think of this moment and feel sorry for the rabbi. The "God of malediction" is a rabbi's burden, yes. And cops, Eliana understood—cops often represent that same God.

Or no God at all.

***

With too many thoughts and ideas and ancient memories rattling around her head, Eliana gave up on sleep and went to sit on the couch by the living room window. The yellowish glare of the streetlamps cast a gray shadow on the empty sidewalk. Queensboro Hill, a small slice of southern Flushing, sat tucked between the Long Island Expressway and Kissena Park. Less than a mile from where she and Danny had lived.

After the divorce, Eliana rented this one-bedroom because it was the first thing she found, but she never felt at home. These "classic" four-plus-one buildings—they were weird. The plus-one refers to a "first floor" which is nothing but a small lobby that opens directly into the outdoor parking area. She looked now at the lot in front of her building, and then at the houses across the street. A hodge-podge: a one-story ranch, a multi-family duplex, and a few larger, odd-looking homes with additional rooms obviously added after the fact, jutting out toward the street at bizarre angles. It was a neighborhood not unlike neighborhoods across the country, working folks proud of their small lawns and well-swept porches. It all struck her right now as a lie. This sweet and peaceful and innocent block, the illusion of safety, while less than two miles away, the park—well, Kissena Park took second place last year for most dangerous park in the five boroughs with over four hundred "serious crimes," including five rapes, forty robberies, and two murders.

Ah, yes, crime stats. What cops do: protect civilians from criminals, separate the good people from the bad. Maybe she should go back to patrol. Give up the dream of working murders. Instead, take the radio runs, clear 911 calls. Be the Band Aid. But that's not fair to patrol, she thought. Cops like Danny are more than Band Aids. "Community policing," coordinating cop-stuff with neighborhood businesses and local residents and everyone working together to address real problems—Danny believed in all of it. The power of dialogue. He pushed for straight talk about tough topics: racial profiling, the culture of poverty, the legalization of drugs, even the underlying economics. Get a few drinks in him and Danny would say pithy things like, "Peace is not the absence of conflict, but the presence of order. That's what cops stand for: order. And that's our role: maintain order so our society can address its conflicts."

Danny's faith, Eliana thought. Faith in maintaining order. That was Danny. And her? What did she believe in? The question caught Eliana by surprise, and with a sudden sensation of panic in her chest she pushed it from her mind, and then pushed herself away from the window and went into the kitchen, where she pulled the small wicker basket off the counter and rummaged through the bills and receipts and unopened mail until she found what she wanted: Vachik Savoyian's address and phone number.

Would he answer his cell phone? Would she hear the roar of the helicopter in the background? No—no need to call. She'd just go to his apartment. And then...?

She had no real plan, but Jack Bayer s voice broke into her thoughts, his words loud and clear. "... *We're playing cops-and-robbers here, and if you don't follow the rules, you can't play!*"

Sorry, Jack, she thought, but I've got to do this. For myself, for my family, for my little sister—I've got to make up my own rules.

Chapter 14

The backseat of Danny's ten-year-old Ford Fiesta resembled a landfill: stained cardboard coffee cups, sticky soda cans, old newspapers, tattered sports magazines, crinkled candy wrappers, bent pizza boxes, as well as a couple of broken umbrellas, old gym shoes, and a few sweatshirts. Danny spent a lot of time in his car. Lately, more than usual.

Tonight marked his fourth straight night of off-duty surveillance. But he didn't mind. He'd eat take-out and listen to the Mets or Yankees, read his phone. Time passed, no big deal. Right now, he sat parked at the end of the block—discreet, well out of sight—but he could still see the door to Eliana's apartment building.

He'd spoken to Jack, who agreed Eliana was in bad shape. "Manic" is what Jack called it. Not a word you usually heard Jack use. He wasn't big on psychological jargon. But Danny understood. Eliana was headed for trouble. Poking around her father's cold case, working murders on her own time—none of it was good. And Danny felt sure that she'd lied to him about being finished with that Queens hooker-tip. That's why he decided to sit on her building. He wanted to help her. He wanted to protect her—from herself.

Usually, the lights in Eliana's apartment went dark around 2300 (not keeping a memo book, off-duty, but Danny still thought in military time). But right now, 2330, Danny spotted Eliana step out of the vestibule and walk quickly through the building's outdoor parking lot to her car, moving with a crisp, clear sense of purpose. No casual late-night trip to the grocery store, Danny knew. A date? The thought made him wince. The other night, unable to sleep, fighting the craving to drink, he Googled: "divorced couples who remarry." He'd not told anyone, but at least admitted it to himself: he wanted Eliana back. A crazy fantasy, perhaps, but...

She pulled out of the driveway, and Danny waited, not wanting to follow too closely. But before he even turned his ignition, another car took off after Eliana, pulling away from the curb in the middle of the block. He'd not seen anyone on the street for well over an hour, so whoever was driving that car had been sitting in it all this time. Alarmed, Danny felt a jolt of energy. An hour ago, he ate half a pizza. Now, he wished he hadn't. He fought back a greasy burp. Overeating, exhausted, yes, the past days he'd slept only four, maybe five hours a night. So had he dozed off and missed seeing the person who got into that car? No, no fucking way. That person had been watching and waiting and was now following Eliana.

Danny started the car. Edgy, tense, he let his right hand go to his gun, resting on the grip as he drove. It steadied him—the feel of solid metal. His off-duty weapon, a 9mm Smith & Wesson, his dad teased him about this, how he resisted the newer guns made of polymer, a synthetic super-plastic. Lighter, less recoil, won't rust or crack or wear out in the usual ways. Cheaper to make too. But Danny insisted on the old-fashioned, the tried-and-true, the feel of metal.

With that same stick-to-the-basics approach, Danny knew this "follow-that-car" bullshit would never fly. Unlike TV, it's pretty much impossible to "tail" a car any significant distance without either losing it or being discovered. The right way to do this: the box system. Four cars, four radios, constant contact between drivers. Put one car a block over on the right, another on the left; one car in front, another following behind. If the target car turns, the whole box turns with it, with the front and back becoming the new "sides," etc. And even better, pick a choke point, busy intersection, a landmark or whatever—and have another team of four cars to take the "hand-off," forming a new box.

But Danny's by-the-book police work stood no chance tonight, so he followed a different instinct. He called Eliana's cell phone.

One ring, two, three... come on come on come on, he thought. Look at the phone, Elly, look at it, see it's me—and answer.

But it went to voicemail. Her message, so familiar, she hadn't changed it in years. Hurried, clipped tones, no name, just: "Sorry—can't take your call." Beep.

He redialed. One ring, two, three... again, voicemail.

Then, on his third try: "What's up, Danny?"

"You're being followed."

"What? Where are you?"

"Following the guy who's following you."

"You—? You've been sitting on my building? What the hell are—"

"I'm just making sure you're all right."

"I'm fine. Look, Danny, I know you care about me, but please—"

"You want to talk about all that right now, or find out who's following you?"

Long pause. She took a breath.

Danny recognized it—her tense, hold-it-in-angry inhale.

"All right," she said, "Four rights. Meet me at Mulberry and Kissena—there's a bus stop. I'll pull over under the sign."

"Got it. And if you're not there in about six minutes—I'm calling a sector car."

"Jesus, Danny, take it easy. You watch too many cop shows."

"Elly—I'm not playing. Somebody's following you."

When they hung up, Eliana slowed down, hoping to read the license plate on the car behind her. It had to be Savoyian. Who else would be following her? But it was too dark, and the car stayed too far back. But Danny was right; right turn after right turn—the car followed. She held to the speed limit as she approached the bus stop on Kissena Boulevard. A residential section of the block, she spotted Danny's car about halfway down. He'd pulled up on the opposite side of the street. If she pulled over, and the car tailing her pulled over too, right behind her, then Danny would make a quick U-turn and box it in. She could imagine the scene: Danny opening his car door, taking cover, gun pointed, and his bark, full of authority, announcing "Police don't move!" then yelling for the driver to stick his hands out the window, followed by another bark, just as fierce, instructing the driver to slowly, slowly, with his hands remaining in the air, exit the vehicle, step away, and lie on the ground, arms spread like a "T." And one last deep-throated yell: "DON'T MOVE!"

She pulled over and waited. Indeed, the tail pulled up right behind her. Whoever the hell's following me it's not Savoyian. Total amateur, she thought, but still, she wished she'd brought her gun. Danny would scold her for that, too. Per the patrol guide (and he could probably quote the section number), "... *all off-duty MOS are required to respond to an emergency or to render assistance* ..." No such thing as a part-time cop, he'd say.

What happened next went down exactly like she'd imagined, except her stomach dropped when she noted the Jersey plates. In a flash of intuition, she knew the driver of the car: Aaron the smoothie guy.

She sat behind the wheel and watched in her rearview mirror while Danny followed the script, finally placing his knee on the center of Aarons back as he cuffed him. All business, the cops cop, Danny conducted himself with his usual precise professionalism. No rough stuff, no pressure from that knee-on-the-back, and once the cuffs were on, and the frisk complete, then Danny helped Aaron to his feet, lifting gently, one hand under the shoulder, the other in a firm grip on the chain between the cuffs. Meanwhile, Aaron twisted his head side-to-side, repeating over and over again, in a scared high-pitched screech: "What did I do? What did I do?"

The words echoed eerily. Eliana, still watching in her rear-view mirror, was asking herself the same question while, simultaneously, her right eye started seeing flashing lights coupled with a zig-zag pattern. Oh shit, she thought, a migraine with aura. In a moment her skin would start to prickle and then, thirty minutes later (or sooner, if she was unlucky), the pounding pain. And, of course, she'd failed to bring any meds.

She closed the bad eye and got out of the car, steadied herself, then walked toward Danny and Aaron. They stood now in front of the headlights. In one hand, Danny held Aaron's wallet. He tossed it to Eliana as she approached.

She caught it and said, "I know him."

This news registered on Danny's face only slightly—eyebrows arching. Pure cop mode, nothing surprised. He nodded. "Cuffs off?"

Eliana hesitated, stopping now just a few feet from Aaron, whose shoulders were slightly bowed, head goose-necked—no doubt Danny had those cuffs on nice and snug.

"You're a cop?" Aaron said, his voice hoarse, weak, faint—as if the cuffs were clasped tight not around his wrists but his neck.

"Yeah," Eliana nodded, and for the sake of protocol, with Danny watching, she pulled her badge from her jacket pocket. But she tried to keep the jacket itself closed so Danny wouldn't notice that she had no gun.

"Cuffs off?" Danny repeated.

Eliana still didn't answer, but leaned closer to Aaron. She saw fear—eyes bulging—but no injury. He looked fine: his short blond hair combed, accentuating his pretty face. "What was your plan? You were going to follow me, and then what?"

Aaron hesitated, looking down at the ground, and in a weak choked voice said, "Nothing."

Eliana tried to open her bad eye, but the flashing light, the zigzag pattern, remained. She twisted her face. "Nothing? No plan? You weren't trying to get even?"

At this—Eliana saw Danny noticeably shift his weight, pulling slightly on the cuffs, which made Aaron tilt forward.

"Maybe fuck up your car," Aaron said.

"Fuck up my car?" Eliana repeated. "You know that's against the law." Eliana threw a quick glance at Danny. "Officer," she said, "if this young man had—"

Danny jumped in, "Criminal Mischief Second Degree—could be a Class D felony."

"And what does the sentencing on that usually run?" Eliana turned now and looked directly at Danny. She really wondered about the sentencing, and also wanted to see if Danny would know.

"Class D Violent—could be two to seven," Danny answered without missing a beat. "It depends if the judge also considers it stalking. Then it's definitely seven."

"Seven years in prison, hmmm." She turned back to Aaron. Now, his fear grew. Eyes bulging wider, nostrils flaring, he started breathing hard. Eliana went on, "Do you have any idea, Aaron—any idea... what jail will be like for a nice-looking young man like you?"

He opened his mouth as if to speak, but then his whole body shook.

"Whoah! Watch out—little puddle here!" Danny yelled. He kept his hand on the cuffs but stepped back to avoid the stream of urine now trickling down Aaron's pant leg. "We got a pisser."

Eliana stepped back also. Aaron was still breathing hard, head lowered, a dark wet circle forming around his feet.

"That's a good sign," Eliana called to him. "That means you're getting the point. That means you're capable of... changing." She stepped further away to avoid the trickle of urine. Then she tried her eye again—no change. She held one hand over the whole side of her face, as if she were blocking out the sun. "All right," she began, "here's what's going to happen, Aaron. As soon as you stop pissing, we're going to take the handcuffs off, and you're going to drive back to New Jersey—and..." She paused, a wave of dizziness. The aura appeared in her other eye—like a camera flash, then faded. She blinked it off. "Then you're gonna start to be a better person. You understand?"

Aaron kept looking down, but he nodded and said awkwardly, stiffly, "Yes, I understand."

Eliana found her own language awkward and stiff. Be a better person? What the hell does that mean? Then, as if answering her own question, "That means no teenage girls, right?"

Another headshake. "Y-y-yes."

"And it means no following people, no vengeance, no getting even, understand?"

"Yes, thank you, I understand."

The "thank you" threw her off. A flash of catering behavior—the little bastard still trying to charm. Made her want to kick him in the balls again.

"Because next time—" she began, and felt her anger rising, a blood rush. Her head pounded—but not the full-blown migraine, not yet. She needed to sit down. She needed to get away, be alone in her car with her eyes shut—that would be soothing. She stepped closer to Aaron, avoiding the puddle, moving to his side. She dialed down her own anger. This was over, yes, over. "Go home, Aaron," she said, and heard the tiredness in her voice. "Everybody deserves a second chance. This is yours."

With a small nod, she motioned to Danny, and while he unlocked the handcuffs, Eliana walked over to Aaron's car. She placed his wallet on the center of the hood. Then she went to her own car and got back in. She rolled down the window, closed her eyes, massaged her temples?

and breathed. The night air soothed the prickling skin on her neck and cheeks. She inhaled and held the count? one, two, three, four, exhale. And again...

A few minutes later, she heard the sound of Aarons car driving away and Danny's footsteps approaching. She opened her eyes as Danny crouched at the side of the car. Eye level, looking at each other, holding still, neither spoke.

"All right, me first," Eliana said, finally. "Ariel had a sweet sixteen party last weekend—guy was working as a caterer. Got out of hand—I straightened it out."

"And...?"

"And nothing. It was in Jersey, a family thing."

"No report?"

"No report."

Danny made a loud swallowing sound. "I don't get over there much, but they have cops in Jersey, don't they?"

Eliana let the comment pass.

"Off-duty assault on a civilian, Elly. That's what happened, right?"

"A family thing—no harm, no foul. You can see the kid's totally fine, right?"

Eliana looked into his face. Danny nodded, wagged his head, pushed his tongue into his cheek and did that little twisty thing with his mouth. It looked as if he were thinking hard about something, or maybe adding a bunch of numbers in his head—pure bullshit, Eliana knew. He disapproved. No concealing it from her.

"So my turn, right?" he said. "Pretty simple, actually. Spoke to Jack. We're concerned about you, that's all."

Eliana turned to him. Tried to open her eye with the aura, and then closed it. She put her hand back over her face.

"You're getting a headache, aren't you?"

"Ahhh, Danny—Danny, Danny, Danny. For a patrol cop, you're really on the ball, ya know? You absolutely ought to be a detective. First you stake out my house, then you follow me, and now you're reading the clues—solving the mystery, huh?"

As soon as she finished this little riff, she regretted it. What had Danny done wrong? He cared about her—that's all. Cared. And what does she do? Instead of gratitude, she gives him this?

"I'm sorry," she whispered softly, letting her head fall forward, pressing the top of her scalp into the steering wheel. The pressure on the crown of her head felt good. She wished Danny would massage the back of her neck. Almost asked him. But that wouldn't be fair, would it? An acrid, sour taste came into her mouth. This headache's gonna be a whopper, she thought. But, strangely, she felt almost glad for it—the pain. The most ancient and pure punishment, she thought. Pain. The way she'd been behaving, she deserved it.

That's how she thought about all this, and she wanted to tell some version of it to Danny, but then he spoke.

"My suggestion is that you take yourself straight home and get a good night's rest."

The tone in his voice—like flipping a switch, hitting the play button. In her mind, she almost heard him say: "My suggestion, ma'am. Pure cop—the essence of Danny. One small part of her wanted to lift her head and say, "Thank you, officer."

But then Danny surprised her. He behaved unprofessionally. He leaned into the window and kissed the top of her head, and whispered: "Let me come over and we'll talk, OK?" She heard the emotion in his voice, a tightness, a small lift in pitch when he added, "Please?" Then he swallowed hard and finished in a firm, low tone. "I just want to help."

They rode the elevator in silence—Eliana disturbed by how deeply grateful she felt for Danny's presence, his quiet, understated strength. The big tough cop watching over and protecting her. She hated it—but loved it. And as soon as they stepped inside her apartment and closed the door, she surrendered. She collapsed into his chest, his huge arms wrapping around her shoulders like a giant canopy offering shelter from—all of it, the whole ugly broken world. What cops do, she thought. And out of the blue came a blast of sexual heat. It blocked out the pain of her oncoming migraine and she led Danny fast across the small living room without saying a word because any pause threatened to reverse everything, to turn the hot buzz in her center back into the dark pounding in her head.

Hurry, yes, hurry, no time for the couch she pushed him to the wall directly opposite the windows. It occurred to her that—who cares. The whole neighborhood could watch. It didn't matter. She almost turned the lights on just for the thrill but instead she pushed Danny up against the wall, pulling his hands to her waist. She watched his eyes slowly close, his head moving forward to kiss her, and she felt her heart pounding as she broke into a slight sweat, moaning, thrusting her tongue deep in his mouth. Then she lifted his hands from her waist under her shirt to her breasts. Reaching back, she unfastened her bra. Danny touched her gently, and her nipples grew large and firm, but she wanted something else. She took two of his fingers in her hand and forced him to pinch her—hard.

Danny resisted.

Her eyes half-open, she moaned. "Do it, Danny. Please, just do it. I want it... to hurt a little." Then she lifted Danny's free hand and slipped two of his fingers into her mouth. As she sucked on his fingers, she unfastened and pulled down her pants and moved her panties to one side, then took Danny's wet fingers and slipped them into her. She watched his eyes roll back and then she pulled his fingers out and fed them to him. "I taste good, Danny? Don't I?" she asked.

He couldn't talk, he just nodded, and she started to rip at his pants, unbuckling, unzipping. His holster and gun tumbled off his belt onto the floor. He didn't seem to care. She didn't care either—about anything, except the hot rush of these feelings as they both unbuttoned and unzipped, their breathing labored and loud, until she said, "I want you inside me, Danny. I want to feel you deep inside." On her toes, Eliana held her pelvis tilted, every inch of her lifted, raised up, breathing hard, soft moans, hard kisses, her body twisting, pressing, a delicious jumble of exposed nerve endings bursting in quick gasps.

And Danny felt ready too. He wanted to thrust himself deep into her center, move with her in that perfect rhythm they once had. That's what he wanted, what he remembered, the sex they used to have. But it felt wrong now. All wrong. He didn't know what to call it, but something was different. The energy driving her behavior. He didn't know what to say, what to do, how to move forward. Then his erection went soft, and Eliana's breathing slowed. Until, after a moment, she stepped away from the wall and pulled up her pants. Danny did the same. Then he picked up his gun, checked to be sure it was secure in its holster. Then they both stood there, flushed, eyes glazed. Finally, Eliana turned on a light and sat down on the couch. Danny joined her. They sat in awkward silence.

"I don't know," he said.

"Don't worry about it."

"Something like that has never—"

"You don't have to say anything, Danny."

"I guess, it's just that—"

"Hey, forget it. I shouldn't have been—"

"I don't want to be your fuckbuddy, you know?"

Eliana looked up. She felt a smile start, though she knew he wasn't joking.

"What? What are you smiling at?" Danny asked.

"Fuckbuddy?"

"You know what I mean."

"Yeah."

"I love you, Elly. I want to be your husband again." He took a breath. "There—I said it. My therapist would be proud."

Now, it was Danny's turn to smile.

Eliana felt tightness in her chest and throat, then a wave of dizziness. Her life was moving in crazy circles. And that phrase—fuck-buddy. Is that what she'd wanted? The crassness made her head pound. No stopping this headache now, she thought.

"I shouldn't have—you shouldn't have come over—and I—throwing myself at you. I—I'm sorry. I'm falling apart, Danny. Really, you better leave. Just leave me alone. I'm sorry that I involved you in all of this."

"Don't be sorry—I want to help you."

"Help me? What are you gonna do—lock me up?"

"Stop it."

"Actually, you know that might be exactly what I need. A little time on Rikers."

"What—so you beat up that kid, OK. Forget it. He went after your niece. It's a—"

"I have to tell you something," she said. "My murder suspect, the hooker tip—I saw him the other night. He followed me out to Jersey and..." Eliana stopped herself. Felt Danny's eyes focus on her suddenly like the beam of a flashlight. She wanted to tell him everything—the video, the helicopter, all of it. But she wondered: could she trust Danny? And then she wondered if she had any choice. She needed help, yes. Vachik Savoyian was dangerous, truly dangerous. She understood this, yet she didn't feel afraid. She needed to get close to this dangerous man because she needed to know what he knew.

She took a long slow breath, then told Danny the whole crazy story.

Chapter 15

The Middle Eastern sun beat down hard on Savoyian standing on a busy corner in downtown Doha. He'd arrived in the capital of Qatar on assignment two days ago. His head ached this morning because the previous night he'd met up with an old friend for drinks and they got going. A depressing conversation. Only way to get through it—sweet cocktails and Sambuca shots.

"Warrior shhpiiirrit," his friend slurred. "All bullshit now. Who needs soldiers if you've got satellites." A big gulp, then he continued, "Remember that SIM card screw-up with Amin?"

"Yes," Savoyian answered, looking into his drink. "Kabul."

"Innocent fuck with the wrong phone, but, hey, SIM cards live in phones—and phones live on persons—and so the TriggerFish, or StingRay—"

"IMSI catcher."

"Whatever the fuck they're calling it now—the tracker-gadgets with their algorithms and triangulated signals beeping a screen five thousand miles away..."

His friend lifted his glass, looking closely, as if inspecting for a crack. Then he looked at Savoyian and said, "Here's to human intel and killing bastards the old-fashioned way."

The two men clinked glasses, smiled, and finished their drinks. And ordered another. And another.

In the morning, Savoyian took four aspirin with breakfast and then killed an hour wandering the alleys of *Souq Waqif,* a fake traditional market. Tourist trap mostly, a maze of tiny shops claiming to offer authentic Islamic merchandise—spices, perfumes, jewelry, clothing. Some honest vendors sprinkled here and there, but Savoyian knew the import/export business in this country concealed millions of dollars in terrorist funding. He located the designated area of contact and waited. There—right on time—a small, stocky dark-skinned man in a lightweight cream-colored suit, a pale blue open-necked shirt, and wrap-around sunglasses. The right outfit. And the signal, yes: checking his wristwatch, right hand. One glance—pause; two—pause, three. He started to walk. Savoyian followed. The handoff would be a blue Buick with a dented right fender.

Moving away from the heart of the market, Savoyian kept the

cream-colored suit in view from a safe distance as they passed a small restaurant crowded with young women dressed in their traditional garb—*abayha*—the simple, black, robe-like dress reaching to their ankles. They also wore black *bourqas*, leaving only their eyes uncovered. Savoyian wore a long white shirt, loose pants, the traditional red-and-white *gutra* headdress complete with a black rope, an *agal*, holding it in place. He fit in, effortlessly.

It's the coin he traded on. His twisted personal history: a once-devout Muslim pretending to be a devout Muslim so he could spy on devout Muslims. These days the way he "used" his identity sickened him. He sometimes felt as if he lived with a slowly spreading cancer, untreatable. But it wasn't always this way. There was a time when his Muslim American identity not only made sense, but it solved all his problems—gave him purpose and meaning. When he joined the United States Air Force at eighteen, he assumed he'd be a professional soldier until he died. In his family, men fought. Savoyian grew up with sacred stories of war—stories about how his father served in the Iranian army. His father, inspired by the promise of Islam—true Islam, the Islam of peace—fought in the 1960s to destroy the Shah, known in the family as "a corrupt leader perverting the true faith." But—then came the tragedy of politics. Or maybe it was a blessing—his father never lived to see the rise of Khomeini and his vicious extremism. Yes, world-historical figures: Mohammad Mosaddegh in the 50s, Shah Pahlavi in the 60s, and Ayatollah Ruhollah Khomeini in the 70s. Distant names, abstract headlines, but not to a little boy whose father believed in "true Islam." Yes, his father believed with all his heart. His father believed until the day he disappeared. Another victim of cruel politics.

A story told and re-told a thousand times—how Savoyian's father took a brave stand against the Shah, opposing the "White Revolution," a period marked by reforms that involved shutting down the free press, imprisoning political dissidents, and torturing and killing innocent people. Meanwhile, the Islamic clergy, after a long silence, found their voice in Ayatollah Khomeini's urging for a return to essential Islamic teachings, a vision of the sacred, the holy. The elder Savoyian, a naturally religious man, was moved, drawn, and wanted to make a difference. Numbers mattered. His uniform mattered. Rank mattered. So dressed in full army regalia, one night Savoyian's father disobeyed his commanding officer and proudly stood in the audience at Ayatollah Khomeini's famous speech at the Feyziyeh School in June 1963. Khomeini insulted the Shah in that speech, and riots broke out, and Savoyian's father wound up in the notorious Evin prison. Never to be seen again.

Politics, politics, politics. What remained: family photos of a brave daddy, a great man, a fighter and soldier whose courage and faith were obvious by the stripes on the shoulders of his uniform. Special stripes: three chevrons, diamond-tipped at the top, with two curved lines at the bottom. His father had been a Sergeant Major First Class, the highest position of enlisted grade personnel. It was a gorgeous uniform.

Of course, for a long time Vachik Savoyian understood none of this. He was three years old when his father died. At six, he and his mother fled Iran and came to America.

Land of the free.

He spotted the big blue Buick as the noise of the restaurant grew faint, though he could still smell the food: wood-charcoal grilled chicken, a trace of garlic and lime hanging in the air. Maybe he'd try the place after work.

A fat man with a thin moustache and swarthy complexion sat in the car. Savoyian opened the door and slipped into the front seat without a word. He didn't bother with a hello or *As-salam Alaikum*, let alone the codename bullshit. A low-level "intelligence asset," as they say, this guy supported visiting field agents, providing forged documents, money, safe-houses, weapons, etc. He'd probably been a common thief or drug dealer or worse, then got caught and "traded-up" to avoid prison. A win-win, if you believed it. Savoyian, after all these years, didn't even like thinking about it. He wanted only one thing: do his job, then go home.

"This guy's son was once a student of mine, right?" Savoyian asked as he opened a manila folder on the seat next to him. Inside were photos, maps, a report stapled backwards, right to left. "If we've got the wrong flicking guy..."

The man didn't answer. He wiped sweat from his forehead, looking upset. Hot on the street, yes, but the stifling mugginess inside the car was even worse.

"Roll down the windows," Savoyian said.

But the man shook his head. Instructions, no doubt. The meeting inside the vehicle must be as discreet as possible—the dusty windows must be rolled up to limit visibility. Keep the engine off.

"Hey, I can't fuckin' breathe in here," Savoyian raised his voice. "Roll down the windows."

The man hesitated, his small dark eyes avoiding Savoyian, making an occasional flick up into the rearview mirror.

"My call—don't worry. A gorilla jumps in here, I'll take the blame."

A loud breath, the man's enormous belly rising and falling, then he turned away from Savoyian and pressed the buttons on his door, lowering all four windows—but only a few inches. It didn't help much. Savoyian let it go.

"This guy—he's the one whose son—"

"I know nothing about the target," the man said quickly in a tight voice.

"This is the whole package?" He held up the folder. "Better be the right fucking guy. And a tool?"

"Under your seat. It is the best I could do at short notice."

"Short notice, yeah—tell me about it." Savoyian reached under his seat and withdrew a small cloth bag. Inside, covered by a colorful square of fabric, was the gun. He needed to check the weapon, but the fabric— he held it up. Absurdly beautiful. A tapestry weaving, he recognized the authentic Islamic style. His mother used to weave by hand.

He shook off the memory, a distraction. The gun. He pulled it out and leaned forward, holding it low to his feet. A Beretta M1951, complete with a noise suppressor. Old, yes, but reliable. He ran through it: tested the spring in the magazine, checked the action, attached the noise suppressor, loaded the full clip and let the slide roll forward, then performed a quick chamber check to ensure a bullet was seated properly. Last step: he slipped on the safety. Ready.

"So we hate this guy because..." Savoyian looked at the driver.

"I know nothing about the target," the fat man said, aware he was repeating himself. They were still parked on the street and the fat man squeezed the steering wheel and looked at Savoyian sideways without turning his head. When Savoyian looked back the man lowered his eyes and put one hand over his belly, as if he were about to burp.

"Right," Savoyian said. "You know nothing—it's better that way."

Savoyian had read the targets dossier on the trip over. Abu Qassam, Lebanese-born, a real veteran, he managed for many years to play both ends against the middle, Sunni, Shi'a, Al-Qaeda, ISIS—a sort of freelance butcher; years ago he personally tortured a British agent in French North Africa, raping his wife and making the Brit watch. Afterward, he killed them both. When younger he specialized in kidnapping wearing the Shi'a jersey. Later he wormed his way out of the desert and into the mountains where he somehow managed an actual face-to-face with a Bin Laden lieutenant, who completely rejected him. Poor Qassam took it hard but bounced back by teaming up with some young ISIS bucks chopping off people's heads.

As Qassam got older, he became more involved in the financial side of things. He also had a son born with cerebral palsy. That's where Savoyian came in. The worst ten-month assignment he ever had. He became Ahmed Yacoub, the beloved first grade teacher of Qassam's son at the Alfarah Center for Special Needs. The son loved him and Savoyian became a favorite in the Qassam household.

The driver pointed to his watch.

"It's almost time," he said.

"What about my flowers?"

"Back seat."

Savoyian took the bouquet of flowers and placed it on his lap as the man started the car. Not an ordinary bouquet—one specially made. And, yes, for once they did it right, he could tell. All-natural, locally grown, he'd researched this himself, telling them to use the *carruthersii* of Northern Qatar, beautiful white flowers with pink specks. And he specifically instructed them to mix these with purple wild petunias and plenty of *jafna,* the thick, forking-stemmed plant from the fig family that would easily conceal the gun in a plastic sleeve nestled against the flowers. To Qassam, Savoyian would appear a kind gentle teacher bearing a thoughtful gift.

They drove into an industrial area of small office buildings and pulled up in front of a one-story structure with an impressive brass sign over the door: CONCORD IMPORT/EXPORT. Strange name, he thought, sounds British. It made him wonder—does MI6 know about this? He pushed the thought from his mind and slipped the gun into the bouquet.

"Six minutes—leave with or without me."

"That's not what I was told."

"I'm telling you."

"But what if—"

"Hey—I'm trying to help you. They don't question people in Qatar. They—you know, *interrogate.* Six minutes. You leave with or without me. Got it?"

The man nodded. Savoyian made a quick scan on the street and slid out of the car, leaning over for a phony wave goodbye, clutching his flowers.

"Look at your watch. Start."

Savoyian turned from the car and walked to the small doorway of the building, counting his steps as he moved forward—twenty-three, twenty-four, twenty-five. He slowed his breathing. Then he settled the flowers in his right hand and turned the handle of the door with his left. When he entered, he closed the door gently behind him.

A curtained room, ornate wooden cabinets on both sides stocked with bottles of wine. The back wall was entirely concealed by thick red drapes like from an old-fashioned auditorium. Not a sound. Suddenly the drapes parted with a mechanical whir, and Qassam like the Wizard of Oz appeared reclining in an office chair behind a large desk. An ashtray held a lit cigar. A bottle of cognac sat next to two glasses. No other people present. That's what took so much planning.

Savoyian stepped forward. Timing was everything. He took three strides to reach the desk. Qassam began to stand, extending a hand in greeting, smiling. "Ahmed Yacoub, *As-salam Alaikum*, how good it is

Standing now at the edge of the desk, holding the bouquet of flowers with both hands to chest height, Savoyian quickly, but not hurriedly, moved the flowers closer. Confusion passed over Qassam's face, and when Savoyian squeezed the trigger hidden within the bouquet. The bullet struck Qassam in the middle of the forehead. *PHUT!* It was barely audible, like a raspy cough. For the briefest moment Qassam froze, his head rocking backward as if he'd merely bumped into something. Then he crumpled to the floor, falling behind his desk, his arms flailing, knocking over the bottle of cognac, the empty glasses and his lit cigar. Savoyian stepped quickly around the desk, fired one more bullet into the back of Qassam's head—not necessary to kill the man, but it would immediately end any possible suffering, and greatly complicate an autopsy, in the unlikely event there was one.

Savoyian felt his heart pounding, the surge of after-adrenaline. He closed his eyes and took two slow, deep breaths and then started moving back toward the door, still holding the bouquet of flowers in front of his chest.

Outside, his heart rate slowed. He walked casually to the car, opened the passenger door and dropped down into the seat. "Take it easy," he said to the fat man. "Don't gun the engine and stay under the speed limit. And roll down the fucking windows."

The driver did as he was told. Savoyian removed the gun from the bouquet and placed the pieces into the cloth bag before tucking it back under the seat.

They drove in silence. Forty-five minutes to the airport. If there was no flight trouble he'd be in New York—how many hours? He tried to calculate, but—unexpectedly—Eliana Golden came to mind. It struck him—the strange web of connection. The hand of God, it seemed. Or was it bad luck? And her sheer physical beauty—should that have any role in what comes next? He felt nothing sexual toward her. At least he didn't think so. Too young, of course.

When he was Eliana's age—goodbye Air Force. After the Iran debacle he came home with a medical discharge and lived with his sick mother. He wandered Queens and worked small construction jobs. He painted houses with a friend from high school and to keep his sanity deepened his faith in Islam, particularly the mystical system of the Sufis. By this time, he'd come to understand that his father had been killed by the politics of Islam, not Islam itself. So he became an active member of a mosque in South Ozone Park where one of the clerics—Ayyan Abbassi, a dear old man with a wise face and big dark eyes—taught about Sufism. Savoyian prayed there every day until, on his twenty-fifth birthday, his mother died of breast cancer. With no one to guide him, he decided to follow—again—in his father's footsteps. Put on the uniform. But this time he'd be a cop.

No trouble finding a doctor to sign off on the PTSD. The burn scars on his neck and back had hardened into thick ropey strips of white skin. A bad experience, you bet. But he was fine now, really, doc. Ready for the streets, ready to serve the community, ready to protect the good people from the bad. Just thinking about being a cop, reading the NYPD mission-and-values statement—he felt a thrill like he experienced reading the Qur'an, particularly the police pledge to "*maintain a higher standard of integrity than is generally expected of others because so much is expected of us.*" This gave him a reason to live the way he was already trying to live. To follow a higher standard of integrity. No drinking, no smoking, the path of a good Muslim. A perfect fit.

But it didn't work out as planned. He never went to the Police Academy. Never even owned a uniform. Instead, when the NYPD learned that he spoke Farsi and had a military background, he was plucked from the mass of cadets by a Joint Terrorism Task Force, a collaboration between the NYPD and FBI. The bosses wanted him so far undercover that attending the academy posed a risk. Two thousand new cops a year—one or two went the way of Savoyian. His assignment: infiltrate Islamist terrorist networks. This was 1983, the year of the U.S. Embassy bombing in Beirut, followed six months later by the bombing of a United States Marine barracks at the Beirut Airport. A historical moment: two hundred forty-one American soldiers dead in Beirut—the worst single-day death toll for the United States Marine Corps since World War Us Battle of Iwo Jima. And responsibility for the attacks was claimed by what the media described back then as "an obscure group calling itself 'Islamic Jihad.'" JTTF brass believed the chain of command ran straight up to leaders of the Iranian Revolutionary Guard Corps, the same distorters of Islam who years earlier had murdered Savoyian's father. Yes, when Savoyian learned of this opportunity to go undercover with the NYPD, he thought: what could be better than to continue his father's fight against those who pervert the true faith? Holy work, holy work.

The Doha International Airport came into view, and the car moved onto the service road and up the ramp for departing flights. When they pulled over at a terminal entrance, the fat driver put the car in park and spoke. "Everything was fine, yes? You will tell your—organization... that I performed well? That I was of use?"

Savoyian hesitated and looked hard at the man whose small dark eyes sat in his big square head like little black bugs, twitching and flitting. He was unable to stop checking the rearview mirror.

"Have you ever killed anyone?" Savoyian asked, surprised at his own question. Dumb, unplanned. He was tired.

The driver shook his head no.

"Yeah, well..."

Savoyian's fatigue suddenly grew worse. *What the hell am I doing talking to this guy? I'm losing it,* he thought. Then he noted that his arms and legs felt heavy. And the morning's headache had returned. Yes, the adrenaline drop. What he needed now: just get on the plane, settle in his seat near the window, and line up the bourbon. Always bourbon on the airplane. Those cute little bottles. He could put away a half-dozen on a long flight like this. And his journal, yes. It would be soothing to write.

He suddenly felt sorry for the fat nervous driver who couldn't conceal his fear. "You did fine," he said, opening the door. "I'll tell my organization that you did just fine."

Chapter 16

The difference between frustration and anger—there is none. It's just easier to admit frustration. A nicer word, though that's part of the problem: the word masks the darkness. Danny's therapist wanted him to think this way: own the darkness, the anger. Accept the feelings. Until you accept the feelings, you cannot limit the actions. This was the point, a key aspect of "the program."

It didn't come easily to Danny, though he tried. He woke every morning to read the words on the 3x5 index card on the night table next to his bed. Following his therapist's orders, he'd copied the Serenity prayer by hand. In blue felt tip pen on a small white card, he wrote:

God grant me the serenity
To accept the things I cannot change;
The courage to change the things I can;
And the wisdom to know the difference.

Now, driving away from Eliana's apartment, trying to make sense of this crazy day—the kid who pissed his pants, the sex that didn't happen, and the story of the nutjob who disappeared in a helicopter—Danny recited the words aloud. *"God grant me..."*

But then he headed straight for Mac's Ale House. He needed a fucking drink. The back of his throat ached, and Mac's had a four a.m. liquor license.

Accept the things I cannot change? Yeah, sure, right—for a cop, Danny thought, that's everything. The whole job. What cannot be changed: violence, cruelty, out-of-control behavior—hell, ordinary rudeness can't be changed. Last tour, there were a dozen noise complaints (always worse in summer), assholes blasting music like nobody else lives in the building— And ask them nicely to—*ahhh fuck it...* Danny thought. Cop-shit. Endless cop-shit, and all those experts with their seminar meetings? Once upon a time Danny tried all that. When he and Eliana were married, attending law enforcement conferences made him feel intellectual, sophisticated, more like his Ivy League wife. Criminologists, sociologists, people whose credentials impressed in a million ways. But they made Danny feel like a tribal outsider observing a strange culture. These well-dressed people with their facts and figures—throwing their theories back and forth. The scene at these academic conferences re-minded Danny of highly trained animals demonstrating tricks at a circus. And those in the audience— policy makers, experts in their own ways, they took their notes and referred to their studies and displayed their impressive memories and giant vocabularies, but... to what end?

Cops don't care about "understanding," not really. We just want to do our job, Danny thought. And everything a cop does—OK, almost everything—is a reaction to something that's already happened. Crime maps are created, right, but only after the crimes occur. His thoughts went on. "Root causes?" Sure. The poverty, the drugs, the despair—and racism? That's another "root," Danny thought. And it's the problem that blurs all other problems. Cover the precinct wall with outstanding warrants—is it the cops' fault that so many of the pictures are Black males? *Ah, fuck it all,* Danny thought, turning down 65th Avenue, anticipating the sight of Mac's Ale House, where he'd gulp a quick shot-and-a-beer, then wait for the warm tang to sooth like a nice hard scratch of an itch. For chrissake, he thought, I can't even prevent Eliana from going rogue, let alone fix society.

When he drew close to the bar, he spotted Fred O'Brian standing outside. Two forty-five in the morning—what the hell? Fred had known Danny for years, knew Danny's whole family. Red-haired Fred, a career bartender, he held his cell phone to his ear, pacing under the green awning that jutted out over the green-trimmed, frosted window.

Danny decided to park around the corner. Seeing Fred threw him off balance. He couldn't just walk right past an old family friend and go into the bar, so he put the car in park and turned off the engine and sat in the dark. *Accept the things I cannot change...* right. His feelings for Eliana—his love. That's what he couldn't change. She'd told him all of it. Savoyian, the hooker tip, and then the hooker being murdered, and then the helicopter. And the dream? She was following a hunch from a dream? It all pointed to what Danny most feared: the curse was back. Eliana's curse: her obsession with her father's disappearance. Crazy. It's like an addiction, Danny thought. Yes, she's just like an alcoholic, and now she has "relapsed."

Which is exactly what he was about to do?

The thought rattled him. He took a breath and held still, recalling how he had tried going for a light tone. "Come on, Elly," he had said, sitting there on the couch, "imagine telling the D.A. your probable cause' is a dream you had. That's not exactly in the penal code."

She didn't answer. She just looked away, swallowed hard. Then they sat in silence until, finally, Eliana moved the conversation in a different direction—backward.

"It's all about Char," she said. "You know, that's what this is about.

She was so little when it all went down."

Danny knew the narrative: Charlotte's "unresolved pain," how her drug problems, her inability to hold a job, her lousy taste in men were directly linked to the disappearance of their father. And somehow Eliana felt responsible.

"Your little sister's all grown-up now," Danny tried to argue, gently.

"And she's not getting better. Wouldn't surprise me if she's using again, and this new boyfriend of hers—"

"Hey, she's gonna date who she wants to date. Eighteen years—that's a long time ago. You're not her mother."

Wrong thing to say. Danny had felt it immediately. His line triggered Eliana's guilt about not "doing enough" when Charlotte was younger. Worried that the adult-Char was now addicted to pain meds, Eliana launched into the old war stories. All Danny could do—sit and listen to how Charlotte, only eight years old when their dad disappeared, wound up cutting herself and attempting suicide—twice—until at fifteen she was hospitalized with a diagnosis of *xenophobic dissociative thought disorder.*

"Whatever the hell that means," Eliana said.

No fan of psychiatrists, Danny knew. Eliana had her own theory about Charlotte.

"The first time I visited her in a hospital—she was like, fifteen, right? And I asked her," Eliana went on, retelling a story Danny had heard a million times. "I ask this little fifteen-year-old girl—I was only like twenty-one, but I felt like her mother, you know—I just asked her what's wrong, and she says, I'm scared.' That's it. She was scared that something bad was going to happen.

"It was that simple," Eliana continued. "She was so scared the only place she felt safe was inside a hospital. And I'd push her, you know, we had this conversation a bunch of times, but I just wanted to be sure, so I'd say, 'What do you mean, Char? What are you afraid of?' And she'd look at me—with that smile. She's really got a beautiful smile when she's not all doped-up. And I could see it—the real Char underneath all the meds. She'd smile at me as if saying, ... *come on, you know what the bad thing is...* 'And finally she'd say it aloud: 'The person who killed Dad is... out there.'"

When Eliana finished talking, Danny remained silent. Eliana sat stone-still, her eyes glistening with tears. "Now, Char blames 'white America' for killing Dad," she went on. "The system. Everything, everyone. She's angry at the whole world."

Danny, unsure what to say, pulled Eliana closer to him on the couch and wrapped his arms around her, kissing her neck. But it was pure comfort and warmth, barely a trace of sexual energy. He held her like that for several minutes. Then, finally, she pulled away and said, "I'm going to take something to help me sleep."

Then she stood, and Danny got up and left. Neither of them said goodbye. They just looked at each other and nodded. Words were not needed.

Now, sitting alone in his car, a thought came to Danny: with all the crazy crap she has pulled in the past week—she could lose her badge. And knowing now what he knew—he could lose his, too.

Unless he did something. But—what? How could he help?

The question triggered the craving, the fierce urgent itch in the back of Danny's throat. He needed to scratch it, to swallow—but his whole mouth, his lips, his tongue. It all felt thick and dry—and he imagined a big scab at the back of his throat. He looked into his rearview mirror at Fred-the-bartender still pacing and talking on the phone under the tavern's green awning. Fred wasn't supposed to be here. He worked only weekends. During the week—he was at PJ Leahy's or Dirty Pierre's or...? *Ahhh fuck*, Danny thought, Fred's gonna try to help. Fred's known me forever and he's gonna think he *needs* to help. He's gonna—

Danny knew his anger was out of line, but he couldn't stop it. The one thing he did NOT want right now was to hear someone say: *don't drink.*

Eliana took an Ambien and went straight to bed. The pill—combined with the comfort of telling Danny everything—helped her sleep, and she woke feeling better than she had in months. Then at nine a.m., still lying in bed, her cell phone rang. No caller ID, one of the precincts, she figured. Good. Going to work would help. But the timing confused her. Scheduled for a four-to-twelve at the One-O-Five—so who's calling? She reached over to her nightstand and answered.

"Hello?"

"Detective Golden?"

No voice she knew. "Yes."

"Frank Alvarez, Narcotics, the Four-Five. Look, there's no easy way to say this."

Eliana paused, took a breath, sat up in bed. "Go on. What is it?"

"We ran a B&B a couple hours ago. Oxy—about two hundred. Ten thousand cash."

"Yeah?" Eliana translated the cop-speak. During a buy-and-bust undercover operation, two hundred OxyContin pain pills were confiscated. The ten thousand dollars referred to additional cash the perp was carrying, or the street value of the pills. It wasn't clear, but it didn't matter. What mattered: why is this cop calling her?

"How can I help?"

"We arrested your sister."

Eliana felt herself stiffen and said nothing.

"Charlotte Golden? Age twenty-six, Manhattan address 32 East—"

"That's her. Buying or selling?"

"Selling. But we haven't moved on it. A guy in crime analysis recognized your last name. You're married to Danny McPartlan, right?"

"Was."

"Sorry, look, you know what we want—"

"Yeah, I get it. I'm on my way."

"Okey-dokey."

"Listen, Velez—"

"Alvarez."

"Sorry, Alvarez. She's your collar, right? I deal with you."

"That's right. You deal with me. And don't worry, I'll be here—I need the OT."

Chapter 17

A long smooth flight, a pleasant bourbon buzz—Savoyian had lots of time to think. A memory came of an absurdly flattering introduction he'd been given many years ago. One of those training days on the sterile campus of those bland grey buildings in Virginia. The idea was to bring a field guy in for show-and-tell, impress the newbies. But the introduction—was he that good? Back then, Savoyian believed that he was.

A DS&T instructor stood at the front of the classroom, motioned for quiet, then said: "Ok, listen up, folks. We have a special guest today, a living legend, a man you're lucky to be in the same room with. To say you can learn something here doesn't begin to describe it. Do what this man does—always, in everything. I mean, think the way he thinks, stand the way he stands, breathe the way he breathes. You're in the presence of a god..."

Savoyian smiled, shook his head, then rose from a chair at the side of the desk. Hushed applause. He moved slowly to the front of the classroom, looked out, took a breath. "All warfare is based on deception," he began quietly. "Sun Tzu wrote those words twenty-five hundred years ago, and they have never been more true than right now, today, at this historical moment. The war on terror—without us, the war on terror cannot be fought. The army, the navy, the air force, Special Ops—all of them, without us, they're like a man without ears or eyes. Nobody— absolutely nobody—matters more than us."

He lowered his gaze, shifted from one foot to the other, then re-centered his weight, lifted his head and continued, speaking even more quietly. "Having faith—by which I mean simply trust—trusting in our ultimate significance, our moral purpose—this will be the key to your success. And, in some cases, your survival. But here's the rub: nobody—in the outside world—nobody understands. Nobody. The true value of what we do—of who we are—is... not just elusive. It's... sometimes even we don't understand it. We manipulate, we lie, we deceive, we pretend that were someone that we are not. We employ kindness—if that works; cruelty if it doesn't. Not because we want to hurt anyone or because we care about anyone. No individual person or moment matters—compared to our deeper goal. Our supreme purpose."

He paused, scanning the classroom. "It's crucial that you are able to name this goal, to define it clearly with every breath you take."

A hesitation, he lifted his hands, chest-high, pressing his palms together, his fingers making a steeple. "So... what exactly is it? Our goal, our supreme purpose—it's simple," he said in a thick whisper. "To shorten the war. That's it. Everything we do is for the sake of peace. There is no example in history of a people ever having benefited from prolonged warfare. In fact, to neglect the use of spies is nothing less than a crime against humanity. Everything we do—even the taking of a human life—is for the sake of peace. Don't ever forget this."

The memory blurred as the white noise of the airplane engine soothed him to sleep. But it wasn't a restful sleep—too much booze. That's why when he deplaned at JFK, he felt a stabbing pain behind his left eye that caused his whole face to twitch. He walked through the terminal's breezeway trying to control the twitching. It surprised him, but he found himself thinking about the detective and her father and what had happened to Kitty, and he wondered if next month—when it came time for the bathtub ritual—there'd be a bullet in the chamber. Then, finally, the supreme purpose would be over. No more killing for the sake of peace.

Chapter 18

The Four-Five Precinct in the Bronx, where Char was arrested, stretches from the Yonkers border to the Throgs Neck waterfront and includes both Co-Op City, the world's largest affordable housing complex, and City Island, a bizarre mile-and-a-half strip of land jutting into the Long Island Sound, accessible only by bridge or ferry. Ah, New York City. Forget the Manhattan hype. Get out to the sprawling boroughs, three-hundred square miles. Manhattan's nothing but a forty-mile sliver. Over the years Eliana had grown to love the outer boroughs.

But she'd never been to the Four-Five. On the front door of the station house grey duct tape formed a large "X" across the doors cracked glass pane. A cardboard sign handwritten in magic marker read: *open carefully—fragile*. She went inside quickly, hardly giving a thought to how the hell a police station door got busted-up like that. Pausing at a waist-high wooden gate, she held up her shield, and asked for Alvarez. The officer at the TS desk pointed up the stairs and said, "I'll call him— go on up."

Waiting for her at the top of the landing stood a light-complexioned Latino man, well over six feet, head shaved, a once-strong body going to flab. His tired face gave off that I've-seen-it-all cop attitude— offset by the dark and alert eyes of one who knows what real danger looks like. Narcotics: guns, drugs, and money, where the perps run, fight, and carry weapons. Sometimes all three. Hardest working cops on the job.

"She's in room three."

Eliana nodded. "Is that—"

"An interview room. You've got privacy."

"Thanks."

"I'm at the end of the hall on the right. Going on twenty hours, so knock hard."

Eliana started down the hall, noting the smell of old coffee, cleaning chemicals, metal, sweat. And she heard the occasional police code murmured in a low voice, computer keys clicking. In some ways, she thought, all precincts are exactly the same. Just then directly in front of her a uniformed cop passed by pushing a cart filled with labeled baggies—evidence. Were the drugs Charlotte sold on this cart? Eliana had an impulse to follow the cart, try to rifle through the bags. And if she found the one with Char's name—no evidence, no case...

Get a grip, she told herself, or we'll both go to jail. Then, Jacks voice again: *"Get off the street... before something bad happens."*

She turned away from the cart and opened the door to a small windowless room with a rectangular table and three chairs. Grateful there was no one-way mirror, no concealed microphone. Just smooth beige walls, totally blank.

Charlotte turned her head but didn't say anything. First thing Eliana noticed, her sister looked cold. Lips blue, shoulders hunched. Her face appeared a pasty white. High as a kite—and just starting to drift down.

"Hey..." Eliana pulled out a chair and sat down directly across the table. "You cold? I can get you a sweatshirt."

No answer, a long slow blink, then: "I'm sorry, Elly. I really fucked up this time."

Charlotte spoke in a barely audible whisper. Bad sign, Eliana thought. The anxious whisper. And the posture—slouching on the edge of the chair, childlike. Her health had always fluctuated wildly, but tonight—maybe it was the baggy T-shirt, but Char's small box-shaped torso looked paper-thin. And the features of her face—Char had their mother's Russian, angular, artsy face, with high cheekbones and a narrow nose—but now grey bags hung under her puffy eyes. Physical appearance, always a touchy subject for Charlotte. Years ago, after Eliana's teenage struggle with cutting, Char followed in her big sister's footsteps, taking it to another level: slitting both wrists, slicing each artery, spewing blood all over the walls of the bathroom in their mother's house. The note she left said simply: *I'm ugly and want to die.* That was the second attempt. The first one: 3000 milligrams of Seroquel, an incident which Char sometimes called her *thirty-six-hour nap.*

Eliana pulled her chair closer. "Tell me what happened, Char." Charlotte looked away, her head turned to the blank wall. After a long moment, she whispered, "Am I going to jail?"

Eliana reached across the table and touched Charlotte's elbow. She flinched, but didn't turn her head. But she didn't pull her elbow away.

"Char? What happened?"

"I'm sorry, Elly—I'm so sorry."

"The cop who called me—he says you had OxyContin. A lot of it. Is that right?"

Charlotte nodded.

"Have you been selling it?"

"Sort of."

"Have you been taking it, too."

"Some, yeah. For headaches, mostly. You know how bad the headaches can get."

"Yeah, I know." Eliana pressed her hand into Charlottes arm, a gentle squeeze. "This headache problem runs in the family, I guess. But Oxy—"

"I know, Elly, I know. You start to need more and more of it."

"And that's what has happened to you, huh? You've started needing more and more?"

"Sort of, yeah."

Eliana nodded, still holding Charlotte's elbow. "You know, we can get you something else for those headaches. A different pain medicine."

"Something strong?" Finally, Charlotte turned and made eye contact. "Oh, yeah, strong. Definitely. Real strong."

For a fleeting moment, Charlotte looked like she might smile, and Eliana imagined herself sliding from her chair and moving around the table and holding her little sister in her arms. But then Charlotte's mouth tightened, and soon her whole body stiffened. "I'm scared, Elly. Jail—it really scares me."

Charlotte sniffled, shivered, then sneezed—cold symptoms? No, withdrawal.

"Listen, Char, it's not like I can make everything go away, but—if you're willing to help, I might be able to take you out of here. Go straight up to Watertown. You remember Good Samaritan Hospital, the rehab center—nice people up there. Remember? Good doctors. I might be able to take you there right now and get you admitted and, you know, get some good strong pain meds to help those headaches—and get you off the Oxy... how does that sound?"

No answer, then Charlotte straightened her posture, spreading her hands out to the side as if she were holding the table down, or preventing it from shaking. After a moment, she said, "I don't want any of Livi's money. That money is dirty."

Not this, Eliana thought, not now. The evils of capitalism, how the American banking system is responsible for their father's death, blah-blah-blah.

"Don't worry about it," Eliana said. "I'll figure out the money."

"What do I have to do?"

"Tell Detective Alvarez the name of the person who gave you the drugs."

Charlotte closed her eyes, shaking her head. "This is so fucked up," she whispered.

"They just want a bigger player," Eliana went on, explaining. "That's how narcotics works. Climb higher up the ladder, a bigger dealer, trying to get as close as you can to the top. You know, the goal is to cut off the head of the snake—get the big-time dealers. That's how it works.

But, you—you wouldn't be involved any further. Just tell them where you got the drugs, and we get out of here. Straight up to Watertown. I'll get you all settled in with the doctors."

But Charlotte didn't seem to be listening to this explanation. She was rocking back and forth in her chair, bending her whole waist, bringing her forehead closer and closer to the surface of the table.

Eliana tried to grab her sister's shoulder. "Just tell the detective the name and address of the dealer who sold you the—"

But Charlotte twisted away. "I get it," she said, rocking back so far her chair almost tipped. "The little white girl goes free—and another Black man gets arrested," she said, and threw herself forward, the chair legs landing with a thud. "That is so fucked up." She leaned back again, then threw herself forward again, farther this time, her face almost hitting the table, and she repeated, "That is so fucked up. So fucked up. This whole country is..."

And this time when she rocked forward—before Eliana could react—Charlotte slammed her face into the table, a loud *thwack* in synchrony with the garbled words "...so fucked up."

When Charlotte lifted her head, one eye didn't open, and blood dripped from her nose and lips; and in the center of her forehead, a large red welt was already beginning to swell.

Chapter 19

Jack Bayer sat with one thick leg resting on his desk, an orthopedic boot where his left shoe should be. Plantar fasciitis, or a heel spur, or—what the fuck, he didn't know what it was. But he couldn't walk for shit. "It's a big move," he said. "And she'll be pissed, that's for sure."

"Better than going to IAB, right?"

Danny had managed to avoid drinking that night at Mac's and after a couple days of thinking he'd come up with a plan: contact the NYPD's volunteer police support network. Known by the ridiculous acronym POPPA—Police Organization Providing Peer Assistance—it was completely confidential. No officials, no supervisors, no investigation of any kind. Nobody loses their badge and gun talking to POPPA. Just cops helping cops, so went the theory.

But he wanted Jack's advice. Which required telling him part of the story—though not everything. The beat-up civilian, the mystery man with the helicopter—no. He told Jack only that Eliana had tailed Savoyian to the bar, and that he'd helped her as backup. That was enough. Jack knew the history, and he cared about Eliana. And he understood cops. "So your idea is to show up with this counselor-cop and—"

"No, no—the cop's just on call. But I go over to Eliana's and confront her."

"When?"

"Soon. Next few days. I go to her place and tell her I'm not leaving until she makes the phone call to POPPA."

"What if she refuses to call, but tells you that she'll lay off the hooker tip?"

"She already told me that lie. And with that girl dead..."

"Yeah, I heard. This is turning into a real fucking mini-series."

"It gets worse. I spoke to a guy in Queens Homicide—the suspect they had in the hooker's death, he turned up dead yesterday."

"Helicopter man?"

"Not clear. Found the guy in his own car—his neck had been snapped. Which sounds like some close quarters combat shit. Maybe ex-military. So helicopter man, maybe. But could be pimp-warfare, too. Who knows."

"Does Elly know all this?"

"Not clear. Last two days, she's not returning my calls."

Bayer slipped both hands under his leg and lifted his booted-foot off the desk with a groan.

"Well, she'll be pissed, that's all I know. You show up at her apartment and start making demands—she'll be pissed."

"Yeah... but I need to confront her, Jack. To intervene. If I don't—who will?"

Danny sat there on the hard-back chair looking at the older man, who said nothing, his eyes lowered. After a moment, Danny gazed absently around the office. Its typically dingy pea-green walls looked like they'd not been painted in thirty years. And the smell—a pungent locker room odor. Bayer himself had apologized for it and left the door open while they talked. Danny looked now into the open work room where about a dozen detectives, many of them in decent suits, stood or sat around their desks. Jackets opened, ties loosened, one guy wore a short-sleeved dress shirt and a bow tie. He pecked at his computer keyboard with a crazy intensity.

Danny turned back to Bayer. "What's the worst that can happen?"

The worst?" Bayer's eyes suddenly came to life, gleaming, an alertness that defied his age. The orthotic boot, the wrinkled face, the drooping shoulders—no matter. He glared like a man ready to throw down. "A haunted cop...?" He hesitated, licked his lips, shook his head. "Wear a vest," he said, then turned away, running a hand through his thinning, grey hair. "And don't get your hopes up."

His voice trailed off, and Danny stood. He started to lean forward over the desk, as if to shake hands and say goodbye. But then hesitated. Jack Bayer had always been on Eliana's side, especially after the divorce. Danny didn't really know what Bayer thought of him.

"Thanks for your time, Sarge. I'll let you know how it goes."

He turned away from the desk and stepped toward the door, then Bayer called out, "Hey, Danny."

When Danny turned around, he saw the older man's eyes puffy with emotion. "When you head over to her apartment, text me. I'll go with you."

Chapter 20

After two crazy days, exhausted from driving but relieved that her sister was in a hospital instead of jail, Eliana resolved to learn more about Vachik Savoyian. She'd heard the news about the suspect found dead in his car and wondered if Savoyian had killed the person who'd killed Kitty. Regardless, she felt sure all this connected somehow to the disappearance of her father. And she needed to get to the bottom of it. Not just for her sake—for Char's.

Her first step was to find out if Savoyian had, in fact, once been in the NYPD. As a precaution to avoid a digital trail, she went in-person to "The Building."

One Police Plaza, NYPD headquarters, sits at the bottom tip of Manhattan like a fortress, twenty-two thousand square feet of concrete choking off a major artery linking the Financial District to Chinatown and the Bowery. Angry residents in the Park Row area have learned to live with the permanently closed thoroughfare, which is necessary, police argue, to protect the 13-level pyramid from attack. Others joke the building needs no protection—because it's so ugly. Too ugly to be attacked. A huge grey slab of concrete. The architectural tradition in which it was designed: "Brutalist." And the names no joke. Eliana researched it. From the French word for "raw," so-called "Brutalist architecture" descends from the modernist movement of the early 20th century. Characterized by "ruggedness," it's understood by critics as a reaction to the lightness, optimism, and frivolity of the 1930s and 40s.

Inside, Eliana passed through security and walked across the cavernous lobby, smiling at a few swaggering chiefs in their bright white shirts, noting a trace of sexual energy in their firm nods. Eventually, she found her way to personnel records, where an old classmate from the academy now worked.

Joanna Holst, a short perky blonde whose computer skills landed her a spot in the Technical Assistance Response Unit, had dated Danny a few times before Eliana met him. The competition lasted barely a month—no hard feelings. At least Eliana hoped so.

She spotted Joanna sitting in a cubicle in a large glass-walled room and without hesitating pulled open the heavy door and walked straight up to her.

"Joanna?"

A pair of bright blue eyes lifted from the screen. "Elly? What are you—? Heard you were on a citywide Vice detail. Did you just walk right in here?"

A little shrug, then Eliana tried for a light tone. "Weak security. Can you do me a favor?"

The eyes darkened. "A favor?"

Prepared, Eliana held out a yellow stickie on which she'd written Vachik Savoyian's name and address. "I need to know if this guy was ever a cop?"

"And you came all the way down here to ask me?"

Eliana had anticipated this question, but now felt unsure how to answer. She nodded without a word.

Joanna shook her head, and then said in a low tone. "Everything I do on this computer is known and tracked and—"

"Please." She shoved the sticky into her friend's palm.

Her friend looked at it. "You don't want anyone to know you're here, do you?"

"That's right."

With her shoulders tensed, Joanna again shook her head and Eliana felt a wave of panic and considered blurting out the story of her father's disappearance. Joanna didn't know, of course. Nobody knew. Only Danny and Jack. Nobody knew how important this was.

"Look, Eliana, I'd love to help you, but, believe me, you're already fucked because the records downstairs are going to show you were here, and if I put this name into—"

"OK, OK, right, I get it." Eliana reached for the little square of yellow paper, but Joanna pulled her hand away. A thought seemed to have just occurred to her.

"But now that you've chosen to involve me, Detective. I'll hang onto this."

Her tone had turned razor-sharp, and in a flash Eliana understood. Or thought she did. Payback for winning Danny all those years ago? Was Joanna that petty?

"In case I need to show IAB that I passed," Joanna continued. "Or call myself?"

Shit, no, Eliana hadn't thought of this. What an error. This wasn't about Joanna's jealousy over Danny; it was her fear of "integrity tests." Internal Affairs uses them to catch corrupt cops. Nobody knows exactly when, where, or how often—estimates are about six hundred each year—IAB undercovers set up controlled situations in which a cop will have the opportunity to do the wrong thing.

"Joanna, no, you don't understand. You think I'm working for *them*?" Her friend spoke in a thick whisper. "I've heard you've been pushing some boundaries. You need to get back in the circle, is that it? I assume those bastards made you do this. I've heard they take advantage of old academy friendships. Just turn around and walk out of here, Eliana. Or I'll call the number myself."

The number, right. 1-800-PRIDE-PD. The anonymous tipline where good cops rat on bad ones.

Without a word, Eliana turned around and walked out of 1 Police Plaza, the ugliest building in lower Manhattan.

She didn't blame Joanna. Integrity tests haunted cops. Her old friend got spooked, that's all. And it occurred to Eliana that Danny should be spooked too. She'd put him in danger just by telling him everything she'd already done.

But it hadn't spooked Danny. In fact, he clearly wanted to help.

The thought gave her a warm feeling for her ex-husband, and also made her resolve to involve him no further. In fact, she had a different idea altogether: Lenny the Locksmith. A family business in the Woodlawn section of the Bronx, good solid Irish Catholics, except for the youngest son, Lenny Jr., the black sheep. He took the family's secret sauce and went to work for himself—Breaking & Entering. Major Crimes hunted two years before catching him, and then Eliana, who worked on the investigation, helped straighten him out. That was partly because Char dated "LJ" for a while, politicizing his criminal behavior by convincing him that stealing from white people was entirely justified. Afraid her sister might end up marrying a felon when he got out, Eliana visited him regularly in Wallkill and explained that she'd be watching every breath he took as soon as he stepped outside.

"I'll give you a choice," she explained. "Option one: while you're locked up, you earn your GED. I'll do what I can to help get you early parole, and then you stay away from my sister and have a life. Or, option two: you come out an asshole, make a play for my sister, and I flush you down the fucking toilet. That means I will put you back inside and make sure you die in a cage. Do you understand me?"

He understood and went with option one, and Eliana kept up her end and helped with early parole. That was three years ago. Now, she hoped Lenny the Locksmith still felt a measure of gratitude. And still knew something about breaking and entering.

Recovering from jetlag, Savoyian sat on the corner of a large bench near a play area in Kissena Park crowded with children. He'd passed the psych eval and was officially on a post-op "vacation." No better place to relax— he loved this park. Slides, swings, climbing equipment, dinosaur-shaped structures made of green plastic—two little Asian girls (twins?) wore identical shorts and shirts and interlocked their feet and hands to make a two-car train, shrieking as they went down the slide.

But Savoyian didn't like the design of this play area: no fence around the playground, too many trees and bushes in the rear, plus basketball and handball courts off to the side with nothing but a patch of grass between here and the street. Poor public safety. Too open, too many benches, too easy to attract adults. Adults without kids. Adults who liked to *look* at kids. Pedophiles.

He looked back and forth from the playground to the illuminated screen of his computer tablet. The website read: U.S. DEPARTMENT OF JUSTICE: NSOPW, and below: a column of photographs, all men, accompanied by their names, with various codes and acronyms.

Fed registry—Meghan's Law. Sex offenders.

And there, off to the side, near the swing set, a middle-aged male, white, six feet, medium build, blue jeans and a grey T-shirt, greasy-looking black hair. The tension in his face—lips pulled backward—same weird smile as the man's photo. He read the name, "Edgar Bristol," and swiped the screen:

Unlawful Restraint (18 Pa. C.S. § 2902)
Interference with Custody of Children (18 Pa. C.S. § 2904) Aggravated Indecent Assault (18 Pa. C.S. § 3125)
Institutional Sexual Assault (18 Pa. C.S. § 3124.2)

Pennsylvania penal code, a teacher in Harrisburg. Savoyian turned off the tablet and rose from the bench, slipping the tablet into the side pocket of his loose-fitting cargo pants. A couple steps, then he stopped to let a tricycle cut in front of him, and when the child's mother apologized, he smiled, nodding.

"Excuse me, Edgar Bristol?" he stepped up close to the man standing at the side of the swing set.

"Yes?"

"I'm just wondering what you are doing at the playground, sir?"

"What?" The man looked surprised, then sprang into what Savoyian called the "fear-dance," wrapping his arms around his elbows, shifting his weight from foot to foot. He noted that Mr. Bristol was extremely pigeon-toed—to the point of deformity.

Savoyian leaned closer. "You have children here?"

"Who are you?"

"Just a guy."

"A police officer?"

"You could think of it that way, if you want."

"What does that mean? Do you have any identification?"

Savoyian knew that Meghan's Law states specifically it's illegal to harass or to intimidate someone just because his name appears on a list of prior offenders. He lowered his eyes. The man's inwardly bent feet pressed together so closely that his toes touched.

"Look," Savoyian spoke in a low tone. "I know who you are, and I know what you've done. OK? I'm not a cop, but—well..."

"If you're not a cop, then what the hell are—"

Savoyian took hold of the man's elbow. "I want to help you," he kept his voice low. "I want to help *you*."

"Help *me?*" the man's voice came out with a breathy half-grunt.

"Yes. Because studies show—well, listen carefully: rapists have a 24% rate of re-offense, child molesters targeting girls 16%, and child molesters targeting boys, 35%. Overall, sex offenders with any previous conviction have a 37% re-offense rate. And it gets worse. 46% of all sex offenders released from prison are re-arrested within 3 years for another crime. Think about it—chances are almost fifty-fifty that you will wind up back in jail."

Letting go of the man's elbow, stepping back, Savoyian waved his arm at the playground, as if pointing out a beautiful view. "Now, I know the name, address, and birthday of every child on this playground. And you need to understand that if anything happens to any of them—I will find you. And then, believe mem you'll wish that I were just a cop."

Savoyian took the man's elbow again. "I'm not trying to threaten or harass you," he continued. "I'm just trying to explain something to you: there are basically two ways to control behavior—positive reinforcement, and negative reinforcement. Question is: what's more effective? It all comes down to pain versus pleasure. Feeling good is nice, but avoiding pain... that's what really matters. Negative reinforcement is far more effective."

The man lowered his eyes and squirmed, his feet now twisting across each other, as if trying to gouge his own ankles. He looked like he wanted to say something, but didn't.

After a moment, Savoyian let go of his elbow, and, still looking out at the children, said, "Mr. Bristol, can you make it to the bus stop on your own, or would you like me to walk over there with you?"

The man uncrossed his feet. "I'm fine," he said quietly. And he turned to leave, cutting through the grass, heading directly for the bus stop. His pigeon-toed condition caused his heels to barely touch the ground as he walked. A strange sight, Savoyian thought. But he found it weirdly poetic: a grown man tiptoeing through a patch of grass, hurrying away from a playground.

Eliana parked down the block from Savoyian's apartment and waited for Lenny Jr., who'd been inside the building for almost twenty minutes. The block was quiet, classic middle-class Queens, featuring nothing but six-story apartment buildings. Precisely six stories, which triggered an intrusive memory. Shortly after her divorce, Eliana dated a fireman from Queens who explained that five story buildings could be built with *semi-fireproof material* but anything higher than five stories required *fireproof construction*. More expensive, of course. But a six-story building always featured an elevator. Status, yes, real status. Eliana tried to remember the fireman's name, then tried to stop thinking about it. Focus, she told herself. Concentrate.

Then she looked at her watch and realized—oh shit, she'd told a detective in Special Victims she'd have something for him by end of tour today. The case involved a thirteen-year-old rape victim—Eliana's task was to search the internet site where initial contact had been made. She'd promised to send her notes and—this would be the second time she'd missed a deadline this month. She gripped the steering wheel tightly. Everything is fine, under control, she told herself, although, in fact, hiring Lenny Jr. to break into Savoyian's apartment went beyond disgracing the badge. It was a felony.

But she kept that thought from becoming fully conscious as Lenny Jr. came into view, walking toward the car wearing a grim expression. He carried a leather bag of tools that resembled an old-fashioned doctor s satchel.

"Who is this guy?" he said, sliding into the front seat. "That door didn't come with the building, I'll tell you that. Underneath the thin wood laminate, its solid steel, fire-rated at six hours and almost impossible to break down, with security bars going three feet in either direction. Even the hinges—practically immune to breaching charges. And the lock? Forget it. That's not an apartment door—it's the door to a vault."

Eliana nodded, disappointed, but also slightly relieved. At least no felony had been committed. She handed Lenny Jr. an envelope.

"Anybody see you?"

"Not a soul." He took the envelope and then quickly stuffed it into his front pocket.

That was good, Eliana thought. But she checked her optimism. Cameras are fucking everywhere. If she hurried, she could still file that report for Special Victims.

Chapter 21

Later that night, Savoyian puzzled over the strange video. He sat on his couch, drinking chilled Smirnoff vodka, watching the video play on his computer. The simple made-in-China hidden camera he'd installed years ago in the hallway outside his apartment had recorded a man wearing a uniformed shirt with the logo: *Lenny the Locksmith*. A simple mistake? A worker at the wrong address? His intuition said no. There was more to it.

Eliana Golden—the bizarre connection.

He knew the steps to take: research this locksmith, investigate the background, track the fella down, talk to him, etc. All this was necessary, maybe even urgent—but it didn't really interest Savoyian. He was in a philosophical mood. The day's "work" at the playground gave him a warm satisfied feeling, but it also left him wondering about his life.

His leather notebook lay on the couch next to him. A thought came to him: *Courage wants to laugh; I would believe only in a God who could dance.* He'd read this somewhere—a philosopher, someone famous, though he wasn't sure who. He picked up his notebook and ran his finger along the embossed Arabic script on the cover, then opened to a blank page and wrote:

—But what is courage? The ancient Greeks had a definition. Courage is what makes a man go into battle. Aristocratic Warriors: Achilles, Diomedes, Hector. And yes, men who go <u>into</u> battle. <u>Into</u> it!

—But then history changes the nature of battle. After the Greeks, a new kind of courage comes along: everyman's courage. Not high-status military heroes but ordinary citizen-soldiers. Phalanx battalions that stand and fight. Hold the ground. Hold it, hold it, hold it!

—And then more centuries pass and along comes the "rational" modern view of courage based on skill. Today, it's technical excellence that produces daring, self-confidence, and mastery. The Special Forces swagger. Those guys tie their shoes with an attitude.

—And it all remains fake because real courage is not a physical test, but a mental one. That's today's courage. Not outer, but inner. A man dies for truth, not territory. And if forced to fight, well, violence is essentially unpredictable. For the individual soldier—it's not human planning but luck that decides whether he lives or dies.

—Which is exactly why I put a single bullet in the cylinder and go one-in-six each month, leaving my death to "Tyche," the Greek goddess of chance.

—But still I cling to the illusion, don't I? The 'vital lie' of control. Yes, I've learned this from the Greeks because nothing in Islam quite compares. (We Muslims and our endless "surrender.") But the Greeks—they invented the "tragic outlook." We must try to control our lives even though it's futile. And all this philosophizing—as if my puny little life could be linked to the great ancient Spartans' and Athenians'.

He sat back and drank, feeling the pleasant incongruity of cold vodka warming the back of his throat, and then his mind again returned to Eliana Golden and her father—the bizarre connection. He wrote in his journal:

—The man measuring the door must be trying to help her. Because she wants to know. She wants to know who I am and what I know and what I've done and... If I tell her...? I do not change anything—or do I? Her father will still be dead, yes. But what changes: the meaning of his death, which is the meaning of his life. Yes, how we die is part of how we live.

—Indeed, here is the divine hand reaching out to me, offering an opportunity to change the meaning of a life. Hers, her father's, and mine too. Perhaps mine most of all.

—A death with dignity is all any soldier wants.

He closed his notebook and sat there on the couch. He felt a deep sense of satisfaction. Then he took another sip of his chilled vodka, as if to celebrate.

Chapter 22

Eliana was supposed to meet a registered informant who promised a lead about getting a gun off the street. And a captain at the Two-Four Precinct in Manhattan wanted her to come by and interview an unlikely prostitute arrested on the Upper West Side. But instead of all this, she sent Savoyian a text message. Yes, she was setting aside her live cases. Disregarding her duties. She couldn't seem to stop herself.

In her text she told Savoyian that she wanted to meet, and he responded so quickly it was unnerving. He suggested two hours from now at a small store-front cafe in Queens on 23rd Street with the odd name *Tost*. Eliana had never been there but knew it was a fifteen-minute walk from Kissena Park, a half-hour from her apartment. She put on jeans, a simple button-down blouse, and a beige, lightweight cotton jacket. No need for a purse. Her pockets would suffice, and she strapped on an ankle holster for her Bersa 9mm, the smallest gun she owned. She wanted to arrive early—a tactical move. Know your environment. Absurd, in a way. She followed this training rule right now even though she intended to disregard it completely as soon as they met. Her goal was clear: get inside this man's apartment.

Even though she was thirty minutes early, he was already there. She saw him from down the block standing in front of the restaurant's glass windows. He seemed lost in his own thoughts. Occasionally he looked up at the buildings or stopped to watch the traffic as if he were a tourist.

When she got close, he waved. At the entrance, he held the cafe door open, stepping back and nodding for her to enter. A corny gesture, but Eliana found herself liking the feeling it gave her. No ironic smile on his lips, no twinkle of mischief—his sincerity was charming, and confusing.

They sat at a small square table by the cafes window. Again, the old-fashioned chivalry: Savoyian pulled out her chair, handed her a menu. She didn't know what to do except say, "Thank you."

"You're welcome," he said, smiling.

Then he opened his menu. Eliana opened hers, but she couldn't concentrate. And she wasn't really hungry. Tired yes, but mostly agitated. This strange man. The bizarre feeling he gave her.

"The salads are good," Savoyian said quietly, then added, "and so is the 'Muscle Milk.'" He peered over the top of the menu and for the first time smiled.

"Muscle Milk?"

"Keep the aging body young." His smile broadened. "Some kind of whey powder concoction, plus fresh fruit. Quite good. But—you— I would say you don't seem to need it. Your muscle tone, I mean. You train regularly, don't you?"

Finally—Eliana thought. A chance to work a game she knew how to win. The oldest one in the book: seduction. She felt herself relax.

"Yeah, I train. And you? You seem to be in good shape."

A half-smile, nodding, he turned back to his menu. She reached across the table and put her hand on his forearm.

He looked up at her, unblinking, and she felt that singular power of holding a man's attention completely.

"I'd like to talk with you about that video," she began, quietly.

No answer. His body was motionless. Then he looked down at her hand on his arm.

"That video could ruin my career," she said.

"I don't want to ruin your career, Eliana."

It was the first time he'd ever spoken her name. And what struck her was the tenderness in his voice.

Just then the waitress approached. A small Latino woman—a teen-ager, actually—wearing black leggings and a brightly colored cotton blouse. They ordered two cappuccinos. She took their order without making eye contact, which, for some reason, Eliana found depressing. The lack of connection, the loneliness in the teen's face—she flashed on Char upstate in the hospital. The clammy chill of Char's palm as she squeezed her hand goodbye. At least it was a hospital, not jail, Eliana thought. Then Savoyian cleared his throat.

"I want to help you learn about what happened to your father," he said, and now it was his turn to lean forward, elbows on the table.

Eliana felt her pulse quicken. "What? You want to—"

"I have resources."

"Yes, I—I—see that."

"It's not what you think, I'm sure."

"What are you, Fed, military...?"

He shook his head. "You know the line: *If I tell ya. I'll have to kill ya...*" A bashful grin, chin lowering, his face transformed into that smiling emoji that brought her back to their night in the bar at Joe & Joe's. But this time she felt much more in control.

"I'm in the mood to take a risk," she said quietly, and shifted her hand on his arm, lifting and then resting it ever so slightly. He stole a glance.

The waitress brought their cappuccinos, setting them down without a word. The silence lengthened.

"I have a question: Why do you want to help me?" she asked.

"Because it's what I do." He answered quickly.

Eliana shook her head and gave his arm a firm squeeze. "That's not good enough."

"That's all I've got."

"What if I say—I want to know you. Really know you."

"What?"

Eliana heard surprise in his voice.

"I want to know you," she repeated softly, and released her grip on his arm, leaving only her fingers resting lightly on his bare skin. As slowly and gently as she could, she moved the tip of her middle finger back and forth, back and forth.

"Nobody knows me," he whispered.

"Why not?"

He started to answer—opened his mouth, then paused. And she watched his expression change, a wave of tension, his cheeks and jaw and lips tightening, as if he were about to cough or burp or... shout. His eyes widened, then narrowed, and then the moment passed. "That's a good question," he said quietly. "And, yes, maybe that should change."

As they walked to Savoyian's apartment, neither of them spoke. Eliana felt a headache coming on. Her body's way of warning her? Maybe. She knew this was dangerous, and knew that she was ignoring—denying— the reality of her fear. A therapist of hers once said: *Ignore your emotions and your body will make you feel the discomfort you deny* Fine, but please not now, she thought, not a headache—not right now. She fingered the small vial in her pocket. Chloral hydrate—the oldest and most reliable of knockout drugs. She'd once shown this vial to her niece Ariel—a date-rape warning lecture. Yes, Eliana had a plan right now. And even if a full-blown migraine hit, she was determined to execute this plan.

Inside, his living room reminded her of a holding cell. Square, four steps wide, four steps long, no window, no furniture, nothing but a beat-up sofa in the center. Crude bookshelves—unpainted wood and grey cinder blocks—lined the three walls. Strange, austere, almost poverty-stricken. Stepping closer, she read one title, *The Encyclopedia of Religion,* and another, *The Genealogy of Morals.* The life of the mind, she thought, the phrase popping into her mind with a stab of pain, the headache worsening. How books once mattered to her—years ago.

She tried to ignore the throbbing and turned from the crowded shelves to Savoyian, who stood near the front door relaxed and calm, his arms hanging at his sides. She hadn't noticed before, but he wore the same kind of snug-fitting dark T-shirt he'd been wearing that night in the bar. His shoulders, chest, abdomen—sleek, grooved with muscle. An attractive older man, yes, but... Her mind again raced: Jack and Danny—they're right. I'm in trouble. I shouldn't be here; I shouldn't be on the streets at all.

"Can I get you something to drink?"

She nodded, "Sure, yes, thank you. If you'll have something with me."

Her gaze went back to the shelves. His books—crammed this way and that, stuffed sideways, two and three deep, overflowing onto the floor. Not even stacked or arranged, not even in piles, more like mounds, pages ripped out, underlined, highlighted, sticky notes and paper clips and... in spite of the mess: a sense of order, purpose. And there in the corner near the window sat a box labeled in black marker:

OLD JOURNALS 1994 TO PRESENT

"Please, sit," Savoyian said quietly, motioning to the beat-up brown sofa occupying the center of the room. Imitation leather, shiny, a wet-plastic look. On either side of the couch, cheap floor-lamps stood like sentry guards with bendable necks. Savoyian turned on one, then the other, their beams of light revealing the small cracks in the cheap cushions. In front of the couch, a make-shift table sat low to the floor—a slab of plywood balanced over four small bricks.

"More coffee? Juice?... Or stronger spirits? What can I get you?"

"Whatever you're having, and a glass of water. Please." She noticed the politeness in her voice. An unconscious effort to control her racing thoughts about that box of journals. 1994 was the year her father disappeared. In those journals she might find—? The pulsing pain behind her right eye increased slightly.

"Then two vodkas on ice. And a glass water." Savoyian said, like a waiter taking an order.

"And do you have any aspirin?" Eliana asked.

"Headache?" His eyes widened—those dark, fiery eyes. They flashed between fierce and friendly as his face jumped from surprise to concern, ending with a look of proud astonishment. "Me too," he said, in a low tone, that inscrutable smile hovering on his lips. "Synchronicity! Mine came on as I was—this whole idea that—well, to be known... that *you* want to know me." He broke off, laughed slightly. "Let me get you the aspirin."

He turned and took a long stride back toward the edge of the room. As her eyes followed him, the architecture of the place became clear. This was a "junior four." Arcane New York real estate jargon, it meant four small rooms: bedroom, kitchen, living room, and a "junior" room that lacks the window required to qualify as a two-bedroom. Around the corner where Savoyian now stood would be the actual bedroom—and another throb of pain hit her, accompanied by a fierce desire to go around that corner.

Savoyian hesitated, one hand on the edge of the wall. He didn't turn around, but spoke over his shoulder, twisting his neck, though not quite far enough to see her. "Before taking aspirin, would you want to try a massage—a shamanic massage? There's a technique I learned from a healer in…"

His voice trailed off as she turned and faced him. She watched his hand sliding slowly down the edge of the wall. Then his arms again hung at his sides, limp and relaxed, swaying slightly. Although she assumed he was inviting her to his bed, Eliana felt a strange absence of sexual energy in him. The quality of his attention burned with a fierce focus, but his body contained a misty, see-through quality, as if in this moment he were living—what? On a spiritual plane, another level.

"Shamanic massage," she said, quietly. "Sure."

"Come. Follow me."

Fighting the pounding in her head, she lifted herself off the cheap couch and stepped forward, telling herself: focus, focus. The plan, the plan.

Savoyian had lived for so long without intimacy—Kitty and the others notwithstanding—that he felt as nervous as a schoolboy as Eliana followed him to his bed. Not sexually nervous—that didn't matter. Or mattered little. It was the embarrassingly ordinary problem of loneliness that made him so nervous. Alone with an intelligent and beautiful woman brought back the period in his life when the isolation of undercover work had first become intolerable. During this time, he developed a strange habit, almost a ritual: at night before going to bed he stood in front of his bathroom mirror and asked: if I am not known, can I be loved? And: if nobody knows my true self, does that true self really exist?

Embarrassing questions. Sentimental, weak. He told nobody. He blamed it all on his handlers. They had left him on his own for too long, and they treated him—and his information—so poorly. *Nobody listens, nobody listens, nobody listens!* And then he suffered an even more brutal rejection.

Asheika Harrack was a thin, small-boned woman famous for having studied in the late 1970s in Jordan with the master himself, the "Godfather of Jihad," Abdullah Azzam. When Savoyian first met Harrack in Brooklyn in 1992, she was talking to a small group of men, her voice low and smooth, tinged with a British accent, as she explained the fundamentals of a "pan-Islamic, trans-national movement." So rare for a woman to be speaking, it was rumored that Asheika had traveled with Azzam all over the world—including more than fifty cities in the United States—to recruit and raise funds. She told of an Islamic movement that transcended the political map of the Middle East, a map, she reminded everyone, that had been drawn by non-Islamic colonial powers, particularly the United States. Her calm, well thought-out arguments were the first crack in Savoyian's idealism—these foreign policy perspectives made sense. The U.S. was partly to blame. He also found her "sublimely beautiful." Islam, of course, forbids all forms of dating and isolating oneself with a member of the opposite sex, but within the confines of mosque life he managed to spend hours with beautiful Asheika. For over a year, they talked. They read. They pored over the news together. He hung on her every word, as a spy, of course, following her like a puppy from meeting to meeting. And if she disappeared for some weeks, he sulked, then greeted her return with uncontained enthusiasm. He felt sure that she knew: he loved her. It was that simple.

Except it wasn't. She pushed him to contribute financially. He did what he could, but he could never come up with more than the "flash roll" limit of $1,500 cash his handlers had given him. Finally, she dropped him— like a cold stone, a piece of dirt, worthless. Where she got the idea that he had more money, he didn't understand. But without money, he no longer offered her anything of real value. Realizing this, his love turned to hate. And in his hatred for her—and his handlers—he began to hate America. He reasoned that Asheika had been corrupted by America the way America corrupts everything it touches, because the key to all vitality in the "free market" rises from a single, essential idea: exchange. Mutually favorable *exchange*. Money makes anything possible, an infinite variety of transactions. And the same "single, essential idea" applies to relationships, all relationships.

He too had been corrupted. Sizing up sources, evaluating who among the brothers in a particular mosque would be worth the investment of his time and energy in *exchange* for their valuable intelligence. Spying, shopping, loving—very little difference. Always the same question: what's a good deal, a decent return on my investment? Two persons make an acceptable match when they feel they've found the best object available on the market, considering the limitations of their own *exchange* values. Nobody admits this, of course, but a life-long friend appreciates in value like a piece of real estate with hidden potentialities that have developed over time. And Asheika? No surprise, really. She followed the same pattern of exchange which governs all other aspects of life in the free-market western world. She spent a little time with Savoyian, examined the goods, so to speak, considered the exchange, and ultimately reached the simple conclusion: not worth it.

This rejection—and this line of thinking—marked the moment

Savoyian lost his way. And he understood perfectly well that he'd been trying to redeem himself ever since. Every daring and brutal act of bravery, of loyalty, of patriotism, or of simple decency to protect the innocent—it's all been an effort to redeem himself. His hatred and anger and frustration led him to commit a true and terrible sin, and ever since he had sought forgiveness, or an end to his life.

And now Eliana Golden stood at the edge of his bed, and he put his hand on her shoulder, and she let it rest there until, gently, he pressed downward, and she lowered her body and then he guided her more precisely, turning her toward him so that they faced each other directly as she perched on the mattress's corner, and he kneeled on the floor directly in front of her.

"An Afghani man, a shaman, a healer I know—he taught me this..."

Savoyian heard his voice trail off. He slid his hand down from her shoulder onto the middle of her thigh. Then he placed his other hand on her other thigh. And he spread her legs slightly apart. She resisted not at all. Then he felt the top of his head move forward and it occurred to him that this was the position of a man about to pray.

Eliana looked down at his kneeling figure and felt his long hard fingers press firmly into her thighs. She flashed on the vial in her front pocket—what if he noticed it? But he quickly moved his hand to her inner thigh, and she experienced an overwhelming desire to surrender, to let go—as if she'd been carrying something terribly heavy and could release it all at once, leaving her hands weak and limp. Free. And in her mind too—nothing mattered but the empty-handed feeling of release. Her thoughts, her emotions, the sensations of her body—the plan to drug him and search the apartment, everything would take care of itself if she just relinquished control.

She reclined flat, letting the bottom of her blouse pull up from the top of her jeans, leaving a strip of bare skin. She felt the coolness of her exposed waist. What now? She found herself holding her breath—too excited to exhale. Would he slowly undo the buttons on her blouse? Unzip her pants? After an intensely long moment, she exhaled with a moan and felt a crazy release as she let her knees spread further apart while in her mind she saw a bizarre black figure—a sorcerer, a witchman—a half-human animal with long black legs and long black arms waving up and down and circling around and around, a primordial creature with a horned head. Antelope horns. Or rams' horns, or...

"To cure headaches," Savoyian said, and his voice broke through her strange reverie. "It doesn't always work. But—do you have something with you, a small object, something you can hold, anything that you associate with comfort and peace and safety?"

"I don't think so," Eliana said, drowsily.

"Nothing? No object that brings you comfort? In your bag—a small object, or a picture on your phone? I've never tried using something digital, but—you must have something with you that carries positive, healing energy."

Her gun. That's what came to her. And it embarrassed her—she'd completely neglected all tactical procedure and made herself totally vulnerable. But she still had her gun and told herself that, if necessary, she could lift her leg, twist, and slide the small weapon from her ankle holster.

"You give me something," she said. "Something of yours."

"Yes," he patted her arm and leaned to the night table. She watched him remove a photo from an old-fashioned, easel-back frame. "My father."

He handed her the picture, and she saw the resemblance immediately—a darker complexion, but the same handsome features, same intensity in his eyes. The man wore full military regalia—but the country?

"Iranian army—before the Shah," he said, as if reading her mind. "I was born in Tehran. See, I'm letting you know me."

She heard the hint of humor in his voice but ignored it. Something about this photo—its power. And for a grown man to keep a photo of his father at the side of his bed...?

"Is he—?"

"Died when I was three years old."

Savoyian took her free hand, massaging the soft fleshy web of skin between her thumb and forefinger. "Lie back, close your eyes. And breathe."

She followed his instructions, holding the photo, reclining, settling back again on the bed. She felt him lean over her, his warm breath on her face.

"What matters is not that that the photograph is a picture of *my* father," he began quietly. "It's the energy, the pattern. What strong fathers do—their potential to be a positive, healing power. The photo contains it, holds it, and together we will transfer this power from the glossy paper into your body."

In another context, Eliana would have laughed. Called this new age psychobabble and dismissed it with a shrug. But now—the way he touched and caressed her hand... he cupped her fleshy web with his palm, then when she felt her skin grow warm, he released the pressure and used his fingers to gently rub the side of her fingertips, one-by-one, up and down, altering the sensation by applying feather-light strokes, side-to-side, then diagonally, slowly, then quickly. Occasionally, he inserted his large thumb and pointer into the "V" between her fingers and applied just enough force for her to feel the stretch as the space widened. Then he'd cup her stretched fingers again in his warm palm and squeeze tightly.

She couldn't help but make the connection: the *Krav Maga* move. "Front Straight Web Strike," hand parallel to the ground, this exact part of her body, this patch of skin between her thumb and forefinger... erogenous zone/dangerous weapon.

"I did a very bad thing to that boy in Jersey," she blurted. "It's something I'm ashamed of. I—"

"Shhhh," he said. "Not now. No self-criticism... not now."

"But what I did—I—"

"Later," he interrupted. "Later..." He took a breath. "How does the photo feel to you? Not in your mind—in your fingertips. Do you feel energy at the tips of your fingers?"

She almost asked him to kiss her. That's what she felt. Not some mystical energy from holding the photo but sexual excitement from the way he was touching her hand. Pure and simple. Good of fashioned lust. Like the other night with Danny—but stronger. She'd almost forgotten what this felt like. So much time playing prostitute... yes, a kiss is what she wanted. A tender kiss. But could she trust this feeling?

He went on talking in that quiet, meditative tone. "You have to let the sensation at the tips of your fingers develop, unfold, let its intricacy happen. All of life, you see, is an interaction—and every interaction contains an implied intricacy, which gets carried forward. In our bodies. The sensation you want to notice, right now, is this interaction between us, between you and the photo—with its intricacy implied, developing, unfolding. Feel the power."

As he spoke, something peculiar happened to Eliana: the glossy cool paper grew warm, and in her mind she saw an elaborately complicated pattern of fingerprints—the arch, the loop, the whorl, and the key identifier, the point where lines from three directions come together, the *delta*—she saw these fingerprint patterns interacting now with the photo. And felt a warmth in the tips of her fingers. Forensics, of course. Crime Scene Units. Every cop learns something about fingerprints. And not just cops. Everyone knows this: we all leave our fingerprints everywhere. All of life—an interaction.

"Feel the power," Savoyian repeated, in a low voice, "the power that draws boundaries, brings order, serves and protects and provides direction to your life. The pain that you feel in your head can be healed by the power at the tips of your fingers—"

He stopped and pushed hard into a pressure point located deep in the "V" of her hand, a small, amazingly sensitive spot—he'd found it so precisely, the exact juncture where her thumb bones joined her wrist, a small space loaded, apparently, with nerve endings. It hurt. The pressure of his strong hard finger hurt her—but also felt good. A subtle, penetrating pleasure.

"Stay with the feeling," he whispered, and Eliana thought that the hard way he hit the word "feeling" contained a strange vibrating note of anger. He wanted something from her, yes—she thought, but not what she imagined. The energy in his voice, the tenderness of his caress, the pain now at the pressure-point in her hand—she experienced a deep hurt but also a feeling of deep release, and with it came with a sense of glimpsed truth, an understanding, grasped, but lost in a flash. The pain in her hand shot up her arm.

What is this, she thought, with a sudden sense of urgency. What is this all about? She opened her eyes and looked into Vachik Savoyian's face, where she found an expression impossible to explain: frowning, inviting, warm, cold, enlightened, savage—that maddening twist in his lips hinting at his smile that was not a smile. And it all struck her now as the mute expression of a man laughing silently to himself, a private joke. An appalling look, she decided—desire commingled with hate. This man should frighten me, she thought, but he doesn't. And it was true: she felt no fear. She felt nothing but a strange feeling of release. With one final hard squeeze, he let go of his grip on her hand and leaned back. Finished.

Slowly, she sat up. Her headache was gone.

They stared at each other. Neither spoke. She put down the picture, and he looked at it. "Archetype of the father—that's the energy," he said quietly, and lowered his head, holding his face in his hands, rubbing his cheeks like someone who's just woken up.

She glanced at the photo lying now on the patterned bed spread. "My headache's gone."

"Good. It's not magic. Just pressure points, and imagery."

She looked around. Everything on this side of the "junior four" was visible from the bed. The kitchen—with its small stove, sink, and refrigerator—sparkled. No dirty dishes, no crumbs, no trace of grease or grime. A small window gave off the incongruent vibe of a homemaker: decorated with country-kitchen style curtains, a frilly flower-pattern, two rods, a space in the middle where a yellowish light shone in from the setting sun outside. A bowl of fruit sat in the center of a small round table with two straight-back wooden chairs. On the other side of the table was the bathroom, set apart by a short hallway of faux-wood tile. A padded workout bench crowded the hallway, the floor around it holding neatly stacked free weights.

She looked now at the quilt on the bed. She hadn't noticed before the intricacy of the design. Simple forms—circles, squares, triangles—

combined, duplicated, interlaced, arranged in intricate polygons, star shapes, multi-sided abstractions. Shapes within shapes—she found it erotic.

"My mother sewed this quilt herself."

"It's beautiful," she whispered.

"Traditional Islamic art."

He stood suddenly, an agitation in his jerky movement. Talking about the quilt upset him?

"How about your headache?" she asked. "Show me that—that pressure point. I'll—"

"I'll try whiskey."

He stood quickly, went to the sink, then opened a cabinet and took out two ordinary water glasses. "Join me?" He lifted a bottle and turned it toward her. "I also have vodka."

The plan, yes. She'd not lost focus. Time to execute the plan. Now. She squinted to read the label on the bottle he held: Knob Creek. "That's fine. Yes, let's drink."

He seemed to suspect nothing. She needed to get the vial of chloral hydrate out of her pocket and conceal it from his view. From her spot on the bed, she watched him untwist the cap and pour in one smooth move. A man used to making a drink. She noted the extreme quiet in the apartment. Heard the whiskey splash into the empty glasses. Then the soft hum of the refrigerator. And a clock, like one you might find in a public school, ticked loudly. It hung on the blank kitchen wall next to a photo of the sun setting over a desert landscape. She heard birds chirping outside. The suburban sounds of the outer boroughs.

"Ice? Splash of water?"

"No thanks."

He stepped toward her, both glasses almost half-full. "Whiskey neat, here you are." They clinked, nodded, a wordless toast. He stood while she remained sitting on the edge of the bed. She looked at her drink.

"This is one heavy pour. Must be four ounces of whiskey."

"Three and one-half. Pace yourself. And don't drink a drop more than you want."

He took a deep gulp, turning his back, stepping slowly to the small round table under the ticking clock. When he pulled out the chair, she thought: Hmmm... all done at the bed? Strange. One minute this guy's making love to my hand, and the next... he sat down at the table, and she watched him tuck in the back of his dark T-shirt. It triggered something, a trace of sexual feeling that lingered, glowing like a crack of light around a closed door. She wondered about the grooves of muscle under that shirt. She could imagine him shirtless—grunting, sweating, legs spread—bench pressing. The neatly stacked weights in the hall by the bathroom—she knew cops who lived this way: they work, they lift, they drink. And, of course, they fuck.

Her own thoughts made her uneasy. Had she become just like these crass men?

She sipped her whiskey, felt the warm pleasing heat in her throat. Then got up from the bed. She slipped the vial out of her front pocket, concealed it in her curled hand, and joined him at the table. They sat in silence, looking out the window, drinking. Eliana counted the floors of the buildings across the street—yes, six stories. But not worth a comment. The silence felt nice, intimate. Outside, sparrows flitted from branch to branch. An elderly Hispanic lady using a bright red walker came into view under the yellowish glow of a streetlamp—dusk had fallen. The old woman inched along the sidewalk, passing directly in front of Savoyian's building.

"So..." Eliana said, noticing that the whiskey had kicked-in, the buzz slowing everything down, like turning off a car, cooling the hot engine of her stupid distracting lust.

She gulped the rest of her drink. Wanted more, but resisted. "So I'm still not sure—did you or did you not tell Kitty that you killed a man?"

"I don't remember what I told her," Savoyian answered quickly. "But I've killed lots of men."

"...Meaning...?"

"It's what I do."

"...In the military, you mean."

"You could put it that way, sure."

"Sure?"

"What's military and what isn't. National security. Fifty shades of grey and all that."

Eliana looked into her empty glass. She wanted another drink and needed to get her hands on Savoyian's. "Should I be putting you in cuffs?"

"You don't have any cuffs."

"You're right. I'm unprepared."

"That's OK. You can't arrest me anyway."

"What can you tell me—about the shades of grey, I mean."

"How many government acronyms can you remember if I start laying them out? An Ivy League girl, you ought to—"

"How did you know I—"

"Columbia University Philosophy major—turned cop? Why? Your family disapproved."

"How do you know all this?"

Savoyian looked away, then took a deep breath. "J-I-A-T-F. Joint Interagency Task Force," he began, "a global, much more comprehensive version of the old JTTF—that's Joint Terrorism Task Force, which dates back to the 1980s, when the NYPD worked with the FBI." A pause, a smirk, then he added: "NYPD is the New York City Police Department—"

"Yeah, thanks."

"And there's JSOC, CENTCOM, NSA, DIA, SAD, and, of course, everyone's old favorite the CIA, and I haven't even begun with the Special Forces: Delta, Rangers, Navy Seals, and ICE and DEA and—then there's the Environmental Protection Police, and—"

"I get it—which are you?"

He looked at her, then stood, went to the counter for the bottle of Knob Creek. He left his glass unattended. She quickly unscrewed the vial and poured in the chloral hydrate. He turned back holding the bottle of bourbon. Then he paused. He stared into the empty glasses. Had he seen her? She felt her scalp tingle, a trace of her headache returning. She lowered her hand closer to her ankle holster. "I've always had trouble fitting in," he said, and poured. Then he put the bottle down and took a quick gulp from his glass.

Perfect, she thought. He'll be out cold in a few minutes. And she'll have at least thirty minutes to search the place.

"Who issues your ID?"

"I can't answer that, but it's a very good—very specific—question. I'm impressed with that question, Detective."

"So... tell me."

"It's not the ID that matters."

"Okaaay. If it doesn't matter—"

"Look, you don't know what you don't know."

"Oh, I see." Eliana reached for her glass, trying to conceal her anger. And why was she angry? Because, in fact, she really did want to know this man. Of course, he was a suspect, or a witness, or...he knew something about her father's disappearance. That was the bottom line. And she was working him to get information. Period. But she felt that he was also working her.

"I'm sorry," he said softly. "I didn't mean to be patronizing. I'm glad you're asking me these questions. I want you to know me."

His dark complexion had paled slightly, his strong posture slumped. I'm a certain kind of soldier," he began quietly. "Started with the Air Force. Operation Eagle Claw—google it. Then—I worked as a mosque- crawler for the NYPD. This was the early 80s."

"Mosque-crawler?"

"I speak Arabic."

"I thought so. From that notebook you had in the bar—"

He smiled, lips going sideways, a drunk's face. "You're good. Wanna be a spy? I could—as the kids say—hook you up."

Eliana thought he sounded serious, in spite of the slur working into his speech, the drug taking effect. "Do I get a helicopter ride?" she answered, and her own tongue felt thick in her mouth.

He laughed, a hoarse, throaty chuckle. She sensed a tender emotion—vulnerability. "I guess I don't think of it like that—a helicopter ride."

"So undercover cop to... some kind of... military intelligence. How do I get from here to there?"

He shook his head.

"How did you do it?"

Again, a headshake. He seemed almost flustered—off-balance in a way Eliana hadn't seen. He licked his lips, then looked away. "Reputation," he said finally.

"Reputation?"

"It's not who you know—it's who knows you. And what they know you for."

He held his forehead, shaking his head slightly. "Oh, my, I feel like I need to lie down. You didn't slip something into my drink, did you?"

Eliana looked at him, met his eyes directly. "You never told me why you want to help me. Why should I trust you?"

He nodded, his eyes glazing over, the drug working. "I get it, yes. You search the place while I sleep. You shouldn't trust me." His speech grew more slurred. "You shouldn't trust anyone because human beings—all of us—we lie. We lie and destroy and kill and pollute and exploit and..."

He paused, breathing harder, fighting to stay conscious. "How do we live with ourselves?" he went on, and she saw that maddening twist in his lips, that hint of a smile that was not a smile. Then he leaned forward. He looked searchingly into her eyes. "I hope you find what you're looking for," he whispered hoarsely, and slumped over.

Eliana caught him by the shoulders before he bumped his forehead on the table, then she folded his hands and positioned him like a college student napping in a library. The association made her smile. It was another strange, incongruous feeling. She adjusted his chair so that if he stirred, he wouldn't fall.

Then she got to work. Twenty minutes, she figured, and looked at the clock on the wall. She didn't want to be here when he awoke.

She went straight to the box of journals. Yellow lined pads with thin cardboard backs, just like the one that he had slipped into the leather binder she'd first seen in the bar. There were hundreds of these pads, and it didn't surprise her that they were perfectly organized by month and year. She found the stack for 1994, the year her father disappeared.

Flipping pages, her heart pounded. *6-26-94*. She read the date written at the top of the page. It was two weeks after her father disappeared.

—Shaved my beard tonight. In a fit of panic. Shocked me how much I now look my father. Being clean-shaven won't disrupt anything tho 'cuz brothers do it for a variety of reasons. Still I felt a pang of guilt—as if clean cheeks are the problem. Re-read the Bihar al-Anwar too, vol 16—in which Gabriel, upon seeing the bearded Adam, says: "This is in response to the supplication you made to your Lord, and it has been granted to you and your male offspring till the day of reckoning."

—That's what this is, a "reckoning." Perfect word. A moment of truth, finality, destruction. The meaning of a life—transformed. Mine will never be the same. Never. The stain, the guilt—permanent. And Allahu Akbar of course of course… but I don't believe it. I don't—can't—or won't…?

—It started with the meeting of The Islamic Society of Bay Ridge. If only I hadn't been there—I'd still have my beard! That's worth a sick laugh and long drink… I recognized nobody at this meeting. But there was this one older man, his beard laced with henna, a very fancy and expensive decoration, complete with an orange leaf pattern reaching from cheek to chin—he sat on an elevated cushion in the center of the floor with about twenty younger men in a circle around him. Hushed but charged atmosphere, very tense. And the big news? Finally, the man in the center started to lecture about how the United States has no right to decide whether or not certain countries and groups of individuals are permitted to conduct business with each other.

All the drama just for this? Sanctions, frozen assets, big fucking deal, I thought. I should have stayed home. And I almost left. My goddamn sinus infection. And I had a fever. I'm sure. But head pounding, ears ringing—I spoke up. On a whim. Didn't really expect them to listen. Decided to explain that bankers run this country. Yes, the Office of Foreign Assets Control, OFAC, operating under the authority of the US. Department of the Treasury, imposes controls on banking transactions and exercises the power to freeze funds, but some banks ignore the controls because it's bad for business. The transactions pass through. No bank wants a policy regulation to cut into their profits.

—How perfectly ironic: my handlers ignore me, but the people I'm spying on hung on my every word.

—The older man nodded and staring a hole through me explained that at one bank—USBC—a Jew there is insisting that his bosses must follow the OFAC rules, and now he is going to the authorities, scheduled to testify at a trial.

—When I didn't say anything, the older guy leaned forward, gave me a hard look, pointed at me. "Why do the banks allow this? If this man is hurting their profits, why don't the banks silence him?"

—The question caught me off-guard, but I recognized the huge intel value and nodded, smiling. "Maybe they will," I said.

That's where the journal entry ended, and Eliana found herself almost breathless with a feeling of urgency. Char, in a sense, could be right, she thought. The bankers killed their father? But that meant someone inside the bank pointed a finger at her father. She strained to recall exactly which bank executives the NYPD detectives had interviewed at the time. And the Fed investigators—they had wider jurisdiction. Had they gone back to those named in the OFAC trial? All of this must be in the files, she thought. Then she thought of Jack. With this new information, Jack could re-open the case. But police procedure—she'd completely violated all procedure. No, she'd gone way beyond that. Too many felonies to count. Using a controlled substance to render an individual unconscious to attempt to steal documents.

She pushed the legal mess out of her mind. Far more important right now was telling all of this to Char. A shudder of guilt came over Eliana as she considered how often she had dismissed Char's "crazy radical ideas."

Validating Char—this alone might be healing.

She turned the page of the journal, then glanced at her watch. Mind racing, she tried to make sense of what she was reading. But the handwriting was a mess. Something about vomiting and being drunk. She couldn't make out the words. The scribbling looked like he'd been drunk while writing.

What she needed was more time. These journals needed to be poured over, read carefully. She took out her phone and started to take a picture of a page, then another, and another. But there were too many. Could she simply take the journals? Fuck it, she thought, and grabbed all of the pads from 1994—eleven in total.

She stood and started to leave, but at the door of his apartment, she hesitated. Her mind filled with an image of Savoyian getting on that helicopter. When he wakes up, he'll be angry, she thought. And she asked herself: *will he kill me?* The question struck her like a dark blow to the chest. In a panic she returned the notepads to the box, then hurried out of the apartment.

Chapter 23

The next day Eliana continued her deception on the job and called in sick, then she drove straight through from Queens to Watertown—four-and-a-half hours—not even stopping for a bathroom break. When she turned into the hospital entrance a little after 4 p.m., she gazed up at the hospitals lounge windows which overlooked the parking lot, and her giddy feeling of urgency broke—pierced by a dark thought. She had no plan. She'd thrown on a pair of jeans and a T-shirt and rushed up here to see Char—but she had no idea if her sister would even want to see her. That happened once. Back when Char was in a locked ward—she'd refused to come out of her room.

But this was rehab—no locked psych ward. And that was years ago. They were past all that, she told herself. This news about Savoyian and the bankers would help Char. And soon she'd be off the pills, and then Eliana would get her back to the city, back into that umpiring school... and maybe she'd even ask Charlotte to live with her. Yes, over the years, Char had always refused this kind of offer, but now...? Roommates, yes. Now, it seemed possible.

The lounge smelled of a flower-scented cleaning solution. Cloying, sweet—a possible headache trigger, but, in fact, Eliana felt fine. Strong, clear-headed.

A nurse brought Char into the lounge, opening the door and nodding officially as if she were giving an order. Nurse as cop, Eliana thought, assuming the worst of the people you serve. The thought depressed her, and she almost said something to the nurse about her attitude, but instead she rushed up to her sister for a hug. Char's small square frame felt thick and solid under her baggy shirt.

The nurse flashed a phony smile. "One hour," she said, then nodded and left the room.

Char stepped out of the embrace and said, "You didn't tell me you were coming, Elly," a hint of anger in her voice.

"I'm sorry," she said.

"That's why Nurse Bitchoff is so pissed."

"Bitchoff?"

"That's her name, really. Or something like that. Because you didn't tell me that you were coming to visit, I had a big fight with her. I told Nurse Bitchoff I wasn't having a visitor, she said I was challenging her authority,' which, according to some write-up in my chart is now one of my issues'."

"Challenging authority?"

"There's a new psychiatrist on the floor who thinks we all have that issue: challenging authority. Like, hello, maybe it's your issue. You're the fucking authority. Ever think of that?"

Eliana fought back a little chuckle, which Char encouraged with a small smile. It looked like their mother's smile—elegant, restrained. Strange how Char had their mother's long angular face combined with their dad's short square body. When she smiled, Eliana saw the trace of a bruise remained over Char's lips from where she'd slammed her head into that table at the precinct.

"Anyway, I'm glad you are here," Char went on. "I have big news."

"You do?"

"Yes. Well, kind of big news. I have a boyfriend, sort of. Not a real boyfriend, but, you know, a rehab boyfriend. He's going to see if he can find a way to walk down the hall that goes right past that window right there. He wants to wave hello to you."

Charlotte pointed to the hallways window, hunching her shoulders, still smiling, but without making eye contact. The energy in her voice, Eliana noted, sounded strong. A nice normal volume. And boyfriend news? Not necessarily a good sign, Eliana thought, but concealed her concern.

"What's his name?"

"Richard—I know, just like Livi's husband. But, believe me, they're nothing alike."

"Oh, well, that's good. We don't need another—"

"Which reminds me—I don't want any of Livi's money involved in any of this..." Charlotte waved her hand in a quick circle, one finger up, like an umpire indicating a homerun. That's what came to Eliana's mind—the umpire hand gesture. She really hoped that someday Char would pursue all that.

"Don't worry about the money. Your job is—"

"I know—off the pills. Stay clean. I know my job. I just don't want any of Livi's money."

"OK, I get it."

"Anyway, my Richard, he's—only twenty-two, we have the same birthday. Same day, four years apart—what a coincidence, huh? He wants to be—he's not sure what he wants to be, but he confided in me that he's writing a novel. About all this." Another homerun gesture.

"He's writing a novel about the hospital?"

"Not just this one. Hospitals, in general. Rehab, psych wards, he's been in a bunch. He had this diagnosis: 'homicidal ideation,' which isn't as scary as it sounds. He hates his father, who used to hit him.

but Richard's totally sweet. I can't imagine him killing a cockroach, let alone another person."

Char looked down, clenched and unclenched her right fist, over and over, then switched hands. An old mannerism, nervous habit. Eliana said nothing. A "homicidal" boyfriend? Char has always known how to pick a man...

They were still standing in the middle of the lounge, so Eliana took a half-step toward the couch in front of the windows.

"I think his family probably has money, though." Charlotte continued. "You know, to afford a place like this." The homerun gesture yet again. "And he agrees it's really not so bad here. He's not trying to write a *Cuckoo's Nest* thing. In fact, he wants to show that it's nice to be around people who are perpetually concerned about you. The way every single day, at least once, sometimes more, somebody asks: do you feel like hurting yourself, how are you sleeping, how is your mood?"

"And how about it?" Eliana jumped in quickly. She knew that Charlotte could ramble on about this new boyfriend for an hour without stopping.

"Me?"

"Yeah—how have you been answering those questions? I mean, you know, how are you?"

Charlotte shrugged. "Off the oxy—though taking a lot of whatever they're giving me to get me off of that. It's all crazy, you know. But—hey, I'm way better than some. Yesterday this girl—she totally lost it. Started to scream and punch the wall until a code one team came. S & R—I hate that shit."

Hospital jargon, Eliana thought. She tried translating but couldn't figure it out. "What's S & R?"

"Sedate and restrain," Charlotte answered quietly, and Eliana could tell that her sisters voice was about to fade into an anxious whisper. "They took her away kicking and screaming," she added, barely audible. "I hate that shit."

Eliana took her sisters hand, and they sat down together on the firm couch in front of the windows overlooking the parking lot. Sunlight warmed the back of the couch. A few potted plants were lined up in the space between the couch and the window.

After a moment, Eliana said, "Tell me some more about Richard." Charlotte didn't pull away—a good sign. Eliana didn't really want to hear about this "boyfriend"—but anything to keep Char from slipping away. The whisper was a bad sign.

"Well... we sit side by side reading and holding hands—when nobody's looking, of course. We're not supposed to get involved with—you know. But this one tech—totally clueless. Plays games on his computer all day. We could probably start fucking and he wouldn't look up unless we grunted too loudly."

Eliana winced a little at this thought, but mostly felt glad for the sound of Char's voice, the defeat of the anxious whisper, at least for the moment.

"Weird thing is that Richie's hands are really rough, which always makes me smile. Like, what? He's sneaking out at night to work the land? His palms feel like they've got these callouses like from raking or something. I call him 'Farmer Rick,' but, actually, it's just skin allergies." Just then the door opened, and a short, older woman came into the lounge, her grey hair in a long braid down the center of her back. Charlotte visibly tensed at the sight of her. Behind the older woman, holding the lounge door open, stood Nurse "Bitchoff," as Eliana thought of her.

"See?" the nurse said. "Only Charlotte's visitor. Just like I told you." The older woman shot a vicious look across the room, then took amazingly small steps toward the door. Finally, she was gone.

"Thank god," Charlotte said with a loud exhale, as if she'd been holding her breath the whole time. "That woman—her name's Lucy. She's truly crazy. Most people here are just, you know, in the middle of some horrible mess because their lives suck and they're taking drugs or whatever to avoid dealing with it—and, well, they just need a little extra help and a nice, safe place to deal with their problems. But Lucy—totally nuts. She claims to have been a back-up singer for Frank Sinatra."

Eliana laughed out loud, and so did Char.

"She walks around screaming 'Fly to the Moon' and it sounds like there's a wounded animal in the room. And if anyone asks her to be quiet, she flies into a rage and starts in with the Sinatra stories. Las Vegas, Caesars Palace. Live at the Sands Hotel. With Dean Martin, too. She says she once gave Dean Martin a blowjob." Charlotte shook her head, then shrugged, as if considering this for the first time. "Maybe that's true—but no way she sang backup."

They both laughed some more and—for a moment—it felt to Eliana like they were just a couple of normal sisters hanging out together giggling stupidly about anything and everything, and Charlotte wasn't a drug addict and a psych patient who'd been in-and-out of mental hospitals half her life for schizophrenic-depressive-borderline personality-bipolar-bulimic-anorexic-whatever-the-fuck-labels... No, she was just fine. She was just Char—warm, witty, alive. With a bright future.

They were still holding hands, their fingers lightly clasped. "Hey, listen," Eliana began, squeezing Charlotte's hand gently. "I have something I want to tell you."

Charlotte yanked back her hand. "What? What is it? Why are you using that tone?"

"What tone? I'm not using—"

"Something happen to Livi?"

"No, no—"

"The kids?"

"No—"

"Then what? What happened? Tell me."

The sudden shift threw Eliana. She wished that she could start over. "Please, Eliana," Charlotte whispered, her shoulders rising, head lowering, that look coming on—the horrible turtle-like thing, the posture, the chin tuck, the stare, eyes blank. It made Eliana feel sick because she recognized it not just from the years and years of dealing with Charlotte—but also from the streets, *Be advised: sensitive site EDP.*

Emotionally Disturbed Person. Or, more politically correct: "distressed."

"Please Eliana," Charlotte whispered again, even more faintly, "it must be serious or you wouldn't have shown up like this. Just tell me, please."

That last little "please" made Eliana's heart ache, as if she possessed all the power in the world, and Charlotte was begging her to be kind, to have mercy. "Well, there's someone I know who—I think—I'm pretty confident... he can find out what happened to Dad." Eliana hesitated. She wanted to say more, but Char suddenly seemed so unstable.

Charlotte held still, the turtle posture unchanged. They stared at each other, then Charlotte leaned closer, pressing her mouth against Eliana's ear. She whispered, "You don't think Dad's alive, do you?" She leaned back.

Eliana looked at her and shook her head, no.

Then Charlotte leaned forward and again pressed her mouth against Eliana's ear. She whispered, "I don't either."

Pattern established. Eliana knew the drill. Charlotte would now speak only by whispering directly into Eliana's ear. A fierce act of control, as one doc had put it.

Mouth to ear, Char whispered, "Is the guy you know another cop?"

"Used to be." Eliana tried to use a full voice, but the distance between them, the power of the pattern—hard not to avoid matching her sister whisper for whisper. "Military now, some part of the military. Intelligence, that kind of thing. He can't tell me exactly."

Charlotte nodded. Then she again leaned forward stiffly, her hips and back rigid. Another whisper: "If you find the guy who killed Dad, you'll kill him, right?"

As if her body were on a hinge, Charlotte leaned back again, staring directly into Eliana's face.

"It doesn't work that way, Char."

Again, Charlotte leaned forward until her mouth was close to Eliana's ear. "But the courts can't be trusted, right? That's what you always say. The courts suck. You arrest bad guys, but the judges let them go."

Another shift of position, bending from the waist, rigid, Char was leaning back and forth like one of those Russian dolls, wobbling.

"It's complicated," Eliana said, and quickly realized that she hadn't thought through what happens if Savoyian brings her face-to-face with whoever killed her father. But then she thought: *I'll make an arrest, of course. I'm a cop, not an executioner.*

She tried to explain how the statute of limitations works. That in New York, like in most other states, lesser felonies have either a six or a three-year statute of limitations. And most misdemeanors, but not all, have a one-year limit. But crimes such as murder and most forms of rape, which are crimes punishable by life in prison, they have no statute of limitation.

"So if your guy helps you find Dad's killer, you'll just arrest him? And that's it?"

The whisper tickled Eliana's ear. She pulled her head away and rubbed her ear.

"Yes, I'll arrest him." Eliana tried to add a measure of firmness in her voice.

Charlotte shrugged. "Not me," she said, finally letting go of the whispering routine. "I'd kill him. And if I went to jail for it—fine. The system—plea bargains, legal technicalities, jurors being manipulated—it's totally fucked up. Look at me—privileged white girl gets treatment' in a fancy hospital while my Black boyfriend—no guiltier than me—sits in jail. That's justice? And how about the credit crisis? Millions of people lose their homes while the bankers—white people—still get their big bonuses? No, there's no justice in this country. If I found Dad's killer, I'd kill him."

As Char spoke, her voice got louder, and her posture improved. Eliana knew where this was going. Over the years, especially back in their *midrash* days as high school students, they'd been through it a million times: Charlotte's interpretation of biblical justice, particularly her obsession with the sixth commandment. With a razor-sharp critical mind, Char turned all this into a gigantic teenage intellectual project. To Char, the biblical prohibition on killing—if translated properly—really means "Thou Shalt Not *Murder*," not "Thou Shalt Not *Kill.*" The confusion involves "philological assumptions."

Eliana could tell what was coming. Wide-eyed, overexcited, her voice now unnaturally loud, Char began laying out the argument she'd been making since she was sixteen. But Eliana tuned out. Instead of hearing Char lecture about the Bible, she now heard a small whisper inside of herself asking: If Savoyian did, in fact, lead her to the man who murdered her father—would it really be enough just to arrest him? If she killed her father's killer, wouldn't that be—?

Ridiculous, she told herself.

"Consider Moses," Charlotte was saying, "the holiest of all prophets, right? But you know the passage, Elly, you know it: Exodus 2, verse 11. That's when Moses kills the Egyptian."

Eliana said nothing.

"What's that, huh? That's Moses taking justice into his own hands. Am I right?" Char was staring at her.

Eliana remained silent. She tried reaching for Charlotte's hand. But Charlotte pulled away. The two sisters just sat there on the couch and looked at each other.

A dangerous and crazy revenge fantasy—that's how Eliana had always dismissed all this. Even though some doctors disagreed, especially this one little curly-haired shrink with an annoyingly nasal voice, he went on and on about "...a possible therapeutic benefit of engaging in theological research."

That was just before Char's senior year in high school, and with this doc's encouragement, Charlotte dug deeper, focusing on the book of *Shmuel*, especially the part where King David kills tens of thousands of men in combat and is honored for it. The celebratory text, Samuel 2, verse 8: *"And David became famous after he returned from striking down eighteen thousand Edomites in the Valley of Salt... "*

OK, fine—back then, whenever Char cornered her to talk about all this, Eliana would concede the obvious point. There's murder, and there's killing—not the same thing. One's a sin, one isn't. She'd say whatever Char wanted to hear if it meant putting an end to the crazy talk about taking justice into one's own hands. And, thinking back to that annoying doctor, maybe he'd been right about the therapeutic value of Char's biblical research. She did, after all, stop trying to kill herself. Yeah, right, Eliana thought, and she could feel a bitter cynicism rise up inside of her, that familiar I'm-a-tough-cop-have-seen-it-all detachment, Char has really "improved," she thought, instead of a suicidal teen she's a drug-abusing adult.

Just then Charlotte stood quickly and said, "I understand, Elly. You're a cop. After all these years, you're probably more of a cop than a sister."

"What? More of a cop than—"

"It's understandable. You've been co-opted by the system." Charlotte stepped away from the couch, turning her back on Eliana. She stood there a moment looking out the window.

Eliana experienced a surge of anger. She got up and grabbed Charlotte's shoulders. She tried to turn her around. Charlotte resisted.

"What did you just say?" Eliana asked. "More of a cop than a sister? How could you—"

Charlotte moved away quickly, positioning herself now behind the couch in the small space in front of the window. Then she hid herself partly behind one of the potted plants and rubbed her shoulders.

"Look, I'm sorry I grabbed you. Did I hurt you?"

No answer. Charlotte continued rubbing her shoulders, then she leaned back slightly, resting her head against the back of the big picture window.

"Char? I'm sorry—I didn't mean to grab you like that."

Char shrugged, then said something, but the whisper was back. "Char, you've got to talk louder."

More whispers, undecipherable.

A vicious power move. Eliana hated when Charlotte pulled this. But, after a moment, she gave up. Eliana walked around the couch and joined Charlotte in the space in front of the window, then she leaned forward and turned one ear.

Still nothing. She leaned closer, her ear now practically touching Charlotte's face. Finally, she heard: "Mom and Livi always said something like this would happen—being a cop would change you. Turn you into—something. But it's OK, Elly. I love you. And I really appreciate everything you've done for me. How much you love me. And none of this—well, it's not your fault that you don't feel these things the way you used to. You're hard now, tough. I'm the same way, really. Tougher, harder. But, well—I still want justice, you know. I still want it for Dad. So if you do find the guy—just tell me, and I will kill him myself. I won't mind going to jail for it. I'm sure you won't give me your gun, but I'll choke him to death. I could do that, you know. I have very strong hands—very strong hands."

Eliana pulled her head back and looked directly in Charlotte's eyes. "Charlotte, you can't talk this way."

"Just—will you give me the man's name? If you find him—I mean, will you just—"

"No. Char—look, you can't—"

"Please, Elly, please... please."

Charlotte's face twisted into a horrible look of pain—eyes narrowing into slits, lips drawing back from clenched teeth, her shoulders tensing as if preparing for a blow. And then Eliana knew what was coming: Charlotte was going to slam the back of her head against the window.

Eliana reached up quickly, wrapping her arms around Charlotte's neck. "Hey, I love you, Char. I love you. And we're getting way ahead of ourselves here. Maybe I shouldn't have started blabbing about all this. You just need—you just need to take care of yourself. That's all that matters. Stay off the pills and get strong and healthy—and then, we'll take it one step at a time, OK? I love you. You know that."

A deep breath, the sound of choked tears, and Eliana felt Charlotte s body relax. "OK, Elly," she whispered, through her tears. "I'm sorry. I'm sorry that I'm so much trouble. I love you, Elly. You take good care of me. You really do, and I love you so much."

Charlotte started to cry, and Eliana felt her own body relax. And then she wondered if she too could cry. She wanted that—to cry right along with her little sister.

But Eliana's tears wouldn't come.

Chapter 24

Alone in her room, Charlotte sat on the edge of her bed and tried to understand what had just happened.

The tragic triumvirate of American democracy, American capitalism, and American racism—this is what Elly fails to grasp, she thought. A cop! Elly became a cop! Of course she doesn't understand this country! She has turned off her critical thinking and refuses to connect the dots, refuses to see the connection between this country's broken democracy, its corrupt capitalism, and its structural racism. But it's obvious, so obvious: the electoral process has been predicated on restricting access to the ballot— just study the history of voting rights! And capitalism? It requires cheap labor, and there's nothing cheaper than slavery. Without it, this country could never have become so rich and powerful. Which leaves racism, the foundation of it all, as it has simply shapeshifted to fit the times— from legally protected slavery to Jim Crow to our neo-liberalism with its emphasis on mass incarceration, which of course perpetuates the...

Charlotte let her thoughts fade and wondered for the millionth time about her boyfriend, whom she was certain sat right now in jail. It's simply wrong—all wrong, she thought, and looked around her hospital room. It contained nothing but the bed, a small table, and a single straight back chair. All of these were secured to the floor to prevent them being moved or used destructively. For the same reason, there were no electrical outlets, just the recessed overhead lighting, securely out of reach. On the wall across from the bed, a single window with thick frosted glass allowed a pale yellow light to enter from outside. Ah, yes, Charlotte thought, bitterly, a basic hospital room like this is designed to maximize safety because we who inhabit these rooms are dangerous. So dangerous. We must be protected—from ourselves! Yes, yes, yes, we need help!

But Elly is the one who really needs help, she went on. Because Elly doesn't get it. She thinks the system can work. Let the guy have a lawyer and put him on trial. Ridiculous. In fact, Elly not only believes the system can work—her job is to defend it! A cop! A cop! She ought to let me help her! She thinks I'm all messed up because of what happened to our father, but—no, she's the one. She's the one who can't let it go. *Yes, what I'd like to do is help Elly!*

With a burst of energy, Charlotte got up and went into the bathroom. There was no door separating it from the rest of the room. She stopped in front of the sink and stood looking at her reflection in the mirror. It was a stainless-steel shatterproof mirror. The bathroom is what bothered Charlotte most about this place. The non-skid floor, the anti-tamper fixtures specially shaped to have no sharp edges, the preset hot water maximum temperature settings on all the faucets, and, most strange to Charlotte, the absence of a shower curtain. As if—what? How do you hurt yourself with a shower curtain?

She leaned over the sink and turned the faucet and splashed her face with tepid water, then she thought again of the visit today with her sister. She felt a strange mixture of anger and excitement, plus a small measure of hope. Yes, if only Elly would let *me* help *her*.

Chapter 25

When Savoyian awoke, he went immediately to the box of journals. Out of order—he knew they'd been read. No surprise. And no anger. In a way that he never could have planned, everything was falling into place.

Not a leaf falls, but He knows. Surah al-An am, 6:59

Crouching near the box of journals, he took out his phone and typed a text message: I WILL TAKE YOU TO THE SCENE OF THE CRIME. Then he hit send. And next he went to the closet near the bathroom and reached for the cloth bag that held his father's gun. He opened the bag and looked at the gun as if seeing it for the first time—or would it be his last? A poetic end to this archetypal weapon, he thought. He spun the cylinder, listened to its familiar soft metallic click. Then he loaded six bullets. No more "Tyche," goddess of chance. Now, a bullet in each cylinder.

Then he went back into the living room and, still holding the gun, sat down on the couch and waited for Eliana to respond to his text message. Tonight. He hoped he could take her tonight, after dark.

To change the meaning of one's life, to change the meaning of one's death—it's possible, he thought. In fact, it's inevitable if one accepts responsibility and follows a course of action and... his thoughts drifted back to where all of this began, his days of "mosque crawling." It involved attending a service, reporting what a particular imam said during the sermon, and then collecting the license plate numbers of the worshipers and tracking where they lived, shopped, and worked. And if not at a mosque, he'd spend hours eavesdropping on conversations in Lebanese cafes, where his knowledge of Arabic dialects could reveal if a customer had lived, for example, in South Lebanon, a region dominated by Hezbollah sympathizers.

In addition to this field work, he had another task, equally tedious: he poured over New York City Civil Court records cataloguing every Muslim in the city who adopted a new Americanized surname. And, whenever possible, he befriended those identified as "high value targets," a term, unfamiliar at the time, which the JTTF had borrowed from the military. Savoyian would find these people at their mosques and spend additional time doing ordinary things with them—sharing meals, watching sports, talking about "life in America." Sometimes, to

get even closer, he rented a room in a home shared by these men, allowing him to spy with an even greater level of intimacy.

To pass as a good Muslim required no effort. Indeed, that part of
the job suited him entirely. In those days, he led a devout life—performed the *salat* five times a day, refrained from smoking and drinking,
wore the free-flowing beard. And the way to walk, the way to pray, the
way to dress—his confident observance made others look up to him.
For example, he showed his less experienced brothers how to navigate
the streets with their eyes lowered, always at the same angle, and to
never make direct eye contact with a stranger, or to look at a woman
below her chin. And how to dress: no pant leg hanging below the ankle—a sign of arrogance. Savoyian explained: "The Prophet, peace be
upon him, once said: 'On the Day of Resurrection, Allah will not look
at the one who dragged his garment out of pride.'" At the mosques,
too, Savoyian taught his brothers how to stand with their feet close
together and explained not to look down when they kneeled for prayer
but to focus on the spot on the floor in front of them where they would
place their forehead.

And when Savoyian himself lay his head down—it was, indeed,
before God. He felt it: a dissolving of the self in Divine Presence,
though he knew better than to use mystical language, not with jihadists. Among followers of the Sufi sect, maybe, but with these young
men—well, Savoyian talked of "jihad" as the battle all devout Muslims
fight within themselves to show their devotion to God. With utter
sincerity, he could say, "You must give everything to Allah. Trust him
completely, and keep nothing for yourself."

And he spoke with such conviction because he himself believed the
words. "Even if you give everything," he went on, "it is not enough.
You must give more. It is not enough to perform the *salat* five times a
day. You must pray constantly, repent at every moment for everything
in yourself that is impure."

A line like this worked on multiple levels for Savoyian. When his
brothers noticed his lips moving slightly, they assumed he was pray-
ing. And often he was. But often he was memorizing a license plate or
phone number or fragment of conversation he would secretly note and
later report.

And what exactly happened to this information? That was the
problem. Not knowing. Week after week, month after month, year
after year, Savoyian met only with his "handler." Or, worse, sometimes
not even that. Just a "dead-drop." An envelope of names and addresses
or a disk of photos placed in a pre-cased hiding spot. A hollowed-out
rock, a fake tree branch, once Savoyian combed through a pile of trash
at the Prospect Park Zoo in Brooklyn looking for a crumpled-up soft

drink can into which he was supposed to drop a small flash drive. A maintenance crew nearly destroyed that drop. But the bigger problem: no contact, sometimes for weeks. And when Savoyian did meet up with someone— an NYPD Detective, a Fed—he didn't even know which. Often, he didn't even know the guy's real name. Back then, the JTTF was comprised of eleven members of the NYPD, and eleven FBI. But Savoyian never met the whole team. Only the "handler."

In cars, coffee shops, out-of-the-way bars, fancy restaurants, expensive hotels—wherever they'd be unlikely to be seen by other Muslims. Savoyian would often travel an hour or more, taking a ridiculously circuitous route to be sure he hadn't been followed. (Surveillance Detection Training—this seemed to be the group's main priority). And then Savoyian would hand over the goods—the folder, the envelope, the list with names, addresses, photos, descriptions—and in return, he'd get: "You're providing very good information. Very good."

But nothing more. A meeting with the bosses?

No, sorry, that might compromise security.

It became excruciating—no matter how many times they met, the procedure felt like day one. The travel, the drop, and, if lucky, a brief conversation—but it never deepened. Over time, the handler changed, but not the conversation. And his frustration grew. By 1992 he felt that he understood and had gained information about Muslims not only in New York City but all over the world. The war in Bosnia had been going on for almost two years, as had the war in Algeria. He'd met dozens of men who'd fought in Afghanistan! He had a source who basically told him that the World Trade Center would, indeed, be bombed.

These jihadists, these holy warriors, these sour-smelling cab drivers sleeping three-to-a-room in Brooklyn basements—they had become Vachik Savoyian's friends. They trusted him, confided in him. That's why... the night he cut off his beard. Ah, yes, he went now to the box and found the journal entry concerning that night. Had Eliana read it? The pages looked handled. Yes, of course she'd read this.

A memory came, a small moment he hadn't thought of in years: after shaving his beard that night he went to his bedroom and took the photo of his father out of its frame. Then he stood in the bathroom looking back and forth from his reflection in the mirror to the picture in his hand.

Amazing—how much a son can resemble his father. And his father's words: "A brave man dies an honorable death; an honorable man faces death bravely."

Yes, tonight, Savoyian thought, tonight I am brave.

Chapter 26

She read Savoyian's text while driving but didn't respond. Bad traffic. Six hours from the hospital to the city. When she finally pulled into the driveway of her building, it was dark. She turned off the engine and got out quickly, but then just stood there, leaning against the warm hood. The summer air felt thick, heavy. Distant thunder rumbled. *Now what?* she thought. Go immediately to the crime scene with Savoyian? Could she trust him?

Something held her back, but why hesitate? After all this, why hesitate now?

Nothing came, except a tight feeling of frustration. Char's reaction—that troubled her. The old revenge fantasy. *I hate that shit*, Eliana thought, and realized Char had used the exact same phrase to talk about the hospital ugliness of "sedate and restrain." Suddenly, Eliana felt the hot summer night closing in on her, her T-shirt sticking to her sweaty skin. She pulled at the collar, wishing for a breeze. *Air conditioning*, she thought, *that's what I need*, and pushed her body away from the cars warm hood.

Then she saw something in the darkness across the street and her cop-sense kicked in. Alarm. Danger. Coming toward her, two silhouettes, both male, about six feet, one average build, the other bigger, walking with a limp. Moving right toward her. As they got closer, Eliana tried to calculate if she could make it into her lobby before they reached her. Outnumbered, she was definitely vulnerable, and the lobby door lock was broken, wasn't it? They could follow her in, and she'd be trapped, even more isolated inside. And—no gun. She hadn't brought a gun to the hospital to visit Char. Didn't want the hospital staff to think of Char differently because her sister was a cop. You never know how that lands with people. Which meant that, once again, she was failing to carry while off-duty. *Be armed at all times when in New York City, unless otherwise directed, or except as provided in P.G. 204-09, "Required Firearms and Equipment."* Danny had tried to drill it into her: no such thing as a part-time cop. The job, yes, not something you *do*—it's who you *are.*

She looked at the two figures coming closer. The threat of attack, yes, that's what she felt. Maybe, now, finally, she'd learn her lesson: *a cop is who you are.* Isn't this what Char had just said? More cop than sister...

"Eliana!"

The sound of Danny's voice should have soothed her. And she immediately recognized the big-bear lumbering shape of Jack, lurching along with his head down. But the sight of these two brought no relief. She still felt tense, threatened, trapped. Her mind raced, jumpy. The Jersey incident, she thought. They've come to warn her about IAB. She took a few steps down the driveway.

"Hey," Danny stopped walking, and when his face caught the yellowish glow from the streetlamp, she noted the tension in his eyes, the concern in his creased brow. Jack hung back a few steps, a bear in the shadows. "Can we talk?" Danny asked.

Eliana hesitated. "Official business, or what?"

Danny shook his head but didn't answer right away. "No. Not really."

"What does that mean? Not really? Danny, do I need a union rep?" Now Bayer stepped forward, his foot scraping the sidewalk. The jerky way he moved showed anger, but he said nothing.

"Union rep? Come on, Elly—*you* think I'm trying to jam you up?" Danny said. "You think I want to hurt you? I want to help."

His voice cracked on the word "he-elp" and—maybe it was just the way the light hit—but Eliana thought she actually saw moistness in his eyes. Danny crying? That would be ironic. She'd wanted to cry so badly just now with Charlotte. Of course—she hadn't cried in... no idea how many years. But Danny—? The cop's cop... the big strong boxer?

The crack in his composure said it all. Eliana knew—plain and simple—she was out of line. These men, both of them, loved her and cared for her and wanted to help. But how? How could they help? Savoyian was going to help her. Could she tell them that? No, because they wouldn't believe it. And suddenly she didn't believe it either. It sounded like a fantasy. *You see, there's this military guy, a spy, special forces—he drinks this Muscle Milk, but I drugged him and read his journal and then...*

It sounded crazy. They'll call EIU. Early Intervention Services. Erratic behavior, unfit for duty. And then: the badge and gun, please.

And counseling services, a psych eval, and, no joke, she could end up in Watertown with Char.

"I'm fine, Danny. Really, Jack, I—I appreciate your concern. Coming all the way out here. You guys—what? You've been sitting on my place all night?"

"I made Danny buy the pizza," Bayer said, and his effort at levity fell flat, which broke Eliana's heart. With his droopy-skinned face, he looked like a tired old dog needing a pat on the head.

"Hey, can we come up?" Danny asked. "We've been kicking around some ideas to get you out of Vice. Let's just talk for a minute."

Eliana looked from Danny to Bayer, then back again. At some level, the idea of them coming upstairs into her apartment pleased her. Neat, clean, orderly. She felt proud of her housekeeping. She'd show them. Everything's fine.

Two bottles of beer, a seltzer for Danny, a bowl of nuts, and some sliced-up cantaloupe. Eliana felt pleased with herself for pulling this off so nonchalantly. Both Danny and Bayer seemed appropriately impressed. Meanwhile, that crazy blast of lust she and Danny had shared a few nights ago hung in the air between them like a pleasing scent. In fact, in her mind, a vague unnamed sexual energy had become paired with the fresh fruit smell of the melon that she'd just so effortlessly sliced up and served. She found herself unable to look Danny in the eye. Also, that pressure point business on the bed last night with Savoyian—that confused things too.

But no awkward silence between the three of them. Talk of "The Job" filled the space. The source of all problems: The fuckin' job.

"You deal with this crap long enough—and, hey—" Jack Bayer shook his head as he spoke, then made that little clicking noise in the back of his throat. "Especially working undercover," he went on, "I remember about fifteen years ago—I had to choose: work narcotics or stay married. After a while, it's just not healthy. You're living on the edge, the extreme edge, and—you, Elly... you've paid your dues. I can hook you up with something else... Intelligence Division, babysitting dignitaries. Give yourself a break."

A hook, yes. Jack and Danny would take care of everything: get Eliana off the streets; get Eliana a POPPA counselor; get Eliana a nice long vacation. Her surrogate father and her ex-husband—taking care of her. How touching, how truly beautiful. She resisted none of it. She called the counselor right in front of them both. Sent an email to her duty captain asking about accrued vacation days. Even completed the leave of absence form Danny had brought with him. That's when she told them about Char being arrested—and then hospitalized. Concerned, but unphased, Danny thought there might be a Family Medical Leave angle to work.

"You need some time to help your sister—makes perfect sense," Jack agreed.

It was too easy. All of it. Playing along with this plan—it cost her nothing. She smiled and nodded and agreed without saying a word about a different plan: to go see Vachik Savoyian as soon as they left. She'd made the decision.

Warm goodbyes. Danny's hug lasted a little too long, she thought. She stepped out of the embrace without meeting his eyes. Meanwhile, Jack rattled off a few one-liners about his foot, including a bit about trying to get a shift at IHOP. Eliana groaned appropriately at the joke, smiled—then finally they were gone.

Alone, relieved—she texted Savoyian. Said she could be at his place by midnight. Not sure why she picked that time, but knew she needed to see him as soon as possible. She also needed to lie down for an hour or so.

He responded immediately: *Midnight perfect. I love traveling at night. Bring your off-duty weapon, your cuff, and comfortable shoes. We're driving to the Catskill Mountains. I will make everything clear.*

Oh god, she thought. *More driving, tonight?* Exhausted, she lowered her phone, felt a weakness in her hands, and experienced a sudden need to sit. She sank down on the couch and looked across her small living room at the empty bottles on the kitchen table. The faint, musky masculine odors of Danny and Jack lingered, mixed with the smell of beer and nuts and that freshly sliced melon.

Sleep—that's what she needed. Especially with more driving ahead. So she took off her pants and changed into a fresh T-shirt, then crawled into bed. But her mind raced and, like a song stuck in her head, she kept hearing Char's whispered words... *I'll kill him myself—I don't care about going to jail. I still want justice, you know... I still want it for Dad...*

After lying down, thoughts and images immediately flooded her head. She was thinking about what it's like to kill. It's what cops are trained to do. And she'd done it—once. Performed her duty and afterwards—well, for those who've never experienced killing, they're like virgins wondering if porn movies are realistic. But the analogy goes only so far, Eliana thought, because killing involves an act of such intensity that it makes sex seem as banal as eating a meal.

"JoAnne Woods."

Eliana said the name out loud softly to herself while lying there in bed waiting for sleep. JoAnne Woods was the woman Eliana killed. An EDP. Symptoms similar to Char at her worst, JoAnne Woods did not "deserve" to die, not exactly. Still, in the jargon of police work, it was a "good shoot."

Eliana had been on the job two years and put out the word: she wanted to learn. From the street, from the perps, the hard way. She went looking for it—asked for a transfer to the Four-Four, a "busy house" in the Bronx. She suffered two concussions and a broken wrist—all three injuries sustained on domestic violence jobs. And still she hungered for more. High-risk patrol calls, that's what she wanted. And, with Danny's help (actually, Danny's father), she sweet-talked her way into a special city-wide Warrant Squad, knocking on doors at dawn.

The night she shot JoAnne Woods, she'd been riding with a pimply-faced detective named Oliver Shaw. A big fat fuck-up, famous for his family connections, he bounced from precinct to precinct for reasons unknown. Everyone hated him. Constantly smelled, carried a bag of French fries wherever he went, filling the air around him with greasy burps. He also possessed a rare gift for obnoxious humor. The previous week he and Eliana had taken a warrant with a woman's name on it, and on the way out of the station house, Shaw stepped up to the desk sergeant, "We've got a situation here, Sarge. Judging by the name on this warrant, the perp's got a vagina. I think she's going to need special care."

The desk sergeant didn't even look up. "That's not even a tiny bit funny, Shaw. But I know your routine. You're just the man for the job, right? A real dick. Get the fuck outta my face. If it weren't for your uncles, you'd have lost your shield and had your ass kicked a long time ago."

Cop culture at its worst. No reaction from Eliana. She pretended to be looking at her phone. Never let station house bullshit bother you. The art of ignoring others—a power all its own.

But five nights later, she and her obnoxious partner caught another female warrant—for JoAnne Woods—and Eliana felt determined to take charge. Maybe Shaw bothered her more than she admitted. The way he talked about women—some cops ought to be fired just for the shit that comes out of their mouths.

Not that Eliana embraced political correctness, especially "gender sensitivity." She had long ago accepted having to prove herself in the male-dominated cop-world—and so prove herself she did. Plenty. By this time, she'd made over forty good arrests, including some hyper-macho guys: a steroid-using weight lifter, a Thai judo expert, and a six-foot- six Golden Gloves boxer, which made Danny roll his eyes. Boxers don't know shit, he reminded her. She'd also arrested PCP freaks, bikers, abusive husbands, crazy wives, angry boyfriends, out-of-control girlfriends, and—well, by now, she'd come to love that special cop moment: the "click-click" of cuffs. Protect the good people from the bad. Or as Jack liked to put it, get the assholes off the street.

And warrants—she was learning. Fast. Talked it over with Danny, who helped her develop a nice smooth "knock and notice" rhythm. Keep it straight and simple. Tell 'em who you are, waive the warrant, and say the magic words: "You're under arrest."

Then, wait. Cuffs—quarter inch out of the case—ready, but concealed.

Whatever you do, Danny explained, do not show your cuffs until the subject has turned around and brought their hands behind their back, palms up.

Most people followed directions. They opened their door, listened, and—nice and easy, no trouble. That's why—well, the "Annual

Firearms Discharge Report" proved—yes, proved—police work's not like the cop shows. Eliana had argued with Livi and her mom, put the numbers in front of them, showed them that the previous year an NYPD-issued gun was fired only seventy-nine times. That's all, the total. Seventy-nine. Thirty-five thousand cops working three hundred and sixty-five days a year responding to 4.8 million radio calls—and a gun was fired only seventy-nine times. And that included eighteen dog attacks, and four cops committing suicide. Do the math, she argued, every cop carries a gun, but how many ever fire it?

But then came JoAnne Woods. The "knock and notice" that went wrong. The door didn't open, the subject didn't cooperate—and PO Eliana Golden became a statistic.

She sensed a problem right away. The home address and location of the crime didn't fit. Woods lived on Manhattan's Upper West Side, but the crime occurred in the Bronx, a mobbed-up karaoke lounge near Orchard Beach. And the charge—aggravated assault with a scissors. She failed to show for the court appearance. The lounge owner, it turned out, also owned the building in Manhattan.

So an hour-and-a-half into her graveyard shift, Eliana stood with Shaw in a brightly lit hallway at 910 West End Avenue, threatening to break down the door of apartment 4-E. Actually, that was Shaw's threat. Eliana knew they didn't have the right kind of warrant for that, but she didn't challenge Shaw's gold shield. Finally, after several minutes of pleading, a three-hundred-pound white female with a sheen of sweat on her skin opened the door. Naked, smelling like spoiled cheese—she stood there grinning.

Classic, totally obvious, no hidden post-traumatic-stress-disorder here. A straight-up EDP. Eliana knew what to do: avoid confrontational behavior; be empathic; do not try to intimidate or frighten. Nothing new to Eliana. This woman was just like her baby sister at her worst.

"Are you JoAnne," Eliana asked, quietly, stuffing the warrant in her back pocket. No need to wave this around.

JoAnne nodded quickly and threw open the door, creating a draft, a rotten smell as thick as smoke. She stood looking at them bug-eyed, motioning to come inside, as if they were guests she'd been expecting. But neither Eliana nor Shaw followed into the kitchen.

"We should put this over the air," Shaw said quietly. "Get a bus and a boss."

"Just hold on," Eliana said, annoyed. "So far, we got unarmed and nonviolent. And we didn't even ask if she's willing to leave voluntarily."

"Yeah, well, just look at her—this could get messy fast."

"She needs a hospital, not a cell."

Eliana went first, enjoying a certain take-charge feeling, a sense of inside knowledge because of her experience with Char. She stepped into the kitchen. Brightly lit, a naked bulb hung from a socket in the ceiling. The white tile floor showed stains of yellow and brown. That explained the smell.

"How are you doing' tonight?" Eliana said, and heard her partner start to cough. "JoAnne Wood, right?"

"Yes, I am Jo—but it's Woods, with an s.' Very nice to meet you. Officer...?" She leaned forward, trying to read Eliana's name.

Her voice was an absurd falsetto, a symptom of meth hallucinations, Eliana knew. She spotted meds on the kitchen table and stepped around the big woman to look at the labels: *10 mg/d of haloperidol; 4 mg/d of biperiden.* Sure enough, treatment for amphetamine-induced psychotic disorder.

"Golden, I'm Officer Golden. How about putting on some clothes, OK? Then we can go for a ride. I want to take you to a doctor. You haven't been taking your medicine, have you?"

No mention of being under arrest. And the tone in Eliana's voice—as if she were inviting this woman out for tea. "JoAnne, have you been taking your medicine?" Again, no answer, so louder: "We're going to take you to a doctor, OK, who will help you take your medicine. First thing, though, is to put on some clothes."

"No thank you," said JoAnne Woods. "I don't like hospitals, and I don't like doctors, and I don't like police stations, either, if that's what you're thinking. And another thing: I'm happy to be naked because I'm protesting that women's reproductive rights are under assault. There is an ongoing attack on immigrants, too." Her words slurred a little, and that high-pitched falsetto made it difficult to understand her, but she continued with a burst of energy. "It's not just immigrants and women—it's everything. Democracy has withered under the emergence of a national security and permanent warfare state. Not only endless wars abroad, but also in the passing of a series of laws such as the Patriot Act, the Military Commission Act, the National Defense Authorization Act, and many other laws that shred due process and give the executive branch the right to hold prisoners indefinitely without charge or a trial."

The smell, the rant, the sheer size of the woman—reason to be alert, to take precautions. But Eliana knew the drill: assess and evaluate. As long as the EDP constituted no threat—to herself or others—no problem. If she refused to leave voluntarily...? Extra cuffs, maybe. The sheer girth of the woman's chest. One pair would dislocate a shoulder. But excessive danger? A call for EMS? Not needed, or so Eliana thought.

Meanwhile, JoAnne Woods paced back and forth, her enormous bare breasts swaying, her crazy falsetto rising higher and higher, as if she were singing a children's song. "Warrantless, warrantless, warrantless. Warrantless wiretaps are just the tip of the iceberg, you now? Because the president of the United States keeps a kill list and claims the right to murder any citizen considered to be a terrorist." She reached onto the table for an article she'd cut from the newspaper. Eliana glanced at the headline: SECRET 'KILL LIST' PROVES A TEST OF OBAMA'S PRINCIPLES AND WILL.

"You see? You see?" JoAnne Woods' voice dropped, and she lowered her head, like a bull about to charge. Eliana stepped back—distance equals safety. But the kitchen was narrow, about five feet wide. Maybe Shaw was right—this could get messy fast. But JoAnne didn't move. She just stood there, head lowered, her chin disappearing into the fat spread of her enormous neck. A freak show—neck gone. Like a hog—nothing but eyes, snout, mouth. No neck.

"Targeted assassinations," JoAnne Woods went on, her voice now a mucous-filled whisper. "By our own government—frightening, yes? Don't you agree, Officer Golden?" Stepping forward, leaning close, one of JoAnne's giant bare breasts brushed against Eliana's arm. "Don't you? Don't you?"

The thick whisper, the awful stench—Eliana looked down and noted a crest of grimy dirt stuck in a crease of fat on JoAnne's thick neck. She moved to the side of the big woman, placed a hand on her elbow. The skin felt moist. *Control the situation*, she thought. But then realized that she'd been listening to the substance of this woman's rant. A mistake. She'd let this crazy woman close the distance. JoAnne Woods was standing way too close. But Eliana was thinking: *the United States does have a kill list, doesn't it? Targeted assassinations—they are awful, aren't they? And her own father, was he—?*

"Drones are killing innocent people every day!" JoAnne yelped, her high-pitched voice cracking.

Eliana's partner stepped up. "Ma'am, let's talk about this when we get to the hospital, OK?"

Pimply-faced Shaw—when Eliana heard his voice, she snapped out of it. Embarrassed—she hoped Shaw hadn't noticed her distraction. Listen and maintain empathy, yes. Do not challenge EDP's perceptions, yes. But interact using your grounded sense of reality. And distance— always keep your distance. Distance equals safety.

"We need you to put on some clothes," Eliana said quickly, trying for a measure of authority in her voice. But it sounded weak.

JoAnne Woods just stood staring at the floor. A moment passed. Then another. A stalemate. An eerie silence. Nothing now but the sound of this huge naked woman's shallow breathing—and the awful, spoiled cheese stench. Then Shaw said something under his breath, and

Eliana heard his equipment belt jingling, his shoes squeaking.

That's when Eliana saw JoAnne's bare shoulders rise, and the enormous woman took a deep breath. Then she started to sing: *"Row, row, row your boat... gently down the stream... Warrantless, warrantless, warrantless, warrantless... life is but a dream."*

"We have a warrant," Eliana said loudly, whipping the document out of her back pocket. But JoAnne had begun to waddle down the hall toward a bedroom in the back. Rolls of jiggling flesh, her wide round buttocks shook in a strange rhythmic synchrony to the sound of the duck-walk, her feet slapping the floor. Eliana watched this so closely that—something strange, it gave her another spacey, distracted, uncertain feeling. Why? Her sympathy for JoAnne right now—it was inappropriate. It was all about Char. But—The Job. She needed to stay focused. Follow the patrol guide. *"Mentally ill or Emotionally Disturbed Persons will be instituted. Once in custody the subject will be removed to a hospital for examination. Once cleared for release by mental health professionals, they should be arrested, charged with the crimes involved, and taken to court for criminal proceedings."*

That's how it works, Eliana thought. Patrol Guide Procedure 216-05. And that's what will happen. One way or the other, the team in Blue always wins. But this woman's rant, the politics, the connection to Char—Eliana needed to clear her mind. She took a breath, then started down the hall, slipping her cuffs a quarter inch out of their case, at-the-ready, Danny's tip. Cuffs ready. Just get this done, Eliana told herself, and started down the cluttered hallway, stepping past a stack of newspapers and magazines. The floor was a natural hardwood—shiny, expensive. It looked familiar. Another distraction. In her own mother's house? Same floors? That's the incongruity. The socioeconomics. Wealthy people on the Upper West Side don't have problems like this. And nice Jewish girls from Teaneck don't join the NYPD.

Yeah, right.

JoAnne kept singing—*"Life is but a dream..."*

Eliana kept moving. Slowly, slowly, down the long narrow hall, she stepped over a pile of unfolded clothes—underwear, socks, enormous bras—then she brushed the wheel of a dusty bicycle leaning against the wall. Behind her, Shaw followed. "Would love to see her ride this," he said, and muffled a laugh. "Picture of fitness here, huh? I just called it in."

"Still un-armed and non-violent," Eliana said. "Let's see if she'll let me cuff her."

"Ask once—then it's over. The boys will be here any minute."

Eliana stopped at the bedroom and watched JoAnne Woods disappear into a large closet, shutting the door behind her. Inside the closet? Did she just let her EDP go inside a—? Major fuckup. An oh-shit moment. Whatever you can't see through, inside of, or around—that's a threat. Why cops hate cars with tinted windows. But Eliana was *no longer a rookie*—she knew better.

It was an error she'd relive in her mind a million times. And what came next: Eliana stood there frozen in place while hearing the unmistakable sound of metal-sliding-over-metal. And she visualized it perfectly: the guns cartridges—bullets—JoAnne pushing the magazine upward into the hand grip, the click indicating its locked into place; then, quietly, the safety lever disengaging, one fat finger pushing downward.

It was a 9 mm Ruger SR9 being prepared for discharge.

And at some level Eliana knew it was absurd, but she couldn't stop herself from yelling: "JoAnne, stop loading that gun! Stop it, JoAnne. Stop it right now!" But it was too late, and Eliana continued to picture it: this naked methed-up out-of-control woman's sweaty hand rising, then pulling the back-slide on top of the barrel—the last step. A bullet had loaded into the firing chamber, and JoAnne Woods was done. Nothing left to do but point and shoot.

Still Eliana did nothing but shout. "Stop it, JoAnne. Stop it! Put down the gun!"

Then the closet door opened a crack, and the barrel slipped through and Shaw screamed "GUN!" and dove forward, hitting Eliana hard at the knees. They fell to the floor with a thud.

The unexpectedness of an attack negates nearly all skill. Later, Eliana would try to work through what happened and think about this. Danny's main point, his criticism of her work in the martial arts. You psych up for training, for competition. You learn breathing techniques, kick-punch combinations, wrist-lock throws—but when facing live fire...?

The first shot made two distinct noises—a blast, then a ping—then the bullet struck the fleshy part of Eliana's thigh. The sharp, stinging pain felt nothing like the dull ocean roar of a martial arts punch. What she'd trained for—yes, useless, as Danny predicted. Wincing, she wanted to curl over the point of impact—and to see it. How badly was she bleeding? She wanted to know. She smelled it, the blood. And that alone froze her. Her blood smelled strangely metallic, she thought. Then she struggled with the intrusion of irrelevant thoughts. Danny had warned her about this, too. She sat there bleeding and thinking about the smell of menstrual blood. Because menstrual blood—well, it's different, right? Not like blood from your teeth or your nose or—what about the blood of a killed dog or run-over cat or—what's that smell?

The mind runs its own way. Danny had told her about the first time he took out his weapon—during a car stop of a stolen vehicle—he felt the gun in his hand and suddenly became obsessed with trying to remember the lyrics to the song "Autumn in New York." The chemical cocktail of stress: the trigger, the effect, it's an unknown combination. Rock climbing differs from public speaking; bourbon differs from wine. And deadly force—it's like nothing else. Unless you've been there, you don't understand.

Hands trembling, mouth dry, knees shaking—they say cops on the street have a miss percentage of 83 percent at three to seven yards. On the firing range—another story. On the range, Eliana boasted 99 percent-plus accuracy.

But right now she could not even make a fist, let alone pull out her gun, aim, and fire. Her legs and arms felt weak, cold, clumsy. The threat—JoAnne Woods—was only five feet away, directly across from her in this tiny bedroom. But the cracked-open closet door, with the black barrel of the gun poking through, appeared as if it were down a forty-foot corridor. Tunnel vision. A perceptual distortion resulting from blood pooled in the internal organs, drawn away from the limbs, the brain. Not just her vision, but her hearing too. The sound of Shaw shouting into his radio—"4-4 Adam! 10-13! 10-13! Shots fired! Officer down! Nine-one-zero West End Ave, 4th floor, shots fired, officer down! Send a bus, officer down, repeat: 10-13 nine-one-zero West End Ave."

He pulled a night table to the floor for cover as JoAnne squeezed off another round. A muffled blast, it sounded—to Eliana—as if it came from underwater.

Vision distorted, hearing turned-off—Eliana remained locked in the mental loop of irrelevance, distracted now by a vivid memory: two kids playing cops-and-robbers on a playground. From her childhood, Teaneck, during Purim—the Jewish Halloween. That's what she called it when she was a kid. In the memory she sits on a bench with her father watching two little boys run around the playground. One wears a black cape; the other a police costume. Squirt guns, hiding behind the slide, ducking under the climbing gym. Finally, the bad guy, the crook in the cape, gets sprayed by the water gun, and the kid in the police costume yells, "Hey, you got shot. You're dead." But the bad guy ignores him and climbs to the top of the slide. Then he unloads his squirt gun on his little friend the cop, who stands there getting soaked, protesting, "Hey! No fair! I shot you—you're already dead!" But the caped perp just keeps shooting until, finally, the nice little kid playing cop does what nice little kids do: he follows the rules. He yells out, "Aaah, ya got me!" And staggers, then curls up, and dies. Right—cops follow the rules. If you shoot them, they die.

The memory passed quickly and with it the freeze, the blur, the loop of irrelevant thought swerved into the light of a strangely clear question: *Am I going to die? Right now?*

Eliana snapped out of it. Crippling stress—gone. In its place: the optimal stage of adrenalization. Studies, heart rate research—she'd read about it, how sometimes a "sweet spot" emerges, the just-right level of stress hormone in the blood to produce an ideal heart-rate of 115-145 beats per minute in which reaction time and fighting skills are maximized. Danny's cynical line, of course: knowing this little medical fact won't help you. But it did. Ah, finally, Danny proved wrong about something. She'd found it. The sweet spot. On her game. Alert, ready.

She reached for her gun. Shoot to kill? No, the line is shoot to stop. And the training is aim center mass; subdue the threat; control the situation. Once her mind had cleared, her actions came automatically. Step one was to release the socket and stud snap on her holster. She'd practiced this hundreds of times, how to press on the plastic hood and rotate it forward, like a safety cap on a medicine bottle. That's what it reminded her of. Push and rotate, two motions, separate and distinct. Then came step two, quick-and-easy, her pointer finger slid out, up, and into palm, perfect position, pointer off the trigger, resting on the side of the barrel. Easy, smooth. Her favorite training wisdom one-liner: slow is smooth, smooth is fast.

The whole sequence—drawing, aiming, firing—took Eliana less than two seconds. Just like she'd trained. And trained and trained. One, two. And it worked: she pulled the trigger and fired a bullet and saw flesh erupt in a little volcano of blood and meat. She'd shot the only bare patch of skin she saw—JoAnne's thick thigh. Looking over her pistol sight, the whole visual field turned red. Bright red—not trickling or flowing but gushing, surging, blood being forcefully and steadily pumped through a small black hole in a fat white leg.

The femoral artery, the main blood supply to the lower limbs, is a continuation of the iliac artery—Eliana had hit it directly. And she knew it. She also knew that arteries are sphincter-like muscles designed to contract and close off. But if the bullet hit at an angle—fired from the floor—the artery might not close. In that case, consciousness would be lost in about thirty seconds. In three minutes—death.

She panicked. Oblivious to her own bloody leg Eliana crawled to the closet as fast as possible, but Shaw got there first. "Pressure on the wound," she screamed and grabbed a belt on the floor of the closet, "tie off the leg. Tighter, Shaw, tie it tighter!"—at one point Eliana heard herself shouting not just at her partner but at JoAnne Woods too. "Don't you die, goddammit! Don't you dare die!"

But it didn't work, and slowly Eliana became aware that she was pushing with all her weight on the bloody leg of a fat corpse. A wave of nausea overtook her. She turned away, leaned into the wall, and vomited.

How much time passed—she didn't know. One minute, five, ten? She couldn't control her stomach. "Jesus Christ," Shaw said, still leaning over the bloody body of JoAnne Woods. "She's dead—she's fucking dead." Then: "I hear the B's downstairs—can you pull yourself together?"

The B's: the bus, the boys, the boss. Ambulance, Emergency Services, a Sergeant. Eliana nodded, wiping her mouth, trying to clear away the dripping vomit. What had she last eaten? Rice and beans, yes, Spanish style, with red pepper. Those little blood-colored chunks—not the torn-up inside of her stomach, no. Just pieces of jalapeno.

She spit. Over and over again, phlegm, mouthfuls of it, she barely noticed that Shaw had crouched next to her, his hands all over her thigh, pressing on her wound. How long had he been doing that? "Lucky she didn't get you where you got her," he said. "You hit the fat lady's fountain there."

"Yeah." Eliana looked over her shoulder at the body, half-expecting it to be deflated, flattened like in a cartoon.

The cavalry had arrived. Radios crackling, boots stomping, the ESU team swarming. Soon Eliana felt Jack Bayer's presence. The Big Bear, his broad shoulders, thick arms, legs the size of tree trunks. She heard his knees crack as he crouched next to her.

"You OK?" he spoke quietly, leaning close. His aftershave mixed crazily with the smell of blood, gunfire, vomit.

"I'm fine, Sarge," Eliana said, then a blast of honesty: "But I feel like I want to cry, and I can't stop puking."

He nodded. "Perfectly normal." Then he put one of his huge hands on her shoulder and said it again, "Perfectly normal."

Eliana hadn't been bothered by the incident in years, but now—desperate for an hour of sleep before meeting Savoyian—these memories kept her awake. Shaw sanitized the report or there might have been disciplinary action, right? And regardless of the report, Eliana knew what really happened. A pointless death. JoAnne Woods didn't *need* to die. If Eliana had prevented her from getting to that closet—?

After Psych Services and all that, Danny, later that week, held her in his arms and said firmly, "Hey, leave this alone. That EDP fired on you first. You did nothing wrong."

But something grated now on Eliana's nerves. Like the noise of a distant yowl, an animal in pain, she couldn't turn it off, couldn't escape the ugly sound. Ah, the sound of a cat howling—that's what it was. Her neighbor from the building next door—crazy Mrs. Willis, an EDP in her own right—she'd begun feeding stray cats, leaving saucers of milk on the front step of her little one-story ranch house. Eliana had asked her to stop. Explained that the cats are going to start coming around looking for food. That crazy old lady, a hunched-over, raccoon-like creature always bundled in mysterious layers of extra clothing, she smiled and nodded—but didn't stop. A lunatic—last summer, she let her son and a bunch of his friends paint her house bright yellow.

Identifying the sound of the cat helped Eliana feel more settled. She looked at her clock: 22:30. She could still get some sleep before going to Savoyian's. If she could only block out the meows. Tactical breathing: inhale, two, three, four, pause; exhale, two, three, four, pause. It didn't help. The cat meow. A groan. Strangely human sounding. Had JoAnne Woods groaned like that before dying?

She climbed out of bed. The goddamn cat—she'd bring it food. Anything to shut off that crazy sick human-sounding meow.

She went to the kitchen and poured a saucer of milk. Then, outside, carrying the small dish carefully with both hands, not a drip splashing, Eliana crossed the street to the bright yellow house. It looked dirty and dejected, the windows closed and dark. Was Mrs. Willis out of town again? That's great—leave me to care for the fucking hungry cats you've trained to come looking here for food. Or was it just one cat? Eliana looked around. She saw only one: a big orange cat crouching near the curb, holding its body low to the ground, its tail wrapped protectively around its feet. A surprisingly good-looking animal, Eliana thought, with a clean, well-kept coat and a big head. Also, a nice, thick neck. But no tags, so, yes, must be a stray.

"Here," Eliana said, "drink up and leave me in peace."

She set the bowl down on Mrs. Willis' front step, and almost immediately the cat scuttled forward with quick little steps and began to lap up the milk. The soft cluck of its tongue made Eliana chuckle, in spite of her annoyance. At one point, the cat paused and looked at her as if to say "What so funny?" Then went back to the milk.

Eliana started home, but before she reached the other side of the street, the meowing started again. She turned back, walked up to the bowl. Empty. The cat stood there, mouth barely open, but somehow still producing the horrible moan. What—more? Bringing more milk seemed ridiculous. In fact, the whole situation seemed ridiculous, and Eliana wished she'd not come outside at all. But the sound of this meowing—?

Noise. That's what this was: a "noise disturbance." And something clicked, a nervous feeling passing over Eliana, an uncomfortable chill. Like any cop with patrol experience, she knew—from countless radio runs—noise makes people crazy. In fact, it's one of the leading reasons people call the police: noisy neighbors. Most cops hate responding to these calls—although, of course, not Danny. Quality of life policing—he believes in it. A quiet neighborhood is a peaceful neighborhood. One of his lines, a pet peeve. Ah, nice pun, Eliana thought now: *pet peeve.*

On impulse, she bent down and petted the cat. Maybe if she moved it to the side of the house, then it would just leave or stop the loud meowing. She started feeling around for the scruff of its neck. Not that she knew how to do this, not really. She drew on vague images of mother-cats carrying their kittens this way. How hard can it be? She placed her hand at the back of the cat's neck, grabbing the folds of loose skin, then she lifted. The cat's eyes widened, its ears flapping backward. No struggle, not at first. In fact, the cat became very still, almost as if it had been stunned. Its paws and hind-legs froze in position, sticking straight out. But then, out of nowhere, came a fierce hiss, head swiveling, hind legs kicking, and the cat twisted backward, sinking its teeth into Eliana's left forearm. She let go of the cat's neck, tried to drop it, but the teeth had penetrated so deeply that the animal hung there, clamped onto Eliana's arm by the sheer force of its bite. Then instinct took over—Eliana's instinct. She used her free right hand to grab the cat by its throat, and she squeezed. It took a moment, but the cat's mouth loosened, and Eliana lifted it away from her forearm to see four small puncture marks in her skin, one for each of the long, pointy teeth. Blood oozed from the dark little holes, and the stinging pain felt remarkably sharp and deep.

Of course, she could have let go now, could have released her grip on the cat's throat and let the animal drop to the ground. The danger had passed. The attack was over. But she didn't let go. She squeezed harder. The cat wriggled, its front paws trying to scratch the hand holding it. But Eliana hung on, squeezing harder. Until the cat's eyes bulged. Then the pressure on its neck forced its mouth to open, and its little pink tongue stuck straight out—stiff, traces of white milk swirling in the tongue's grainy pattern. And then Eliana squeezed harder. And harder. Life remained in the animal. Cutting off blood to the brain takes time. Cops learn about chokeholds—legal by NY State Penal Codes, illegal by NYPD policy. But, in fact, right now Eliana had no sense of choking technique. She was just squeezing as hard as she could, rotating her hand slightly, feeling the tiny bones in the cat's neck twist and break like little twigs cracking off a branch. Then, finally, the cats bulging eyes turned a damp, golden red, and its body convulsed in one last spasm—front paws and hind-legs jerking wildly. And it was done.

She'd killed the animal—a pointless, utterly senseless act of violence. What began as an effort to help turned into... what? She heard

Char's voice, the accusation: you're more cop than sister. And the twisted logic of revenge, how Char had said: I still want justice, you know... I still want it for Dad... So if you find the guy who killed dad. I'll kill him myself. I don't mind going to jail. I'll choke him to death. I could do that, you know. I have very strong hands—very strong hands.

This is all crazy, Eliana thought, but she couldn't slow her thoughts. Violence works. It obviously works. Like Danny once said, *Fuck the Hollywood crap. Movie characters need tortured reasons and justifications for their behavior, but real criminals, perps, assholes—they use violence because it's the most efficient way to get what they want.* The cat was bothering me so...

But, of course, she'd not meant to be violent. She'd not meant to kill the cat. She was no killer. She'd meant to help the animal. She'd fed it! Just quiet the damn cat, that's all she'd wanted to do. Solve a problem. But then—*how?*—she didn't mean—suddenly—*why* had she—? A murderer. She'd taken an innocent life. But, no, she thought, that's not me. I'm not a murderer. I'm a cop! But if she found the man who killed her father, that man wouldn't be innocent—killing *that man* would be justified.

Eliana felt her muscles tighten, her pulse racing. She breathed. Control the heart rate, control the stress. Yes, she told herself to breathe, and with each breath she calmed. Her mind quieted. What's done is done, she thought. What matters is now. Cops learn this—deal with the problem in front of you. Everything else... distraction.

She held the dead cat straight out in front of her—stiff. It looked like a big stuffed animal, but heavier. She'd broken the law. That's what she needed to deal with right now. Cruelty to animals—a misdemeanor, a one plus one. Thousand dollar fine, plus one year max in jail. But this—it could be considered "aggravated cruelty," couldn't it? A felony. She'd had a case once, went to court. "...*Cruelty with no justifiable purpose, such as the intentional killing or causing of serious physical injury to a companion animal....* "A five plus five.

The thought chilled her. Physically—although the summer night air was warm, a cold dampness penetrated her whole body, and she began to shiver. She brought the dead animal close to her chest, as if it were alive, as if it could warm her. Then she looked around the crime scene. That's what it was, really: a crime scene. She bent down and picked up the empty bowl—evidence. Then she checked for drops of blood from her wound. She looked at the ground. Where she stood, on the patch of sidewalk in front of the steps of the yellow house, a portion of the cement had buckled and cracked, leaving a black line like a small, crooked scar. The dirt showed. A few tiny weeds grew. But no blood, not a drop anywhere. She looked at her wrist. The cat bite oozed, but it didn't drip blood. That was lucky. It hurt like hell, but—no blood. Yes, very lucky. And she realized that—without even trying—she'd become totally calm and alert. Tactical breathing, situational awareness. Her training had kicked in. Good cops—the truth is—depend on this, more important, perhaps, than anything else in their lives: good training.

And it worked, thank god. Eliana looked both ways now, scanning the quiet block—no witnesses. More good luck. She crossed the street. Calmly, slowly, carrying the dead cat in her arms. Yes, she understood. She felt in control. She knew exactly what needed to happen. Hide the body.

Chapter 27

They drove in silence. Two hours, no radio, not a word. Silence and the summer darkness. Pointless to ask questions, Eliana thought. What he knows, I'll know—when he chooses to tell me.

That's what Eliana had decided. No playing detective with Savoyian, no interrogating. All that felt irrelevant. Nothing mattered but this unlit stretch of Route 17—the darkness. It soothed. In daylight, this part of the highway—a two-lane section at the northern tip of the county's Black Dirt Region—offered river views, rolling hills, sprawling vistas. And there were apple orchards not far off this highway, which brought back memories. Her whole family, before her father's disappearance, used to drive out here to pick apples for *Rosh Hashana*—the Jewish New Year. They'd spend the day at the orchard and return home with baskets for their synagogue. The tradition called for apples dipped in honey, and every year her father's line was the same: "Ah, fresh apples—a fresh start. May it be a sweet, sweet year, indeed!"

Indeed.

A funny word. A word of emphasis, a word used to amplify something that's true. Her father was like that, she thought. Not an original thinker, not a creator of new meanings, but a man who wanted to emphasize what's true, what's already there. "Our tradition," he once said, "contains such wisdom it boggles the mind. When I feel lost and confused—I like to remind myself: the tradition *knows*, I'm the ignorant one. The way forward is always there—it's that sometimes I find it difficult to see."

The way forward, right. Or forward and backward. North this morning to the hospital, then South back home, and now North again, upstate to the Catskills—her eighth hour on the road. No wonder Eliana's head swam, the double yellow line occasionally rising off the pavement, coming at her like a wave. But she insisted on being the one to drive. Savoyian offered. When he first got into the car, he'd been absurdly friendly, chatty, asking about her gun and cuffs and entering an address into the GPS as if they were a young couple going off on a holiday. He said nothing about being drugged or the journals or anything. He'd brought a small navy-blue gym bag bulging with notepads. And did he have a weapon? She wondered about that. Her Bersa 9mm was strapped to her ankle.

"Midnight," he announced, "no traffic, no worries. I've brought some things to read aloud." And he pulled out a large metal flashlight, like the ones cops use on foot patrol, heavy, thick. It doubles as a perfectly effective nightstick. Savoyian leaned forward, clicking the heavy flashlight on-and-off, smiling, as if he'd invented this clever piece of technology.

Eliana didn't laugh, but she felt relaxed, more or less, considering the crazy stress. It had taken much longer than she'd expected to wrap the dead cat. She'd wanted to put the cat inside one of those extra thick plastic garbage bags like the kind used by contractors to haul trash— but she didn't have any of those bags. Almost went to the store to buy some, but leaving the dead cat alone in the apartment didn't feel right. When she started to lay the animal in the bathtub, seeing it there in the empty white basin gave her such a creepy feeling that she decided to skip the heavy bags. Instead, she just put the cat down in the center of the living room rug on a beach towel and tore a bunch of small plastic bags into strips, then wrapped and taped and wrapped and taped until the dead animal resembled an odd-sized package prepared for shipping. Actually, it was prepared for burning. She stuck the package in a corner of the car's trunk. She'd find an incinerator somewhere upstate and badge her way thru, explaining as little as possible, then toss the cat and be done with it.

The flashlight now clicked on. After such a long stretch of silence, the sound startled her. Then a rustle of pages. She glanced sideways at Savoyian hunched over, shining the single beam of light into his bag. Then he pulled out a notebook, sat back, cleared his throat, and read:

It is the existence of the victim's pain and loss—echoing forever in the soul of the killer—that is at the heart of the killer's own enduring pain.

He folded over the page, clicked off the flashlight, and looked out the window. A long moment of silence, then: "Have you killed anyone, Eliana?"

The question—its bluntness—threw her.

"Yes," she said, quietly. "I have killed." And waited.

He nodded, and she thought he'd ask for details. But instead, he said, That's unusual—for a cop, I mean. So few fire their weapons even once during their whole career."

Eliana nodded, grateful. Hardly anyone, except other cops, understood this. Not her family, that's for sure.

"I remember my shock at learning most soldiers don't fire their weapons either," Savoyian continued, "even in the middle of combat."

"That's true?"

"Oh, yes, very true," he said, with a little cough and a laugh. But then he quieted and turned again to look out the window, almost pressing his face against the glass. He mumbled, "A new field of study, so to speak: killology."

"What?" Eliana strained to hear him.

"Killology," he said louder, but still not turning to look at her. "The scholarly examination of '*the factors that enable and restrain killing*. 'Lt. Col. Dave Grossman, former Army ranger, psychology professor at West Point." Eliana remained quiet, her eyes on the road.

"Out of every hundred soldiers in a firefight," Savoyian continued, returning to a mumble, "only fifteen to twenty actually discharge their weapon. Pathetic."

"I can't hear you."

Savoyian turned his head slightly. "You'd think, hey, this is war—soldiers fight, right? They should all be shooting, every single one of them. But—no. Most soldiers don't shoot. Only about twenty percent are natural killers. The rest—well, it's World War II data. The numbers are a little higher now. At least that's what the research shows."

Eliana felt herself drawn into this more deeply than she wanted to be. The suggestion that soldiers don't easily kill—?

"The eighty percent—it's *not* like they panic and run," Savoyian went on. "They're willing to risk their lives. They'll rescue, get ammunition, run messages—they just won't fire their weapons at the enemy, even when the enemy is firing at them." He paused, then turned to her. "Does that surprise you?"

"Yes. Or, no. I guess not, in a way. Killing is hard. Most people can't do it, I guess."

"Right, except that's not true either. In fact, with the proper conditioning and the proper circumstances, almost anyone can—and will—kill."

Savoyian turned away again, lowering his chin, crossing his arms over his chest, folding into himself. He let his notebook slide off his lap onto the floor of the car. Then he turned away again, staring out the window. Eliana looked closely at him, taking her eyes off the road. He swallowed hard, and she noted the protruding lump of his large Adam's apple. Something about the particular angle of his neck, combined with the dim greenish light from the car's dashboard—it made his throat look thin, unhealthy, vulnerable. She flashed again on the feeling of squeezing the life out of the cat, the small bones in its throat cracking like twigs. What had she done? Now she swallowed hard, fighting the feeling of guilt tightening her own throat. Then she felt the cat bite on her left arm. It ached—throbbed, if she focused on it. An infection spreading, no doubt.

"The truth is," Savoyian went on, still looking out the window, "the history of warfare is the history of creating better killers. More effective mechanisms for enabling and conditioning men—and now its women too, of course—to overcome their innate resistance to killing their fellow human beings."

His head remained turned away from her, and he gave off a distinct feeling of defeat. Until now, she realized, his dark intensity always contained a twinge of bravado, a subtle hint of pride in his own understanding, as if he wanted to say: *I've studied. I've contemplated—I know something important!* But now his head leaned into the car window; his shoulders sagged; his mouth hung partly open. And all this transmitted something else, Eliana thought. A broken man, beaten. Glancing back and forth at him as she drove, she experienced a weird desire to push back, to urge him *not* to surrender to his despair, but to fight back.

"You mean, we're getting better, then? Better soldiers."

"Sure," he answered without moving a muscle. "You could put it that way. Better technology, better soldiers—better at killing." His voice sounded tired.

Eliana again felt a desire to—what? Cheer him up? Slap him on the back like she sometimes saw the guys in the station house do at the end of a tough tour? Shake it off, buddy...

"Better training all around, you mean," she said.

"Conditioning, I prefer to call it," Savoyian went on, his voice barely audible, almost as bad as Char's anxious whisper, Eliana thought.

"A soldier can be dazed and exhausted and almost completely unable to function, but still do precisely what is expected—if it has become automatic enough."

Somehow all this now made Eliana feel accused. Strangely, wrongfully accused. The killing of JoAnne Woods—yes, her training had, indeed, kicked in automatically. But no cops could do their job—hell, none of us could live our lives—without this carefully cultivated capacity to focus on the task at hand. Call it "conditioning," fine. Call it whatever you want, she thought, straining to contain a gnawing feeling of anger.

She accelerated, pushing eighty miles per hour. They drove again in silence, Savoyian gazing out the window, motionless. Like a dead man, Eliana thought, angrily. She disliked—no, hated—the unfinished feeling of the conversation. Finally, she said, "Well, if our soldiers are getting better, that's bad news for the enemy, right?" Her voice was louder than she'd intended.

"The enemy?" Savoyian answered quickly, coming to life, snapping his head toward her. She felt him staring, and so she turned and met his eyes. Bloodshot, dark, but glaring with intensity—a sneer of contempt. She tried to look away, but couldn't. His eyes held her. She didn't notice the car drift over the double-yellow line. Neither of them noticed. The road was empty, no oncoming traffic. Then, suddenly, the distant glare of a truck blasted their faces with white light. She jerked the steering wheel back, pulling the car into its lane. Then she focused straight ahead. The truck passed. Savoyian hadn't flinched.

"I have been involved in disrupting forty-seven terrorist plots since 9/11," he began, his voice steady. "And there were others before then. Abu Khabbab al Misri, Emerson, Winfield Begolly, Manssor Arbabsiar, an Iranian-born U.S. citizen—I could list them all. Chemical weapons that were discovered, explosives about to be shipped, crates of automatic rifles ready for distribution; and the deals involved not just holy warriors perverting the peace of Islam, but drug cartels, greedy businessmen, and, of course, angry lone wolves..."

His voice trailed off, but he took a breath and continued, "Do you believe there's such a thing as an innocent American?"

"Of course," she said quickly. "There are innocent people all over the world. Most people. Most people are basically good and innocent and—"

"I've saved them," he cut her off abruptly. "I've saved innocent lives. Countless innocent—"

He stopped and seemed to get flustered, rubbing his chin, then his nose, and then his ear, and then back again to his chin, a sudden nervous tic. "It's all the paradox of prevention," he said in a low voice, as if he were talking to himself. "Nobody would ever know what I do until I don't do it."

Eliana glanced at him from the corner of her eye as his voice trailed off in an angry swallow. "Our exit is coming up next," he said, very quietly. "We're close."

They drove through the Woodland Valley State Campground before winding onto an unpaved service road taking them deeper into the thick dark forest. Savoyian motioned, pointed, saying almost nothing but an occasional "turn, here." Soon they were off the road, squeezing down trails, passing signs with icons of green tents and the words printed in white block letters: "CAMP HERE." But they went further, creeping slowly, moving deeper into the darkness, inching down the trails meant for hikers, not cars. Branches hung in front of the dash, scraped the side windows. Still, Savoyian pointed, grunted, and they didn't stop until, finally, Eliana felt the car wedged between two trees and a bank of thick bushes. A feeling of claustrophobia spread across her chest and back.

"OK," Savoyian said. "This will do."

Eliana put the car in park and turned off the engine. Total darkness. But it lasted only a moment, then Savoyian opened the passenger door, activating the car's inside light. Without a word, he got out. Took his gym bag with him. Eliana got out too, and when she closed her door, the darkness was again complete. They stood in silence. Eliana took a deep breath. An apple scent filled the cool, dry air. Or was it her imagination? The power of memory? She didn't know. She just stood there now waiting for her eyes to adjust. Trees lined the vista, the thick branches adding texture to the horizon. She looked through the trees to the sky beyond. Nothing but more darkness. The sky—a black bank of dark clouds. Then her vision blurred slightly, and she saw a path revealing itself, a small thin clearing going deeper into the dark woods. *This is where my father was killed?*

The thought made her shudder, but not with a chill. In fact, her body overheated suddenly, and she broke into a stress-induced sweat. Pinpricks of moisture stung her neck, face, under her eyes.

"He didn't suffer."

Savoyian said this as if she'd asked the question, but she hadn't said anything. Or had she? Her arm throbbed from the cat bite, and she felt impossibly tired.

"You mean my father?"

"Yes."

The sound of his voice hung in the darkness, and Eliana stood there, puzzled, trying to see his face. She leaned forward, straining. The darkness stabbed at her eyes. Squinting, she wiped away the stinging sweat, and leaned closer. Nothing but the shape of his head hung like a ghost in the thick darkness, his chin tucked, the features of his face impossible to see. Just then a gust of grassy-smelling wind distracted her, and she imagined millions of tiny pollen particles landing on her like 9/11 dust. *Not that again,* she feared. *Associations to 9/11? Please, not now. Not the burning-tower, not the falling buildings, not those crazy intrusive dream-images of disaster. Not in my head now, please.*

She felt helpless, the panicky feeling of claustrophobia increasing, and she started to cough, choking on a faint smell of fire buried in the breeze. Her imagination again? Burning towers? Or a campfire? It could be real, she thought. Someone, somewhere, someplace nearby— could be sitting around a campfire.

The thought calmed her. Clarify, divide, take one step at a time, and separate the elements, she thought: danger, and the fear of danger. Not the same thing. She found her voice.

"How do you know all this?"

"Drugged. And—he never woke."

Savoyian started to walk away, but Eliana grabbed him by the arm. She suddenly felt angry, impatient, and unsure of herself all at once—a terrible mix of emotions. "Tell me—more," she demanded. He shook his head, refusing, then started to turn away. "His work at the bank, right?" She tightened her grip just above his elbow. It reminded her of how only a couple hours earlier, she had used her bare hands to squeeze the life out of a cat. The memory made her shudder at the pure horror of it.

"The bank, yes," Savoyian said. "But there's more." He shook his elbow free with a hard tug, then clicked on his flashlight and started to walk. Eliana followed, stepping onto a spongy, narrow trail of dark earth. Her heart started to beat terribly. The flash of anger and uncertainty and the memory of the cat—*What am I doing here?* she thought. *What am I doing?*

They walked for several minutes in silence following no discernible path. The deeper into the darkness they travelled, the more Eliana felt layers of dead pine needles and twigs cracking softly under her feet. The sound reminded her again of choking the cat, breaking its small bones with her bare hand. Just a few hours ago that was? Hard to believe. Just then a gust of wind blew, rustling leaves, making a sound like water rushing. She looked up into the dark sky and thought she heard the tall trees creaking and groaning as if they too experienced some incomprehensible suffering.

Unsteady, her mind racing, she found herself now silently reciting a biblical passage—in Hebrew, English, back-and-forth, one of the Psalms, a fragment:

...But the Lord is my defense; and my God is the rock of my refuge. And He shall bring upon them their own iniquity, and shall cut them off in their own wickedness...

The verse didn't end there, she thought. Or did it? The ancient past, her Jewish life, a God of justice. She didn't believe, not really. But justice—her father died for justice. And JoAnne Woods—a good shot. An out-of-control EDP, right? She fired first. It was kill or be killed. Justice? But the cat—the senseless cruelty of killing the cat? A mistake—

No, a tragedy. All killing is a tragedy, she thought. But it's not. Savoyian killed terrorists to save innocent people. That's what he was just saying. She suddenly realized she was alone in the dark. Lost in her thoughts, she'd let Savoyian get too far ahead. She couldn't see the flashlight. She couldn't see anything but the darkness of the thick woods. A wave of panic hit her like a gust of hot wind. Help! Help! She almost called out—but the embarrassment, the feeling of dependency... a lost little girl in the woods. She just stood there, remaining silent. Then he called in a low tone, "Over here."

The path had twisted back behind her, winding up a long slope straight through a thick grove of birch, beech, and maple trees. She turned and followed the light, steadying herself. She touched the trees as she passed them, finding their solid strength comforting. Her father had taught her to recognize the species of trees—the texture of the bark, the color and shape of the leaves. But she couldn't be sure in the darkness, not really. And it was so dark. She looked up. The thick leafy branches blocked the moonlight. The sky now appeared darkly purple, like the color of bruised skin.

Finally, they reached a small clearing. Savoyian cast the flashlight beam in a small semi-circle. Pinecones dotted the ground like spilled trinkets. A large wood beetle crawled across a fallen log.

"About a hundred yards up, to the left. There's an abandoned well."

He said this as if its meaning were self-evident. Eliana considered a moment, then it occurred to her: the body.

"Sulfur fires," he went on, eerily anticipating her thoughts. "Burns hotter than—well, even the pulp tissue inside the teeth—its... gone." He turned and looked in the direction of the well. Eliana half-expected to see flames and smoke, but, of course, nothing but darkness extended as far as her eyes could see.

"It was here? They took my father from the city and—"

"Yes."

"An Islamic hit, wasn't it? Because of the trial. Your journal—I read."

"I know—"

"They wanted—"

"An abduction—that's what I thought it was going to be. Just an abduction."

"You—you were there?"

He looked away and took a step back from her. The flashlight continued to shine into the center of the small clearing, its beam falling over the brown earth, illuminating the piles and piles of pinecones. Such perfect geometrical shapes. Eliana's father once took her into the woods and delivered one of his famous nature-lectures about how the pinecone is the evolutionary precursor to the flower, and how its classic cylinder-form spirals in an exact Fibonacci sequence, referring to the famous formula discovered by the Italian mathematician Leonardo Pisano Bigollo, in which the number in a series always equals the addition of the last two numbers, starting with 0, and 1, and continuing infinitely: 0, 1, 1, 2, 3, 5, 8, 13, 21... The point, her father explained, is that nature contains its own sacred symmetry. And the pinecone, he went on, is where we get the name for the pineal gland, the geographic center of our brain, which governs our body's perception of light, among other essential functions. That's why the pinecone is a symbol of "enlightenment."

Years later, Eliana would look back on this kind of lecture with disdain—or, worse, contempt. During her college days, this sort of talk served as a perfect example of everything she wanted to leave behind. A kind of Jewish intellectualism, she thought. This endless analyzing, abstracting, squeezing a moral meaning out of every encounter.

But now—she heard Savoyian swallow hard. The darkness concealed his face. Then she heard the distinct click-click of a gun's hammer being cocked. He shined the flashlight into her face.

"I'm not going to hurt you," he said quietly. "I'm going to show you—and you must follow my directions precisely. Precisely—do you understand?"

No, Eliana didn't understand. She didn't understand at all, but she couldn't speak. A wave of dizziness hit her suddenly, and her legs trembled. She'd come alone into the woods with this dangerous man. No backup, not even a plan. It proved that Danny and Jack were right. She was unstable, out of control. She needed help. Like Char. In fact, she was no better than Char, no saner than her drug-addicted little sister slamming her face into the table—how ironic. It was out of love for Char that Eliana was doing all this. At least that's what she told herself. Rescue her poor innocent wounded sister—her life's mission. But now it was Eliana who needed to be rescued.

The truth of all this gripped her with a spasm of terror, a stabbing pain deep in her chest. She tried to breathe, but couldn't. Then her neck tightened and her scalp tingled and her arms and legs grew heavy. *I'm going to faint*, she thought, and lowered herself to one knee, placing both hands on the ground. That was her training kicking in—avoid injury, prevent the fall from a blackout. Crouching now, she looked into the white beam of the flashlight.

"I'm not going to hurt you," Savoyian said again. "Just do exactly as I say."

Eliana noted that he was breathing heavily, a wheezy noise rising above the sound of the wind in the trees.

"I'll leave you alone," she went on. "I promise that I will leave you alone."

"Your gun," he said, in a hoarse voice. "You have one on your ankle, right? Take it out and put it on the ground. Slowly."

She reached into her ankle holster, removed her gun, then slid it on the ground toward Savoyian. He lowered the flashlight, stepped forward, picked up the gun, seemed to inspect the weapon, then threw it into the thick dark woods.

"Now turn around. Your back to me, your head lowered, your chin tucked—touching your chest. I need the back of your head exposed."

She followed his instructions and positioned herself exactly as he asked.

"Pay attention here," he said, and she felt the barrel of the gun press against the back of her head. "The Triune Brain Model," he began. "Forebrain, midbrain, hindbrain. It's important that—" he stopped. The wheeze in his breath grew worse. *An allergy attack*, Eliana wondered?

But then he swallowed and, impressively, recovered his poise. "The hindbrain controls heart rate and respiration," he said, and his tone now sounded clinical, a teacher giving instructions. "A trauma to the forebrain can be survived with damage limited to reflexive processes and organs that receive impulses from both the sympathetic nervous system and the parasympathetic nervous system, although the SNS and PNS generally work opposite each other. But a trauma to the hindbrain—" He paused again, then pushed the barrel harder into her head. "That's why it needs to be right here. So there's no survival—and no suffering. Just death."

He stepped back, and she felt the pressure release from the back of her head. And, after a moment, she turned around and watched him set the flashlight and gun down on the ground. Then he turned his back to her and lowered himself to his knees.

She stood quickly and picked up the flashlight and the big heavy cowboy gun. What had just happened? She stared at him kneeling on the ground with his back to her.

"You should handcuff me," Savoyian said, without turning around, his tone flat, matter of fact. He brought his hands behind him, palms up. "Before any adrenaline-dump kicks in for me," he said, as if she'd asked a question. "If I get a rush that I cannot control—I'm trained, of course, never to give up, with my hands free, you could be in for a very bad time." He paused, took a deep breath, then went on: "I've been eating my gun for months one bullet at a time telling myself... about God's will. He laughed suddenly, a snorty sarcasm in the guttural sound. "And each month I lived I'd tell myself, 'Well, there's nothing divine about justice—it's a purely human problem.' But now—now, finally, I am the faithful man I've always wanted to be, the one who believes, quite simply, that you are an agent of God's will."

"What—"

"I am responsible for your father's death—and I'm prepared to be punished for it."

Everything had happened so fast—too fast, like the world itself had been flung forward, careening off its axis. Yet now, in this moment, it all seemed to slow, stretching into an unbearable, suffocating stillness, like a dream where your limbs feel as though they're moving through water. Or her dream—the recurring dream of the pulverized concrete from the fallen towers, the sky filling with white dust mixed with drops of red blood, swirling and thickening the air, making it impossible to breathe. She became aware of her clenched jaw, then gasped, gulping down a quick breath. The feeling of disorientation overwhelmed her. For a moment, she wasn't sure where she was or what had just transpired—only that she was there, in the dark woods, holding a flashlight, her hands trembling as she shined its narrow beam on the back of Savoyian's kneeling body. He was still—deathly still—as if the weight of his own confession had turned him to stone, his hands raised behind him like some ancient offering to gods who no longer listened. *Hadn't he confessed?* she asked herself, the words echoing, circling back like they didn't belong to her. *Yes—he confessed.* But the moment felt strange, unreal, as though time itself had forgotten to move, leaving the past, present, and future impossible to separate.

Police procedure, make the arrest, control the situation. That's what she knew to do. Protocol. Follow protocol. She took out her cuffs and side-stepped to his right side, and then grabbed two fingers on his right hand, twisting hard so the narrow part of his wrist faced upward while in one smooth motion she pushed the single bar of the metal bracelet hard against his bone. It clicked shut—a perfect speed cuff. Then she switched sides. Grabbed and twisted two fingers from the other hand and cuffed the left wrist. Lastly, she gave the small metal chain between the two bracelets a little tug.

Then she stepped back and stood behind him, fighting her own feeling of disorientation. She looked at the back of his head. "What do you mean you're responsible? Exactly what—"

But he cut her off and without turning around said, "In the bag there you'll find a phone with a number and our location taped on it. When it's over, call the number. It will go to voicemail. Report the coordinates then leave the area and get rid of the phone. They'll come for my body."

The flashlight and gun suddenly felt heavy, and Eliana's whole left arm throbbed from the cat bite. She heard Savoyian exhale loudly, then watched his head flop forward, chin to chest, like a worn out, loose necked doll. The back of his neck was fully exposed.

But she stepped in front of him and shined the beam into his face. "I need to know exactly what happened."

He lifted his head and looked at her and Eliana thought his face registered an eerie calmness, no trace of fear. Alert, awake, his eyes were steady, brow relaxed. The only sign of stress was a trace of sweat shining in the crisp V of his widow's peak hairline.

"I... am responsible," he said. "That's all that matters. Your father's death was my fault. I must be punished."

"Suicide by cop? Right, sure... I get it. This little song-and-dance routine so I position the gun just right. But I need to know exactly what happened to my father. *You* killed him?"

Savoyian paused, looked down at the ground, then gazed up at her, squinting into the flashlight's beam of white light.

"Just punish me—and be done with all this. Go help your sister. I have money. It's for you. The instructions are in the bag. Take the money and go and have a life. Move on from all this."

Eliana felt a flood of rage. No—not this, she thought, not the ancient message to "move on." She stepped forward and pressed the long barrel of the gun directly into Savoyian's kneecap. "This is my life," she said. "And if you don't tell me exactly what happened, I will put a bullet in your knee, and then one in your other knee, and leave you here to bleed to death. You want to suffer for days?"

She saw this register, his eyes widening, an unmistakable wave of fear.

"What—a miscalculation? Didn't think I was capable of torture? Try me."

She watched him lick his lips and turn his head slightly to avoid the flashlight's beam. She removed the gun from his kneecap and stepped back. "Go on," she said.

"I thought it was just going to be an abduction," he began. "One of the men in that cell—he'd been trained in Algeria, he knew about kidnapping. They knew where your father lived—" He stopped and looked at her directly, squinting into the light. "Where you lived."

Eliana felt her arm tremble and saw the beam of light shake. She gripped the heavy metal flashlight more tightly, squeezing so hard that the cat bite throbbed. With her uninjured arm she held the big awkward gun. She forced herself to focus.

"How did you get him into the car?"

Savoyian's face registered puzzlement, as if she'd asked an irrelevant question. The look angered Eliana. She was about to repeat herself when he said, "Chloroform. There were two cotton cloths soaked in it. And we had syringes." He paused, then added, anticipating her question. "Haloperidol and lorazepam, probably. Or some earlier generation of those drugs."

Hearing this information gave Eliana a hollow feeling, which angered her further, as if he were right—these questions were, indeed, irrelevant. But she pushed on.

"Where did—"

"The parking lot of the grocery store," Savoyian said, again anticipating her thoughts. It was unnerving, this way he had of controlling the tempo of a conversation, even now.

Eliana took a deep breath. Slow. Slow down, she told herself. But her mind raced, and she imagined the parking lot of the grocery store where her father would have gone, the kosher one, of course, Dovid's Market, squeezed between a kosher butcher and an old-fashioned barbershop. Gone now. Everything gone. Every inch of the mall covered now by a sprawling Stop & Shop, but that night—she imagined her father walking from his car, taking his small jerky steps, lost in thought, worrying about the argument he'd left behind at home. Did he notice anyone approach? Did they use a diversionary tactic? Hadn't anyone else in the mall noticed the collision of two grown men in a parking lot? The attacker must have come from behind, she thought, but in Eliana's mind now she saw her father's face, his nose being covered with the chloroform-soaked cloth, his eyes snapping wide open. Bright, ferocious. Her own eyes resembled her father's—everyone said that. Instinctively, he must have held his breath, which would have forced the attacker to push the cloth down harder against his nostrils until— yes, Eliana felt now as if she were the attacker, and she could see her father's cheeks twitch for some seconds under the cloth until finally his eyes dim and his body grows limp and...

Her own arms felt heavy as she told herself to control her thoughts and focus. "Did he ever become conscious?"

Savoyian twisted his shoulders, as if he wanted to gesture with his cuffed hands. A restless moment of agitation—it passed, and he took a breath and regained his composure. "No."

Eliana wasn't sure she believed him.

"Look—you can figure this, right?" He swallowed his words in a rushed, flustered breath. Again, it was a moment of agitation, and again he worked to restore his composure. "It's not complicated, really. Undercover cops have snorted cocaine or injected heroin or god-knows-what-else in order—"

It clicked. The meaning of what he was saying. Eliana exploded. Two quick steps, and she swung the heavy flashlight into the side of his head. She heard the loud *thwack* of metal striking bone and watched him fall to his side.

"You killed my father to avoid blowing your cover?"

She stood over him. In her mind saw herself kicking him in the ribs over and over or maybe going for the groin or eyes or...

But he didn't resist. He didn't curl into a fetal position. In fact, he let himself lie with his chest and face exposed. It gave her pause. She stood there breathing hard, looking down at him.

"Beat me," he said, breathing hard. "Go ahead. I deserve it. Because it was more than just protecting my cover. Worse, much uglier."

She turned away and walked a little into the woods. No thoughts, numb. She clicked off the flashlight and looked around. The trees swayed like a huge black curtain—impersonal, cruel, absurd. She waited a moment, then turned the light back on, moving the beam in a steady circle, as if she were patrolling a park. Finally, she walked back to Savoyian. He had pulled himself back onto his knees. More questions, get the facts. Do what detectives do. Investigate.

"What's worse and uglier? Keep talking."

Savoyian shook his head. "It doesn't matter."

"No, it does matter. And I think I know. Because killing my father made you who you are. Your reputation, right? You had credibility and so that made—"

"I tried to tell my handler."

"And?"

Eliana could picture the scene. A hotel room somewhere anonymous. Midtown, or maybe upstate. After taking a circuitous route to make sure he hadn't been followed, Savoyian would have sat there in the sterile room explaining to a faceless bureaucrat that he'd just killed an innocent man—a good guy, a whistleblower. And the handler—in her mind, Eliana saw a face like Richard's, Livi's husband—a mindless self-absorbed scared shitless functionary horrified not by the injustice, but by what this major fuckup might mean for him. The universal law of any social hierarchy: shit splashes back *uphill.* If someone at the bottom screws up, someone a bit higher gets blamed.

"I was sick with guilt," Savoyian said hoarsely.

"I read about it. Your journal."

Savoyian shook his head. "I deserve to die for what I've done. Please."

He said this with a trace of insistence in his voice, as if he were arguing the point. It made Eliana think: yes, he's trying to win an argument with himself about the value and meaning of his life. Vachik Savoyian is a soldier who feels guilty about an innocent person he once killed. A single act that's destroying him, making him suicidal. It's not killing itself that bothers him. Targeted assassination, Obamas pet project. That's fine. In the car, he boasted about the innocent lives he has saved. He talked of "doing more good than harm." Yes, she understood. Everything felt perfectly clear. This dedicated soldier in the war on terror—he has a stain on his soul. And he wants Eliana to wipe it clean. Moreover, the bizarre symmetry of their linked lives is that his sin involves her suffering. All these years, almost her whole life, it's not been her father's death that has destroyed her—but the meaninglessness of his death. Not knowing who killed him, or why. But now she knew, and Savoyian's punishment would be her freedom. Could it be that simple?

Yes, she thought. *He wants to die—and he deserves to die. And I will kill him. It's what he wants. Redemption, freedom from the past. I can kill him and then—yes, it's what Char wants too. Savoyian's death will...* Eliana's thoughts trailed off. She felt her body shake with a mix of fear and excitement. After all these years, she realized she could finally do the one thing she wanted most—to help her little sister.

Her heart pounded, and there was a thudding in her ears. Rising blood pressure, she knew. The flashlight started to shake again. She gripped it tighter, but that made the cat bite throb worsen. Take a long deep breath, she told herself. Then she tried to notice her heart rate. It was dangerously high. Could be approaching two hundred beats per minute, she thought. Motor control starts deteriorating at around one hundred-fifty beats, so—next, her vision and hearing would go. And the flashlight—she didn't know if she could keep holding it, let alone the big heavy gun.

Breathe, Relax, Aim, Sight and Squeeze—BRASS. Training acronyms, a way of life. No need to sight, though. She stepped forward fast and placed the barrel of the gun gently against the base of Savoyian's skull. Yes, she knew the anatomy. She turned off the flashlight. Complete darkness. The darkness of the woods—a great darkness. Perhaps this was, indeed, the whole difference. In the city there's no darkness like this. Nobody will understand—but, fine, nobody *does* understand. Ordinary people, "safe citizens." They couldn't possibly know what she knew—what Savoyian knew. The mere thought of it, how people go about their business with this absurd feeling of safety— it offended her. It sickened her. They might judge her harshly for taking the life of Vachik Savoyian, the man who destroyed her family, but he understood. And she understood. Yes, together, they'd found a truth that now required her—simply—to kill.

Chapter 28

Danny hadn't been fooled. He knew Eliana too well. She'd gone through the motions—talking to the counselor, requesting days off—but he knew. It was bullshit. In the end Eliana would do what Eliana wanted to do. So he sat now sipping cranberry juice and soda water at Mac's Ale House trying to feel good, at least, about this: not drinking. His second night in a row at Mac's, but this time red-haired Fred-the-bartender didn't even open his mouth. Just set down the glass of bubbly fruit juice without a word.

Mac's—a good old-fashioned cop bar, hard to find these days, even in Queens. A few were left on Staten Island. Red vinyl booths lined one wall, a handful of tables and chairs were near the pool table. The juke box was loaded with oldies—right now Springsteen wailed about "The Darkness on the Edge of Town." The Police Athletic League once owned the building and Danny's favorite thing about the place was the small mildew-smelling weight room in the basement. Cops would earn their beers by lifting first, then come upstairs with a sheen of sweat on their foreheads, chalk dust on their palms. Now, Danny recognized a few detectives at the bar, but nobody he worked with. Most cops avoid drinking in their own precinct. Don't shit where you eat, as they say.

The solitude suited his mood. Lonely, frustrated—he couldn't stop thinking about Eliana. Their first date, near the Two-Four Precinct, the Upper West Side, an innocent walk through Riverside Park, warm and sunny, they'd strolled through the highway underpass to get closer to the river, then stopped near the tennis courts at 96th Street, where they stood in front of an open bench, its hard metal covered with a thick coat of rubbery blue paint. That's when she popped the deadly question: "Why did you become a cop?"

He didn't answer. He stared at the bench. He wanted to sit with her on that bench, but there was a wet spot in the middle where someone had spilled a can of Coke. Eyeballing one side, then the other, he measured where they'd both fit. Finally, he took her elbow, and they settled close together, their arms touching. It was her choice to get *that* close, to let their arms touch. And when the soft smooth skin on her bare shoulder brushed his rough hairy arm like a butterfly-kiss, he didn't just spring an erection—he felt a surge of sexual energy like the hot buzz of exposed wires, a quiver from his toes to the top of his scalp.

Her question didn't surprise him, exactly. They'd eaten lunch at Ollie's and talked about the bar incident with the college boys two weeks earlier, and details about Eliana's martial arts training, plus her plans for the Police Academy. But she talked so easily and fluently and seemed so articulate that it made Danny feel—well, inferior. A working stiff, hopelessly "blue collar." Which is just a dumb label, he thought. And now she wanted to know why he became a cop? The truth: because of his dad and his dad's dad and his dad's dad's dad. But what kind of dumb answer is that?

No, he wanted to say more. Much more. And now, with this ever-so-slight physical contact, arms touching, the mood shifted. Something about this woman... the way a long silence with her could feel so comfortable, effortless. Danny said nothing but lost himself in the Hudson River view, admiring the green-and-grey cliffs of the Jersey Palisades.

"It's such a beautiful day, isn't it?" he said.

This embarrassed him further—instead of answering her question, he'd made a dumb comment about the weather. Get a grip, he thought. Behind him, he heard the high ping and thwack of tennis balls. Tennis—a rich man's sport.

"Yeah, it is really a beautiful day," he repeated, trying to shake free of this foggy feeling of self-consciousness. Another long silence. She didn't seem to mind, which made him even more nervous. Finally, he threw himself into it the way he might take down a perp's door. He blurted, "I'm really intimidated by you."

"By me?" She laughed, and—out of the blue—punched him hard on the arm.

"Hey! What's that for?"

"Because you're being a jerk."

"What the hell—? Assaulting an officer—I could lock you up." He slid away from her, trying to get a clear look at her face, and slid right into the puddle of soda. "You don't know me well enough to call me a jerk," he said as a warm wetness seeped into the butt of his pants. It made him feel—well, like a jerk.

"I think I do."

"Yeah?"

"Want me to 'run it for you?'"

"Run it?"

"That's a cop line, right? Picked it up from a show." She smiled, her full lips twisting as if to hold in a laugh. Danny fought the urge to lean forward and kiss her right on the spot. Then she took a breath, lips straightening. All business. "So you meet this Columbia University girl who says she wants to be a cop," she began, a calm even tone. "You think she's out of her mind, but, hey, you're a cop—you deal with crazy people for a living. And this nutjob—well, not only is she quite attractive but can fight too, which is a big-time turn-on for a macho guy like you. The problem is: she's just exactly the kind of girl you've always thought beyond your reach. Jewish, you figure, wealthy and, you know, those Ivy League kids—another world, right? And so what happens?"

She met his eyes, then lifted a finger for emphasis, pointing accusingly. "Instead of trusting who you are, valuing your experience, appreciating what you have to offer—your insecurities kick in and—"

Danny raised his hand. "That's enough. I get it." He heard the edge in his voice, and he knew Eliana heard it too. Her eyes narrowed. She looked out at the river.

"I'm sorry," she said. "I don't mean—"

"No, you're good. I'm ready to confess, OK? You're right. I once thought—lawyer or professor or writer or something—but... hey, a cop's what I am. And all I am. And all I'll ever be."

"And there's nothing wrong with that."

"Sure, to you. Because you got a thing for—"

"No, I don't have a thing for cops. A buff, or whatever the hell you call it. That's what you were going to say, right? What I have a thing for is the law—because the law... is what makes it possible for human beings to live together."

Danny didn't answer. He just looked at her.

"Maybe you don't see it anymore," she continued.

"The importance of the law?"

"That's right."

"I don't want to burst your bubble, but, believe me, it's complicated. The law doesn't always work the way it's supposed—"

"I understand that. But I'm talking about you. Your life. It must have been part of the reason you became a cop in the first place, right? Because
you believe in the power and importance of justice? And I know—Ivy Leaguer, remember? Law and justice are not the same thing. I get that."

Danny shrugged, unable to think of anything to say. But her voice—even now, arguing, chastising, whatever—her voice had this timbre: musical, reedy, like the earthy sound of a saxophone, not wailing but controlled and clear, full of feeling. It made Danny want to tell her all about the pressure, the burden to live up to his fathers and grandfathers and great-grandfathers celebrated NYPD careers. And more: how in high school he'd wanted nothing to do with police work and had won a poetry contest and dreamed of attending a school like Columbia where he'd celebrate his family—their Welsh roots—in some other way, his own way, not chasing perps but reading poetry. Dylan Thomas—that was his favorite poetry. He loved Dylan Thomas the way most kids love a ball player. And the castles. He wanted to tell Eliana about the castles in Wales he'd dreamed of visiting since he was a boy, especially the *Harlech*, with its double-ringed wall that withstood the longest siege in British history during the English civil war in 1642, and the *Dolbadarn* castle on Mount Snowden, built nearly four hundred years ago by Celtic soldiers defending and protecting themselves from the invading Norse. Danny dreamed once that he stood inside *Dolbadarn*, leaning against its thick stone wall, his hands in the grooves of the rough rock where generations of men—warriors—maintained an unshakeable commitment to defend and protect. They paid a price—suffered. That was the subject of his poem, the high school award winner. Silly adolescent stuff, yes, Danny knew the line: "To be eighteen and a poet—is to be eighteen." But as an adult, in secret, he still occasionally re-read and tinkered and quietly recited his award-winner, titled: "Their Unshed Tears."

Sentimental? Cheesy? Would Eliana take him seriously? The way she talked about the law, the way she looked at him now, her thick dark lashes defining her large wide eyes ... so open and trusting, yes, she'd understand, Danny thought. But still he hesitated to speak. Another long silence. Traffic sounds. Cars whooshing down the West Side Highway. And from the park: a high-pitched female voice on the tennis courts called, "Out!" And from somewhere else, way in the distance, barely audible—the familiar, faint scream of a siren.

Eliana lifted her eyes, encouraging him to say more. But he just smiled, then watched her slip her tongue over her deliciously full lips.

"OK, here's my philosophy of life," she began. "The way I see it," and she paused and smiled with a sheepish, aw-shucks look in her eyes that made Danny laugh.

"Your philosophy of life—I'm ready."

"The human condition is defined by sex and aggression," she began, "but most people aren't honest about either one."

Deep breath, Danny felt glad to be off the hook. Her philosophy—this would be fine. Much easier to talk about the "human condition" than his own little life.

"Sounds good so far," he said, "sex and aggression define our lives. Got it. But for most people—that's not such a big deal. Aggression gets controlled, sex gets satisfied. I don't know that justice and the law—let alone cops—have much to do with it."

When she nodded and looked away, Danny regretted what he'd just said. A troubled expression on her face. He watched her jaw clench, then relax, then clench again. And one eyebrow twitched, lips tensing, as if she were about to whistle or whisper or mutter something to herself. Since Danny had slid back away from her into the puddle of

Coke, their arms now no longer touched. Suddenly, she seemed terribly far away. And Danny felt responsible. He sensed a dynamic at work: his insecurity. It was driving a wedge between them right this moment. Because he feared that she wouldn't take him seriously, he'd gone on the offensive, dismissing her, shrugging off her ideas about the "human condition" as "not such a big deal." He tried to think of a way to apologize.

"My dad was murdered," she said simply, holding her gaze on the river. "Actually, disappeared, but I'm sure he was murdered. My sisters— well my little sister, especially, she's been pretty traumatized."

Danny immediately put his hand on Eliana's shoulder. He didn't know what to say—so fell back on the standard cop line: "I'm sorry for your loss."

A deep stillness had come over her. Danny felt it under his palm— her shoulder motionless, stone-cold, not the slightest twitch or sign of life in the muscle, as if his hand were resting on a cement ledge. "Maybe that's why I called you for lunch today." She shook her head, eyes lowered now, a look of embarrassment. Then she removed Danny's hand from her shoulder and abruptly stood. Danny could tell she was about to leave. "I—I'm sorry," she stammered, then rushed her words. "I really—it's just that meeting you—and then—I don't know—something got me going... thanks for lunch, and, you know, I'll let you know how things go for me at the Police Academy. Maybe we can get together again some time."

She leaned over and gave Danny a quick kiss on the cheek, then turned away.

But Danny stood quickly and grabbed her by the wrist. Gently, but firmly. He pulled her toward him. "Don't become a cop."

"What—?"

"Because you're the victim of an unsolved crime. It's—that's not the way it works."

Her jaw jutted forward slightly, and the way she stood, her weight centered, head still—an impressive pose, almost intimidating. It caught Danny off-guard. Just moments ago, she'd seemed so vulnerable. Delicate. The incongruity confused him. He couldn't think of what to say, except: "The job, I mean. It doesn't work that way."

She laughed, shaking her head, a swagger that again made Danny feel disoriented. Her shifting energy, her contradictions—he couldn't keep up. Naive but sophisticated, vulnerable but confident, wounded but strong. "Cops solve crimes, right?" she said. "Isn't that what cops do?"

Danny felt outmaneuvered and a little angry not just because of the "duuuh-uhhhh" tone in her voice but also because of the warm wet stickiness in the seat of his pants where he'd sat in the puddle of Coke. "Yes," he said. "That's what cops do—partly. But.

"But what?"

"Look, I see what's going on here, and I am sure you see it too. Cops solve crimes, yes. But it's not like the movies or TV. You're talking about a very old crime and about a family situation and—that's not what cops do."

"You don't think justice heals?" she snapped back.

Again, Danny felt off-balance and didn't know what to say. So innocent, he thought, she is so innocent!

He watched her shrug. Then she looked down at the ground, folding into herself so completely that the physical change was again transformative: her brash swagger melting.

"I don't know," she said quietly. "Maybe you're right, but if justice doesn't heal, then—then what's the point? What's the point of anything?"

Danny stepped back and looked out at the river. *A justice that heals?* Who talks this way? No cop he knew.

The streets will destroy her, he thought, and a slow wave of sadness passed through him as he looked out at the river and watched the sun drift behind a cloud. The dark sky turned the water a dull grey, like the color of cement. He couldn't articulate it but knew what he wanted: to stop trying to understand this woman, stop trying to figure her out. Instead, just defend her and protect her and—yes, be as close to her as humanly possible.

She started to turn away again, but he grabbed her shoulder and pulled her toward him—and she didn't resist. "Let me help you," he said, and the words surprised him. She seemed surprised too. Her eyes widened, then narrowed. He stepped closer to her, and what happened next came easily to him—taking charge. He leaned forward, eyes open, holding her gaze until their foreheads touched. Then he looked down at her lips, as if stealing a glance at something forbidden, and then — gently but firmly—with the tip of his finger, he lifted her face and, as subtly and softly as he could, he brushed his lips across hers, not kissing exactly, just tasting, pausing, noticing. Then he came back to looking again into her eyes, checking one more time to be sure—yes, it was right. And, slowly, their barely-touching-lips pressed harder, a pleasing pressure, an exciting hint of force, until her tongue found his, and he moaned softly, and she matched his moan with a moan of her own, and... Danny knew. This was real. This was... love.

Yeah, sure—he thought now, sitting with his cranberry juice and soda. Love. What a word. He'd been right about his love for her, sure, but he'd also been right about the streets and what they would do to her. *A justice that heals...?* No fucking way. The streets destroyed Eliana. And his love never meant shit because he'd failed to do the one thing good cops do: protect the innocent.

Chapter 29

The fear of being tortured—the panic it triggered—came as a surprise to Vachik Savoyian. He had miscalculated—twice. It hadn't occurred to him that Eliana would make such a threat; and he hadn't expected to feel such terror. That's why it soothed him now to feel Eliana pressing the gun firmly into the base of his skull directly in line with the brain stem. No pain. His annihilation would be complete.

He'd always wondered, of course, if it's true that one's whole life flashes before one's eyes in the final moments before death. For Savoyian—no. What flashed before his eyes was not his whole life—only the long blurry episode of his days after the killing of Neil Golden.

When he returned home from the Catskills, Savoyian felt nothing but panic. On an impulse, he went into the bathroom and shaved off his beard. He didn't know why he was compelled to do this, but with his cheeks shaved he no longer looked into the mirror and saw a soldier in the war on terror. He saw a murderer. And something else, equally threatening to his sanity. Leaning over the sink, looking more closely into the mirror, he saw buried within the features of his face—another face. Like a double-exposed photo, one image super-imposed on the other, a second pair of thick, dark eyebrows, deep-set eyes, another long thin nose. Someone else's dark, swarthy Persian face. His father—staring at him with anger and shame and disbelief. And at that moment, the unrelenting nausea of guilt began.

The next day it reached such a pitch that he did not know what to do with himself to escape the torture except walk along the crowded streets of his neighborhood like a drunken man, jostling strangers, ignoring their looks. His thoughts were jangled in confusion, mirroring his movements. Stepping forward, stopping short, turning around. A backpack in his face, an elbow in his side, an impatient frown from an unknown person. He'd start to apologize, begin to mutter "sorry, sorry," but the absurdity! Sorry—for this?—when... no. No words, no exclamation, nothing could express his agitation.

He walked for blocks and blocks. When he reached the cemetery on Woodside Avenue, he stood there for several minutes looking at the tombs, headstones, monuments to the memory of the dead. Then he switched over to Queens Boulevard, where after another few blocks he found himself standing in front of a dark narrow tavern with an old-fashioned wooden shingle on the door: Hurleys. The entrance required descending four steps, and somehow this idea appealed to Savoyian—the feeling of being underground. He stood there staring at the wooden sign when two drunken men with crew cuts and large round pink faces came out of the door. They talked at the same time, overlapping, their tattooed arms wrapped around each other's shoulders. But they also punched each other in the chest as they spoke.

"—The fuck you don't know what the fuck—"

"Fuck what-the-fuck I haven't been so fucked up since I don't fucking know the fuck when—"

They mounted the steps, froze momentarily to look at Savoyian, then continued past him, cursing, hugging, punching. Savoyian watched them stagger into the flow of people on the sidewalk, then he went down the steps.

Until that moment he had never been inside a tavern. Had only tasted liquor once, with his Air Force platoon, a million years ago. But now he felt tormented by a burning thirst and longed for a drink of something cold. He stood at the bar, pointed at someone else's empty Heineken bottle next to him, and waved his money. He stood there and drank the first bottle, then ordered another, and another. Dizzy, he attributed the sudden feeling to lack of food and sleep. But he didn't go home. Instead, he sat down at a sticky little table in a dark and dirty corner and drank two more beers.

The dizziness increased, but then, strangely, he felt better. His thoughts became clear. The solution—it was simple. Tell the truth. Don't cover it up. Go to the police. But, of course, I am the police, he thought, so—? Better to meet with his handler, yes. Explain exactly what had happened. That's still going to the police and still telling the truth, he reasoned, but they understand the situation so—so...? What will happen, he wondered. Jail, of course. But you can sleep in jail, right? That sounded fine. He'd tell the truth and go to jail, and sleep.

When he stood up from the sticky little table, the room spun. So he sat down and waited an hour. Or maybe two hours. He wasn't sure. But eventually he made it home—and made the call.

Two days later, he sat face-to-face with his handler and confessed. He told him exactly what happened. He started with the meeting in Bay Ridge when the abduction—as he thought it was supposed to be—had been planned. He'd almost missed the Bay Ridge meeting entirely. Sick. A sinus infection. He should have stayed home. But instead, he loaded up on cold medicine and entered the building's large meeting room, where immediately he sensed something was different. A group of older men sat on cushions in the center of the floor with a group of about twenty others sitting in a circle round them. The older men all had long beards laced with henna. One man, clearly in charge, sat on a cushion slightly higher than the others. He had a long angular face and wore scholarly-looking wire-rimmed glasses. Savoyian knew none of these men, but he knew they held rank. Could tell by their posture, the hushed atmosphere, the way the younger ones sat quietly waiting. Finally, the man in the center passed around an article explaining that the United States had no right to decide whether or not certain countries and groups of individuals are permitted to conduct business with each other.

Savoyian knew the argument. Sanctions, frozen assets, etc. He glanced at the article and thought he should be home in bed. His head ached, his ears rang, and he couldn't concentrate. He also couldn't stop thinking about how futile this undercover work seemed to be. He never knew what happened to the information he provided. He never knew if he was actually helping. Sitting there in the circle, the feeling of frustration merged with another old familiar ache, Operation Eagle Claw. Nobody listened to him then. He'd failed to help. And into his congested, pounding head came that sick, haunting image of a broken helicopter propeller in a dry lakebed. The soldiers who died that night—good men. But he had lived. Why? Lived to do what?

Then he started to shiver. A fever, yes. The back of his neck tingled. He wondered: should I just get up and leave? But his legs felt heavy. He didn't want to make a big show of dragging himself out of the meeting like a wounded man. And now someone in the circle was explaining in detail: the Office of Foreign Assets Control, OFAC, operating under the authority of the U.S. Department of the Treasury—imposes controls on banking transactions and exercises the power to freeze funds. Many banks ignore the controls, and the transactions pass through. But others—yes, one bank, in particular, USBC, a Jew there, he insists that this bank follow the OFAC rules.

The talk carried on this way for several minutes until the man sitting on the cushion in the center paused and looked around the room, then announced, "There is a hearing scheduled. And at this hearing, the infidel wants to present his information."

The room fell silent.

And now—sitting there in the dark woods with his father's fully loaded gun pressed against the base of his skull—Savoyian's memory reconstructed the moment: the feeling of the shiver from his raging fever, the pain in his congested head, the ringing in his clogged-up ears, and the dry-mouthed, heavy-lipped way in which he spoke, half-expecting his words wouldn't be heard at all because—nobody listened to him. Why should they? Who was he in all this? Back then—he was nothing. No reputation. He was a failed soldier, a cop without a uniform, a devout Muslim pretending to be a devout Muslim so he could spy on other devout Muslims.

"We need to interrogate this compliance officer and find out how much he told the FBI and to what extent FinCen is involved," he said, speaking loudly, as if he were giving a lecture. Then a stillness came over the room, and he recognized his error—the suspicion his words had aroused.

Nobody had named the investigative agencies—and FinCen? The Financial Crimes Enforcement Network. Jargon.

The man in charge sitting on the highest cushion in the center of the circle tilted his head slightly to the side, a small barely perceptible gesture. Then he adjusted his wire-rimmed glasses and nodded.

"Very impressive," he said quietly.

"*Alhamdulilah*," Savoyian answered quickly, using the longer, more formal version of "praise be to God."

Two nights later, still fighting his raging sinus infection, Savoyian found himself driving north from New Jersey to the Catskill Mountains, with Neil Golden lying drugged in the backseat. Two men accompanied him. They spoke to each other in an Iranian dialect known as Pamiri. Savoyian struggled to follow their conversation, but he didn't like the tone. Finally, the man sitting in the passenger seat took out a sheet of paper and turned on his flashlight. Savoyian recognized the scribbles on the sheet—it was his handwriting.

"Did you lose this?"

Savoyian hesitated. The sheet contained a list of numbers and letters. License plates. He never should have written them down.

"The paper is yours, yes?"

"Yes. I was wondering what had happened to it. I was careless."

"You wrote this?"

"It's a list of license plates," Savoyian said quickly. "I copied them down because I think we are under surveillance. I want to see if these cars continue to be parked near the mosque. There were five cars, right?" The man sitting next to him said nothing. He turned off the flashlight and leaned back in his seat. Savoyian focused on the road in front of him. He'd answered quickly and forcefully, hoping by his tone and manner to establish a position of strength. But in his chest, he felt the weak, hollow, unsteady feeling of fear. This was a dangerous moment. The silence lengthened. Savoyian's head hurt, and he envisioned the clogged nasal passages beneath his cheeks thick with pus, spreading pain across his face, stabbing behind his eyes, deep into his ears. He could barely smell anything, but the sweet, slightly medicinal odor of the chloroform hung in the car. The man sitting in the back with Golden shifted his weight and coughed. He started to say something, but the man in front cut him off.

"You need license plate numbers to recognize cars that are parked near the mosque?"

"No," Savoyian said, firmly. "I don't 'need' them, but its more precise." They didn't believe him. Savoyian sensed it. But the conversation was over. Nobody spoke again until they had parked the car and carried the still-drugged Golden to the small clearing in the woods. Savoyian held the flashlight; the other two men had done the lifting and carrying and now set Golden down in the dirt on his back, and then they looked around as if checking out the view. Savoyian, familiar with the Catskills, knew that in the daylight the thick woods would be a fantastic sight to behold. But the darkness now offered nothing but the ragged borderline of trees swaying between moonlight and shadow.

The taller of the two men, the one who'd trained in Algeria, spoke first.

"We need to kill him," he said.

"No," Savoyian answered quickly. "We need to talk to him. We need to know exactly what evidence there is."

The two men looked at each other. Savoyian saw the communication pass between them, although neither spoke. It was a slight rise of their shoulders, a tilt of their heads. Yes, this was a dangerous moment. Savoyian knew it. He felt it in his body—a start of his limbs, an acceleration of his heart.

"Our contact in the bank," he blurted, feeling his words rush. "If we know the evidence, then we can reach out to our contact and—"

The taller man stepped forward. Lanky with a severe angular face, he stood now as straight and emotionless as a pole. His thin arms and legs appeared even thinner because of his loose-fitting multi-pocket workpants.

"We have a contact inside the bank, right?" Savoyian went on, trying to keep the tight feeling of fear out of his voice. "If we find out what—"

"You go back to the car. We will conduct the interrogation. Then, we will come to get you, and you will kill him. You don't have a problem with that—do you?"

The man reached into the long deep front-pocket of his baggy pants and took out a gun. He showed it to Savoyian, then put it back into his pocket. As a rule, they never carried handguns. It was unnecessary and could only cause trouble, turning a routine traffic stop, for example, into a larger incident. The gun was a Taurus nine-shot .22 caliber revolver— Savoyian couldn't help immediately identifying and categorizing the weapon. The cognition came without effort. A small gun, the Taurus was known for its reliability—being a revolver means if there's a misfire you just pull the trigger again to bring a good bullet under the pin. But it's an amateur's weapon. A .22 caliber has far less recoil than a larger, more serious gun. Still, although the bullet makes a small hole going in, it will kill a man.

Working to conceal his sense of panic, Savoyian looked over at Neil Golden lying on the ground. The motionless figure shocked him. The body of an innocent. In the moonlit darkness, it appeared a blank shape, an empty vessel—but one that contained all the meanings of life and war, the illusions of victory and defeat, the soldier-hero vanquished by his own strength locked in combat with the irreconcilables of life, death, love, hate. And hope. The hope that war can settle the matter.

Savoyian turned and silently walked back through the woods and sat in the car until the men came for him, motioning with a flashlight that it was time. He'd heard no screams. The interrogation, apparently, hadn't involved any torture. He hoped that after talking to Golden they had injected him with another sedative. That would make it much easier.

As he followed the men back to the clearing, he considered protesting further, arguing again that killing Golden wasn't necessary. But he knew that would only arouse more suspicion. It was clear: Golden couldn't be saved. And if Savoyian resisted doing the killing, the terrorists would kill them both.

"Here."

The man who'd trained in Algeria held out the small caliber handgun. The other man, standing at his side, lifted his larger gun, a 9mm Glock, and pointed it at Savoyian.

"What's this about?" Savoyian said, flicking his head casually toward the man pointing the gun at him.

"Precaution."

Savoyian smiled.

"Yes, of course, I see." Savoyian shook his head, still smiling.

"It's time to kill the Jew."

Savoyian nodded yes. And he knew what needed to be done. Undercover work is acting. He needed to play the part—and play it brilliantly. Later, he'd wonder about the impact of overdosing on decongestants and cough syrup. For two days he'd been swallowing fistfuls of pills and gulping straight from the bottle. But it wasn't drugs that gave him so much energy; it was the transformative power of performance—the high, the adrenaline rush, the athlete's thrill of competition, the rock star's roaring crowd. Soldiers experience a similar blood-passion, though darker, a response to danger, the fear of injury, the threat of violence. War is the ultimate performance pressure.

"You should turn off your phones and wait for me in the car," Savoyian said quietly. "What you don't see, you can't describe, and if your phones are off—"

"Yes, you make a point. We'll return in five minutes." He extended his hand. "Here."

Savoyian took the small gun, and the two men left. Then, alone, he turned and focused on the prone body of Neil Golden lying in the dirt, face-down. Golden, sedated again, was lying there only about fifteen feet away. A patch of shadow separated the two men. It was caused by a large tree branch blocking the moonlight. Time to kill the Jew, Savoyian thought. Yes, time to kill the Jew. Smoothly, not allowing himself to think about it, he glided into the darkness of the shadow and crouched, then crawled on his hands and knees, keeping his face low, as if he had to conceal himself, as if Neil Golden might spring from the ground and fight back. After crawling a few feet, Savoyian looked up.

The moonlight broke through the big swaying branch and he gazed out into the dark woods with fascination. The trees were alive, yes, with an existence as acute as his. He felt the aliveness of his own body. His throat was tight, aching, swelling as he gulped hard. He wanted to taste the night air. He wanted to absorb the earth-plant-human kinship at a cellular level, a level that destroys distinctions. And, yes, after a moment he felt the earth breaking apart, minerals and chemical compounds dissolving, mountains evaporating like huge dark clouds under the noon sun, evolution reversed. Back to the beginning, the primeval fireball, the origin of all violence, the Big Bang. The idea made him almost giddy. How the universe began: shots fired! But that's science not religion. *In the beginning God created the heavens and the earth. And the earth was without form, and void; and darkness was upon the face of the deep...* Darkness, yes. The trees were a blanket of darkness. He thought now about Golden being a Jew. And how Judaism, Christianity, Islam—one religion evolved out of another. Or failed to evolve. Kill the Jew. That was the order. Neil Golden was a man of deep faith, right? Savoyian wondered, then he looked up at the sky through the trees at the shimmer of the moonlight. It wasn't a full moon. It was an off-kilter sphere, imperfect, the shape a child might draw. He stared at the glow of the moon with a crazy unconscious absorption until his mind quieted. Then he pushed on.

He moved closer to the body. A twig snapped under the weight of his knee; the sound startled him. But he pushed forward, lowering his eyes. Another twig snapped. He parted the pile of twigs with his hands, and then crawled more slowly, trying not to make a sound. Finally, he drew within an arm's length of Neil Golden's body. With his head turned to the side, Golden looked like a man sleeping on his stomach. But the flesh on his face was stretched and taut. A reaction to the drugs? Suddenly Savoyian thought he heard the sound of voices—the two men coming back so soon? If he didn't kill Golden, they would kill him. He held still, listening. There was a soft scratching noise—like a scrabble of claws against tree bark. Just a squirrel, probably. Then came a gust of wind and the whoosh of the trees swaying. It sounded vaguely like a wave breaking on a distant shore. The image pleased Savoyian: the round ocean, the living air, the dark night sky. A fragment of a poem drifted into his consciousness: ... *in the mind of man there's a motion and a spirit that impels all thinking things, all objects of all thought...* Wordsworth, right? He couldn't have explained it but for at least a minute he couldn't get the line out of his mind and he was wholly paralyzed, not breathing, afraid to even swallow for fear that something horrible would happen the moment he indicated any sign of life. The poem. Why lines of poetry now? How had he, Savoyian, ended up a soldier and not a poet? All he'd ever wanted to be was a poet.

He breathed, finally. It was impossible to turn back. They would kill him if he didn't kill Golden. His fear of moving forward was great but not so great as his fear of turning back. He could not think it out. He extended his arm, and then moved one knee. Then again, and again. He felt his body heating up. Perspiration smarted his eyes. The seconds passed like individual units, almost as if he heard a clock ticking. In his mind, he felt strangely self-aware, capable of seeing several parts of himself all at once, like a trick mirror with multiple reflections. Image within image within image, both old and new. The old image: a devout Muslim pretending to be a devout Muslim in order to spy on devout Muslims. But now he saw this too: an American pretending to be a terrorist about to fire a bullet into the head of an American fighting terrorists. He wanted to shake his head, to clear his mind, as if he were adding a list of numbers and knew there was something wrong with his calculations. If only he could shake his head or flex his limbs all this would become clear to him, but now he was caught. There was no going shaking or clearing or going back. If he didn't kill this man, the terrorists would kill them both—period.

He drew closer to Golden, within arm's reach. The gun's barrel could be placed now at the back of Golden's head, but as Savoyian lifted his arm the weapon felt uncomfortable in his palm. Alien. He did not know how to hold it. His thumb seemed to be in the way. Where should he put his thumb? A ridiculous question. He knew how to hold a gun—he'd been trained. But he thought: A knife. I should kill him with a knife. Then there would be no sound. He suddenly feared the sound of the gun firing, the disturbance it would cause in the deep dark quiet of the night. But he had no knife. So he looked again at the gun. It was a toy gun. It was not real. None of this was real. It's all a silly game. The thought made him giddy with relief and he slid forward and quickly pressed the gun into the back of Golden's head. Then, dumbly, with a strange deliberation that was almost leisurely, he pulled the trigger. Somewhere in the great vast forest a firecracker popped, then the body in front of him thrashed. It reminded Savoyian of an insect still writhing after being squashed. And it was irritating—why was the body making this unnecessary trouble? He had to kill this man, right? That's all. He had no choice. So what was this movement in the body? Hadn't the bullet gone far enough into the brain? Did he need to fire another shot to kill this man?

No. The moment passed. Neil Golden was dead.

***

And then came the opportunity. After two days of being sick with guilt, including the night he wandered the streets and wound up drinking alone in a little sticky-floored bar in Queens, Savoyian reached the conclusion that the only way to restore his humanity was to admit his guilt. So he spoke to his handler.

His name was Matt Smith, although this might have been an alias. Savoyian had been working with this handler for about six months. Usually, Smith embodied pure business and polish, polite and formal to the point of sounding phony, but after Savoyian told him what he'd done, Smith paced the hotel room, cursing, pulling on the collar of his well-fitted white shirt. He'd already loosened his tie. That came first. While still seated, his initial reaction was very cool: a hard swallow, eyes narrowing, one hand slowly rising, he loosened the top button of his shirt, then executed a small controlled tug at the tie. But the poise didn't last—a chunk of ice melting into a nervous puddle. He kept asking Savoyian if there might be some mistake—if maybe he'd failed to prevent Neil Golden's murder, but not actually committed the murder himself.

Gradually, as they went through the story over and over again, Savoyian understood what mattered most to Matt Smith: not that an innocent man had been killed; not that Savoyian needed to be held responsible for the crime; not even that the overall investigation, the years of intelligence Savoyian had gathered, had now been compromised. No, what mattered to Matt Smith: covering his ass. Savoyian chided himself for not anticipating this. Smith wanted first and foremost to avoid any inquiry that might "splash back," holding him or anyone else on the JTTF team responsible. But denying responsibility also created a problem—because someone higher up the ladder must be held responsible. And, of course, if the press found out about this story...

"OK—" Smith wiped the top of his lip, then swallowed and wiped it again. "You haven't told anyone about any of this, right? I will take care of it. Just go home and don't do anything until you hear from me."

Savoyian nodded. The peace of mind he'd achieved by confessing— gone. A twinge of nausea had returned, a clot in the back of his throat. It disgusted him—Matt Smith's naked self-interest. And he should have seen it coming: "plausible deniability," always a factor, allowing the government to claim no knowledge or involvement. But, in this case, the concept applied fully. In fact, Savoyian recognized that, on one level, an injustice had been done to Smith and the other members of the JTTF team. They didn't all deserve to go to jail. In a sense, Savoyian alone was fully responsible. He was the one who pulled the trigger.

But then something happened. On his way out of the hotel, Savoyian stopped and stood for a moment in the lobby. They'd met at the St. Regis Hotel, one of New York's fanciest—not clear why. His "intelligence briefings," for all these years, had always been held in unlikely locations, but here? The lobby featured marble floors and wide stone columns and mellow walnut furniture. Decadent, Savoyian thought. Excessive luxury and opulent American wealth—pure decadence. But so what? What does it matter? What does any of it matter? Whether he goes to jail or not, Neil Golden's still dead. Even if the whole JTTF team goes to jail, nothing's changed. Another team will be created, and that team will pick up right where this one left off. But without everything Savoyian knew. And he knew plenty. And that's when it occurred to him: the great and terrible idea. With the credibility among terrorist groups that he had earned by killing Neil Golden—he could penetrate. He could use his reputation to climb higher, to get closer to "the head of the snake." He could be a great weapon in the War on Terror. And that would make him a great force in the redemption of true Islam. Indeed: the killing could be worth it.

He went home and waited for Matt Smith's call. But it never came. Two days later, the man named Matt Smith died in an MVA—motor vehicle accident—on a remote highway in upstate New York, just outside of Binghamton. Foul play? Coincidence? Divine intervention? Savoyian only learned of the death at the end of the week when he met with a new handler: a female federal agent from Washington. She introduced herself as his new "case officer." New terminology, Savoyian noted. She claimed to know nothing about "Matt Smith" except that he'd died in a car accident. And she didn't even mention Neil Golden. What she wanted to discuss: a new assignment, a new job. No more NYPD, no more JTTF. Similar work, but better pay, deeper cover, more impact. Much more impact.

"Your reputation," she said quietly, "is extraordinary."

And what about the murder of Neil Golden?

Vachik Savoyian didn't ask. And the woman from Washington didn't tell.

Chapter 30

All she needed to do was pull the trigger. But her mind jumped again to the dead cat, the feeling of squeezing its throat. Should she choke Savoyian to death? She lowered the gun and shined the flashlight on his neck. She could use a strap, she thought. Tell him to take off his belt and then—

"You want to die," she blurted the statement matter-of-factly, the words coming without thought, as if she needed to remind herself that all this made sense. Killing him was the right thing to do. She couldn't possibly arrest and process him. The whole case was hopelessly tainted. "It's understandable that you want to die," she went on, "that makes sense."

Savoyian didn't answer. He remained still.

"My sister tried to kill herself. When she was a teenager. In some mixed-up little-kid way, she felt responsible for what happened to our family."

Now, Savoyian lifted his head and turned to look at her. The flashlight lit his face. He started to open his mouth as if to speak, but just swallowed.

"There's something so perfect about all this, isn't there? You killed my father, I kill you. An eye for an eye."

Savoyian still said nothing.

"But it's a little too easy, in a way. That's how it comes to me suddenly. That all this—I kill you, and then what?"

A memory came—sharp, like a shooting pain. A twinge in her neck made her shiver. She remembered the sound of her father's voice that night, the last night she saw him alive. How he argued with her mother. She didn't want him to testify. She asked why he had to do it, and the whole house seemed to shake with his booming shriek: *"JUSTICE! THAT'S WHY..."* And a few minutes later, standing at the door, his chin up, calmly, deliberately, he quoted Torah: *"The wicked flee when no man pursueth, but the righteous are bold as a lion..."*

Her mind came back to the present. "How many terrorists have you killed because of the 'reputation and access' and all that black ops mysterious helicopter crap that was your reward?"

Savoyian didn't answer.

"How many have you killed?" Eliana repeated.

"It's not a question of—"

"A number! Goddamn it, give me a number!" Eliana shouted, her voice cracking. She pressed the gun into the top of Savoyian's knee.

"Twenty-eight. Twenty-eight high value targets."

She stepped back, pulling the gun away and letting the flashlight's beam wander aimlessly, lighting up the dark leaves and thick tree trunks. She felt her energy rising and falling as if she were trying to lift something impossibly heavy—then giving up. A fatigue settled over her, but she went on talking, hearing the tiredness in her voice.

"One good person—who happened to be my father—in exchange for twenty-eight bad people. That's war, isn't it? The heart of it: a calculation. Those terrorists you killed would have killed—who knows how many, right? So killing them saved lives. That's the way to think about it. And killing my father helped you kill them, so my father helped save lives. Is that how I should think about all of this?"

Savoyian continued to remail silent. Eliana said, "I'm asking you—is this how I should understand it? My father helped save lives. Is that right?"

"I suppose, yes. But I'm sorry for what happened to your father. I'm sorry for—for everything. I'm sorry for who I am."

Eliana laughed, which surprised her. It came from someplace she didn't completely understand. A short quick unexpected burst, like an involuntary cough. "You don't get to be sorry. That's not an option—for a soldier. A soldier doesn't get to be sorry for who he is."

Then, as if following the unexpected momentum of the laugh, she found herself now reaching into her pocket for the key to the cuffs. The actions now seemed to come of their own volition, almost as if she were not choosing but following, obeying, surrendering to a force greater than her own will. "No, soldiers don't get to be sorry," she went on, but quietly, mumbling to herself. "Soldiers fight. Soldiers are doomed to fight and kill and..." She kneeled now, fumbling with the flashlight to shine it onto the cuffs. Then she freed Vachik Savoyian's hands.

She stood and moved in front of him and laid the big heavy old-fashioned cowboy gun on the ground between them. She shined the flashlight on the long black barrel.

"Do it yourself," she said, quietly. "If you want to kill yourself, do it yourself. But it will be an act of cowardice."

Then she turned off the flashlight, letting the darkness surround them both. A strong breeze picked up, and she took in the earthy smell of decomposing leaves and rotting wood and the faint stench of a skunk. After a moment, she started to feel so weak that she feared she'd collapse, so she lowered herself to her knees and crawled toward the trunk of a huge tree at the dark edge of the small clearing. It seemed far away. She crawled slowly. The ground felt damp and cool against the palms of her hands. At one point, her knee landed on a small rock, sending a sharp twinge through her leg. But she pushed on. When she finally reached the log, she turned around and leaned against it, trying to settle into a reclining position.

Exhaustion overwhelmed her. Sleep. That's all she suddenly wanted. Nothing else but to sleep, to shut her eyes and sink into the darkness of a quiet mind, dissolved, done, free from all this, yes, free. It was like a desire for death and made her wonder if simple fatigue is at the center of accepting the incomprehensibly dumb-awful mystery of death. Exhaustion. That's all it is—simple exhaustion.

The pain in her throbbing arm seemed trivial compared to this all-consuming feeling of being depleted. Too tired to continue, that's all. Then she heard Savoyian breathing heavily and almost as if she'd fallen asleep and was yelling in a dream, she heard herself call out into the dark thick night sky.

"I want to find those goddamm terrorists and the banker who was working with them because somebody inside tipped them off about what my father knew. I want to find them, especially the banker, and you can help me. Do you hear me? You can help me."

She stopped and pressed her head backward into the bark of the tree. At some unconscious level she expected a sensation of hard sharp scraping pain on the back of her head. But the trunk of the huge dark tree was moist, mossy, surprisingly soft. She somehow found the energy for one more outburst: "But if you don't want to help me, then fuck it. Just go ahead and kill yourself," she said, and knew now that she was done. She closed her eyes.

Savoyian heard her words and sat there motionless kneeling on the ground. The wind blew through the trees and the sound whistled in his ears and it was like the high-pitched whine of an engine gunning, and he thought about how he should have died long ago burned by the flames of the C-130. Then he looked up at the dark sky and thought he saw something flash, a tiny blip of frosted translucent white. He knew something about meteorites and black holes and without really thinking wondered if he'd just seen a tiny remnant of a star that had burned out for the last time.

She won't kill me, he thought. *She wants to keep me alive to help her continue her investigation.* He considered this. It made sense. It was rational. But it gave him a hollow and empty feeling. He wasn't sure he could do it. Of course, there were records and notes and—his thoughts stopped short. He looked back up at the sky and wondered if he had imagined that flash of light. A falling star? Or just rock dust, some tiny piece of nameless matter burning up, disappearing, vaporizing before it can even hit the earth's surface. It's all in my mind, he thought. And then he looked at his father's fully loaded revolver, and a great wave of sadness overcame him.

She won't kill me, he thought again. And then he lay down on his back and tried to sleep. But he felt strangely alert. He kept thinking: *I'm* alive, yes, I'm alive... I'm still alive... alive.

***

The dream: Eliana is in New Jersey, digging a grave. For the cat. And for her father. Yes, for both of them. And Savoyian is helping her. Or no—it's her sister, Charlotte. Or the three of them? Yes, together, the three of them. They are in the backyard of her parent's house, and they crouch in the dirt with small shovels, like sand-toys, and Savoyian is saying something to her, trying to explain about the size of the shovels, but his voice sounds far away—

"I managed to turn around the car."

The words startled her awake. He stood in front of her. In the light of day, the sight of him—alive, real, not a dream image—made her feel dizzy. The sunlight hurt her eyes. She looked around. The woods were thick—the trunks of the trees stretching upward, their branches basking in the sun's glow.

"We should go," he said.

"Yes," she answered, and made eye contact with him. He turned away and started to walk. Before standing she let both of her hands grab a handful of dirt, and squeeze. Her dizziness passed. The earth felt warm to her touch, but it didn't please her, although she felt like it should. In fact, she felt a twinge of guilt as she realized how badly she wanted to get back to the city, back to the sound of traffic, the smell of exhaust, the concrete-and-steel feel of police work.

When she stood, she spotted her gun on the ground.

"I found it for you," he called over his shoulder, as if he had eyes in the back of his head.

Quickly, automatically, she moved to pick it up and check the safety. Then she holstered the weapon.

When they pulled out of the campground onto the highway, Savoyian rolled down his window, leaning his head out to inhale the smell of hot pavement and road tar tinged with the odor of cow manure. A good natural honest smell, he thought. Fertilizer, agent of growth. He looked out at the wide-open pastures. Barley and corn. And tall stalks—Timothy hay? He couldn't be sure. Barbed wire fencing marked the plots. Yellow canola flowers dotted the side of the road. The land reminded him suddenly of Ukraine, and he wondered now when he'd return to that part of the world. Then he felt an urge to be out in these fields right here, working the land, caring for it. And the road too. He could imagine himself at the side of the road straightening the leaning white mileage posts nearly lost in the tall grass growing in the ditches. That would feel good, the long strong stems of the plants scraping his legs and arms as he worked to straighten the mileage posts.

He flashed on the face of a new asset, a man named Jan Moham-mad. HUMINT, as they say. That's human—as opposed to electron-ic—intelligence. Mohammad was trained in nuclear engineering and had access to valuable information. A courageous person, too. Savoyian recalled the man's focused dark eyes, and how he wore the local neck scarves favored by men in the Panjshir. A light cotton fabric, white with a black pattern—which identified the wearer as a supporter of the old Northern Alliance, particularly the faction once favored by the late Ahmad Shah Masood. Of course, few westerners would understand all of this. Savoyian—well, it was his job to know.

Afghanistan—yes, he'd return there next, most likely, but other places were possible, including (a long shot) Paris. Ah, romance, a blast of silly fantasy: walking hand-in-hand with Eliana along the banks of the Canal Saint-Martin. No—he'd better plan on Afghanistan. And he might be there for months, so winter rains needed to be considered too. Also, invariably, he would travel the final leg (lately it's been over the Pamir Mountains) by helicopter so space for personal gear would be limited. Extra fuel, generators, weapons, communications gear, and so forth—all that would dictate how much additional weight in per-sonal items he could bring. Last time, Operation Neptune Spear, back in '09, the team had required water purification kits, entrenching tools, knives, compasses, and an absurdly heavy piece of radio equipment—which meant half the personal gear he'd brought with him had to be discarded at a staging point almost 200 miles from Abbottabad. And while the target lived like a regular Joe in that nice little Pakistani villa, Savoyian's team holed up in a makeshift Afghani compound with... oh, yes, memories of the toilet facilities came rushing back, how twelve grown men shared a hole in a cement floor. Disgusting. A cracked por-celain square about four inches high was fitted around the hole, and a pair of raised footprints pointed away from the wall. Follow the foot-prints, lower your pants— but don't lower them too far or they'll touch the wet floor or the filthy porcelain—then squat, lean back, brace your-self with one hand pressing against the wall behind you, and aim. Yes, look carefully down between your legs, and aim. Because if you don't hit the drain hole dead center—splish-splash. Cold shit-soup drip-ping down the back of your legs. Why not build slit-trenches outside?

Because at least inside—repulsive, uncomfortable, unsanitary—their little shithole was private, concealed, hidden. Which meant, relatively speaking, it was safe.

Savoyian's intestines twisted now just thinking of all this. He looked again out the window at the fields of barley and corn. Yes, Afghanistan. Or would it be Pakistan, Turkmenistan, Uzbekistan, or Tajikistan? Algeria is possible too. His contacts in cells over there were always about to pop. But none of this would be his call, of course. He'd just follow orders. And he'd take his shit wherever he's told.

Chain of command.

"I'm still working," he said, turning to look at Eliana, whose face was like stone and implacable and impossible to read as she focused on the road in front of her. She held both hands on the steering wheel—ten and two, like a student in a driver's test, straight from the manual. "I'll help you," he went on. "You're right, of course. There was someone in the bank helping the terrorists. It will be difficult, but—yes, I'll help you. We can try to find him—all of them."

Eliana's chin lowered in a small barely perceptible nod, but she said nothing.

"If you're serious about it, though," Savoyian went on, "it can't be like this."

He paused and tried to read her expression, but nothing changed. She kept her eyes on the road. "Chain of command, I mean. You'll have to get yourself back in the good graces of the NYPD. A proper investigation will mean the FBI, DOJ, counter-terrorism—all that. If you're serious about justice, your investigation—then, yes, that's fine, I'll help. But you'll have to follow the rules. Even war—we tell ourselves—has rules."

"Really?" she said, and Savoyian noted that although her voice was calm and low, her grip on the steering wheel had tightened. She didn't say anything more.

They drove in silence, then stopped for food at a small diner with a scratched-up Formica counter. A tall glass case filled with doughnuts was directly in front of them, and a tired-looking, middle-aged waitress rested her pad on top of it.

After they ordered, Eliana turned on her cell phone. She had a bunch of missed calls from Danny, three from Livi, one from Char. And this gave her an idea—a crazy thought. But it felt connected to the dream. Digging a grave in the yard. It felt connected to everything. She excused herself and went out to the parking lot. Behind her Savoyian was asking if she wanted more coffee. She called out "Yes" without turning around.

Danny answered on the first ring.

"Hey, how are you?" The tone in his voice—soft, gentle. But intense.

"I'm OK. Long story, but listen, Danny... it's all true. This time, really. I found him. Savoyian. He did it. He took me to the scene. A campground up in Ulster. We're right near there now."

In the long silence that followed, Eliana imagined the look of disbelief on Danny's face. His cool, thin-lipped gaze, his steady blue eyes. But the loud raspy breath she heard him take didn't fit with all that. He sounded out-of-breath, off balance. In a word: vulnerable.

"Jesus Christ," he said. "Just stay where you are—I'll come and—"

"No—no. That's not what I want. Listen, Danny, this is—this is *everything.*"

She didn't know where to begin. How to explain it to him. But Danny—Danny would understand. Danny would make this happen.

He loved her. The idea seized her now, flashing in her mind like lightning. Then a sharp crashing pain hit the side of her head. But it wasn't a migraine—no. She had bumped her head with the edge of the phone. The pain passed in an instant. Freedom, freedom, she thought, and shuddered—oh, god, it felt so perfect.

Savoyian had turned his phone back on while Eliana stood in the parking lot. Not his regular phone—this one belonged to CENT-COM. Seventeen messages, including three from RDJTF. Rapid Deployment Task Force.

He didn't listen to the messages. He just sat there staring at the phone. A vague restlessness troubled him. Then he found Eliana beside him; she had come up noiselessly and sat down on the stool at his side. The waitress brought their food—identical orders, scrambled eggs and toast. Another synchronicity! But he said nothing—the mood all wrong for levity. They ate without speaking, though Savoyian stole glances at Eliana, thinking her face looked thinner and paler, and she showed signs of being in serious pain, grimacing slightly when she used her left hand. The bandage on her forearm looked bad. Pus oozed from one side. She'd never told him the reason for the bandage.

A final sip of coffee, then she swiveled her stool and faced him directly. "The *Diagnostic and Statistical Manual of Mental Disorders*—the DSM—it's the 'Bible' of psychiatry," she began. "You know it?"

All this felt totally out of the blue to Savoyian, but he just nodded. "I know *of it*, yes. Not in detail."

"Well, it specifically states that if the cause of stress is human, the stress is more severe."

"If the cause of stress is human—OK. Where are we going with this?"

"Human versus non-human. Like natural disasters. The DSM says that posttraumatic stress disorder is relatively rare and mild in response to natural disasters—even traffic accidents, it's much less."

"And so...?"

"My sister. My sister, Charlotte. She suffers from—"

"PTSD."

"Let me finish."

She paused, and Savoyian knew she'd lost her train of thought. He felt bad for interrupting. He waited. Told himself to simply wait, give her space. But the silence lengthened, and she said nothing. She looked unsteady on the stool, almost like she might faint. Then, when her eyes grew glassy with the threat of tears, he said finally, "Where is your sister now?"

"In a hospital, a rehab facility. But my ex-husband—he's going to bring her to my apartment. They'll meet us there." She spoke without looking up. He watched her closely as she licked her lips, then swallowed hard. "I want you to—to tell my sister that you killed our father. Don't lie to her. Tell her that it was—tell her about working undercover. She's very smart. She'll understand all of it in a flash. Make it clear she's in no danger. And make it clear that our father's death is a civilian casualty that made possible great military victories. Tell her that understanding this simple fact should help us go forward now... forward."

Eliana's voice trailed off into a barely audible whisper, and she lowered her face as if she were looking at something on the floor. Savoyian looked down too, then leaned close to her, extending his hand—but timidly, the way you might reach out to pet a small animal, hoping that you don't frighten it away. At the far end of the counter, the cash register rang, followed by a clatter of change hitting the tabletop. Behind him, he heard the clunk of a coffee pot sliding back into the urn slot.

Eliana looked up. "Can you do this?"

"Of course," he said, quietly. "Of course, I can."

And he moved his hand a fraction of an inch closer, palm up. He wanted so badly to reach out and touch the tips of her fingers. But he didn't dare.

Chapter 31

Danny didn't push back, although he felt Eliana's idea sounded crazy. He just went along—worked out the logistics. Location, timing, length of the drive—plan backward, set the objective, yeah, sure, he could do his part: bring Char to meet Vachik Savoyian at Eliana's apartment. 1600 hours.

Within fifteen minutes of the call, he was on his way to Watertown, where he badged his way through some hospital red tape, and met with Char. He made almost no effort to explain anything to her. Instead, he got Eliana on the phone again and let the two sisters talk directly to each other. He started to leave the room, but she said, "Would you stay?"

"Sure, if you want."

He watched Char's face as she made the call.

"Elly?"

Her eyes widened, and then she stared blankly at the wall, her mouth open, breathing as if she had a stuffy nose. Then came a squint of concentration, eyes narrowing. And she rubbed her face, massaging her wide flat cheeks almost as if she had a toothache. "OK, Elly, OK, sure, yeah, I—I'll go with Danny."

She hung up, then handed Danny back his phone. "Wow," she said softly, and shook her head. "She found him. The guy who killed my father. At least that's what he says." She looked directly at Danny. "You think it's legit?"

Danny held still, silent.

"If it is him," Charlotte went on. "I just want to kill him. You know, get it over with."

"That's not how it works, Char," Danny said quickly.

"Yeah, I know. We have this *criminal justice system.*"

Charlotte looked around the small room, gazing from one corner to the other. Danny almost asked what was on her mind. Then she suddenly blurted, "You know, Danny, I wish you and Elly had never gotten a divorce."

The bluntness of the comment surprised Danny, but he just smiled. "Yeah, me too."

"I mean, even though you're a cop and everything—you have always seemed like, you know... just a really good guy."

Danny nodded, then looked away. "Come on, we've got about four hours on the road."

They drove most of the way in silence, with nothing but polite exchanges about a bathroom stop, adjusting the air conditioning, songs on the radio, the weather. When they reached Eliana's apartment, Danny saw that her parking space under the building was empty, so he knew they'd arrived first. He pulled into a spot in front of the building, and they sat watching the neighborhood's late afternoon activity. It was almost four pm, but with school out for summer there were no buses crowding the street or kids standing on the corner. Just two boys jumping on and off their skateboards, rumbling down an apartment building driveway; and two houses down from Eliana's building, a woman in nurse's whites stood on a house porch, steadying a wheelchair for an old man in a bathrobe. Then, right in front of the car, a man in a suit and tie walked up tugging on a dog leash. He called out to his German Shepherd, as if to an employee, "That's fine, Bill. Let's go. We're on a schedule."

Charlotte turned to Danny, "Don't you think dogs should have dog-names? You know, Sparky, Bubbles, stuff like that. What if someone named Bill goes over to this guy's house? 'Bill, nice to meet you. This is my dog, Bill.'"

The long awkward silence broken—Danny felt a little relieved. And Char's voice sounded fine. Eliana had warned her this might trigger the bit with the anxious whispering. "I've got an aunt we call Bubbles," Danny said. "She actually looks a little like a poodle."

Charlotte laughed, then sighed. "Yeah, well—it's a mixed-up world."

Danny smiled. Playful, funny, smart—nothing about Char seemed "off." Looking at her right this moment, he'd never peg her as a chronic EDP. She wore a perfectly "normal" outfit: jeans and a pullover collared shirt, a pair of running shoes. And her small square frame appeared strong and solid. It made Danny wonder: if this meeting with the government spy-guy comes off, what kind of life will Char have?

Then she went on, "Do you ever feel like this whole country is just—you know, totally broken?"

Danny laughed.

"I mean, you know the whole thing—the system: capitalism, democracy. All of it. We are all totally fucked up living in a totally fucked up system."

"Yeah, well, I don't know if we are fucked up because of the system or the system is fucked up because of us. I mean, you know, human nature can be pretty dark."

"Right," Char said, very quietly, and her posture slumped as she turned and looked out the window. "Human nature. That's the counterargument."

The low tone of her voice and her slumping posture worried Danny. He didn't want to provoke her anxiety and bring on that horrible whispering-thing Eliana had told him about.

"No matter what, though," he said, his voice full, "no matter how messed up things are—a good person doing a good job can still make a difference."

Char sat up with a small burst of energy. She turned away from the window and looked at Danny. He felt relieved.

"Is Elly a good cop?" she asked. "I don't mean good' like good-cop/ bad-cop.' I mean, is she good at being a cop?"

"Excellent."

"Really?"

"That surprise you?"

Charlotte shrugged. Danny watched her look down at her hand, opening and closing her fingers into a fist—three times, first one hand, then the other. He recalled the gesture from years ago. Odd, definitely— but harmless. Suddenly, she looked up and said, "Elly was trying to explain to me over the phone that this guy says my dad was like a civilian casualty in the global War on Terror. She thinks maybe we can get some kind of plaque or something. You know, like maybe that my dad died a hero. I mean, my dad was trying to do the right thing."

"Yeah, he was. And maybe we can work that out. A plaque." Charlotte looked again at her hand, started to open and close her fingers— then stopped. "Anyway... it was a long time ago." Outside, the guy with the dog said something to his dog and gave the leash a hard yank. "There goes Bill," Charlotte said, looking out the window.

"Yep," Danny said. "And I think the guy even picked up Bill's poop."

Charlotte laughed softly, then said, "You think I could be a good umpire?"

The abrupt question took Danny by surprise, but he answered without missing a beat. "Absolutely. You'd be great."

Danny imagined Char wearing an umpire's uniform. Blue shirt, grey pants, her stocky body—a good fit, hunching over home plate.

"If I could get to the majors—I'd be the first woman," Charlotte went on.

"Is that right? No women?"

"Have been six in the affiliated minor leagues, but none have made it to the Big Leagues. Pam Postema—she spent a bunch of years in Triple-A during the 1980s, and, after being fired, she filed a sex discrimination suit against the MLB. But still—she didn't make it. Settled out of court. I'm not sure of the details."

"Hmm—you'd make history."

"Yeah, well... did you know that a pitch that bounces to the plate cannot be hit?"

"Really?"

"Yeah, it's against the rules. Like a dead ball. I've studied all this stuff—online. It's good—the online stuff, but, of course, I've gotta get out there and call some games."

Danny concealed a grin. The phrase "call some games" came to Charlotte so effortlessly that it made him smile. But he didn't want Char to think that he didn't take her seriously. In fact, at that moment, Charlotte becoming Major League Baseball's first female umpire seemed entirely possible.

"Yeah, being a good umpire is really about a quality of attention," she went on. "Which means, you know, that you have to really care. You have to care that the rules are followed. And, of course, you have to *know* the rules. All the rules. And it's funny, how I usually can't stand rules. I think the so-called 'rules' in our society are totally screwed up, but—baseball. I love it. I love studying the rules in baseball." She looked straight ahead out the car's front window and took a deep breath. "Try this, Danny," she said, still looking out, as if there were a game going on right in front of her. "The batter's up—no balls, no strikes, one gone. Runners on first and second. Batter hits a pop fly between third and home. Third baseman gets under the ball, then lets it drop untouched just barely into foul territory. But the ball then rolls *into* fair territory. The umpire rules an infield fly and declares the batter out."

Char turned her head and looked at Danny, an impish grin on her face. "Right call?"

***

Savoyian picked up the tail about ten miles north of the Tappan Zee Bridge. A blue BMW, it hung two cars back. He knew who it was. Not their names, specifically. Names don't matter. What they wanted—that's what mattered.

"Eliana," he said, quietly. "You should get off at the Nanuet exit. I need to—well, there are people behind us, and I need to talk with them." Eliana glanced into the rear-view mirror. Then she pulled off the highway at exit eleven: *Nyack - South Nyack - US Route 9W.* She followed a blue-and-white sign with a gas pump icon. As she drove, Savoyian looked at his phone, scrolling messages, then he reached into his pocket, took out his keys.

Sure enough, the blue BMW was right behind them as they pulled into the gas station. Eliana parked off to the side, stopping behind a big white camper van. The van's driver was using the air hose, filling a tire. At the gas pumps in the center of the station, a pale, slump-shouldered attendant with dirty blond hair seemed to be lost in his phone. The BMW, which parked a short distance behind them, turned on its emergency flashers. Eliana noted that two men sat in the car, apparently waiting for Savoyian.

He finished working two keys off his ring and held them out to her. "I'm sorry," he began, "but I have to go with these men."

He waved the keys slightly, as if that explained something. Eliana just stared at them. *Abloy* keys. She recognized the brand. Used on disc tumbler locks, springless, nearly impossible to pick. And these keys—four sets of teeth. Added security. Almost every house in Finland uses them, the *Abloy* lock-and-key system. She'd read about it somewhere—a law enforcement magazine, a website. It didn't matter.

He pushed the keys hard into her palm and went on, "Front door, and my apartment. Inside, there's money hiding in plain sight. A shoe-box in my closet. Close to three hundred thousand dollars. Untraceable. Use it to—whatever. Help your sister. Give her the money and tell her that—"

"Who's in the car?"

"I—I have an assignment. I—" Savoyian's voice clotted with a sudden, jerky stop. Eliana watched his eyes well-up, and he hunched his shoulders as if about to choke. Then he coughed, a dry hard cough. "Tell your sister..." His voice was tight, raspy, like he needed water. But then he closed his eyes and took a deep breath, and the moment passed. "Tell your sister everything, and tell her about *my* father too," he said quietly, his composure restored. "And the ritual with the picture, the healing ritual—*you* know, the visualization and the pressure point. Do it with her. You remember the pressure point? For your headache?"

Eliana didn't answer. Savoyian grabbed her hand, the good one, the one that didn't ache from the cat-bite. And he pushed down somewhere in the soft fleshy web of skin between her thumb and forefinger. "Right there," he said. "Feel it?"

Unable to speak, with everything seeming to happen at once, Eliana nodded her head yes, and he released the pressure on her hand and continued, "Tell her about the picture and the archetype of the father, the positive-father, the power of authority, boundaries, all that—but tell her that when we can do it for ourselves, when we value ourselves for the right reasons, then we have it. Within ourselves—order, peace." He looked away, swallowed hard, then went on, "I—I... it's too late for me. There's such a thing as too late, you know. But you—and your sister..."

"You said you would help me."

He looked at her directly. "Yes, I want to help you. I will. But I have an assignment now."

Eliana felt her throat tighten. She wanted to say something, anything, but no words came. The cat. She suddenly wanted to tell him about the cat and that she—yes, she was... a murderer too. No different from him, really. And so she lifted her throbbing arm as if to start by explaining about the spreading infection from this cat bite, but he took the gesture as the beginning of an embrace, and he leaned forward and kissed her on the cheek, like a father saying goodbye to his daughter.

When he got out and closed the door without looking back, she watched him get into the car behind her where the two men were waiting. She could make out the figures, but nothing else. Then the car drove away, and she just sat there staring straight ahead, both hands on the steering wheel, as if she were waiting for some kind of instructions. A numbness settled over her. Except for the throbbing pain in her arm, she couldn't locate a single feeling. Finally, she started to drive again. She got back on the highway going south, toward the city. She fingered the thick metal of the keys Savoyian had given to her. Then she told herself that when she got closer, she would stop to text Danny. She'd send Savoyian's address, and they could all meet there. And then—?

She didn't know. There were no clear thoughts. All she knew is that her arm tingled and throbbed. She also experienced a strange sense of heat rising behind her eyelids. But mostly she felt nothing, replaying in her mind what had just happened, how she'd watched in the rearview mirror as Savoyian got into the backseat of the BMW, which pulled away—not with a screech and a dramatic skid, the rear end of the car fish-tailing, as she half-expected from the movies—but slowly, almost cautiously, as if the driver wasn't sure of the proper direction. And they headed north, away from the city, which confused her.

She stopped once on the other side of the Tappan Zee to use the bathroom and texted Savoyian's address to Danny. She didn't explain. He shot back a thumbs-up emoji, no questions asked. Then about forty minutes later the three of them stood outside of Savoyian's building. Char looked nervous, but she gave Eliana a strong hug and said hello in a good, full voice. Obviously, they wondered about the missing Savoyian, though neither said anything until finally Danny asked, "So is this guy coming out here?"

He flicked his head in that familiar manner of cops, a gesture that Eliana thought always communicated a subtle feeling of two worlds: us and—flick. *Them.*

"No," Eliana spoke now while holding her left arm, trying to conceal the bandage. Its edge oozed a yellowish fluid, and the throbbing pain was worse.

No fooling Danny. He stepped right up for a closer look and said, "You got an infection here—what's going on?"

"Not now," she said. "Let's go inside. I have keys."

Eliana moved quickly to the building's door, with Charlotte following so close behind that she kicked Eliana's heels, almost tripping them both.

"Sorry—sorry, sorry," Char said. A familiar feeling came to Eliana. An old family pattern surfacing—the little sister getting in the way.

When they reached the upstairs hallway, Danny stepped around both of them and brought their movement to a halt. A classic cop-move. Take charge, control the situation, it came to him so effortlessly. Beyond training—it was in Danny's DNA.

"How about I go in first?" He started to reach for his weapon.

Eliana shook her head. It almost made her smile. "The apartment is empty, Danny. He's gone."

"Gone?" Char's voice sounded choked with alarm. "What do you mean—gone?"

"Let's go in," Eliana said.

She stepped around Danny and worked the keys in the fancy lock, then threw open the door, and they all stepped into the windowless front room filled with books. Exactly as she remembered it: the big clumsy sofa, the cheap floor-lamps, the makeshift table created from a slab of plywood balanced on a stack of bricks. She walked quickly around the corner, leaving Danny and Charlotte in the front room. The bedroom— neat, tidy. Her eyes went to the patterns of the multicolored quilt spread over the bed, smooth, without wrinkles. And again, exactly as she had the first time, she inched forward, drawn, transfixed by the artwork in the fabric. She recalled something he'd read to her while driving up north, something from his journals about the elements in Islamic art, the use of geometrical, floral, and vegetal designs in a repetition known as the "arabesque," a symbol, he explained, of the transcendent, indivisible and infinite nature of God. But Islamic artists—to emphasize that only God can produce perfection—introduce intentional mistakes in the patterns, deliberate inconsistencies, a way to show humility.

She stared into the quilt, looking for the "mistakes." Reds and autumn browns, various shades of blues and greens, and the shapes: circles, squares, triangles—combined, duplicated, interlaced, arranged in intricate polygons, stars, multi-sided abstractions. Finally, her eyes lifted from the quilt and settled on the framed photograph of Savoyian's father sitting on the night table. Savoyian had turned the picture toward the edge of his bed, as if moments ago he'd been sitting there looking at it. The brave father, the military man, stripes on his shoulder, a Sergeant Major First Class in the Iranian army, which, Savoyian had explained proudly, was the highest position of enlisted grade personnel.

Eliana looked closely at the picture, and her feeling of rage came on slowly—building, rising, like distant thunder getting closer and closer. She didn't understand it. But she felt it. Rumbling, pounding. It was in her ears—blood thudding. And then her pulse beat faster, harder, with a distinct sensation of increased strength spreading through her body. She felt capable of reaching down and lifting the whole bed, tipping it over with one hand. But instead, she crouched slightly and took her gun from its ankle holster. An edgy, twitchy feeling—more rage coming. The picture, Savoyian's father, her father, brave fathers everywhere with their stories and wars and laws and—she hated all of it. The suffering it caused was too much. She'd become a cop to become one of them: a hero. But right now she hated the whole ugly world of heroes.

She lifted the picture off the night table and propped it up on the pillows of the bed, then she stepped away as far as she could, until her back touched the wall behind her. Alone, free—she took a tactical breath. She heard Danny and Char say something to each other in the other room, their voices muffled. Then she lifted her gun. Shoulders square to the target, feet apart, her weight slightly forward on the balls of her feet— training, ah, training. Head high and still, chin pointing at the target, ears in front of shoulders, shoulders in front of hips—she preferred the "Isosceles Stance," toes facing straight ahead, as opposed to the "Weaver Stance," the body angled. And recoil—none of that Hollywood onehanded crap. Though her non-shooting hand felt weak and achy from the spreading infection of the cat-bite, she set the butt of the gun in her left palm, wrapping the forefinger of her left hand around the outside of the trigger guard, supporting the weapon. Then she executed her "relationship of sights." Yes, just as she'd been trained. Inside combat distance, seven yards, she knew to focus the gun's front sight on the target. In combat shooting, this is the most important fundamental. *"The eye can only focus on one object at a time. It cannot keep the rear sight, the front sight, and the target in focus simultaneously."* She'd trained hard and long and knew this—so well. The shooter must concentrate on the front sight, yes. And there it was: equal light, equal height. A perfect sight-picture. She squeezed the trigger—a booming noise, a surprise. You pull the trigger but you still cannot know the moment a gun discharges. She pulled again and again until she emptied the magazine— seven bullets aimed directly not at Vachik Savoyian's father in a military uniform but at all the men in all the military uniforms in all the wars in all the unstoppable awful history of the world.

Then she dropped her gun and collapsed.

Chapter 32

She wound up in the hospital. The Marworth Treatment Center for Uniformed Professionals in Pennsylvania specialized in alcohol or chemical dependency. But Danny's family had contacts, so the docs made an exception and took in Eliana with the diagnosis of complex post-traumatic stress disorder. She spent eighteen weeks there.

When she wasn't attending group or talk therapy, she wrote in a journal. The doctors approved. Journal-writing can be healing, they explained to Danny. And Eliana too said it made her feel good. Almost like being a student again, she said. But with no grades, no requirements. One of the therapists, a slim-hipped woman with stringy blonde hair, had studied philosophy and appreciated that Eliana's writing included things like quotes from Nietzsche: *"Beware that, when fighting monsters, you yourself do not become a monster... for when you gaze long into the abyss. The abyss gazes also into you... I love only what a man has written with his blood. Write with blood, and you will experience that blood is spirit..."*

When he came to visit, Eliana showed some of this writing to Danny, who didn't pretend to understand it. At one point, Danny had a chance to talk to the therapist himself and asked about it. Monsters, blood, spirit—? The doctor explained that Eliana's diagnosis involved "a high degree of desensitization to violence," most notably demonstrated by the incident of cruelty to an animal, which had made Eliana feel like a monster.

"And it's not just that she was a police officer," the doctor went on, "Eliana has experienced violence as an essential part of her life ever since the disappearance of her father. She is struggling to integrate that reality, the reality of violence." The doctor paused, then concluded. "She still wants to be a cop. And maybe she can. She's strong, and capable of being deeply honest with herself. I'm hopeful that she'll make a full recovery."

As the months passed, both Danny and Charlotte visited often, especially Char. It was good for them. The reversal of roles: Char caring for Eliana—that started, in fact, right after the shots. Danny would never forget it: that little picture frame shot to pieces, shards of glass everywhere, bullet holes in the pillow on the bed, and the acrid smell of gunfire in the air. After emptying her gun, Eliana crumpled to the floor, crying hysterically. They both rushed into the room, of course, but Char got there first. Wrapping her arms around her big sister, comforting her, kissing her forehead, saying over and over again, "If s OK, Elly, you're just upset, but I'm here with you—you're just upset, that's all, but I'm here with you, it's OK, it's OK."

Danny knew someone must have heard all those shots and would call the police, so right away he stepped outside to wait in front of the building, holding his badge in the air. When the first sector car arrived, he didn't even try to make it go away. "Can't un-ring this bell, I know," he told the sergeant who had responded to the call. "But it's my ex— she's on the job..."

It went over the air as an OIS. Officer Involved Shooting. Which meant a full court press, and soon the whole block swarmed with crime scene investigators, detectives from the Borough Shooting Team, guys taking measurements, collecting evidence, interviewing potential witnesses. And, of course, IAB—Internal Affairs Bureau—quickly discovered way too many loose ends: the dead cat in the trunk, the money in the closet, the story of the mysterious government agent? The more they learned, the more Danny felt certain they'd sink their teeth into this one. They'd want Eliana out—for good. If not in jail.

Danny's father helped find an attorney for Eliana, someone to help out the union guy. But even the lawyers thought she'd never again be considered "fit for duty." And the money in the closet? That didn't look good.

But then everything changed. A few weeks after the incident, while Eliana was still in the hospital, a couple of expensive suits from Washington showed up, and within days, the IAB case against Eliana disappeared. Someone, apparently, knew the right people. Eventually, after completing treatment, a deal was offered: Eliana would lose her detective's status and never again work undercover, but if she wanted to be a cop—a white shield, in uniform, on patrol—the job was hers. Even that took convincing. Once the Feds dropped out of sight, the NYPD wanted Eliana behind a desk. Danny and his family called in every favor they could to help get her what she wanted.

And on her first day back, nine months after her night in the woods—nine months without a word from Vachik Savoyian—Eliana and Danny worked a detail together, the Cinco De Mayo Celebration at Orchard Beach.

They call it "the Bronx Riviera," although Orchard Beach is just a one-mile strip of sand in the northern part of the borough, a man-made shorefront allowing access to an inlet that connects, eventually, to the Long Island Sound. Food stands, a couple of playgrounds, a large parking lot, and twenty-six courts for basketball, volleyball, and handball. No Riviera, that's for sure. But it's a public beach in the Bronx, and that's something.

When Eliana spotted Danny at roll call, her stomach churned with a fluttering mix of nerves and desire and the tentative stirrings of love, uncertain yet hopeful. Their renewed contact during all this had been full of warmth and care. And much, much more. They saw each other often, sharing meals, going for walks, being careful to avoid anything physical from developing. Then two weeks ago Danny came right out and told her that he'd been researching divorced couples who remarry.

"It's not as uncommon as you'd think," he explained. "Some research shows about ten to fifteen percent of all divorced couples reconcile. And we perfectly fit the profile for success because there was no infidelity, no abuse, and no financial conflict. Basically, our problem was just—me. My insecurities, my feeling inferior, inadequate—all that. And how instead of talking about it—I just worked and worked and worked. And drank."

Eliana quickly pushed back that she had plenty of issues too, but then she didn't know what else to say. His straightforwardness impressed her. She loved him, yes. But in a deep and complicated way. And she found him attractive, yes—in an embarrassingly uncomplicated way. But... marriage? She just nodded and said, "We'll talk some more, OK?"

A week passed. They met for breakfast twice, but neither of them brought it up again. Then last Sunday they drove an hour up to Yorktown Heights, where Char was completing the first phase of umpire training at a girls' softball tournament. Turned out to be a bigger deal than either of them thought. When they arrived, the size of the parking lot surprised them both. There were several different fields, with busy mobile snack carts and kiosks scattered around the park selling hotdogs and ice cream and popcorn. Families were everywhere, and Eliana soon learned that among the people watching were college coaches. That explained the tense feeling of drama—scholarship money. Eliana hadn't anticipated such a vibrant and energetic scene, but she found herself enjoying it. She took in everything: the anxious, cheering parents armed with sunscreen and water jugs; the silent, scrutinizing coaches with their clipboards and rosters; and most of all, the feeling of wholesome, ordinary family life. It made Eliana think about Livi and how she wanted to stop judging her sister so harshly.

She and Danny bought popcorn and found the field where Char was working and took seats on the back row of an aluminum bleacher along the third baseline. They settled in. The sky was fair. The warm summer air, soft. The feeling between them—nothing but tender and intimate. As they shared the popcorn, their hands kept bumping when they reached into the bag for a handful. At one point, they both reached at the exact same moment and let their fingers lightly clasp, then they laughed and looked each other square in the eyes. Danny spoke first.

"You're making me feel like I'm in eighth grade," he said.

"Yeah, I get that." Eliana laughed some more, then felt an urge to lean over and kiss Danny on the mouth. But she resisted. Instead, she lifted her hand away from the popcorn and looked away. A strong memory was coming, but she wasn't sure that she wanted to let herself feel it.

"Danny," she began in a quiet but clear voice. "This might seem like a crazy time to talk about it, but—if we did... you know, try again... Would you consider..." The feeling of fighting off the memory grew stronger. It was like trying to block out noise coming from another room. She felt herself fidgeting on the hard aluminum bleacher, as if she were working a kink out of her back. Her therapist had told her that flashbacks would be inevitable.

"You OK?" Danny asked.

She said nothing, trying to sit still and calm herself. The memory was coming now.

"Would I... what, Elly? What is it?"

The memory broke through, and she saw herself in her childhood home, standing at the top of the stairs, looking down at the living room. Her father stood at the front door, one hand on the knob. He was looking at her mother, who stood with her back to him. Watching the scene in her mind, Eliana took a breath and waited. If the memory went forward, her father would start to speak. He would quote Torah. She knew the passage: Proverbs 28.

But, after a moment, Eliana's mind cleared. In a low, calm voice, she turned and looked closely at Danny.

He was leaning forward, his eyes calm but intent, locked onto her. "What is it, Elly?" he said, softly.

"Would you consider converting to Judaism?"

She saw the immediate surprise on his face—his lips forming a small 'O' shape, eyebrows lifted, a slight backward tilt of his head. "You would want that?"

"I don't know," Eliana said. "I'm not sure. I'm not sure what I—"

"It's OK if you want that. I'm just—a little surprised."

"Yeah, it surprises me too. But my father, he—well, I think my father got his strength and courage from being Jewish. And, you know, I've cut myself off from all that."

Danny was nodding his head, a blank look on his face. "Honestly, Elly," he stammered, "I don't really know what it would mean to convert—"

"You don't have to answer me, Danny."

"No, I'm happy to answer. I mean, I'm open to exploring it. With you. Together. That's what matters to me. Being together."

And they left it at that—with so much more to talk about. But they somehow silently agreed to turn their attention back to the softball game. Eliana experienced it as a cop move. Focus on what's in front of you. After a tough moment, especially, all that matters is what's in front of you. The next call on the radio, so to speak. They watched the game, then took Char out for a burger, and, later, said goodbye with a kiss on the cheek. But now, here they were. On her first day back in uniform, Danny and Eliana were, indeed, together. Neither of them had told the other that they would be working this detail, and, of course, it wasn't entirely their decision. Supervisors pulled from various precincts to cover events like this. So, a coincidence? Or, no, synchronicity! The word jumped into Eliana's mind. And the irony—not lost on her. It was Savoyian's word.

She had thought about Savoyian a million times and had been through the familiar "stages" of anger and grief about not hearing from him. She wasn't sure what her therapist or Danny or anyone *really* understood whenever she tried to explain about him. Who—or what?— was Savoyian *really*, in the end? The man who killed her father, yes. And a soldier in the War on Terror, yes. And if he ever reappeared, then he would be—what? Could Savoyian come back and help her find those guys in the bank who'd been working with the terrorists? There must have been someone, right? With Savoyian's help, could Eliana find them and bring them to justice? Could she still be a hero?

But... she felt done with all that. No more heroes. At least for the time being. Now there were only ordinary people, all of whom face the same struggle she does: how to live with pain and loss. She was learning—one day at a time. She was learning that peace with the past and hope for the future are impossible without coming to terms as openly and intimately as possible with the cold hard sad beauty of the present. That's how it came to her—*the cold hard sad beauty of the present,* those strange words. Her life, her real life, her life right now: she was a cop; Char was doing better; Danny loved her. And this: she had begun, once again, to find meaning and value, even a kind of strength, in being what she was and always would be—a Jew.

Thoughts like these hummed somewhere in the back of her mind as the afternoon wore on. Close to a dozen cops and another two-dozen auxiliary strolled up-and-down the beach's cement promenade. Eliana felt good, comfortable in spite of the heavy blue uniform, the duty belt, the baton. "The complete rookie package," she'd said to Danny, smiling. But she didn't mind.

She was too busy enjoying the briny sea air mixed so deliciously with the smell of smoky hot dogs and burgers. City smells and beach odors like perfume! She loved it. Also, because of the holiday, a few Mexican and Dominican restaurants had set up food-stands and carts, including one of Eliana's favorite's, *Estrellita Poblanos*, which featured a blue-corn spicy taco chip.

It was a perfect summer day, and there were hundreds of families out with their coolers and lounge chairs set up in the sand. Plus, water toys— brightly colored buckets and pails—dotted the beach. By four p.m., it was packed, and Eliana walked back and forth on her post at the north end of the beach. Then she stood for a while at the edge of the boardwalk where the cement meets the sand and just looked out at the horizon. Not a whitecap in sight—nothing but gentle waves rolling inland, dissolving into soft foam on the shore.

So peaceful. So beautiful. So innocent.

Until it wasn't.

She heard the sound of—what? At first Eliana couldn't tell. A fire-cracker? An automobile backfiring? No, of course not. It was the sound of a gunshot. And then a child's scream. The scream of someone horri-fied. Eliana turned quickly. A little way down the promenade, she spot-ted a small golden-skinned girl, maybe eight years old, with long dark hair and a wide flat face. The girl stood between two vendors—one selling sunglasses, the other snow-cones. The snow cone cart had been knocked over. The little girl wore loose-fitting dark shorts and a bright blue tee shirt, and she held her elbows, hunching her shoulders, suck-ing air, screaming. Several adults were running in different directions, shouting, grabbing up their children.

Eliana moved toward the chaos, breaking into a run as the girl's screams—throaty, guttural—continued, rising now above the other beach sounds as if carried by the wind, anointed with some special power. People stopped what they were doing. Parents stood; children froze. A small crowd formed around the screaming child.

Eliana ran harder, one hand gripping her heavy duty-belt, her ba-ton slapping against the side of her hip. Then her radio crackled: *all units, beach area six, 10-10, shots fired, repeat: beach area six, all units, shots fired, be advised: no description of shooter, proceed with caution.*

Coming now from the opposite side, Eliana saw Danny running too. And behind him, a whole wedge of blue uniforms. Yes, all these cops, she thought—running toward the gunfire, toward the sound of the screams.

Hoping to help.

The End

About the Author

Walter B. Levis, a former crime reporter, lives in New York City. His articles have appeared in *The NY Daily News, The National Law Journal, The Chicago Reporter, The Chicago Lawyer, The New Republic, Show Business Magazine,* and *The New Yorker,* among others. He is author of the novel *Moments of Doubt.* His short stories have appeared widely and have been chosen for a Henfield Prize and nominated for a Pushcart Prize. His website is walterblevis.com.

www.ingramcontent.com/pod-product-compliance
Lightning Source LLC
Chambersburg PA
CBHW060355030726
47497CB00003B/725